"A strongly told tale with a fascinating hero. This series should eventually rank with *Little Big Man*. An impressive voice. An impressive first novel."

—David Nevin,
New York Times bestselling author of *Dream West*

"I found the novel to be very well researched and heartfelt, as if Mr. Sinclair Lewis were living the story himself. His sense of time and place is on the mark. He's a writer with a flair for fine storytelling and most certainly has a wonderful future in historical writing."

—Earl Murray,
author of *Thunder in the Dawn*

"Lewis's debut novel displays a strong sense of people, places, and time that yields a convincing and compelling historical novel."

—*Booklist*

FORGE BOOKS BY J. P. SINCLAIR LEWIS

Buffalo Gordon
Buffalo Gordon on the Plains

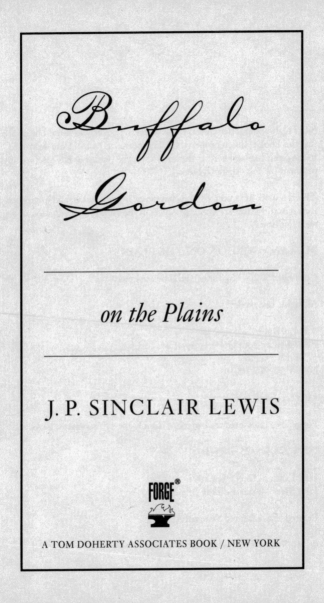

Buffalo Gordon

on the Plains

J. P. SINCLAIR LEWIS

FORGE®

A TOM DOHERTY ASSOCIATES BOOK / NEW YORK

This is a work of fiction. All the characters, organizations, and events portrayed in this novel are either products of the author's imagination or are used fictitiously.

BUFFALO GORDON ON THE PLAINS

A Forge Book
Published by Tom Doherty Associates, LLC
175 Fifth Avenue
New York, NY 10010

www.tor-forge.com

Forge® is a registered trademark of Tom Doherty Associates, LLC.

ISBN 978-0-8125-7011-3

First Edition: December 2003
First Mass Market Edition: July 2010

Printed in the United States of America

0 9 8 7 6 5 4 3 2 1

To my daughter,

Charlotte-Jeanne Sinclair Lewis

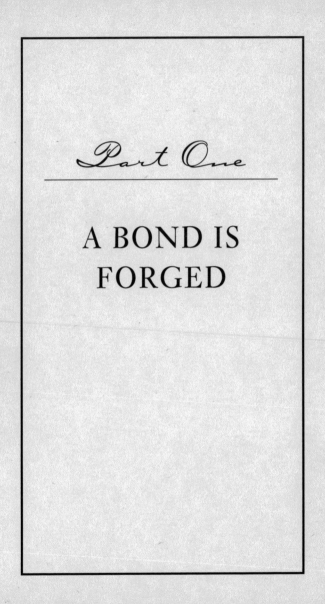

Part One

A BOND IS FORGED

One

AUGUST 1868.

"Medicine Bill" Comstock and the scout, "Sharp" Grover, were on the trail toward Fort Wallace returning from their disastrous meeting with the Cheyenne Dog Soldier leader, Turkey Leg. The scouts had been sent to talk peace with Roman Nose and the Dog Men, but Roman Nose had refused to meet with them and only one of the Cheyenne warrior societies' leaders, Turkey Leg, agreed to parley with them.

The meeting, which took place at Turkey Leg's lodge, went badly. The Dog Man leader had refused to smoke the pipe that Comstock had brought and spent the next twenty minutes shouting at the two white men. His anger was not directed particularly at Comstock and Grover, but at all the white men and their ways. He spoke of the broken treaties, the mass killing of the buffalo to satisfy the white man's lust for their hides, and the bad spirit of the iron horse that was bringing thousands of whites to the frontier to despoil their land. He also harangued them for the indiscriminate murder of children and squaws by the *ho' nehe*,* the pony soldiers, and the theft of their land by greedy settlers who insulted them and treated the *Tsitsitas*† as if they were coyotes.

---

*Soldiers
†The People

Medicine Bill was taken aback by Turkey Leg's tirade and tried to tell him that yes, there were many white men who had bad hearts but that there were others that shared his view of a world where both races could live in harmony. Turkey Leg scoffed at this assertion and swore that there would be no peace as long as the whites continued to treat the *Tsitsitas* with contempt.

The meeting ended in cold silence and both Comstock and Grover became nervous in leaving the Dog Man camp. Medicine Bill asked Turkey Leg for an escort to see them through their immediate territory and the warrior leader agreed to provide seven braves to accompany the two white scouts from the Dog Soldier encampment and out of the land under their direct control.

"I don't like the way these braves are looking at us," cautioned Sharp Grover as he cradled his Spencer more tightly in his arms. He looked at the seven braves who were about a hundred yards away on his right and hoped that they kept their distance.

"Oh, I'm sure they probably just want our animals, and not our hair," mocked Medicine Bill as he patted his big mule's neck. "Besides, they're Turkey Leg's Dog Men, and we have his assurances for safe passage."

"Still, I'll feel a whole lot better when we are out of this territory."

"Well, it won't be long now," replied Comstock as he pulled out his gold pocket watch that his father had given him when he was a boy. The scout clicked open the lid and gazed at the tiny hands to determine the time. The timepiece glistened in the dying summer sun and one of the braves saw the bright light.

"Five-thirty, we should be out of Dog Man territory in about twenty minutes if we continue at this pace," remarked Comstock. He looked at the face of the watch and admired its fine craftsmanship. The scout never grew tired of delighting in holding and looking at his family heirloom and he prided himself that it was the only item of luxury that he owned.

The Dog Man looked intensely at Comstock's timepiece and told his companions to look in the direction of the two white men. They chatted heatedly among themselves for a few seconds and Grover became concerned that they were now agitated.

"They're goin' to come after us!" Grover pulled back the lever on his Spencer, placing a round within the chamber, but before he could cock back the hammer, a hail of bullets had hit Comstock in the chest and liver, and Grover was wounded in the thigh as the Dog Men charged them, screaming, *"Hye, hye, hye!"*

Both Comstock and Grover fell off their mounts, and the beasts fled. Medicine Bill was spitting dark blood from his mouth and chest while the seven attackers were fast approaching.

"Jesus!" hollered Grover as he picked himself up from the ground and quickly placed the butt of his Spencer to his shoulder and aimed the weapon. He squeezed the trigger and managed to drop one of the charging Dog Soldiers' war ponies. The remaining braves reeled in shock from the barrage of bullets that came their way and reined in their ponies to retreat into the nearby brush.

"Bill!" Grover moved closer to the dying man.

"Black blood! They got me this time fo' sure."

"You best save your breath . . ."

"So much to say, so, so little time," interrupted Comstock as he cracked a painful grin. He was still clutching his timepiece but now the gold object and its chain were stained by blood.

"Take this. I don't want this fine watch to hang around the neck of some treacherous buck."

Sharp Grover took the watch reluctantly and placed the object in his vest pocket. When he turned around and looked into his friend's eyes, he saw that he had already expired from his wounds.

Two

OCTOBER 1868.

Brevet Major General Eugene A. Carr of the Fifth United States Cavalry was in a cantankerous and frustrated mood. Not only was he riding a horse that had an abrupt gait that made his backside and shoulders hurt, but his escort was two companies of black soldiers from the Tenth Cavalry!

The general had been out for days in a fruitless search for his regiment and was becoming impatient and curt with the officers of his "African" escort. The hero of the Battle of Pea Ridge and a veteran of the Vicksburg Campaign, Eugene Carr had been offered a commission after the war to command either the newly formed Ninth or Tenth Negro Cavalry. Like George Custer, however, Carr had chosen a lower rank in a white regiment rather than lead blacks. Not that he had anything personal against Negroes. After all, he had fought for their freedom, but he did not believe that they could be soldiers, and certainly not cavalrymen.

The general had arrived at Fort Wallace a few days ago after leaving his staff position at the War Department in Washington. He was sent to lead the Fifth Cavalry and was now looking on the Kansas plains for his regiment that had departed twelve days earlier under the temporary command of Major William B. Royall.

"Damn my fate!" whispered Carr to himself as he gnawed on

his teeth to prevent from crying out from discomfort when his rough mare abruptly shifted her gait and great weight to the left to avoid an abandoned gopher hole. "Darkies, always darkies," he emphasized under his breath and thick oval beard that covered half of his silk black cravat. The general briefly glanced with his quick eyes at Nate and Jesse who were riding near him, and shook his head in distaste and resignation, and in a low voice that was not meant to be heard, said, "What's the army coming to?"

Nate heard Carr mumbling to himself and although he could not hear all of the words clearly, he sensed that the general was ill at ease being escorted by black troopers. The senior officer avoided all contact with the men in his escort and talked contemptuously to Captains Carpenter and Grail. Nate didn't care though if Carr stayed away and avoided eye contact with the men and behaved as if the Colored troopers did not exist.

He had seen these types of officers before. He remembered during the war, when he was in the infantry with the First Kansas Colored Regiment posted at Fort Scott in 1862. So many white officers were ignorant and condescending toward black volunteers that they talked to them and treated them as if they were dogs. Nate chuckled incredulously to himself as he thought about how one shave-tail officer of Irish descent from Massachusetts would always reward a recruit with the words "*Good* boy! That's a *very good* boy!" The officer would repeat the sentence over and over again as if the men never heard him the first time.

"Sergeant Major!" beckoned Captain Louis Carpenter as he raised his arm, signaling the command to halt. The commander of Carr's escort saw a small creek to the north, and considering it was almost twilight, Louis Carpenter decided to bivouac his two companies and get an early start in the morning.

Carpenter called for Nate to come up. Nate squeezed his thighs against his horse's flanks and cantered to the head of the column where Captain Carpenter and General Carr were.

"Sir?" queried Nate as he pulled up next to his commanding officer. He gently pulled on the reins on his new coal-black, three-year-old gelding, Frederick, and maneuvered the animal skillfully. It was Cara who had planted the idea to name the gelding in honor of Frederick Douglass. Nate had met his son during the war and often spoke to Cara about how he would like to someday be as articulate as the famous abolitionist. When Cara suggested the name of Frederick to him, Nate at first was appalled. But then he reflected on the idea and decided that Cara was right. He had purchased the animal from a Mexican some weeks before who badly needed money. The Mexican had preferred to sell to Nate because he hated *Norte Americanos* and did not want to sell his beautiful animal to a gringo. Consequently, when Nate inquired if the animal was for sale, the Mexican obliged him and only asked for thirty dollars when he knew he could get much more from a gringo.

"We will bivouac here for the night," ordered Carpenter. "I want you to see that the number of sentries on the picket line are doubled, and pick your best men. I want the horses as well grazed as possible before sundown and watered in the creek." Nate was about to turn his mount around to execute the orders when Carpenter called him back. "Oh, Sergeant Major! No cook fires, no pipes, and no talking."

"Aye, sir," replied Nate smartly as Frederick reared slightly on his hindquarters. Nate smoothly and almost effortlessly brought the animal down and departed at a gentle canter to inform Jesse and the other noncoms of Carpenter's bivouac orders.

"Doubling the sentries won't prevent those men from sleeping on duty," scoffed General Carr as he sat smugly on his horse.

"I assure you, General, my men do not sleep while on duty," snapped back Carpenter.

17

"If you say so, Carpenter. As far as I am concerned, I think our prospects of finding my regiment are growing dimmer by the hour and that this excursion into the Kansas wilderness has been fruitless. Now if my escort would have been all white, I am certain that I would have found my command by now."

"General, with all due respect, locating anything on the plains that *moves* is very difficult," retorted Carpenter, who took that last statement as an affront. "And if I may be permitted to say, sir, half of these men were with me when we located Forsyth's command on the Arikaree."

"You might have located Forsyth, but it was his scouts that led you to them," responded Carr dismissively.

Captain Louis Carpenter did not wish to argue with the general who was a Medal of Honor recipient and possessed much national prestige. But like his commanding officer, Benjamin Grierson, however, Carpenter knew better. He had every confidence in Company H and Company I. Both of them had been with him when he saved Forsyth's pitiful command from annihilation by Roman Nose's hordes of Cheyenne warriors.

II.

Nate, Jesse, and the scout, Sharp Grover, were standing near the horse picket line. The horses were quiet and most of the mounts were asleep due to fatigue from the day's thirty-five-mile-long march. Nate and Jesse had completed overseeing the grazing and watering of the horses, and placed pickets around the perimeter of the bivouac area. Nate had also ordered that the men keep their Spencer repeaters at hand rather than stacking the carbines, as was customary. The soldiers were in hostile territory and the ravines that covered the High Plains were still crawling with hostiles and especially the *Hotame Ho' nehe*, the dreaded Dog Soldiers. After supervising those tasks, Nate and Jesse walked among the troopers and watched them eat hardtack and dried vegetables, such as onions and tuber roots, in silence. After the meager supper and as darkness enveloped the landscape, one by one the soldiers pulled their wool sleeping blankets over their bodies and fell asleep.

Nate had wanted to talk to Sharp Grover in private ever since leaving Fort Wallace, but the opportunity had not presented itself until now. He had first met the scout when he led Carpenter and the troopers of H Company to Beecher Island to rescue the wretched survivors from the fight with Roman Nose and Cougar Eyes, but had not seen him until they were departing Fort Wallace to look for Carr's Fifth Cavalry.

It was what Nate thought he overheard Grover tell another scout regarding Medicine Bill Comstock, however, that motivated Nate to speak with him. As the troops were preparing to leave Wallace, Nate was in a hurry to see that his men were equipped and saddled when he suddenly crossed paths with Sharp Grover and another scout. He only caught the last part of their conversation, but the comment that Grover made to the other scout regarding Comstock bothered him and kept ringing in his head. *"Don't worry, I don't expect to face the same fate as Medicine Bill!"*

"Scout," queried Nate in a grave manner as he approached Grover. "I need to know something about what I heard you say back at Wallace."

Sharp Grover was taken aback by Nate's directness and for a moment wondered if this big black noncom was a snoop. But Sharp remained appreciative of the men of Company H who had come to their rescue at Beecher Island. He remembered how one trooper willingly gave him all his bacon from his saddlebag when he was half crazed with starvation. Sharp was a soft-spoken polite man who thirsted for revenge against the Dog Soldiers.

"Back at Wallace, I believe you mentioned something 'bout Medicine Bill."

"You ain't heard, Sergeant?" replied Grover, looking up at Nate. The moon was out and there was a soft glow that made the scout's wide-brimmed hat look ridiculous on his small head. Grover, for his part, thought Nate's skin looked like he was dark blue in color rather than black, while the whites of his eyes made him nervous.

"He got killed, Sergeant-Major. Them deceiving, lying, thieving Indians betrayed our trust and tried to *kill* us!" Grover paused for a moment and sighed; he had taken a nip from a flask he carried in his saddlebags and was feeling melancholy. Grover had taken a liking to hard liquor ever since the horrors he had witnessed on that sandy island on the Arikaree. "If it was not for Medicine Bill's *body*, them bastards would have kil't me too."

"What happened, scout?" Nate asked softly, but without exhibiting any emotion.

"It happened about a month before the island fight on the Arikaree when Lieutenant Beecher sent us to parley with Turkey Leg. The lieutenant *really* believed that if Comstock and me could talk to Turkey Leg, we could convince him to put a halt to his warriors' raids and ravishments of the settlements *all along* the Saline and Solomon Valleys. Poor Beecher, God rest his soul." Sharp bowed his head and tipped his hat in reverence as a gesture of respect for his recently departed commander. Nate noticed that Grover's breathing became heavier as he continued with his story. "*Beecher*. He—he thought that if we could *reach* the chief at his camp, and tried to smooth things over, the bloodshed would stop."

"Did you see Turkey Leg?"

"Oh, we saw the ol' cuss alright. And he was madder than hell. He told us that the raids and bloodshed was right because the white man broke every treaty he had ever made and that the pony soldiers were the killers of women and children. And what's more, the bastard was not prepared to stop in what he considered was just cause for the invasion of Cheyenne lands."

"Did you try an' talk to him as Lieutenant Beecher ordered?" asked Nate in a tone as if he were addressing a recruit. Nate's sudden authoritative demeanor startled Sharp Grover. The scout became unsure whether he should feel insulted or defensive because maybe Medicine Bill and Grover had, in fact, failed in their mission to communicate with Turkey Leg.

"The man would not hear us out! He told us to leave and when Medicine Bill told him that he did not trust his warriors to obey the truce, Turkey Leg appointed an escort of seven of his young braves to escort us out of harm's way. Well, we got out of the village all right, but once we were on the open plains near the limit of their territory, the savages pointed their carbines at us and opened up with a blast of gunfire." Grover paused and sighed. "Medicine Bill first got hit in the chest and liver. To this moment, I can still see his blood pouring out of him. I myself was slightly hit in my right thigh."

Nate's mouth and left eye winced. He had told himself not to show any emotion, but visualizing his friend's death startled him, and made him angry.

"How did you get away?"

"*Luck*. Medicine Bill's body took the brunt of the first volley, and since the warriors were busy reloading their single-shot carbines, I had time to dismount and grab my Spencer. I threw myself to the ground using Comstock's body as a breastwork and started to work that hammer and lever for dear life shooting at rapid fire at the red heathens. They withdrew in confusion but not before they rode off with our mounts. For the rest of the day, I had to defend myself and hide behind Medicine Bill's body, for the Cheyennes kept shooting at me from a distance. When night came, the firing stopped, and I decided to crawl away and make my escape back to Fort Wallace."

"What about Medicine Bill's body?" Nate had visions of his friend's body being robbed and stripped by the braves, and this bothered him more than Comstock's murder. Since he began fighting Indians, Nate had wondered why it was so necessary for the hostiles to strip and mutilate the dead in such fiendish ways.

"Never found," snapped Grover, a little defensively. "I tried to find his corpse with a few other men who would return with me, but we just could not locate it. I shudder to think. I guess the wolves took care of him after the Cheyennes got done with him."

"Yeah, probably," mumbled Nate, deep in thought.

"You know, Sergeant"—Grover's voice became softer, trying to reassure Nate and himself—"out here"—Grover took his arm and waved it against his chest as if he were in a parley with an Indian—"on the plains, people and animals die and disappear real quick. And maybe that's best."

"Yeah, maybe," said Nate, slowly bowing his head, and as he turned away, the right side of his face caught the moonlight and Sharp Grover noticed a huge tear pouring down Nate's cheek.

III.

Turkey Leg was a guest in Cougar Eyes' lodge. The Dog Men sat in silence while eating a hearty meal of venison, potatoes, thistle, and wild grapes that Cougar Eyes' squaw, Willow Branch, had prepared for them. They sat near the fire in the center of the lodge staring at the tiny cook fire's smoke clouds that gently climbed and disappeared into the smoke hole and vanished in the brisk night. The strong scent of cooked food and human body odor permeated the air. Both warriors finished eating at the same time and placed their clay bowls near the edge of the fire. Cougar Eyes then ordered Willow Branch to leave the tipi and immediately reached for his long polished stone pipe. He then removed his beaded tobacco pouch that was made from buffalo scrotum from the corner of his parfleche and pinched some tobacco from it and lightly packed the bowl. Completing this ritualistic task he bent his torso near the edge of the cook fire and seized a twig that he had placed there earlier and touched the tiny piece of ash wood to the bowl and drew deeply from his lungs. Turkey Leg's eyes widened with envy when he noticed the hue of his host's very finely polished stone pipe as Cougar Eyes flamed the opening. He took deep breaths and on the third hit passed the pipe, stem first, to his guest and friend. Cougar Eyes' usually obedient wife was again ordered by her husband to leave the tipi for the warriors wished to discuss things that did not concern a squaw.

"I must clean up first," snapped back Willow Branch, irritated that Turkey Leg was visiting her husband. Willow Branch did not like him. She considered Turkey Leg rude and curt, and was disappointed that her husband considered him a friend, for she knew in her heart that Turkey Leg was a rival to her husband.

Willow Branch noisily removed the clay bowls and left the tipi to go outside and wash them, but deliberately left the door unflapped as a means to protest Turkey Leg's presence. A cold surge of air entered the tipi, causing the tiny flames of the cook fire to flicker and the Dog Men to shudder. Cougar Eyes quietly got to his feet and closed the flap but his guest had become irritated by his host's woman's actions.

"Your squaw is insolent, my brother!" Turkey Leg became irked that the warmth of the tipi was now diluted by this sudden burst of cold air. "If she were my squaw, I would have used my elkhorn quirt to beat her."

"She is proud, that is true, my brother, but I like that quality in a woman. To break her spirit is like breaking the spirit of a fine young pony."

"Perhaps, but a fine young pony like a woman needs the control of a strong and steady hand," retorted Turkey Leg, taking a deep hit off the pipe and savoring the tobacco.

Cougar Eyes wanted to abandon this line of conversation. Turkey Leg was not the only fellow warrior who criticized and teased him regarding Willow Branch's impertinence and his lack of physical discipline to instill obedience.

"Why did *your* Dog Men from *your* warrior society betray the two white scouts you had promised safe conduct from our camp?" inquired Cougar Eyes methodically, taking back his pipe from his guest. He was referring to Medicine Bill and Sharp Grover's visit to their camp.

Turkey Leg remained motionless for a moment as his eyes sharpened. "I promised them safe conduct from the camp that is true, but I never promised them safe conduct from my braves once they were out in the open."

Cougar Eyes listened patiently and remained silent, sensing that his guest was becoming annoyed with his questions. He passed the pipe back to Turkey Leg in an effort to placate him.

"Besides, how many times have the *Ve' ho' e** betrayed their words?" Turkey Leg took such a deep hit from the pipe that Cougar Eyes could see the glow of the burning tobacco.

"I think it was bad medicine that the scout Medicine Bill was killed in such a way. He was white, that is true, but he came honorably to us and he was killed dishonorably. He came in peace and wanted to leave in peace, and he spoke our tongue. He was also always fair with the *Tsitsitas*." Cougar Eyes stared into the campfire and added with a sense of melancholy and foreboding,

---

*White man

"But what I find most troublesome, my brother, is that he was a friend with *Tsehe esta'-ehe*,* And *he* has the power to harm us."

"I am tired of the words and promises of the *Ve' ho' e*, I rather die like *Voo' xenehe†* than to live with the *Ve' ho' e* like a beggar. They are like locusts, stripping our land and leaving us nothing."

"I agree with you, my brother, but I saw the nighthawk in a dream last night and he told me that something is going to happen to the *Tsitsitas*."

A man's voice was heard from outside the tipi. He asked if he could enter Cougar Eyes' lodge. It was Wolf Man or, as most of the believers of his new medicine were now calling him, *Ho ho I tu i* (Bullet Proof).

"*Ni'istsihnsts,‡* my brother." Cougar Eyes had been expecting Bullet Proof; he wanted to know what Turkey Leg thought about his new and apparently invincible medicine of making men bulletproof.

Bullet Proof quickly unflapped the lodge's entranceway and stepped into the warmth of Cougar Eyes' tipi.

"Flap the door," snapped Turkey Leg, who again became aggravated that another burst of cold air drifted past his body.

Bullet Proof was carrying a buffalo hide that came from a young bull. The garment was delicately draped over his left arm with the coat of soft fur facing outward. Bullet Proof seemed to give great reverence to the robe.

"*Haaahe,*" greeted Cougar Eyes as he moved his hand across his chest.

Bullet Proof took his place to the left of Cougar Eyes. He was dressed in fine trade-cloth black leggings with a wide red stripe

---
*General George Custer
†Roman Nose
‡Come in

down the sides and his red tunic was tied off at the waist with a captured yellow silk cavalry sash. Like Cougar Eyes and Turkey Leg, Bullet Proof wore a silver pictorial with suspended *najas*. What earned him respect, however, were the two eagle feathers whose tips were dyed in red horsehair, which identified him as a warrior.

"My brother Cougar Eyes told me about the medicine you have in preventing the *Ve' ho' e* bullets from penetrating your *hotoa' e* robes," said Turkey Leg eagerly.

"It came to me in a vision when I went to the lands of the Utes," stated Bullet Proof confidently. "In the vision, an old buffalo bull showed me the way to treat the hides of young bulls and make them impervious to the bullets of the *Ve' ho' e*."

"Were you purified before the vision came to you?" asked Cougar Eyes, who placed a fresh pinch of tobacco in his stone pipe. He wanted to be sure that Bullet Proof did all the proper *Tsitsitas* customs and rituals. The recent death of Roman Nose and the belief that it was because he tasted food from a cast-iron pot made by the *Ve' ho' e* only added to Cougar Eyes' trepidation.

"I made the great sweat in the willow lodge, and I fasted for three days in the land of the Utes when finally the vision came."

Cougar Eyes misplaced the twig he had used previously to ignite his stone pipe, so he decided to seize a tiny charcoal from the fire with his hand and place the burning ember into the bowl. He took a deep hit to get the tobacco burning while Turkey Leg and Bullet Proof gazed at the hue of the pipe. Cougar Eyes savored the tobacco by blowing the smoke out of his mouth slowly. He then rested the pipe on his lap and spoke with respect to Bullet Proof.

"The people want to believe in your courage, my brother. Many of us witnessed your strong medicine during the fight with the *Ve' ho' e* scouts on the Arikaree. When you were shot through

26

the breast and the bullet came through your back, you were not harmed. When you dismounted your war pony and touched the ground with your hand and rubbed the hand in front and back, you stopped the bleeding and closed the wounds. We are glad to see that all is well."

Bullet Proof nodded his appreciation to Cougar Eyes.

"Two of your *Hotame Ho' nehe* from your warrior society and who are also my relatives have come to me and asked if they can wear the bulletproof robes in our next fight against the pony soldiers." Bullet Proof knew that this information would surprise his host. Cougar Eyes was the leader of his warrior society, the *Mai gho-moi.** So, for Cougar Eyes' braves to go directly to him outside the society was a breech in protocol and undermined the cohesion of the Dog Soldier society.

"Who are these warriors?" demanded Cougar Eyes, irritated that his authority over his braves in the *Mai gho-moi* might have been compromised. His eyes became sharp and his body stiffened.

"My uncle, Bobtailed Porcupine, and my cousin, Breaks The Arrow."

Cougar Eyes puffed heavily on his pipe, then handed it over to Wolf Man. "They are my best warriors. They have been with me in many fights against the *Ve' ho' e* and the *Mo' ohtae-Ve' ho' e.*†

"Then you will not object if they are the first to charge the pony soldiers when we meet them?" Wolf Man returned the pipe to his host.

Cougar Eyes thought for a moment on what Wolf Man had just said. On the one hand, he resented that two of his Dog Soldiers went behind his back. On the other, he was eager for Wolf

*The Red Lances
†Black White Man

Man's new name Bullet Proof be truly earned by demonstrating that he had indeed with the help of the spirits found a way to treat buffalo hides to become impervious to bullets.

"I will watch in anticipation when Bobtailed Porcupine and Breaks The Arrow charge the pony soldiers in your hides, *Ho ho I tu i.*"

IV.

Nate was making an entry into his journal. His wool bedroll was converted into a tiny tent supported by several cottonwood branches that he had found along the creek. His body was resting on its left side on the ground as if he were an infant. His left hand supported his head while he wrote furiously with his quill as a stub of burning wax flickered close to his face. Because they were in hostile country and ordered to have no lights burning, Nate made sure that his provisional wool structure was tight. Over the years, he had perfected this practice so well that no light could be seen from the outside, just like he used to do with his mother when they were slaves to avoid detection. All during the war, as long as he could find some light, he would sneak away for a few minutes or no more than a half hour and find a private spot to write a few words in his journal. Erecting a temporary structure with his bedroll and a candle for lighting was all he needed.

> I cannot get Cara out of mind. The features of her face, her perfume, and her voice will not leave my head. I long to feel the touch of her raven hair and the soft-ness of her brown skin. The worst time is during the day when we ride over endless miles of prairie so a man's mind either becomes completely dull by the mo-notony of the terrain or becomes distracted by personal

thoughts. At night, at least, I can write down my thoughts about Cara, and this clears my mind. I don't like being distracted from my duties, but since this woman has entered into my life, I find my mind has been made captive.

General Carr is a cold, ambitious, and arrogant man. I have been watching him for several days, and I have concluded that he is a man in a hurry! He has an aura of great confidence, but is impatient and condescending. I know that he won the Medal of Honor during the war and was fighting the hostiles when I was just a slave, but he shows nothing but contempt for us and even disrespects his subordinate officers.

V.

It was an hour before reveille and General Carr, unable to sleep because of restlessness and frustration, instructed his orderly to wake Carpenter, Grail, and Sharp Grover and have them report.

Grover was the first to arrive. He cradled his Spencer repeater in his arms as if it were a baby and his eyes flashed hawklike about Carr's tent. Carpenter and Grail followed quickly, dressed in full field uniform and wearing Army Colt .44s. The orderly had brought a lantern earlier and attached it to the central support pole of the tent after Carr instructed him to keep the flame low and the flap door closed until daylight.

"I have decided that we need to send out another small reconnaissance patrol with Mr. Grover, farther downstream of Beaver Creek." Carr's tunic was open, the lapels buttoned back, revealing a blue vest. The lighting of the tent was poor, and Carr's eyes squinted at a map of the northwest area of the Kansas frontier that was unfolded neatly on a camp table in the center of the tent.

"General, we have already reconnoitered in that area and found no evidence that the Fifth Cavalry was anywhere nearby," argued Carpenter, concerned that Carr was now going to dispatch tiny patrols of his command to search for his regiment. Carpenter preferred to keep his two companies together and send out deep flankers to pick up trails or sight roaming bands of Dog Soldiers rather than dispatching small and vulnerable squads into hostile territory.

"Except for the tracks of a single Indian pony that were sighted yesterday by Mr. Grover!" retorted Carr in an irritated tone of voice. "Therefore, I have decided to send Mr. Grover out again, with an officer and two of your best men, and pick up those tracks and follow them."

"*Sir!* I would like to volunteer," barked Captain Grail, standing crisply at attention.

Carpenter's eyes rolled, and he thought to himself, *Damn fool is going to get himself killed. What is the purpose of this?* Carpenter turned and faced General Carr. "Sir, would it not be best to return to Fort Wallace and wait for your regiment there, rather than continuing to search blindly?"

"I am not sending out Mr. Grover to locate the Fifth Cavalry," responded Carr calmly, rolling the map and placing it in its carrying tube. "I am inclined to agree with you that the column should return to Wallace. But first I want to follow up on those tracks that were sighted yesterday and locate hostiles."

Carpenter was not afraid to run into Dog Soldiers. He had over a hundred forty men under his command and felt confident that his two companies could fight off any attack. What concerned him, however, was that the command was not out to seek engagement with the elusive Cheyennes while trailing a dozen wagons and pack animals. Carpenter believed that conditions were simply not conducive for taking the offense. He had also witnessed the horrifying results on Forsyth's crack scouts after they had engaged hundreds of Dog Men on the Arikaree, and he wanted to avoid a similar fate.

Well, he thought to himself, *best to assign my two top men for this task if the general wants to find Dog Men.*

"I recommend that Sergeant Major Gordon and First Sergeant Randolph go with Captain Grail and Grover, General. They have the most experience in my command. If there are Dog Men out there, they'll find 'em."

"Good, good!" replied the hero of Pea Ridge. His mood had now become enthusiastic at the prospect that if he could not find his regiment, at least maybe he could engage some hostiles and that his foray on the Kansas plains was not for nothing.

"Don't worry, General, we'll find some Dog Men to kill," blurted Grover, eager to avenge his dead comrades of Beecher Island.

VI.

Nate was on top of Frederick, while Jesse was making a tack adjustment to his McClellan. They were waiting for Grover and Captain Grail near the horse picket line. Carpenter had told Nate that he was relying on him to follow orders, and to remind Grail if need be to avoid all contact with the hostiles if they were spotted.

The late October air was brisk and the horses' breath poured from their nostrils resembling thin clouds while they snorted and eyeballed each other. Nate's horse, Frederick, was acting up. He kept chopping on his bit and lowering his head abruptly to the ground, jerking the reins. "*Stop it,*" commanded Nate loudly, smacking the brute on the side of his head after the animal had repeatedly ignored his commands to behave.

"I *tol' you*, that hoss is too frisky," boasted Jesse teasingly as his own gelding, Cailloux, stood calmly. Jesse's horse was a government-issue, wind-blown relic of the war. He had spent weeks fattening up the animal and giving the horse extra attention and, with Nate's supervision, a lot of ring work. He had named the gelding after Captain Andre Cailloux, who was Jesse's senior company commander in his old wartime regiment, the First Regiment, Louisiana Native Guards. Captain Cailloux, a freed man of color and a respected citizen of New Orleans, was much admired by Jesse. During the battle of Port Hudson, Andre Cailloux, who had his left arm shattered by a minié ball, rallied his troops in both French and English and was finally shot to death while leading a charge against Confederate breastworks.

"I like the look of his eyes. Big an' bright," responded Nate, staring into his horse's eyes.

"An' full of promise, I'm sure," teased Jesse cynically as he mounted Cailloux.

Sharp Grover and Captain Grail appeared from the other side of the camp and when they saw the two noncoms ready to depart, they broke into a trot to catch up.

"Mawnin', boys." Grover smiled as the brim of his wide sombrero moved in the breeze. The scout easily balanced his Spencer repeater on the front of his saddle, frontier style. Nate nodded and Jesse smiled and returned the greeting.

Nate suddenly was reminded of his now-dead friend and mentor, Medicine Bill. Not that Grover looked or even dressed in the same manner as Comstock. It was the way Sharp Grover held his carbine and the relaxed manner he carried himself in the saddle while his quick eyes seemed always to be searching the ground and horizon that made Nate compare Grover with Medicine Bill.

"Take the point, Mr. Grover," commanded Captain Grail as he raised his hand toward the southwest.

"Let's go find some Dog Men," boasted the young scout, spurring his horse forward.

VII.

Cougar Eyes, Turkey Leg, Breaks The Arrow, and Bobtailed Porcupine were crouched behind some tall brown buffalo grass on a slight incline about six hundred yards from where Company H and I were bivouacked. They observed Nate, Jesse, Grover, and Captain Grail leave camp and turn south for Beaver Creek. The sudden cry of a meadowlark broke the stillness of the air and briefly drew Cougar Eyes' attention away from watching his prey. The Dog Men's ponies were cropping grass a few yards behind where the warriors were secluded and painted for war.

Cougar Eyes was holding a model 1855 Colt revolving rifle that he had acquired in exchange for his beloved Henry repeater. Initially, the Dog Soldier had reservations in trading the fifteen-shot Henry that he had captured at the Fetterman Fight for the inferior, older Colt, but decided that if he wanted a rifle where ammunition was plentiful, he had to make the trade.

The Dog Men were dressed in warm, dark clothing to protect themselves from the late October air and winds. The warriors wore heavy shirts made from trade cloth with paisley patterns, cowhide vests, and silk scarves stolen from *Ve' ho' e* homesteads. They also wore tight leather leggings and thick beaded moccasins, and all the braves possessed blankets that were either draped over saddle pads or wore them over their backs.

Cougar Eyes recognized Sharp Grover immediately at the head of the group but squinted his eyes toward the last man that covered the rear who was riding a good-looking young black horse. He was the biggest of the pony soldiers and after identifying the wide yellow chevrons on the man's upper arm, sharply remarked to Turkey Leg, *"Hotoa' e Gordon!"*

"It is good then! We will kill some *Mo' ohtae-Ve' ho' e*," responded Turkey Leg as his eyes sharpened and he touched the braid of human hair on his bow-lance.

VIII.

"Thinkin' 'bout your woman?" jested Jesse as he moved Cailloux next to Nate's young gelding. Jesse had noticed that Nate looked melancholy this morning. Not that his silence was unusual, but it was the sadness in his eyes that betrayed his despondency.

"I . . . can't git the woman out of my mind," responded Nate awkwardly as he shifted his weight in the saddle. It was clear that he was a little uncomfortable talking about affairs of the heart.

"Oh, hell, you'll be with her soon 'nough, my man!" responded Jesse, trying to reassure his companion.

"It's a hell of thing, Jesse. My mind keeps a-wonderin' and it scares me," confessed Nate.

"Nuthin' like *a good fight* to clear your head, just you wait."

"Yeah, it's 'bout the *only* time that I don't think 'bout Cara," acknowledged Nate as he took a deep breath and was about to look over the western horizon when he heard an abrupt sound of two successive thuds. Suddenly Sharp Grover's horse reared up on its hind hooves and neighed in pain. Nate noticed immediately that two arrows had hit the rump of Grover's horse and the terrified animal nearly threw its rider, forcing the scout to seize the animal's neck to avoid being thrown.

He frantically shouted, "Whoa! Whoa! Whoa!"

Nate next heard gunfire and the rest of the men turned to the northwest and saw a party of howling Dog Soldiers coming toward them at a full gallop.

"They're trying to *cut us off* from the camp!" shouted Sharp Grover. With great effort, the scout had managed to regain control over his horse but had to pull hard on the reins and had to force the animal into a tight circle to slow him down. The horse, however, still pranced violently about in pain and bled profusely from the two arrow wounds.

Nate saw that Captain Grail was paralyzed with inaction due to fear. He had seen that look before. Shavetail white officers buckling under the pressure of battle and unable to give orders. He knew that this officer, who had volunteered to find Dog Men, was now suffering from the same fate of incertitude. Grail had never seen a band of fast-moving painted ponies with howling warriors brandishing lances and rifles charge him out of nowhere. Nate galloped the few feet that separated him and the commanding officer and placed his horse in front of Grail.

"Sir! The scout is *right*. We've *got* to return to the camp 'fore they cut us off an' bring up more Dog Men!"

Grail stared at Nate with motionless eyes while Nate took stock on how far the Dog Soldiers were from cutting them off. Grover's horse was still whining in pain as he thrashed his head from side to side and danced madly in an effort to be free of the arrows that protruded from his haunches. Jesse had drawn his Army Colt and held the weapon fully cocked in the air, getting ready to aim and fire, but was having trouble controlling Cailloux who smelled the Indian ponies and was beginning to misbehave almost as badly as Grover's wounded mount.

Finally, Grail came out of his frozen state of mind after Nate again strongly suggested that they ride as fast as possible back to the bivouac area.

"Yes, yes," he stammered. "We must retreat back to the safety of the camp, Sergeant Major. Follow me!" Captain Grail dug his spurs into his mount's flanks and the animal bolted, blowing off Grail's straw hat from his head.

With Grail in the lead and Jesse and Grover following closely behind, they galloped their mounts as fast as the animals would move as dozens of bullets buzzed by them as if they were a horde of indignant bees. Nate decided to hold back Frederick and cover the retreat. He first maneuvered his horse to face the attackers and then swung his Spencer to his shoulder. He slowly raised himself in the saddle by pushing down on the stirrups and cocked the repeater and began firing at the Dog Men. He only managed to get off five rounds when Frederick started to become excited by the Indian ponies and wanted to run with Cailloux back toward camp. Nate obliged him. If he did not move immediately, the Dog Men would cut him off from the camp and he would find himself alone. He calmly returned the Spencer to his right side by adjusting the carbine sling and then pressed down on the visor of his kepi and touched spur to flank. Frederick bolted and Nate could feel his mount's strength and power between his legs as he leaned forward and pressed his thighs forward, encouraging the animal to gallop faster and faster.

Cougar Eyes saw that his prey was getting away. He became awed when he saw *Hotoa' e Gordon's mo'ehno'ha* move so swiftly. Cougar Eyes briefly admired the animal's long and sleek body as it moved like the wind and decided that he wanted *Hotoa' e Gordon*'s mount.

Nate had caught up with Jesse, Grover, and Grail, and although the soldiers were moving fast, they were losing the race with the Dog Men's swift ponies to reach the camp.

Captain Louis Carpenter heard the sounds of gunfire and knew immediately that Grail had been ambushed. He wasted no time and ordered thirty men to horse. The troopers were saddled and ready within a minute and Carpenter, leading the way, charged out of the bivouac area, heading toward Grail who was within sight.

When the Dog Men saw that Carpenter and his troopers were coming at them, they abruptly halted their war ponies, turned them, and retreated behind some ravines that were near Beaver Creek.

*"Noxa'e!"** shouted Cougar Eyes as he motioned Turkey Leg to halt his pony. "I will send Breaks The Arrow and Bobtailed Porcupine to tell our brothers to join us in attacking the pony soldiers."

"Yes! All the Dog Soldier societies must participate."

"We want to wear Bullet Proof's robes in the fight against the *ho' nehe*," clamored Bobtailed Porcupine.

"Then go. Turkey Leg and I will wait here."

IX.

General Carr had watched Carpenter and his thirty troopers drive off the Dog Soldiers. The general was mildly impressed with the speed and diligence of "Carpenter's *brunettes*." He had not expected the men to move as quickly as they did when the order was given "to horse." He observed that the troopers exerted expert control over their mounts and seemed genuinely enthusiastic as they charged the Dog Soldiers, something that the general had not seen since the war. He noted, however, that there were only a few warriors and that they retreated as soon as they spotted Carpenter's men.

"General, I think we should get the column moving and cross the north side of the Beaver." Carpenter was breathing heavily, he

---

*Wait

was still feeling the adrenaline going through his body due to the brief chase.

"I concur, we should make for Fort Wallace," confirmed Carr. "If the few Cheyennes that might be around this vicinity won't fight, I prefer to return to Wallace and await my regiment there."

As soon as Captain Grail, Nate, Jesse, and Grover made it back to the bivouac area, Nate went up to Sharp Grover's wounded horse. The horse's haunches, legs, and rear hooves were soaked with blood and the animal was breathing heavily. Nate approached the beast carefully, speaking to him softly. He examined the point of entry of the arrows and determined that the projectiles were fired into the sky in an arc angle, entering the animal's flesh from above.

"You know whut to do with them arrows, don't ya?" asked Nate, concerned about the animal's painful ordeal.

Sharp stood in front of the horse holding the reins tightly.

"No! I've never removed an arrow."

Nate did not have much time. The order was given that the men, wagons, and mules were to move out at once and cross the Beaver to the north side. Jesse was already busy seeing that his men were following orders, so amid the sounds of wagons being hitched and driven off, mules packed, and companies forming up, Nate went to his saddlebag where he kept a pint of two hundred proof whiskey and removed the bottle and pulled out his Bowie. He then gently poured a small quantity on both ends of the huge blade and looked Grover in the eyes.

"I've done this before."

"Go ahead! Cut 'em out. I'll try an' keep him still," said the scout with a nod. He forcefully pulled the top of his wounded horse's head toward his mouth and prepared to bite down on the animal's left ear. It was a trick that his father had taught him when he broke horses.

Nate smoothly caressed the horse's neck with his left hand as he made his way toward the haunches where the arrows protruded.

Grover bit down on the animal's ear and held it there, applying sufficient pressure to force the horse's body to freeze.

Nate then placed the slightly curved tip of his Bowie knife along the side of the shaft of the first arrow and slowly and skillfully plunged the blade into the horse's rump following the length of the shaft until he reached the rear of the arrowhead. Then, with his left hand holding the bottom of the shaft at the point of entry while holding the Bowie with his right, Nate gently worked the blade to remove muscle and hide away from the arrowhead. Satisfied that nothing would obstruct the removal of the arrow, he yanked it from the horse's flesh. The horse briefly kicked, jerked his head, and neighed, but Grover kept his teeth on the animal's ear so the beast remained relatively calm. Nate repeated the process with the second arrow while Sharp Grover kept biting on the horse's ear. Completing the removal of the two arrows, Nate ordered Grover to release his teeth from the horse's ear and inquired anxiously, "Got any black powder?"

"Just what I got in my shells."

"Break out two of them an' remove the heads," he commanded hurriedly.

Grover knew exactly what to do. On Beecher Island, during the fight with Roman Nose on the Arikaree, the scouts had used gunpowder to spice up putrid horse and mule meat in order to hide the stench and decomposition, and used it to close and disinfect wounds. Grover removed two Spencer cartridges from his ammunition pouch and used the tip of his hunting knife to pry the lead bullets from their casings. He then carefully handed the shells to Nate and watched him pour the black powder on the two wounds. Once again the animal kicked and bucked violently but then calmed down.

"He'll be all right—he'll be stiff an' sore, but he'll be all right."

X.

Nate made his way toward the head of the column to where Captain Carpenter and General Carr, along with Company H, were spearheading the crossing of the Beaver. Company I covered the rear where the wagons and mule train were having trouble keeping up with the troopers because the fording of the Beaver proved to be more difficult than anticipated. Carpenter and Carr were on the north side of the Beaver watching the wagons negotiate the creek when Nate appeared and saluted. He then turned to Carpenter.

"Sir, I think the Dog Men will return in great force an' attack the column in the open."

Captain Louis Carpenter concurred with Nate's assessment. He considered Nate a seasoned Indian fighter and valued his opinion more highly than most officers who were stationed on the frontier and who could only dream in equaling the experience of Sergeant Major Nate Gordon, or as he was rapidly being known among his men, *Hotoa' e Gordon*.

"How *did you* come to that conclusion, Sergeant Major?" bristled Carr, sizing up the upstart noncom with great skepticism.

"Well, sir . . ." Nate was about to explain his reasons when shots from multiple carbines rang out toward the south in which several bullets hit the ground near Carr's skittish horse's hooves, sending up patches of turf and dried buffalo grass into the air and spooking the general's mount.

"Sir! Ov'a dare! . . . *Hoss-tiles,*" hollered Carpenter's orderly, Private Reuben Waller, pointing toward the south.

Approaching at a gallop, some two hundred howling warriors were coming at the troopers and wagons from the south side of the Beaver. Their eager war ponies' hooves splashed and sprayed the water of the creek into the air while they rapidly unloaded their carbines and pistols at the troopers of Company H who were posted at the head and flanks of the column.

"Dismount. Form skirmish line. Fire at will," bellowed Carpenter, raising himself in the saddle. The bugler sounded the order and the men rushed from their mounts to take positions on the line. Hundreds of arrows were shot from the Dog Men's bowlances at the full length of the column and some braves waved blankets hoping to scare the mules and horses away from their handlers.

Nate had placed himself at the center of the skirmish line holding his Spencer at the ready and clamored encouragement to his men. *"Pour it in, boys ... Let 'em have it."* The Cheyennes, however, kept their distance from the column. After the losses they had incurred at the fight at Beecher Island and other engagements with the pony soldiers, they learned to keep out of harm's way from the deadly repeaters. They were perfectly content to fire at the *ho' nehe* from a safe distance and await reinforcements.

"Should we not circle the wagons, Captain?" asked Grail, firing his army Colt wildly at the Dog Men without much effect. He was becoming concerned about the number of warriors amassing against them. General Carr was standing next to Carpenter and eyeballing him. Although he was Carpenter's senior officer, he was not directly in command, and the general was curious to see how the rescuer of Beecher Island would react to the pressures of an attack by superior numbers.

"No, *mister,*" retorted Carpenter, aware that Carr was scrutinizing his behavior and decision making. "I will not be trapped like some frightened turtle retreating into its shell! The column will continue to advance along the banks of the creek while Company H protects our front and flanks." Carpenter quickly unfastened the lid of his well-worn leather binocular case and elegantly removed the field glass and brought it to his eyes. "And Company I will cover our rear and protect the pack train," he added, training the binoculars on the sniping Cheyennes. *"Now,* execute my orders, Mr. Grail."

"Sir!" saluted the captain. He mounted his horse and touched spurs to the mount's flanks and galloped down the column barking orders to the noncoms.

The column moved slowly but steadily, in order for the skirmish lines to keep pace with the wagons and mule train. The troopers would form a skirmish line, the men kneeling or standing up, and fire off several rounds. They were then ordered to cease fire and march for several yards and fire again, all the while keeping the wagons, horses, and stock in a protective cocoon.

Cougar Eyes and Turkey Leg were mounted on their finest war ponies shooting at the *ho' nehe.* Cougar Eyes, unlike many of his fellow Dog Men, took his time shooting his Colt carbine revolver. There was a slight cold October breeze that occasionally bent the eagle feathers and warbonnets of the warriors' headdresses, bow-lances, and shields. Many *Hotame—ho' nehe* warrior societies, such as Cougar Eyes' Red Lances, and Turkey Leg's Crazy Dogs, as well as the Foxes, Shields, and the Elks, were present. The Dog Men came from camps all over the upper Republican River Valley and many were anxious to see if Bullet Proof's powerful medicine on his treated buffalo robes would work against the bullets of the *Ve' ho' e.* Although most of the warriors preferred shooting their bow-lances, carbines, and a variety of pistols at their enemies from the natural protection that the creek offered, such as ravines, cottonwood trees, and river brush, a few younger Dog Men charged the column. Eager to count coup and prove their bravery, the young bucks would gallop their ponies toward the column, yelling profanities or blowing bone whistles.

"Steady, boys! Keep a *sharp* eye. Aim fo' the hosses if you can't see the braves," encouraged Nate and Jesse as they walked directly behind the skirmish line that protected the column's flank. "Don't waste ammo!"

At around noon, the sniping from the attacking Cheyennes ceased.

"Looks like the savages had enough of our superior fire-power," commented General Carr to Carpenter dryly.

Carpenter was not convinced, and was miffed that the hero of the Battle of Pea Ridge thought that only superior firepower was responsible for holding off a mobile force larger than his own and who also possessed formidable weaponry. He nodded his head in contempt and thought to himself, *My God, man! You should know better than most! Didn't you take note of the discipline on the line? Or the coolness that the men displayed?*

"That might be true, General," replied Carpenter cautiously as he slowly scanned the horizon with his binoculars. "But I don't think we are done for the day." Carpenter also found it hard to believe that the Cheyennes would content themselves with this little insignificant fight. They had not charged en masse nor did they succeed in running off any stock or even taking coup. Surely, he contemplated, either the Cheyennes had disappeared only to regroup at another location and await the column in ambush, or they would be back momentarily after possibly being reinforced by other Dog Soldiers.

The wagons and stock continued moving southward along the creek while the troopers that formed the mobile skirmish line remained dismounted, keeping their Spencers ready in case the Cheyennes decided to return. Carpenter continued to look through his binoculars searching at every ravine, knoll, and clump of vegetation that bordered the banks of Beaver Creek. Satisfied that the area was currently free of Cheyennes, he ordered Private Reuben Waller to request that Captain Grail, the scout, Jesse, and Nate come up.

Ever the eager attendant, Reuben Waller galloped his horse to where Nate, Jesse, and Grover were located and told them to report at the head of the column. He found Captain Grail in the rear with I Company and relayed the orders.

"Looks like the captain needs our advice." Jesse smiled as he took the reins of Cailloux from the handler.

Carpenter, Grail, General Carr, Nate, Jesse, and Grover were again at the head of the column. "I want to reach Wallace by tonight, Sergeant Major. How're the horses holding up?" probed Carpenter as he gazed at Nate's fine mount. Although the captain was mounted on a Thoroughbred, he was a little envious that his main noncom's horse was such a fine animal and wondered if maybe Frederick was faster.

"Sir, Wallace is seventy-five miles 'way an' some of the mounts suffered wounds during the snipin' but none seem to be mortal." Nate paused and reflected for a moment and thought about Cara. "Yes, sir. We can make Wallace tonight."

"Excellent, Sergeant Major. Have the men mount up in column of twos. I am counting on you and First Sergeant Randolph to keep the column moving at a fast walk and you, *scout,* to keep an eye out for any signs of the hostiles. I don't want to run into another ambuscade."

XI.

By a stream that had a little flowing cascade, Breaks The Arrow and Bobtailed Porcupine sat on a grassy spot around a small fire that bellowed a thin stream of smoke. They were waiting for Bullet Proof to come to the ceremonial site with his specially treated buffalo robes. The structure was arranged in a semicircle that was made of a double ring of cottonwood poles topped by a beamed willow branch ceiling. Wearing a buffalo head mask, Bullet Proof entered the structure's entranceway that opened toward the east. Draped over his right arm were two small buffalo hide sashes from a four-year-old bison calf.

"Did you fast and are you purified?" demanded Bullet Proof.

"Yes, my brother. We have not taken food for two days and have visited the sweat lodge. We are prepared to receive the robes and attack the *ho' nehe,*" responded Bobtailed Porcupine confidently as his comrade, Breaks The Arrow, slowly nodded his head in approval.

"Ne'aahtove!* Before you wear these sashes, you must first listen to what I have to say," instructed Bullet Proof, very seriously. Bobtailed Porcupine and Breaks The Arrow fixed their eyes on Bullet Proof and prepared to listen with great reverence.

"You must wear the sashes in the following manner. The hide of the head must be placed on your right shoulder in which one horn faces forward and the other one protrudes from the back. The shoulders and forelegs of the sash must pass your breast and back and meet under the left arm."

"Will you join us in the fight?" inquired Bullet Proof's uncle, Bobtailed Porcupine.

"No, my uncle. I will watch you and Breaks The Arrow from the nearest high point so I may be able to direct your movements. Now, this is most important. I will first send out you, Breaks The Arrow, and then you, my uncle, one at a time. Both of you must ride a circle around the *ho' nehe* four times. First, at a great dis-

---

*Listen to me

tance, then each time a little closer. If, on the fourth encirclement, you are not killed or wounded, we will know that my medicine works. Only then can you ride into the *ho' nehe* and run them down without fear of their bullets."

XII.

Nate and Sharp Grover were riding on the left flank of the column with H Company. They were moving at a fast trot, but Nate could feel the powerful tug on his reins from Frederick's desire to gallop at the head of the column because he wanted to be first.

Both men were scanning the ravines and horizon for any signs of hostiles. "I'm pretty certain that they're going to try again, but with more braves joinin' in the fray," remarked Grover as he adjusted his Spencer carbine so the weapon would be perfectly balanced on his lap. Although the scout's horse was stiff from the two arrow wounds, the animal nevertheless had managed to keep up with Frederick.

"I think that the captain has taken that into account," responded Nate as he raised himself in the saddle and turned to view the middle and rear of the column. He wanted to be certain that the men were keeping a taut formation and that there were no stragglers. As he gazed at the cavalcade, watching the men ride in column of twos shielding the wagons from attack, he thought that the procession resembled a giant maneuvering snake as it made its way southward. Nate noticed with satisfaction that the troopers' facial expressions were tight, revealing a seriousness of purpose. They sat firmly and confidently in their McClellan saddles while the horses moved at a strong canter rhythm breathing deeply as their hooves pounded the sandy ground along the banks of Beaver Creek. With the exception of snorting horses and the clatter of the supply wagons in the rear, the column moved quietly. Nate was concerned, however, that the clanging and jangling sounds of tin cups, canteens, rifle slings, and Blakeslee cartridge boxes would carry for miles and reveal their location.

The troopers' horses were the first to notice the close proximity of the hostiles. Many of the cavalry mounts started to snort and act ornery, alerting their riders that danger was lurking nearby.

"Oh, my heavens!" exclaimed Sharp Grover, shielding his eyes from the bright sun as he stared at hordes of hostiles.

"What's the matter?" asked Nate, still oblivious that the scout had just detected hundreds of mounted warriors amassing along the column's flanks. The warriors were difficult to see at first because the position of the sun blinded the troopers and enabled the Cheyennes and their ponies to blend into the landscape.

"Over there! Can't you see them?" repeated the scout anxiously, aggravated that Nate had not spotted the Dog Men.

"Yeah, I see 'em." Nate had to squint and raise his hand to his kepi's visor, but sure enough, toward the west and in front of the column, hundreds of Dog Men formed a straight line that resembled a rope that was quickly encircling the column. By now, other troopers had noticed that they were being surrounded, and when a loud war whoop was heard at the head of the column, General Carr was not the only soldier to feel the hairs on the back of his neck rise. For the Medal of Honor recipient, this was not the familiar Rebel yell that he had frequently heard during the war, but a bloodcurdling cry that sounded as if it were coming from Hades. Dozens of other warriors joined in by screaming and insulting the *Mo' ohtae-Ve' ho' e*, while others blew on their bone whistles and pranced their ponies in a provocative manner.

Captain Louis Carpenter was thinking about Beecher Island. He did not wish to be caught in the creek bottom while yielding the high ground to a superior force. He noticed a small knoll in the distance. If the order was given right away, the column could reach the location and make a stand.

"Captain Grail," beckoned Carpenter. Grail was staring at the amassing Dog Men and tried to swallow and respond, but found that his throat was too parched to moisten his mouth and tongue.

"S-s-s-*sir?*" sputtered Grail, finally managing to raise some spit from his glands to respond.

"We will advance the column to that knoll," explained Carpenter hurriedly pointing toward the northwest. He had to yell at the top of his lungs in order to be heard because of all of the commotion. *"Dismount, form a defensive perimeter by circling the wagons into a horseshoe. The opening of the horseshoe must face the creek. Do you understand?"*

"Sir." Grail snapped off a salute and turned his mount to ride over to where Nate and Grover were, and repeated the orders. The Dog Men started to shoot their carbines, pistols, and hurl hundreds of arrows into the column causing the teamsters and many of the men to curse and seize their Spencers and army Colts to shoot back.

"Hold yo'r fire till we reach the knoll. Hold yo'r fire," commanded Nate as the column started to pick up speed, throwing clouds of dust, buffalo grass, and clomps of sandy soil into the air.

Jesse was in the rear with I Company firing his Spencer at the encroaching Cheyennes from his saddle. Led by Cougar Eyes' and Turkey Leg's warrior societies, the Dog Soldiers were waving trade-cloth wool blankets trying to spook the wagon teams and were pressing the rear of the column, trying to cut off some of the vehicles. Jesse bellowed that the company proceed without him as he covered the rear with a squad of troopers. They formed a horizontal line with their horses and worked the hammers and levers of their Spencers, firing as rapidly as they could in an attempt to slow down the encircling warriors.

Carpenter's command reached the crest of the knoll, and within a few minutes the men had unhitched the mules from the supply wagons and placed the vehicles in a horseshoe-shaped defensive perimeter with the stock and horses within the enclosure. The troopers were then ordered to form skirmish lines outside the enclosure and fire at will.

Nate was busy pulling on the tongue of a supply wagon that he had just unhitched in order to move it closer to another wagon when a bullet penetrated his left cheek, almost cutting the flesh all the way to the bone. He cursed loudly but did not release his grip on the tongue of the wagon even though his first inclination was to touch the wound. On the contrary, he refused to yield to the burning pain and pulled the wagon even faster into place as a means to vent his anger at being shot in the face. When he had positioned the vehicle to his satisfaction, he pulled out his bandanna and commented in a rather cavalier manner to a nearby trooper who stood openmouthed at the sight of Nate's gaping facial wound, "Damn blood always makes a *mess.*"

"By Jezuz, Sarge . . . You're shot in the *face,*" responded the trooper in horror.

"No I'm not, boy! It's just a graze, now stop wastin' time an' git your black ass on the line where you *be-long.*" Nate placed himself behind the wagon for cover and pulled his bandanna from in between his brass buttons and placed the soothing cotton cloth to his wound cheek and winced. He then felt a clump of flesh hanging from the rear of the wound in between his bandanna and cheek. "This one is deep!"

Jesse and his rear guard squad came charging through the skirmish line. The skirmishers nearly fired on Jesse and his fast retreating troopers, for they at first did not recognize them through the haze of gun smoke and dust. Grover had to yell several times at the troopers to hold their fire until Jesse and his men had entered the relative safety of the enclosure.

"Git on the firin' line," commanded Jesse to his squad as he gave the reins of Cailloux to the handler and unflapped his holster to retrieve his Army Colt because he had almost exhausted all of his ammunition for his Spencer.

Hundreds of Cheyennes were shooting at the cavalrymen at all sides of the perimeter. Although the troopers kept a hot fire on their foes, the Cheyennes kept their distance and managed to kick up so much dust that the troopers had a hard time aiming at the fast-riding warriors mounted on excited war ponies.

General Carr, standing next to Carpenter, was carefully firing his side arm, a .41-caliber Lefaucheux revolver. The nonpercussion French weapon was imported during the war and issued to officers serving in the Western Theater. The general was very fond of the revolver because he had used it during the Battle of Pea Ridge.

"Why don't they charge?" he yelled to Carpenter, puzzled that the Cheyennes who seemed to outnumber the command by at least two to one would not rush at one point at the perimeter and try to cut the defenses in two.

"They are probing our defenses for weakness," yelled back Carpenter, trying to make himself heard through the din of hundreds of war whoops, deafening gunfire, panic-stricken neighing horses, and ear-piercing bone whistles.

XIII.

Breaks The Arrow and Bobtailed Porcupine were ready. They sat majestically on their war ponies and wore Bullet Proof's buffalo sashes around their torsos. They were waiting on top of a nearby ravine watching their companions attack the *ho' nehe*. With them were Bullet Proof, Turkey Leg, and Cougar Eyes, who had returned from the attack to watch his Red Lance warrior society members wear the magical bull robes against their enemies.

"The *ho' nehe* are *Mo' ohtae-Ve' ho' e* and *Hotoa' e* Gordon is certainly there," pointed out Cougar Eyes as he pointed his Colt revolver carbine toward the wagon enclosure.

"Will your robes work against the bullets of the *Mo' ohtae-Ve' ho' e?*" asked Turkey Leg, concerned that the majority of the pony soldiers were Black-White Men.

"Guns and bullets are the creation of the whites, not blacks," riposted Bullet Proof defensively. He had to respond quickly, fearing that the warriors would lose heart and his personal prestige might be reduced if he hesitated in giving an answer to a question when he was not certain of the answer.

"Remember what I told you, my cousin." Bullet Proof was worried that Breaks The Arrow and Bobtailed Porcupine would not heed his instructions that were crucial in making his buffalo sashes infallible against the *Ve' ho' e* bullets. "You are to circle the *ho' nehe* four times. Each time tightening your approach to condition the sashes to become impervious to their bullets. If you are not dead or wounded on the fourth approach, then and only then may you strike."

"Heehe'e," responded Breaks The Arrow confidently, while his war pony's front hoof scraped the sandy ground in front of him. The animal's head, front, and hind legs were painted in a pale green that resembled delicate blades of spring grass while the flanks, stomach, and rear were painted in a bright yellow.

Breaks The Arrow's entire face was painted in pale white made from chalk, while a lone red-tipped eagle feather tilted toward the left at the back of his head. The bull hide was properly worn per Bullet Proof's instructions. One horn facing the front and the other facing toward the rear. Around his neck was a medicine necklace made from imitation bear claws of carved horn.

His legs were covered in single-piece beaded deer leggings that matched his moccasins. For weapons, Breaks The Arrow carried the traditional Dog Soldier weapon, the bow-lance. His quiver was stuffed with arrows in anticipation of killing many *ho' nehe* once he was inside the enclosure. He also carried a very long lance and a buffalo hide shield decorated with an encircling stream of hawk feathers tied to a piece of red trade cloth.

*"Epeva'e!"** shouted Bullet Proof in approval. He raised his hand and shouted *"Noheto,"* commanding Breaks The Arrow to proceed. The Dog Man touched his heel to the war pony's flank and charged toward the *Mo' ohtae-Ve' ho' e*, assured in the belief that he would take many coup.

XIV.

All of a sudden there was a lull in the fighting. The hundreds of Cheyenne warriors who had surprised the column and pressed their advantage against the cavalrymen's flanks, front, and rear and who had continued to pressure them with long-range gunfire had, without warning, ceased. The Dog Men had moved to take positions on different high points, out of range from the troopers' guns because they wanted to get a good view of Breaks The Arrow's and Bobtailed Porcupine's rides against the *ho' nehe* and try out Bullet Proof's magical bull robes.

Nate and Sharp Grover were standing near the middle of the column. Nate had tied his bandanna around the middle of his face so his facial wound was covered. The rag was soaked in dried blood, but the scout noticed that Nate did not seem to be bothered by the injury.

---

*It's good.

"Why don't you let me clean that nasty wound and stitch it," offered the scout.

"Best wait till after this fight is ov'r," replied Nate, surprised that a white man had offered to care for his wound. Not since he was a runaway when Jean le Fou patched up the ghastly gator laceration on his arm had a white man offered to help him. He turned to Grover.

"Thank you, I appreciate it, scout. I'll go wash it, now that the Cheyennes are takin' their time." Nate walked over to Frederick and removed his canteen. Feeling great sympathy for his sergeant, the horse handler offered Nate a fresh white handkerchief from his saddlebag.

"I got it, Sarge. I got it." The trooper untied the knot at the uninjured side of Nate's face and slowly removed the bloody bandanna. He winced when he saw the nasty gash on Nate's face but remained quiet for he did not wish to alarm his sergeant. The trooper poured a large amount of water over the clean white cloth and approached Nate's face hesitatingly.

"Don't worry, boy. You go on 'head. I've been hurt worse," said Nate dryly, even though he felt pain and discomfort when he spoke. He wanted to smile, but the wound was too deep for that kind of expression.

"You might have seen worse, Sarge, but I sure hasn't," responded the trooper as he gently applied the wet handkerchief to Nate's facial wound, and delicately wiped away some of the blood and dirt that encrusted the wound.

"Whoo-we. Look at dat," clamored a trooper on the skirmish line. In the distance, about two hundred yards away, Breaks The Arrow was circling the enclosure at great speed.

"Kill that man!" commanded Captain Grail, outraged at the savage's impertinence The troopers started firing at the warrior, but Breaks The Arrow kept riding around the enclosure blowing on his bone whistle.

With the help of the horse handler, Nate had replaced his bandage and had returned to the line when he heard the troops firing at what appeared to be a lone rider.

Breaks The Arrow was on his third ride around the *ho' nehe* enclosure at about one hundred yards and feeling exhilarated. He could hear the wild cheers of pleasure and encouragement from his companions and fellow Dog Men on the nearby ridges and felt proud.

The spirits are with me, he thought to himself. *Bullet Proof's magic is true.*

Breaks The Arrow had ridden around the soldiers three times and hundreds of rounds had been fired at him, none doing any significant damage to his body. Although he felt the bullets pass closely by his head and several of them grazed his arms, legs, and both hands, his horse remained unharmed and he was looking forward to riding around the enemy on the fourth time. He was within fifty feet of the horseshoe enclosure and he could see the faces of the *Mo' ohtae-Ve' ho' e* through the gunfire smoke, and see their rifles pointed at him. He defied them by yelling insults and screaming war whoops as they emptied their Spencers and Colts at him. When he passed the rear skirmish line and was about to turn his pony into the horseshoe to take coup and kill, he felt a sharp pain in his lower back.

Nate saw the warrior stiffen on his saddle pad for a moment and then collapse to the ground. He had watched this brave man take on the whole outfit and admired his efforts. He did not fire his Spencer or take out his Walker-Colt to take a shot at the lone rider. He decided that he did not want to take part in a mass shooting of a courageous individual who was sacrificing his life.

"Here comes another one," hollered Private Reuben Waller,

proud that he was the first man to see the warrior coming. Riding at great speed, Bobtailed Porcupine was circling the enclosure at about two hundred yards away.

Nate noticed that he was wearing a buffalo sash in the same manner as the previous Dog Man, and wondered if this was co-incidental or related to some Cheyenne warrior custom.

"What do you think they are doing?" asked Nate as Grover stood watching the brave.

"Not sure," replied the scout. "Probably some Dog Man warrior society manner of dress."

Nate nodded, but did not quite believe Grover's simple explanation. *Why would they sacrifice two braves in such a way against superior firepower? No, there must be another reason,* he mused.

Bobtailed Porcupine failed to heed Bullet Proof's instructions. He was too eager to get close to the *ho' nehe* and shoot his carbine to avenge Breaks The Arrow's noble death. He shot at the *Mo' ohtae-Ve' ho' e* with his carbine, and then pulled out an arrow from his quiver and affixed it to his bowstring. As his warhorse galloped around the horseshoe encampment, he shot off several arrows into the soldiers, giving a loud war cry each time before releasing the bowstring. Like his relative, however, many bullets flew past him without finding their mark. Nate was amazed that although the troopers were firing their seven-shot Spencer repeaters at one lone rider, the Cheyenne brave kept circling them defiantly, shooting arrow after arrow. Several of the men on the skirmish line halted their fire to watch Bobtailed Porcupine maneuver his beautiful horse, and Nate overheard one man comment with admiration, *"Man!* That Injun ken *ride!"* The trooper had exhausted the ammunition in his Spencer Blakleslee tube and decided to amuse himself by gawking at Bobtailed Porcupine.

First Sergeant Jesse Randolph, however was not impressed with Bobtailed Porcupine's ride. Jesse did not like the Cheyennes.

Ever since he was trapped for hours in that railroad cutting and hounded, taunted, and severely jabbed by Dog Men's lances, he had sought revenge against them. Every time he removed his uniform and undergarments he would see the dozens of scars that were inflicted on his body when he was trapped by the fiends, reminding him that he had personal scores to settle with the Dog Men. Jesse planned to fix his sights on Bobtailed Porcupine as he approached his line of fire and wait until the warrior was directly in front of him before squeezing the trigger. Bobtailed Porcupine was fast approaching and Jesse took a deep breath and was about to shoot when suddenly the Dog Man's horse turned abruptly and headed directly toward him. Jesse still held his breath but thought to himself, *Now I got you—you son of a bitch!* He waited until the Dog Soldier was within a hundred feet of him. He fired, and Bobtailed Porcupine's head violently snapped back, propelling his body to tumble from the rump of his horse. A loud cheer went up from the skirmish line and several troopers tossed their forage caps into the air in celebration of Jesse's accurate shot.

Cougar Eyes, Turkey Leg, and Bullet Proof became distraught. They had witnessed, along with hundreds of their fellow Dog Soldiers, the killings of their two friends by the *Mo' ohtae-Ve' ho' e*. The worst aspect of this failed venture was the disappointing results of Bullet Proof's magical bull robes.

Cougar Eyes was incensed by the wild cheers of the soldiers at the expense of his two killed Dog Soldiers. He screamed a war whoop and bellowed. *"Noheto,"* and charged down the ravine. Sharing his anger and thirsting for revenge, most of the warriors who had been spectators followed Cougar Eyes and charged the soldiers, en masse.

The troopers of H and I Companies were prepared to repulse the attack. They held their Spencers ready and awaited orders.

Captain Carpenter held his Army Colt in the air, fully cocked, finger on the trigger, patiently waiting for the warriors to come within the effective firepower range of the Spencers. The Dog Men's painted war ponies were coming fast, and Carpenter could feel the ground slightly tremble beneath the leather soles of his boots while many of the cavalrymen's horses started to become restless as their handlers struggled to keep them from bolting.

"Prepare to fire," barked Carpenter. Although his voice was raised, it was calm and confident. Nate and Jesse repeated the order down the skirmish line behind the men's backs with encouragement, and the troopers obeyed instantly by placing the stocks of their Spencers to their shoulders.

"Steady, men! I want discipline and accuracy," reminded Nate. The Cheyennes were about one hundred yards away, firing rifles, pistols, and hurling hundreds of arrows through the air, most of them landing within the protective enclosure, raising havoc among the horses and causing the mules to bray uncontrollably and buck madly.

"Aim," Carpenter wanted to wait until the Cheyennes were about fifty yards away before giving the order, for he wished to maximize the impact of his superior firepower. When he finally saw the painted detail on the bodies and faces of the warriors and their war ponies, he gave the order.

"Fire!" A thunderclap of .52-caliber repeater carbine fire filled the air as the skirmish lines opened up. A large cloud of gun smoke began to take shape in the crisp fall air and drifted down the line and roll against the ravines, carried by the prairie's October winds.

Nate watched five warriors fall from their horses and dozens of war ponies crash into the sandy ground as they neighed and whinnied in pain from receiving multiple gunshot wounds. The horde of warriors charged past the horseshoe encampment as if it were a wave breaking on a rock. They rushed by and discharged their weapons while shouting war whoops.

Amid the horde of warriors galloping past the skirmish lines, Nate recognized Cougar Eyes' stallion. Although the war pony was painted in yellow, the Dog Man's mount was close enough for Nate to identify the animal by the wide blaze on his forelock. The warrior rode the same animal when they had first fought each other on the banks of the Saline River. His nemesis was attired in a red-spotted war shirt and yellow buckskin leggings with red fringes. When Cougar Eyes rode past, for a brief moment, their eyes met, and Cougar Eyes gave out a bold yell and raised his Colt revolver carbine in the air as a sign of defiant recognition.

XV.

"Over here, General! This one's still alive," shouted Sharp Grover. He was staring at Bobtailed Porcupine who was lying immobilized in the brown buffalo grass, and although the Dog Man was shot in the head, he was still breathing and could talk. His companions had been unable to retrieve his body before Cougar Eyes and the other Dog Men had withdrawn. Disillusioned with Bullet Proof's medicine, and hesitant to confront disciplined firepower from the *Mo' ohtae-Ve' ho' e*, the warriors had lost heart and had retreated back to their camps.

Captain Carpenter and General Carr were examining some of the dead Dog Men when they heard the scout call out.

"You say he's still alive?" inquired the general, hopefully. He quickened his pace toward where Grover was standing with the body.

"I want to question him." Carr looked into Bobtailed Porcupine's face that was caked with war paint, dust, sweat, and fresh blood. The general immediately saw that the head wound had blown out his left eye and that the round was lodged within the socket.

"Can he speak?"

"I can try and speak to him, General, but I don't talk Cheyenne," replied Grover.

"I thought you spoke both Cheyenne and Sioux," inquired Carpenter, feeling that he had been misled by the scout's credentials. Nate and Jesse walked over to Carpenter as he was addressing the scout. They wanted to report that both companies were prepared to move out and that the supply wagons were hitched up and ready to roll.

"No, sir," responded Grover defensively. "I never said I spoke Cheyenne, only Lakota."

"Beggin' the captain's permission, sir, but I believe that the scout here might talk to the man by usin' signs," advised Nate, staring at the body of the ravished Dog Soldier. Looking at Bobtailed Porcupine's blown-out eye reminded Nate of the time he found Corporal Mathias Pridgeon's corpse tied to a cottonwood tree with his eyes pecked out by buzzards.

"Can you do that, scout?" interrupted Carr.

"I can try, General. What do you want me to ask him?"

"Ask him where their camp is located and how many braves they have?" Carr believed that he could deal with a wounded Cheyenne in the same manner as if he were interrogating a Confederate prisoner of war.

Grover knelt down next to Bobtailed Porcupine and started to try to communicate with the gravely wounded warrior by maneuvering his hands, arms, and fingers as he spoke a few words of Lakota for emphasis.

"How many warriors are in your camp, how many lodges?"

Nate turned to Jesse who was standing next to him.

"See how this buck is wearin' the same kind of buffalo robe as the one who was shot first?"

"Yep, I noticed the same thing. Damn if I know why," replied Jesse, half interested in his companion's observation.

Bobtailed Porcupine remained mute. Although he was gravely wounded and in agony, he understood perfectly what the *Ve' ho' e* scout was saying. The Dog Soldier knew he was slowly dying and he certainly had no intention of telling these *Ve' ho' e* anything that might endanger his companions and relatives. Grover, however, eager to earn his generous monthly scouting pay of seventy-five dollars, was insistent. Asking the dying man over and over again where his village was located and the number of warriors.

"He's not goin' ta say anything to us, General," said Grover finally, exasperated at his efforts to communicate with Bobtailed Porcupine. The warrior just stared with his one good eye into the scout's face with burning loathing, and Grover was beginning to feel uncomfortable. Nate was struck with how calm the Dog Man was, even though he was gravely wounded and obviously in great pain. With the exception of the contemptuous expression he had on his face, he remained completely motionless.

Captain Carpenter was becoming fed up with this pathetic line of questioning. He was anxious to get the column moving and make for Fort Wallace as soon as possible. As far as he was concerned, trying to get information from a dying Indian who has no incentive to tell them anything except perhaps lies was a waste of time. The two companies had expended a lot of ammunition, and he was concerned that the Cheyennes might return in even greater numbers before nightfall and attack them again.

"Sir, we are wasting valuable time. The column is ready to move and I intend to use what daylight we have left and proceed toward Wallace."

"Well, yes, I suppose you are right," replied the general,

scratching his beard in contemplation. "I suggest that we put this bastard out of his misery, but I would not waste a bullet on him."

"I'll take care of it, General," volunteered Jesse as he pulled out his hunting knife.

"Very well, First Sergeant, I will leave you to dispatch this man," replied Carpenter, businesslike. "General, I propose we mount up and lead the column back to Wallace."

As soon as Nate and Jesse were alone with Bobtailed Porcupine, the Dog Man gave out a long moan. "Better git it done right quick, Jess."

"Right! Afta all, 'twas my shot that wounded him, so I best finish the job." Jesse stooped over Bobtailed Porcupine and placed the blade of his hunting knife near the Dog Man's jugular vein and sliced it open, resulting in an outpouring of blood. The warm liquid quickly formed into a pool in the sandy soil. The next action Jesse undertook dismayed Nate.

"I'm goin' git me a *souv'nir,*" stated his companion enthusiastically. He placed the blade of the hunting knife against Bobtailed Porcupine's head and began to slowly move the knife back and forth, cutting into the flesh just under the scalp as if he was removing the skin of a fish.

Nate's face bore a quiet expression of disparagement at his friend's actions. As he listened to the sound of ripping skin, he thought to himself how much Jesse had changed since coming to the frontier. He remembered how only a year ago the very discussion of taking scalps would render his friend's stomach nauseous and he would have to control his instinct to vomit. Now, the son of a bitch was behaving as badly as the so-called savages or hard-bitten frontier white men.

"There you go!" commented Jesse triumphantly, lifting the scalp from Bobtailed Porcupine's skull. He removed his handkerchief from the inside of his shell jacket and snapped it open on the ground. He then placed the bloody hairpiece in the middle of the cloth and folded the handkerchief as if he were wrapping a delicate slice of cake for transportation. He then wiped the blade on his sky-blue wool trousers and placed the knife back into its leather sheath.

"One last Dog Bastard to worry 'bout, eh, Nate?"

"Yeah right," replied Nate halfheartedly.

Three

Packs of wolves howled among the nearby ravines along Beaver Creek near where the column had encamped for the night. The beasts had smelled the blood of dead Dog Men and horses on the battlefield and had descended onto the site. The packs came to devour the corpses of the war ponies and lick at the pieces of human flesh or at the pools of dried blood that stained the brown buffalo grass where the bodies of killed Cheyennes had lain. The wolves were disappointed, however, that there were no human remains, for the surviving warriors had returned to the battlefield after the soldiers had departed, and retrieved all the bodies for burial. After feasting on the remains of dead ponies, the carnivores decided to follow the column at a safe distance, hoping that the humans would yield their next repast. Their bellies filled, and stimulated by the full moon, the wolves were now communicating with each other by howling on the crests of nearby ravines.

The column had bivouacked after it became dark, and the wagons and stock were arranged in a defensive perimeter with a strong night guard placed all around the camp, and sentries for the horse picket line doubled.

The men of Companies H and I were allowed to have cook fires and the first hot meal in days. Nate was sitting on a camp chair next to a supply wagon. Jesse had placed a lantern on the tailgate and was stitching Nate's wound. He had cleaned the nasty gash with warm water and soap and used some of Nate's one hundred and ninety proof whiskey to disinfect the gash. Much to Jesse's amusement, Nate had almost squealed in pain from the sting when he poured the alcohol on his wound. He noticed that his friend gnashed his teeth together so firmly that the only sound that came from Nate's mouth was a very loud growl.

"Don't think I cared fo' your *behavior* today, afta the fight," commented Nate accusingly as Jesse moved the long needle and thread through Nate's skin to seal the wound. The threading had reopened the wound again, and blood was seeping from the gash. Anticipating Nate's fastidiousness in keeping his uniform in a state of "perfect regulation," Jesse had placed a towel against his companion's shoulder to protect his blouse from being stained.

"What you mean, my *behavior*?" riposted Jesse as he pulled the needle tautly, so the opening would be tightly held together.

Nate winced in discomfort. "You takin' scalps an' behavin' like them so-called savages you always talkin' about!"

"Shit. That's nuthin'. Everybody out here does it," fired back Jesse as he closed the final stitch on Nate's wound.

"You a *soldier* not a gawddamn heathen or some white man that's been out here too long," criticized Nate. The grin that had been on Jesse's face because he had enjoyed seeing his sanctimonious friend wench with pain disappeared. Nate took a big gulp from the one hundred and ninety proof whiskey and corked the bottle.

"Not tryin' to knock you down, Jesse. I just don't want to see you as a bitter man lookin' to satisfy your need for revenge 'cause of what happened to you in that hole." Nate passed the bottle to Jesse as an afterthought, and as a means to reach out to him in a friendly manner. "Thanks for stitchin' me up."

"Wound still needs to be bandaged," replied Jesse, removing the cork from the neck of the bottle.

"Private Waller done tol' me that he got some of the surgeon's bandages. Guess I'll go an' make him dress the wound."

Nate tried to smile at Jesse's kindness but the pain of the wound was too acute.

II.

General Carr and Captain Carpenter were sipping coffee near the cook fire discussing the day's events when Nate appeared. The two officers were hatless and had relaxed their attire for the evening. General Carr's double-breasted frock coat was wide open, revealing a fine white linen shirt, while Captain Carpenter had changed from his field uniform into his fatigues in order to be more comfortable. As usual, Carpenter's orderly, Private Waller, was standing at ease near Carpenter, ready to jump at his charge's command for more coffee or to stir the fire, or prepare the captain's bedding.

"Ah, Sergeant Major!" beckoned Carpenter, cheerfully raising his tin cup in the air as if he were about to propose a toast. Carpenter had Reuben Waller pour a shot of bourbon into his coffee cup, so consequently the captain was feeling a little warm and euphoric. Nate walked over to where the officers were sitting. When he came close enough into the light of the fire, the officers noticed Nate's nasty wound.

"How are you feeling, Sergeant Major?" inquired Carpenter, rising from his chair. "Would you like some coffee?"

"No, sir, thank you, sir. The sergeant major's wound is much better, sir," replied Nate, standing at attention.

"At ease, man, at ease," commanded Carpenter. Nate noticed that his commanding officer wore a funny grin on his face and wondered if Reuben Waller might have spiked his coffee too many times with hard liquor. A man who appeared to be light-headed and mildly jovial had replaced Carpenter's usual sharp and professional demeanor.

"I was very pleased with the way the men conducted themselves today, Sergeant Major," commented General Carr, pointing his tin cup at Nate. The general was sweating and Nate wondered if he too had a few nips from a bottle. "The men stood firm, and I will mention this in my dispatches." The general then turned his gaze toward Carpenter. "How many warriors did we kill today?"

"Ten! And many wounded," boasted Carpenter. "And only three wounded on our end," he added, holding up three fingers.

"The sergeant major thanks the general," responded Nate, surprised to hear such praise from the general, who only days before would not even have addressed him.

"Better have that wound bandaged," added the general.

"Yes, sir, fact is I came over to see if Private Waller could do it."

"Of course! He is at your disposal, Sergeant Major," offered Carpenter as he staggered a little on his feet. His voice was high-pitched, convincing Nate that the captain was indeed feeling his alcohol.

"Thank you, sir."

III.

Nate could not sleep. The burning sensation in his face was too overwhelming for him to try to close his eyes. He decided that it would be best to make an entry into his journal to get his mind away from the pain.

Many howling wolves are keeping us company tonight. They do not sound as threatening as the ones that attacked my camp last winter and attacked my mules, injuring Pvt. Filmore Alexander. As I listen to them converse with one another, I almost envy them. Their lives are so simple, free of hate.

I saw Cougar Eyes today at the fight. We briefly locked in to each other's eyes and although his gaze was fierce and I could tell his blood was running hot, I did not feel that his gaze was hostile to me personally. I certainly bear him no personal loathing, but he is a hostile.

One of the wounded, Pvt. John Daniels of my company, was shot through the neck during the fight. The surgeon said he will survive, but doubts if he will ever talk properly again.

Seems as if General Carr has had a change of heart concerning "us brunettes." This evening, the man praised the boys for their steadfastness against the Dog Men, and will mention us in dispatches. Will he?

I think I'm going to ask Cara to jump over the broom with me. I have given this matter much thought and I have decided that I cannot live without her. Every time I am far from her, my heart becomes anxious to return to her presence. When I finally see her, my heart jumps and pumps faster, but when I am with her, I feel at peace and less restless. I think I am ready to assume the responsibilities of a husband and father, although I have to admit I thought that I would always have one love: the army.

After Nate had completed making his entry, he took another gulp of the hundred and ninety proof whiskey and wrapped himself in his wool blanket and rested his tired body in a fetal position on the sandy ground. He placed his head on the seat of his Mc-Clellan saddle, the bandage facing the stars. He stared at the embers of the dying cook fire as the throbbing pain of his wound subsided slightly. The October night air was crisp, and he scrutinized the thin clouds of his breath every time he breathed. Although the incessant howling of the wolves continued among the nearby ravines, keeping many of the men awake with apprehension, Nate was not bothered by their cries. Soon he was fast asleep.

Nate dreamed about Jacques Napoleon Gaches. The young and dapper octoroon gambler from Natchitoches whom he had helped hide from the two henchmen of his creditors on a steam paddle wheeler on the Red River. In the dream, he was squatting on top of the onion dome of the pilothouse facing the stern of the steamer *Belle de Jour*. He was watching Jacques Napoleon Gaches fight off two attackers with a bullwhip as he stood his ground on the edge of the roof on top of the cabin deck, his back facing the huge, menacing, churning paddle wheel. Like all of Nate's dreams, however, the action moved at a painful pace and his legs felt as if they were mired in a bog, helpless to intervene, and he could only shout: "Watch out, Gaches! Watch your left—the man's got a derringer!"

Jacques furiously cracked the bullwhip at the two white men who were trying to push him off the roof and into the blades of the paddle wheel, while the calliope played "Amazing Grace." Only the music that came out of the pipes was so loud and strained that the noise drowned out Nate's baritone voice and gave the scene a surreal quality of anxiousness and desperation. Nate kept hollering: "Watch the man! Watch the man with the derringer!"

"Sergeant Major! Wake up," beckoned Private Reuben Waller, holding a tin cup of fresh coffee in his right hand while gently shaking Nate's shoulder with his left.

"What? What time is it?" Nate's eyes popped open. He was

disoriented because he was suddenly awoken from the nightmare, and then stunned that he had slept so long after he saw that the sun was already high in the sky. Troopers were mounting their horses as officers and noncoms barked orders while teamsters snapped their long reins on the rumps of their mules to get them moving. Nate was usually the first man up in the morning, and in the field he could never properly sleep past four-thirty. In addition, he was thirsty and his facial wound still pained him and the fact that he had to be awoken by an enlisted man was embarrassing and he felt unprofessional.

"Past reveille, Sergeant Major. They be no horn callin' this mawnin'. I know you were dawg tired last night so's I lets you sleep long as possible."

"What the hell are you still doin' lyin' on the ground still wrapped in your bedroll? What you waitin' fo'?" mocked Jesse as he led Cailloux by the reins. "I ain't bringin' your sorry ass break-fast in bed like you were the mas'a, just 'cause your face got cut!" Still feeling a little bitter that his friend had scolded him the night before over the scalping of the dead Dog Soldier, Jesse became delighted that he had caught the great *Hotoa' e-Gordon* over-sleeping and unprepared to move out with the column. Jesse's mount nuzzled the ground for grass and managed to crop a few blades before his master yanked his head up to keep the bit clean.

"What 'bout the boys?" asked Nate, grabbing the tin of hot coffee that Reuben Waller was holding. He placed the rim to his lips and sipped with care while sniffing the aroma.

"The company is gettin' ready to mov' out. I took the liberty of waterin', feedin', and brushin' down your mount. I'll take your saddle and bridle now, and tact up your hoss."

"Are you brown-nozin' me, Private?" questioned Nate as he sprang from his bedroll fully dressed with the exception of his high-top boots that he had removed the night before and the three top unfastened brass buttons on his cavalry shell jacket.

"No, Sergeant Major." Reuben Waller picked up Nate's McClellan saddle, bridle with curb bit, halter, and link with his right arm and with his left grabbed the horse blanket and saddlebags.

Nate took a few gulps of the coffee and handed the tin to Jesse. He then quickly buttoned his jacket, slipped on his boots, and grabbed his saber belt. Although the belt was heavy with the huge holstered Walker-Colt revolver, carbine cartridge pouches, and Bowie knife, Nate had developed the habit of swinging the saber belt around his waist in one swoop and attaching the brass U.S. buckle with one smooth, elegant movement.

"Thank you, Private." Nate took the reins from Private Reuben Waller. "And thank you," he repeated again as his eyes softened when he handed the tin cup back to Waller. He was grateful that Carpenter's orderly had found the time to bandage his wound, wake him up from his deep sleep and nightmare, and had given him coffee, as well as saddling his horse.

While Frederick was vigorously swinging his long tail from flank to flank, Nate tightly rolled up his wool blanket and fastened it to the rear of his saddle. The column was moving out and the sounds of men, horses, and wagons on the move made Frederick eager to go and caused him to scrape the ground with his right hoof while plunging his neck and head up and down.

"You sure do everything with *style*," remarked Jesse, envious that his friend always did things in efficient elegance even when he was wounded and in pain. Reuben Waller brought Frederick up to Nate and handed him the reins.

Nate wanted to smirk at Jesse's cynical comment, but the wound on his face was too tight and tender for that expression, so he grudgingly grunted approval and placed the toe of his boot in the stirrup and lifted himself into the McClellan. He adjusted his saber belt and holster so the pommel of his Walker-Colt properly protruded from the left hip, allowing him to have immediate access to the weapon at an instant. Nate then adjusted his carbine sling, pulled on the visor of his kepi, and looked at Jesse in a patronizing manner.

"Yeah, I know I'm good! Now, hand me my Spencer."

IV.

The column moved at a leisurely pace southward, on the east bank along the North Fork of Beaver Creek toward the Smoky Hill Road where they would follow the trail home to Fort Wallace. Carpenter had ordered that flankers be dispatched in front and along the flanks of the column to search for pony tracks and other indicators of hostile activity. First Sergeant Jesse Randolph, with a squad of men from H Company, was assigned the task of covering the rear of the column and keeping the wagons and stragglers moving. Carpenter was concerned that the supply wagons, always trailing behind the rest of the column, would come under sniper fire from vengeful Dog Soldiers, or that a wagon or some of the mules in the pack train might be cut off and snagged by the Cheyennes.

Nate had received permission from Carpenter to accompany Sharp Grover as one of the flankers who were to take the point. Nate wanted to be away from the clouds of dust and swarming flies that the column produced and that had plagued him most of the morning because the insects were drawn by the dried blood of his facial bandage. Most of all, Nate wanted to avoid conversation because his wound was sore and it pained him when he tried to utter a word or move his mouth. He knew that the scout was good company in this respect, because Grover chose to remain silent most of the time when not spoken to, and preferred to scrutinize the ground and horizon for Indian signs.

Nate was disturbed by his nightmare of the previous night. His mind kept turning back to the scene where he found himself squatting helplessly on the onion dome of the pilothouse watching Jacques Gaches wield his bullwhip at his three attackers. As he stared at Frederick's notched ears that were attentively pointing forward, he realized that it was the first time in a long while that he had thought about the gambling octoroon dandy.

"What a bettin' fool he was," he muttered to himself, shaking his head disapprovingly. His mind reflected for a moment as he gazed at the brown buffalo grass, and with an air of acknowledgment whispered to himself in recognition, *"Well, I do owe 'im. Then again, he owed me too."*

The sky was gray and the clouds were low, accentuating the flat monotony of the High Plains. He felt hypnotized by the terrain as the throbbing discomfort in his cheek forced him to slightly close his eyes to escape the pain.

Nate's thoughts turned to the days when he was a runaway and when his friend, the Cajun alligator hunter Jean le Fou, hid him in his pirogue for days in order to take him as far north as he could on the Calcasieu River.

"I will take you dare, *mon ami noir*, I know de way. We will travel togeder, tru de by-yo's in my pir-ogue," insisted the Cajun.

They paddled through the murky marshes, and at night, as they made their way through the bayou, they stayed with Jean le Fou's friends and relatives at Cajun fishing villages where they feasted on pork, catfish, crawfish, and rice and consumed local distilled hooch.

They navigated the hundred-fifty-mile voyage through Bayou Lafourche and Bayou Teche and arrived at Calcasieu Lake where they entered the Calcasieu River to go north. Because the waterway had considerable commercial boat activity, and groups of mounted patrollers with dogs constantly searched for runaways along its banks, the pair traveled at night and hid and slept during the day among oak, gum, and cypress trees that grew along the banks of the Calcasieu River. They then paddled their way past the river port town of Lake Charles for another seventy-five miles where Jean le Fou deposited Nate on the eastern bank of the river near the entrance of an old Atakapan trail that led to the Red River and close to Alexandria.

"*Suit le chemin, mon ami.* It will take you about two days to reach *la Rivère Rouge.* Go east!" Nate remembered fondly when they bade each other farewell.

"*Toi! Toujours bienvenue chez moi!*" The gator killer smiled, extending his hand to Nate.

"*Merci, mon ami,*" replied Nate, clasping the hand of the man who had given him food and shelter and had risked much to accompany him as far north as he could in his quest for freedom.

Nate followed the old Indian trail east, toward the Red River and the port town of Alexandria. The night was filled with stars, so he was able to see the pathway sufficiently to keep up a good clip. He knew that if there were patrollers coming down the path, they would carry lanterns, alerting him of their approach, buying him time to hide in the brush and thick woods that bordered the old Atakapan trail. Jean le Fou was generous in providing Nate with a haversack filled with biscuits, dried fruit, and vegetables, a change of clothes, needle and thread, a flint block, and an old but clean towel and wool blanket. Nate rolled up and transported the blanket across his left shoulder and strapped the ends so the item would remain tight. His plan was to travel all night and find a secluded place in the woods or some abandoned farm building at dawn and rest and wait until dark to make the final run to Alexandria. Jean le Fou told him that he then should try to sneak onto a paddle wheeler that was heading north toward Shreveport, jump ship at the town, and then proceed north, on foot, toward the Arkansas border, which was about a forty-mile trek.

The first day spent in the woods in hiding went without incident. Nate devoured some of Jean le Fou's biscuits and dried fruit. His generous Cajun friend had also provided Nate with tobacco and a clay pipe, but although he wanted badly to have a smoke, he dared not strike a match to burn the tobacco in the bowl for fear that the aroma might draw attention to himself. He decided instead to try to sleep for the remainder of the day. At dusk, he left the woods and struck the trail for Alexandria. The Atakapan trail ended at a cleared field that had its cotton harvest picked last fall. Nate noticed the redness of the soil and thought to himself, *Prime cot'on country.*

At the end of the field, he noticed bright lights in the distance. He paused for a moment thinking that it was the lights of a large plantation house, the last place he wanted to be near, but then he saw clouds of black smoke and sparks in the sky and concluded with some relief that it was a steamer heading for Alexandria. He ran toward the lights of the paddle wheel intending to reach the levee and follow it into town when he noticed more bright lights to his left, only these lights were concentrated in one compact area with many more lights spreading out throughout the countryside. Nate whispered to himself with contentment, *"Alexandria!"*

As he followed the levee for several miles toward the town, the lights grew larger and brighter as he neared the port. He decided that he would wait until dawn to enter the town and hide until then, among a clump of gum trees. His plan was to follow the levee into town and reach the waterfront when the steamers were taking on cargo, passengers, and fuel and where he expected to blend in with the other blacks and sneak onto a steamer heading north. His greatest fear was to be stopped by patrollers demanding to see his pass, or if someone would somehow realize that he was a runaway and report him to the authorities.

He crept carefully but steadily along the bottom of the low levee until he approached the edge of Alexandria where he straightened up, increased his step, and pretended to be on some important mission for his master. When he entered the waterfront area, he could smell burning wood being stoked in the boilers of the steamers and see belching black smoke pouring out of the stacks and sparks being dispersed by the flared crowns. A steamer blew its whistle and made him jump. The sound was deafening and shook the small town. A moment later other steamers blew their whistles in response, and soon the waterfront and the port of Alexandria became a dueling cacophony of screaming steam. As the sun rose, dozens of men, mostly black, started to descend on the waterfront to move hundreds of bales of cotton, and barrels filled with cider, molasses, and salted pork, and sacks of grain. Within minutes, the waterfront of the town was abounding with teamsters hauling freight, men pushing huge wheelbarrows transporting sacks while others rolled barrels.

Nate walked past a human chain of singing brawny black men moving heavy bales of cotton onto a paddle wheeler called *Belle de Jour*. Although the men were dressed in rags and most were barefoot, Nate thought that their strong voices and prideful singing to the rhythmic beat set by the "man" on the line was inspiring.

> "I am climbing Jacob's ladder,
> I am climbing Jacob's ladder,
> I won't be here fo' much longer."

As the men sang, Nate saw his chance. He decided to sneak onto the steamer behind the human chain and find a spot to hide among the mountain of hundreds of bales of cotton that were being stacked on the floor of the hull from stern to bow, reaching all the way to the cabin deck. Without hesitation, Nate made a left oblique and hurried past the human chain of singing black waterfront workers and past the white overseer who was too busy talking to his employer to have noticed him, and stepped onto the steamer *Belle de Jour*. He then marched toward the bow of the paddle wheeler where two young black boys were stacking bales of cotton in between the hog chains that supported the shallow wooden draught hull. Nate approached them and smiled.

"Where is this big boat goin'?" The boys stared at Nate and his bulging haversack, dumbfounded.

"Goin' north towar' Shreveport," responded the youngest boy finally, gawking at Nate.

"I need a place to hide."

The boys looked at each other and the older one nodded at Nate. "Git in!" he commanded.

He turned his head toward an empty space in between the tiers, which they were about to fill in with a bale. Without saying another word, Nate jumped into the space within the cotton tiers and maneuvered his body into the space, which was big enough to accommodate his huge frame with some room to spare. He sat with his knees up against his chest while the boys looked about to see if anyone was watching. Satisfied that they were clear, they quickly placed a bale on top of two lower bales that were the front and back of Nate's hole, sealing off the enclosure from the top. They then rapidly started to build another tier of cotton bales to wall up the side to completely hide the stowaway. In between the side wall, they left a crack about a foot wide for Nate to see and receive light.

Although Nate was not entirely in darkness in his walled-up hiding place, he felt apprehensive.

"Damn! I feel like I'm in a tomb," he whispered to himself.

There was another, smaller crack that faced the river among the stacked bales of cotton that allowed him to see the activities on the waterfront and riverbanks from his secluded space.

It was not long before the stern-wheeler got its boilers up to steam and the remaining bales of cotton were loaded on *Belle de Jour*. Nate noticed with dismay that several companies of well-equipped Confederate infantry, marching single file, boarded the vessel. He could hear the Rebel officers barking orders to their men on how they had to watch their manners and language on board the steamer because there were civilian passengers and children on board. Nate could hear them march up the stairwell to the cabin deck and take their positions at the bow of the paddle wheeler directly above his hiding place. Soon after the whistle of *Belle de Jour* blew, signaling that the vessel was departing. Her stacks coughed up black smoke and it seemed that the vessel wheezed and blew its nose as the boilers built up pressure. Nate was so taken by surprise by the blasts of steam that he banged his head against the upper cotton bale that was the roof of his little tomb. Suddenly the steamer's iron pitmans started to drive the cranks, which in turn rotated the large stern wheel in reverse. Nate could feel the vibrations and hear the humming sounds of the boilers and hydraulics in the engine room as the boat maneuvered away from the levee and moved itself to steam up the Red River.

Nate spent the day looking at the riverbank out from his little crack in between the cotton bales. He gazed at the river plantations, farm buildings, and livestock grazing on the levees, but sighed whenever he saw the occasional throng of slaves toiling under the gaze of a mounted overseer holding a whip and, lately, armed with pistols or rifles. All of the activity on *Belle de Jour* took place above him on the cabin deck where the dining room and parlors and sleeping accommodations were located. When he grew tired of watching the banks he concentrated on listening to the sounds of women's chatter and children playing and running up and down the double stairway in the forecastle. He particularly enjoyed hearing the well-heeled male passengers swap dubious stories as they smoked cigars and spat in iron cuspidors. They would talk about how the Yankees would never come down this far, and how much the war was costing them, but in the end they were sure that "their boys" would defeat the blue rabble. Nate also listened to the Confederate soldiers who were bivouacked directly above him. At first they were chatty in their enthusiasm to be traveling by steam rather than marching. They joked about how the other boys had to march for miles on dusty or muddy roads, or through swamps and thick forests while they rode like "millionaires."

At dinnertime, the aroma of cooking food coming from the galley was so overwhelming that it overpowered the smell of burning boiler wood, and Nate started to salivate. The smells of broiled beef, fried sausage, roasted chicken, boiling vegetables, and rice mixed with tomato sauce made his mouth water so that he hurriedly removed some dried fruit from his haversack and devoured the food with ravenous delight. He chewed his meager repast while listening to the clatter of porcelain dishes and utensils and the sounds of huge pots and pans being dragged and manhandled over stoves in the galley as waiters hollered for their orders. Nate also listened to the murmur of many conversations deriving from the dining room, broken at times only by boisterous bursts of laughter coming from the bar where the men were drinking and swearing and talking about "the niggers."

Later, after the passengers had completed their dinners, they strolled along the covered cabin deck to take air and digest their huge meals as they gazed at the lights of farmhouses and plantations that dotted the banks of the Red River. Nate deduced that the Confederate officers were not with their men, for the soldiers were talking among themselves on how they favored that officer so-and-so over that officer so-and-so, accompanied by laughter and insulting remarks regarding their leaders' characters. Nate assumed that the officers had probably preferred the company of several single young women he saw board the stern-wheeler back in Alexandria.

After all the passengers had retired to their cabins, Nate heard a Jew's harp being plucked by one of the Confederate soldiers. The twanging sound helped pass the time and reminded Nate of the "quarter" at Mas'a Hammond's plantation when ol' Ben Horry would play his Jew's harp after supper during those long hot summer nights.

"Quit playin' that goddamn t'ing, Osborne, 'fore I throw you in the river," barked a soldier to his friend, startling Nate who was drifting into sleep.

"I can't sleep," retorted the Jew's harp player. "Helps me to relax."

"Well, if you gots to play som'ting, blow on your harmonica."

"Stop waggin' yo'r tongue and arguin' like a bunch of cooped-up ol' hens," ordered another soldier whom Nate assumed was the head sergeant.

"What do you want me to play, Sarge?"

There was a moment of silence as Nate listened to the humming of the boilers as the stern-wheeler rotated its paddles in the river water.

"You know what I want to hear, son. You know which tune," egged on the sergeant. He adjusted his wool blanket around his body and neck to ward off the damp night air as he lay on the deck.

"Sure, Sarge, I know what you want."

The musician located the harmonica from his haversack and gently placed the reed part of the tin and wood instrument to his mouth. Within a moment, an amiable, doleful melody poured forth from the tin and wood instrument. Nate could hear one of the

Confederate soldiers sob while another soldier started to softly sing the words of the song:

> "The years creep slowly by, Lorena,
> The snow is on the grass again:
> The sun's low down the sky, Lorena
> And frost gleams where the flowers had been."

Nate listened attentively to the sad music and lyrics of the song. The soldier who was singing had a deep voice and placed much emotion in emphasizing the words.

> "One hundred months have passed, Lorena,
> Since last I felt that hand in mine;
> I felt that pulse beat fast, Lorena,
> But mine beat faster still than thine."

Nate heard a soldier sniffle, and cry out pathetically, "I wanna go home!"

"Shut up! We all want to go home," retorted a comrade.

As Nate listened to the song and the verbal exchange among the Confederate soldiers, he became surprised that these boys were homesick and seemed tired of the war. A year earlier, when the state of Louisiana had broken away from the Union, he had seen many young white boys and men march past Mas'a Hammond's plantation with much fanfare and bravado as they went off to form regiments. He remembered clearly how they loudly boasted to any-body who would listen, white or black, that *"we goin' to whip the Yankees by Christmas!"* Now, these same patriots appeared to be spent and disillusioned with the "cause."

At around midnight, *Belle de Jour* turned onto the Canes River heading for Natchitoches. Nate overheard the pilot bellow to his apprentice that they were now on "the Kanes" and to watch for floating debris. Nate felt the engine slow down and heard another man call out to the pilot, "Mark five, suh." There would be a pause and then he would hear him again inform the pilot, "Mark six, suh." Nate looked out from the crack and noticed that the lights on the bank of the river were closer, indicating that the river was much narrower than the Red, and from what he understood, shallower because the pilot kept asking for the depth.

For the rest of the night, *Belle de Jour* carefully maneuvered its way along the numerous narrow bends of the Canes, and by dawn, Nate was awoken by the loud whistle announcing that the steamboat was approaching Natchitoches. Jean le Fou had told him that Natchitoches would be the next river town after Alexandria and that the steamer would have to travel up the Canes in order to reach the old Spanish settlement.

The sun was rising and a beam of light poured through the crack in between the cotton bales that faced the river. Nate reached into his haversack and retrieved a biscuit, which he intended to be his meager breakfast. He peered out from the crack and saw the tiny town of Natchitoches, which was much smaller than he had imagined, and wondered if there were going to be any passengers leaving the steamer or people seeking passage to travel north. The sounds coming from the galley told Nate that the cooks were busy preparing breakfast, and soon the smells of boiled ham and fried potatoes, onions, peppers, and okra made his mouth water so much that he violated his own resolution and reached for another biscuit.

Only a few passengers disembarked from the steamer. Nate could hear families descend the forecastle and walk down the stage gangplank onto the levee, their children stomping their feet on the stage while workers unloaded barrels of molasses from the stern of the vessel and rolled them down the stage. Nate gazed at the activities on the waterfront and noticed that the area had many stands of stacked rifles and military horses with Confederate infantry and cavalry milling about as a field kitchen handed out plates of grits and bacon. *Belle de Jour* did take on a few new passengers but no extra cargo, and the Confederate soldiers, much to Nate's dismay, remained on board.

Belle de Jour's stacks belched smoke and Nate felt the stern-wheel paddle go into reverse. As he watched the levee move away from the steamer, he spotted a tall, thin man who was running as if Lucifer were in pursuit. He wore a long black cape and a dark purple felt broad-brimmed hat and carried a medium-size leather bag. His legs took great strides as his boots crashed into puddles of water or leaped over obstacles as if he were in a race. His long black cape snapped in the breeze, reminding Nate of a crow fleeing on its feet. He focused on the man's face and saw that he was a very light-skinned Negro and surmised that he was probably a freed octoroon.

A hundred paces behind him, two white men were giving chase. They were both dressed in dark suits and wore hats. The man in the lead was tall and lanky, while the other was short and heavy. Nate watched in astonishment as the fleeing man with the cape seemed to be heading for *Belle de Jour*, even though the vessel was now quickly moving away from the levee. The tall pursuer who was ahead of his colleague drew a derringer while the other slid off the wooden part of his cane with his left hand while holding the curved handle with his right, revealing a long and very pointed sword. As the tall man with the derringer aimed his tiny weapon at the fugitive, the steam whistle of the vessel blasted, and Nate could see smoke emerging from the barrel of the pocket pistol. The round missed the man with the cape, however, as he leaped like a fear-stricken cat onto the deck of *Belle de Jour*, leaving his pursuers in a state of rage on the levee.

The action had been so quick that no one on board the steamer noticed the event. The pilot and his apprentice were too busy getting the vessel on its way, and the crew too preoccupied in attending to their duties while most of the passengers were either having breakfast or were still asleep. The two companies of Confederates who were directly above Nate also remained oblivious because their attention was turned to their tin plates, devouring their first hot breakfast in weeks. Nate could hear the sounds of hurried steps made by heavy boots coming toward him. He assumed it was the fugitive. The pacing of the boots went back and forth along the narrow pathway in between the tiers of cotton bales and the engine room. As he listened attentively, he deduced that this man was seeking a place of concealment.

"Pisst! Pisst! Hey! Ov'r this way," whispered Nate from behind the tier of cotton bales that shielded his hiding place. The man with the cape froze. He had his back turned to the mountain of cotton and looked about him. Nate could hear that he was trying to catch his breath after his fantastic escape from his tormentors.

"Pisst! Hey! Ov'r here," beckoned Nate a little louder. The fugitive looked about him but remained uncertain where the whispering was coming from.

"Here! Behind the bale of cotton!" Nate positioned his legs against the main bale that entombed his secluded place and started to kick and push out the giant cube. The man with the cape turned his back and noticed that a bale of cotton was moving toward him, and for a moment thought that divine intervention was upon him. He elegantly turned his head toward the stern and bow of the steamer and saw that the deck was clear. He seized the ends of the bale with his black leather gloves and pulled at some cotton that was protruding at the ends of the bale. Nate pushed with his feet on his end, and within a moment the bale was dislodged sufficiently for the man with the cape to enter Nate's little tomb.

"Come on in! I'll make room fo' ya," whispered Nate eagerly. He was anxious to have some company and a potential partner who might be of help to him in his own flight. He decided that this octoroon dandy, obviously running from enemies, was a good bet.

"Just close the hole behind ya." The desperate man, chest still heaving from the chase and eager to hold up in a safe place, briefly gawked in amazement at Nate's smiling face. The dandy tipped his index finger at the rim of his hat and elegantly folded the cape with the grace of a prince, so the garment would not be entangled with his feet. Without saying a word, he stepped into Nate's snug hole and both men then grabbed the bale of cotton that was just removed and strained to lift it back into place. Accomplishing that task, the dandy smiled and extended his gloved hand to Nate.

"My name is Jacques Napoleon Gaches. Whom am I addressing?"

Four

Cara de Quervo Zarata and Mary Pugh Daniels were inside the newly constructed washhouse at Fort Wallace beating loads of laundry with short wooden paddles that resembled beaver tails. They pounded on the wash on long tables to beat out excess water from the linens to get them ready to hang. Mary Pugh had kept her wash paddles when she had left the plantation after the war and gone west with her children. She had given one paddle to Cara as a gift and reminded her to take good care of it because, "*Lot a* sweat *an'* pain *had gon' into dem wen I was a* slave."

The laundry business at Fort Wallace was proving to be lucrative. Cara and Mary Pugh had all the dirty laundry they could wash and iron and despite the long hours, their work was never done. Mary Pugh had noticed Cara's strength, stamina, and unabashed will to "*ganar mucho dinero,*" and proposed that they form a partnership. They agreed to act as a team and share all the profits straight down the middle.

The officers and their wives constantly brought them their clothes to launder as well as their children's. They also brought them their linen tablecloths and napkins, towels and doilies. Consequently, Cara and Mary Pugh were busy from before the bugler sounded reveille until past tattoo, scrubbing shirts, pants, undergarments, dresses, table linens, and curtains. Although the October air was brisk and the winds cut through most clothing, the interior of the washhouse was always extremely humid with hot vapors coming from the huge cast-iron cauldrons where the laundry was soaked, and from permanent fires that heated the pots. Adding to the torridity in the room was the constant back and forth movement of large women's arms pressing down on their hot irons.

Besides the usual chatter among the laundresses that usually involved fort gossip, and the sounds associated with laundering clothes, songs from slavery times mixed easily with melancholy Mexican mariachi tunes. Mary Pugh would frequently sing her favorite song at a high voice that dominated the large washhouse:

> "Abe Lincoln freed the nigger
> With the gun and the trigger;
> And I ain't going to get whipped anymore.
> I got my ticket,
> Leaving the thicket,
> And I'm a-heading for the Golden Shore!"

After a while, the song penetrated into Cara's mind and she started to hum along with Mary Pugh as her delicate hands worked the huge bar of soap against the soaked clothes while rubbing them vigorously against the corrugated surface of the washboard. When she was not humming along with Mary Pugh, or singing a song in Spanish, she obsessed about Nate. She missed him terribly, and felt anxious all the time. At night, before going to bed, although dead tired from toiling all day long, she could not help but visualize his strong face.

She knew that he would be returning sometime this evening because yesterday an Osage scout who had been recently in the field with Custer's Seventh Cavalry had brought news to Fort Wallace. The Osage had seen "Carpenter's *brunettes*" with General Carr, returning to the fort after a brief fight against fanatical Dog Soldiers along the Beaver. It was Mary Pugh who had broken the news to Cara.

"Your man is a-comin' for sure, for I ov'rheard that scout with the turban an' feathers on his head tell some officers."

When Cara learned that the column was in a fight with hostiles, her chest heaved with trepidation. She tried pressing Mary Pugh for additional details regarding the fight, fearing that her man might have been wounded or killed, but Mary Pugh would simply reply: "Child! No one knows nuthin' and if you knows nuthin', you gots to keep your mind on your work, an' the Lawd will see you through!"

II.

Antonio Vasco and his painted whores were camped near Fort Wallace. The fat Creole pimp had led his little band of traveling prostitutes to the post the day before, hoping to conduct some fruitful business with lonely and sex-starved troopers on their paydays. Although he was warned that the area around Wallace was not completely safe from Indian attack, the prospect of cashing in on such a large garrison's payroll became irresistible. His old portable wooden bordello had burned down in a fire a few months back, so he now resorted to using large tents and dividing the interior with blankets to form tiny spaces where the customers and his *Nymphs du Prairie* could conduct business.

Vasco wanted to go to the fort and do a little advertising. He only had to tell a few troopers or one or two noncoms to get the word out that he was open for business, and that his "bitches were the best meat along the Smoky Hill Road." He had given orders to his Mexican helper, Miguelito, and the hookers to pitch the tents and get things ready for this evening. Vasco always paid close attention to army payroll days, and it just so happened that this was the day that the soldiers were going to get their monthly thirteen dollars.

He rode through the front gate slouching in his saddle dressed in his usual gaudy manner. A dark pink frock coat that was heavily soiled with dust and dried mud and an overly tight purple and green silk-striped vest that made his large paunch resemble a mound. His black pants were stuffed in Mexican boots and his head was crowned with a felt stovepipe hat. The two black sentries at the gate laughed at his appearance, and one of them commented, "Mister, you look like my ol' mas'a's *peacock*."

Vasco ignored the comment and got down to business.

"Boys, my name is Vasco! *Antonio* Vasco," he announced with pride as he straightened his obese frame in the saddle. "I run the finest sportin' establishment west of the Missouri. You'll find my bitches tasty, clean, and cooperative in every way. We camped about two miles from here, on the Smoky Hill Road. I would appreciate it if you boys would pass the word."

"Sure, mister. We'll pass the word if we can get some fo' nuthin'," one of the sentries said, grinning.

"You send me bizness, my friend, and we will see," snapped Vasco, fully intending not to give anything away for free. He touched his Mexican spurs to his horse's flanks and rode toward the parade ground. As he walked his animal through the fort taking care in avoiding any officers, he told every enlisted man he encountered about his whores and the reasonable prices for their carnal services. Vasco was on his way out of the fort and returning to his camp when he passed the washhouse. He saw the door creak open and became startled when he saw Cara de Quervo Zarata step out. She was taking a break from the work and heat and wanted to get some fresh cool air. Although she had wrapped herself in a long wool white shawl, and a red bandanna covered her head, Vasco immediately recognized her because of her size, beautiful round eyes, and stunning face. At first Cara did not notice him because she was enjoying removing the bandanna from her head and running her hands through her hair and letting it blow in the breeze. Vasco halted his mount and stared at Cara. He had never gotten over the fact that Nate had taken her away from him and the loss bothered him greatly. He often told himself that if he should ever run into her again, he would take back what he believed was still his property.

Only when Cara tied the bandanna back around her head to keep her hair in a bundle did she notice her former tyrannical master and tormentor gawking at her from his horse not fifty feet away.

"Los Nacarra!" she uttered to herself in horror. Her heart jumped and her large round eyes became even larger due to fear. She ran back into the washhouse slamming and barring the door. Her chest heaving, she braced her back against the door and whispered, *"Imposible!"*

Antonio Vasco had no intention of following her into the washhouse. He knew that this was not the time or place for what he had in mind.

III.

Captain Louis Carpenter's column arrived at Fort Wallace as the bugler sounded Retreat. The colors were being lowered and most of the enlisted men were in their barracks waiting for the bugler to sound Tattoo. Nate, still wearing his bandage that was caked with dried blood and dirt, was riding with Sharp Grover in the middle of the column. The troopers, like their mounts, were tired, dirty, and hungry, and though they were happy to be back at the fort, they were too exhausted to show any emotion. Even Nate, who usually ordered his men to look good and tighten up when returning from the field, was too tired to give encouragement. He did notice, however, that the troopers looked like professional, seasoned cavalrymen, and he felt proud of them.

Most of the wives and children of the officers, along with their barking dogs, came out of their houses and ran toward the column to greet their spouses and fathers. Cara was still in the washhouse and feeling the effects of seeing Vasco's face. Her anxiety disappeared, however, when she heard the pandemonium outside and realized that her *Amor* had returned. Mary Pugh saw that Cara wanted to bolt and find Nate, but noticed that she was apprehensive because of her earlier shock of seeing her former tormentor.

"Well, what you waitin' fo', child? Go on, git! Go see your man," she urged, opening the door.

Cara wiped the perspiration from her face with her apron and ripped off her bandanna from her head to allow her long black mane to fall gracefully against her slender back. She then elegantly wrapped her shawl around her shoulders and ran from the washhouse, her long raven hair blowing in the wind. She headed toward the parade ground as fast as her moccasin-clad feet would carry her where she saw a column of troopers dismounting, and military wagons being unhitched from their mules.

Nate had halted Frederick and was about to dismount when he saw Cara in the distance running toward him. He saw her hair fly in the air as her delicate body seemed to float closer and closer to him.

He decided that rather than waiting for her to reach him, he commanded Frederick to canter in her direction. He came within a few feet of Cara when he abruptly reined in his beast and leaped effortlessly from the saddle. He then seized her in his arms and lifted her tiny body off the ground. Cara turned her head and placed her lips against Nate's while seizing his face with her tiny hands. They kissed as if the two of them thought that they would never see each other again.

"Mi amor!" repeated Cara, over and over again with great joy, and when she felt Nate's blood-caked bandage, became overcome with concern. *"Qué pasó?"*

Her eyes grew soft with tenderness, and she wanted to hold Nate forever. Nate breathed in her body aroma deeply, as if she were a blossoming rose. Cara's strong scent was so erotically over-powering that his neck and back shivered. He placed Cara back on the ground as if she were a porcelain doll, but continued to hold her in his arms as he stooped to be at her level. Looking into her eyes, he maneuvered his huge, powerful hands on her face and stroked every feature as if he were a blind man. He then gently stroked her head, feeling the strands of her silken hair in between his fingers that were rough and dirty and smelled of horse and gun oil. Although Cara's heart was thumping rapidly against her lover's breast, she felt secure and protected, and confident that nothing could go wrong now that *Mi Amor* had returned.

IV.

Antonio Vasco was combing back his oily black hair in front of the mirror in his tent. He was in a very bad and brooding mood. He had returned from Wallace to find that the big tent that was supposed to serve as the place to conduct business between his whores and the troopers was only partially erected. Miguelito nervously tried to explain that the high winds made it too difficult for him and the wenches to set up the large canvas, but Vasco, enraged that his establishment might not be ready and open for business, kicked and slapped the Mexican and screamed at the whores. After he had his tirade, he realized that he had no choice but to help erect the tent because there were no other able-bodied men or women to help in securing the big canvas.

As he sucked in his huge gut to button his vest, he thought about Cara and how much he resented that *"dirty nigger sergeant"* for taking her away from him. Seeing her for the first time since she went off with Nate a year ago brought back the memory of the insulting episode, and reminded him of his longing for Cara and his need to possess the half-breed wench again. He wanted her back, and his mind raced on how he could achieve this. He was not sure if Cara was still under Nate's protection or if she was alone, or even where she lived on the post. He did know that she was a laundress, hence employed by the army.

He cursed her under his breath.

"The bitch. Leaving me after all I done for her! How dare she!" He then whispered to himself confidently as he admired his corpulent face in the mirror, "I'll find out where you live."

He pulled out his gold chain watch from his vest pocket and clicked open the lid to check the time. It was still early and customers would only be coming later. He hurriedly put on his frock coat and told Miguelito to saddle his horse and bring the mare to him. Vasco then ordered the Mexican to mind the place for a while, and that if anything went wrong while he was away, threatened to thrash him. The kowtowing assistant brought Vasco his equally chubby horse and the Creole pimp mounted the animal and started down the road toward Wallace.

His plan was to talk his way past the sentries and inquire where the laundresses were staying. He would present himself as a relative of Cara's, and if challenged would make up a story that he carried news about a sick relative of theirs. He approached the main gate and halted when one of the sentries demanded to know his business. There were several oil lamps hanging on posts, and one of the two sentries carried a lantern and placed it above his head to see who the visitor might be. Vasco noticed that the sentry who carried the lantern was young and probably green and gullible.

"Good evening, kind sirs." Vasco smiled. "Could you direct me to where the laundresses are lodged?"

"Why do you want to know that?" demanded the other sentry.

"I am a relative, sir. I have important news to convey to my cousin," responded Vasco as he shifted his great weight in the saddle. "You gentlemen would not happen to know her? Her name is Cara de Quervo Zarata."

"The Mexican half-breed?" questioned the trooper with the lantern.

"Yes, that would be her," responded Vasco good-naturedly.

"Well, most of the fort's laundresses are niggers and they stay near that darky regiment at the other end of the post," explained the sentry.

"Ah! Yes of course." Vasco was quickly becoming high-spirited and pleased with himself that he was close to success and pleasantly surprised that the sentries were so cooperative. "And how would I find them?"

The sentry with the lantern held the light in the air and pointed toward the parade ground.

"Cross the parade ground and bear left. Pass the officers' quarters and the hospital and make a right at the commissary. When you pass the bakery you'll see the barracks for the Tenth, and across that will be a house with a double porch, and *that's* where the nonmarried laundresses are quartered."

"Thank you, kind sir," replied Vasco, delighted that he now had precise directions. He calmly walked his horse past the sentries and crossed the parade ground and then proceeded toward where the Tenth was lodged. When he passed the bakery, he smelled the aroma of bread being baked and the sounds of the workers beating dough on wooden tables accented by laughter and verbal banter. In the distance he spotted a big building that he assumed was the barracks of the black troops and looked for the house with a double porch. Vasco smiled when he saw several lighted windows on the second floor of a house that fitted the sentry's description. He approached the building and dismounted and tethered his horse to a corner beam that supported the second-story porch. He listened attentively for any noise, and most particularly for voices that might guide him toward Cara. After a minute of silence, he became frustrated that no noise was coming from within the structure. He did not want to go inside, fearing that if he had to search the house, room by room, a scene might occur that would alert his quarry and call attention to himself. He decided to peek through the windows where there was still a light, and see if he could locate her.

He discreetly started to peer into several windows that had their curtains drawn, but glowed from burning lamps inside. Vasco, however, could neither hear nor detect any movement from within the rooms, so he was in the process of tiptoeing toward a third window when he heard faint sounds coming from behind him. He halted and lifted his fat head to listen. The sound was faint but he could hear a moanlike quality to it. After a moment he realized that the sounds came from the second floor. Vasco turned around and made for the exterior stairway that led to the second-story porch. He tried to place each foot delicately on every step, but most of the wooden planks creaked loudly under the pressure of his great weight. He started to perspire out of nervousness and fear of being discovered. Every time a board would creak, he stopped and listened for any sounds that meant trouble for him, but all he could hear was the persistent murmur coming from one of the rooms upstairs. When he managed to reach the second story, the moaning sounds became clearer and louder. He reached the edge of the middle window where the sound was coming from and noticed that the curtain was not entirely drawn over the window. He slowly moved the right side of his head to where only half of his face was exposed, and peered into the room with his right eye.

The wick in the oil lamp was turned down very low, but there was enough of a glow in the room that enabled Vasco to see inside. His eyes widened, and his mouth gaped, as he gawked at the bronze flesh of a petite naked woman thrusting her pelvis back and forth as if she were posting on a horse. He immediately identified the woman as Cara. His face tightened, and his eyes became angry as he watched her skin glimmer while the soft hue of the light in the room threw her shadow onto the opposite wall. Her delicate arms were straining forward, and Vasco could hear her nimble fingers move her nails to scratch and dig into what he recognized as skin and hair of a man's chest. Her body was soaked with perspiration and her long black hair was wet and tangled from effort, and fell over her shoulders. She continued to moan and Vasco overheard her repeatedly cry out in a tearful, almost desperate voice.

"Love me! Please love me! *Mi amor.*"

Vasco could not fully see who was beneath Cara, but then he noticed two huge erect black arms reaching out from the bed, the large hands gently holding her waist, and assumed that it was Nate. *"Bastardo!"* he whispered to himself as he stared resentfully at Cara's breasts, her nipples firm from excitement. The window was slightly open and the body aroma of the two passionate individuals' sexual exertions began to seep from the room and Vasco could not help but smell the redolence of their excitement. *"El bastardo,"* repeated Vasco again, becoming increasingly irate. He continued to gawk as her thrusting pelvic movements quickened, as if she were now galloping, and her breathing became more intense and concentrated. He wanted to watch more, but the window of the room began to steam up, obscuring his vision. At first he thought that it was the frost because the night was chilly, but when he tried to rub a little hole on the glass pane, he realized that it was the steam and heat of the interior of the room that had fogged the glass.

"Who are you? What you doin' here?" hollered Mary Pugh Daniels as she stood near the foot of the stairs, her hands placed defiantly on her waist. She had heard Vasco's movements when he was climbing the stairs and decided to go outside and see who it was. Vasco became so startled that he nearly lost his balance and almost fell. He had been so absorbed by his voyeurism that he had not heard her approach. He knew he was caught in the act and that any verbal excuses would not pass muster with this large, authoritarian-looking black woman. In addition, he certainly did not wish for Nate to be disturbed and have him come out of his room. He decided to bolt and make for his horse. He managed to move his obese body fast enough to pass Mary Pugh and seize the railing of the stairs as a means of support and wobbled down the steps. He went for his horse but the animal became spooked by his hurried movements and Vasco could not calm him long enough to get a foot in the stirrup. The animal pranced in circles and Vasco was becoming more desperate as Mary Pugh was making her way down the stairs. He finally calmed his mount sufficiently to get his boot in the stirrup and grab the pommel of the saddle. With tremendous effort, he managed to heave his great weight onto the seat, his paunch resting on the seat. He was too exhausted, however, to lift his other leg into the left stirrup and contented himself with urging his horse to move by yelling at him. His mount, though, refused to move and Mary Pugh had now descended the stairs and was running toward Vasco. She was waving her arms in outrage and fast approaching the horse as Vasco con-

tinued to urge the animal to move. Mary Pugh's size and abrupt movements with her arms finally startled the horse enough where he suddenly bolted and cantered toward the gate as Vasco grunted in pain every time his stomach bounced on the seat of the saddle.

Five

NOVEMBER 1868.

Well, the orders have come down from General Sheridan to move against the Indians, and I feel sick. Little
Phil thinks he can destroy the Cheyennes and the other
tribes by launching a three-pronged attack against the
hostiles in a winter campaign. I am to report with
Company G, to Fort Lyon, Colorado Territory, along
with Companies B, F, and K, and report to Brigadier
General W. H. Penrose of the Fifth Infantry, where we
are to form part of his attacking column. The main
column is under General Sully and General Custer, and
the third one will be under General Carr. An officer
told me that the expedition's purpose is to surround the
Cheyennes, Arapahos, and Kiowas, and destroy them!
He wants to do what he did to the Secesh. Render them
poor and helpless. Our column would proceed toward
the North Canadian and join up with General Carr.

Nate reflected for a moment and grinned sarcastically before
continuing in his journal.

Can't wait to see Carr. Maybe he will talk to us now
that he knows that black soldiers can and will fight.

My heart is weary when I think that I have to leave Cara so soon! It seems that every time I get real close to her, I have to leave. When I told her that I had to go, she started to weep and carry on how I might not come back. I felt bad and told her that I won't be gone for long and that Fort Lyon is only a four-day ride from Wallace. I hope that when I return I will have enough time to do something permanent. I want her, I want her . . . forever!

I don't know, I feel that this is going to be another General Hancock disaster, and I don't relish the prospect of being in the field in winter, on the plains. From a paper point of view, the plan seems sound. Converging from all directions at the same time to overwhelm the hostiles looks good, but after last winter I know that too many things can go wrong.

Nate paused and held the quill in his giant hand. He looked out the window and noticed that with the exception of a few scattered lanterns hung on some of the walls on nearby barracks and the interior lights of the bakery it was pitch-black. The bugler had sounded taps a few minutes ago, and though he could not see much outside, he could hear the winds blowing, slamming against the exterior wall of the noncommissioned officers' quarters. Each time a gust of wind came rolling in and hitting the building, the structure would feel as if the walls and roof would collapse, and he could feel the cold air penetrating the walls and window casings. He thought about the inevitable travails of the upcoming winter campaign and quickly dipped his quill into the bottle, fearing that he might lose his train of thought.

Don't Little Phil know that the horses and mules are going to suffer? And that we are probably going to lose a lot of them? Don't he know that the men will move slow and be thinking more about staying warm than looking for hostiles? Hell! Even during the war, the armies would avoid a winter fight if they could, 'cause of the impossible conditions. Nevertheless, I will do my duty, and I am sure that the men will do their part, but chasing Indians in snow, ice, and howling winds will be a harsh task.

II.

PALO DURO CREEK, COLORADO TERRITORY.

Wild Bill Hickok was curled up in his blanket vigorously rubbing his fingers so they would not freeze. He feared that the ice-cold air and glacial winds that had slowed the circulation in the tips of his fingers would prevent him from using his revolvers. He had joined General Penrose's command at Fort Lyon as a scout for one hundred dollars a month, and now, shivering in his blanket, cursed his plight. Wild Bill's only consolation in view of the current predicament that he and Penrose's column found themselves in was the overly generous salary that the army was paying him. The plainsman never had enough money. Even though he was being paid a deputy United States marshal's salary, and supplemented his income with card games, his expensive taste in clothes, lodgings, and women never allowed the gunman to put any money away. Consequently, he was frequently forced to scout for the army not because he particularly enjoyed hunting Indians for weeks on end under arduous conditions, but because the army needed experienced men to chase hostiles and was ready to pay a premium.

"Thought you might like some hot coffee," offered Nate, holding a steaming tin in his right hand. Although Nate, as well as all the troopers, black and white, wore their regulation sky-blue great-coats with cape, the wool garment was not sufficient in insulating the men from the frigid winds, and many of the troopers' boots were falling apart due to the ice and moisture. To fend off the cold and to reinforce their collapsing footwear, the men sliced pieces of hide from dead horses and mules and wrapped them around their freezing feet. The men also wrapped bits of clothing around their heads and hands, and stomped their boots and clapped their hands together, going about the business of surviving until the arrival of General Carr.

"You mean hot dish water?" responded Wild Bill with a smile as he lay wrapped in his blanket looking up at Nate who seemed like a giant from his perspective.

"I've seen worse coffee!" cracked Nate, looking at Hickok's stiff long hair and catlike mustache that had become frozen from the wet snow and glacial winds. He was thinking about the war, and how most of the time there was no coffee for black troops and how they were forced to improvise by substituting for the cherished bean with chicory, tree bark, or be content to drink hot water.

"I bet you have!" Wild Bill unfurled his blanket in one quick elegant movement and stood up, revealing his buckskin outfit. His .36-caliber Navy Colt revolvers were strapped at each end of his waist, the butts of the revolvers facing outward. He straightened his buckskins and after he had stretched, picked up his Bowie knife and wedged the weapon in between his belt and stomach.

"Thank you, Sergeant Major." Wild Bill took the tin of coffee from Nate and held it in his hands, rubbing his fingers hard against the metal to get the numbness out.

When Wild Bill took a sip from the watered-down coffee, a shot rang out.

"There goes *another.*" Nate grimaced, turning in the direction of where the horses and mules were tethered. Although he had seen hundreds of horses and mules shot during the war, he could never fully immunize himself from witnessing such sad actions or bury the pain in his heart when engaging in it himself.

"How many you reckon have been shot?" inquired Wild Bill as he continued to rub his hands on the tin.

"Not sure, but I figure that more than two dozen or so horses and mules have already been put down. Lawd knows how many more are goin' to meet the same fate." Nate was thinking about Frederick. He had become increasingly weak and his ribs were showing. Nate felt horrible every time his horse would stare at him, begging for food. Nate knew if he stayed here much longer, he might also have to shoot his mount.

"Poor bastards!" exclaimed the plainsman as he sipped on his tin of dishwater coffee.

"Better this way. They all freezin' and starvin' . . . and I can't *bear* to look at them and have nuthin' to give them to eat."

"This is one *hell* of a situation we've gotten ourselves into. I'd do *anything* to get away from here," lamented Hickok as he stomped his feet on the dirty snow. "Being holed up in this god-forsaken place freezing on half rations, with no fodder for the horses and mules. That ain't what I signed up for!" Hickok took another sip from the tin and gazed at Nate. "Got to hand it to you boys though. You all bein' paid a miserly thirteen dollars a month and puttin' up with frostbite without much of a gripe."

"Yes, sir, them good boys." Wild Bill looked at Nate's breath as it poured out of his mouth. It reminded the gunfighter of a bellow of white smoke pouring out of a locomotive. "But you know Mr. Hickok, most of these men are former slaves and *they know* all 'bout hardship, pain, doin' without, and the *lash*. So a little snow, cold, and not enough food ain't too far away from slavery times, 'cept now we get paid, same as a white soldier is paid, and we damn proud to wear the uniform of the *United States Army.*"

"I see that the wound on your face is healin' nicely, but you goin' to have a nasty scar," remarked Wild Bill, trying to shift the direction of the conversation.

"Ain't the first, nor will it be the last." Nate smiled. "Besides, the way I figure it, the scar just makes me look more of a bad ass."

"And that is important to you, uh, Sergeant Major?" baited the plainsman.

Nate thought for a moment and then cracked another smile. "The same way you wear your guns, Mr. Hickok, it's a way of tellin' folks that *you dangerous.*" Nate pointed his finger at the gunfighter for emphasis. "And when you dangerous, people respect you."

Hickok kept his lips on the rim of the tin as he held the canister in both hands, feeling its warmth. He liked what Nate had said, and concurred completely.

"Tell you what. How about I ask Penrose if you and me can go out on patrol, and see if we can find some pony tracks?"

"I like nuthin' better, and if we can't find any tracks, maybe I can find some forage for my horse."

III.

"I think you a *fool* fo' not takin' this extra blanket," lectured Jesse as he stood shivering next to Frederick's head. Nate could hear Jesse's teeth chatter uncontrollably because the cold had penetrated his greatcoat and clothing as he saddled his horse and checked his accoutrements.

"Don't need it," insisted Nate, thinking that Jesse might need the blanket more.

"You more stubborn than an ornery mule. You might have to spend the night out . . ."

"We just goin' fo' a couple of hours," interrupted Nate as he tightened the cinch and worried about how much weight Frederick had lost. It disturbed him that his ribs were sticking out. "Besides, I ain't taken no spare blanket with me when other men could use it more. We'll be on the move, while you all have to stay here, freezin'." Nate mounted his horse and then looked at Jesse. "I'm sick of waitin' for that good ol' boy, General Carr, to come rescue us."

"Ready, Sergeant Major?" inquired Wild Bill as he maneuvered his mount next to Nate and Frederick. He had slipped on a pair of tight leather gloves that were practical for quick gunplay, but were poor insulators from the cold and knife-cutting wind.

"Let's go!" confirmed Nate, tapping his spurs gently on Frederick's flanks as he pressed down on the visor of his kepi to shield his face against the freezing gusts of blowing snow.

IV.

Antonio Vasco and his Mexican assistant, Miguelito, were riding on the trail that led toward Fort Wallace. They rode in silence, the only sound coming from the creaking of leather due to the cold and the crushing of their horses' shod hooves on fresh snow. It was an hour before the bugler was to announce evening stable call, the time that Vasco learned was when Cara usually left to go and have her supper at the laundress quarter with the other single laundresses. Vasco was wearing a velvet black cape that enveloped his corpulent body and a beaver hat that protected his head and heavily pomaded hair from the cold and wind. Miguelito was wearing his long and thick wool poncho with green and yellow stripes and a brown felt sombrero that had many little rips all around the wide crown. His long straggly black hair fell all the way to his shoulders, leaving grease spots on each shoulder.

Vasco's plan was simple. He had learned from several troopers of the Seventh Cavalry who had come to frequent his establishment that Nate had departed along with several companies of the Tenth on a winter expedition against the Indians. He was also assured that Cara usually was the last one to leave the washhouse, and considering that the building was close to the main gate, Vasco decided to abduct her as she left the building to have her supper at the laundresses' quarters.

Vasco had instructed Miguelito to use the dark green silk sack that often served to hoodwink young women whenever Vasco was in a major town and needed to replace one of his horizontal workers. Miguelito had become quite adept in sneaking up behind unsuspecting victims and hurling the silk sack over their heads. As the victim struggled with the sack, he would sweep his prey with a short oak pole at the back of the knees, forcing the body to collapse backward. He would then whip out his rope and quickly tie the sack around the woman's waist with her hands by her side, forming a transportable bundle.

Getting past the sentries was not a problem. They were all recurring customers, and anticipating that he would need all the goodwill he could develop at the post, he gave occasional freebies to those troopers who were frequently on guard duty at night.

"Evening, Señor Vasco," said the lone sentry with a big smile. He had recognized the owner of the traveling bordello immediately, and wanted to be polite and accommodating to him due to Vasco's recent generosity in granting ten minutes of free carnal enjoyment with one of his girls.

"Good evening, my friend," replied the pimp, smugly. There was a full moon and the night was cold and crisp. The sentry had trouble seeing the face of the visitor because Vasco and his horse's breath made huge sparse clouds that slowly dissipated in the thin night air.

"I have business. May I pass?"

"Don't pay me no mind. Just watch for the officers." The sentry smiled eagerly, hoping that Vasco would not forget his co-operation the next time he visited his establishment.

Vasco and Miguelito rode their horses through the gate and headed for the washhouse. Vasco could see that several laundresses were hurriedly leaving the building as they wiped the perspiration off of their faces and necks. They came out in pairs, some laughing, while others moved slowly and stiffly, indicating fatigue.

"We will wait here," ordered Vasco. The two men tethered their horses to a hitching post behind an enormous pile of stacked wood that was adjacent to the washhouse and served as fuel to boil the water for the cauldrons.

"How long do we have to wait?" whined Miguelito who did not like the cold and was anxious to get on with the matter at hand.

"Shut up," snapped Vasco as he tightened his cape around his neck. He was also impatient, but knew he had to wait for Cara to leave the building. There was a lull where there was no activity coming from the washhouse. With the exception of the sounds made on the fresh crisp snow by a few soldiers going about their business and the occasional civilian scout or tradesman riding by, there was no activity near the building. Vasco could see that the smoke from the chimney indicated that a strong fire was still burning, so he assumed that some washwomen, and hopefully Cara, were still inside. At eight o'clock, an hour before the bugler was to sound Tattoo, Mary Pugh Daniels stepped outside. Vasco recognized the big black woman who had nearly snagged him the night he had watched his former concubine mount and ride Nate in a state of rapture.

"Mi dios! Qué negresa mas grande!" exclaimed Miguelito as he stared at Mary Pugh.

"Encerrar!" chided Vasco, fearing that Mary Pugh might hear them and come after them the same way she tried the other night, and he certainly did not want to repeat that sad event.

"Don't be too long now, child, or your suppa goin' git col'!" hollered Mary Pugh, closing the door of the washhouse behind her. She slowly made her way down the path toward the laundresses' quarters, pressing her chin against her chest to protect her face from the cold gusts of winds.

Vasco's heart began to race. He anticipated that now that Mary Pugh had gone to supper, Cara was sure to follow. Knowing how fastidious she was, he decided that she was probably tidying up or finishing a load of laundry before closing up. The two men continued to wait behind the woodpile in the cold and Miguelito's toes started to freeze.

"Qué pasó?" he complained, stomping his feet on the ground to improve his circulation. Vasco raised his arm and was about to smack him against the side of his head because he was making too much noise and was becoming insubordinate when he heard the door of the washhouse creak open. He could see that the door was left open but no one was coming out. For a moment he feared that maybe it was not Cara, or if so, she was being very cautious in stepping outside. Vasco was growing so impatient that he wanted to go and see, but when he heard a woman humming and recognized that it was Cara's voice, he checked himself. When he spotted a petite foot clad in beaded deerskin booties stepping onto the snow, he knew it was Cara. She finally slowly walked outside carrying a bundle of neatly ironed and folded linens. Vasco quickly glanced around to make sure that there was nobody around and ordered Miguelito to move.

"Vete!" commanded Vasco, slapping the Mexican on the back.

Cara never saw or heard Miguelito approaching. So adept was the Mexican in creeping up to his victims that the suspects rarely realized what was going to happen to them. He tiptoed and crouched like a brigand as he came up to Cara from the rear. When he was close enough to his prey, he snapped open the sack and jumped in the air to throw it over her head, sending the pile of neatly folded linens flying into the snow and mud. He then took his oak pole and whacked Cara at the back of her knees forcing her to fall on her backside. As she lay on the ground struggling, he whipped out his rope. He took the piece of twine and wrapped her hands and feet together, hog-tied style. The bag was so tightly fitted to Cara that her screams became muzzled and all she could do was wiggle. Satisfied that she was now immobile, he then hoisted her up against his left shoulder and scurried back to the woodpile like a chicken thief in the night.

Vasco was holding the horses, waiting anxiously. When Miguelito returned, Cara was mumbling loudly through the green silk sack and was still wiggling furiously. This alarmed the flesh peddler, for he was afraid to draw any attention to himself. Miguelito tried to silence her by covering her mouth with his hand but it was not enough. Vasco saw the futility of this and raised his right hand high in the air and formed a fist. He then punched Cara in the face, knocking her senseless.

"Now you are *mine* again, you bitch!"

V.

Nate and Wild Bill Hickok were about thirty-five miles from Palo Duro Creek. They had decided to extend their scouting duties well beyond the limits of prudence in order to have a better chance in finding Indian or cavalry tracks and a greater opportunity to kill game if they were fortunate enough to run into a deer or buffalo. They had been out the whole day, however, and only saw one trail of single tracks made by an unshod horse, which they deduced was made by a lone Indian hunter because the tracks indicated that the pony was carrying killed game. The two men were also unsuccessful in finding any forage for their horses because of the deepness of the snow and failed to spot any game. As evening approached, there was an ominous silence that prevailed over the prairie. There were no sounds coming from birds or moving water from nearby streams and creeks, and even the winds had died down to such a point that the air was completely still.

"Did I tell you about the time last year when I had to interpret for General Sheridan and a bunch of Cheyennes, Arapahoes, and Sioux?" quizzed Wild Bill, trying to make conversation to pass the time. He had told the story on quite a few occasions and had forgotten whom he had told.

"No, sir," replied Nate, anticipating another one of the plainsman's great yarns.

"Well, last spring, General Sheridan wanted to have a parley with some of the chiefs, and since I know sign language and a little Cheyenne and Lakota, he wanted me to translate what he wanted to tell them. So, there we were in this big old army tent with the chiefs dressed in their finest and these newly arrived shavetail army officers from back East, and the general wanted to make a big impression on the Indians. So he instructed me to tell them that the white man has many large boats with huge paddles and can navigate in any river. He also told me to make clear to them that one of these large boats could carry the whole Sioux nation. Well, the chiefs were not convinced. They just stared at us in disbelief and continued to puff and pass the pipe around. The general then told me to tell them that the white man has many iron horses, and that the trains can transport more buffalo meat than all the tribes on the plains can in one year. Well, the Indians were still not impressed and told me that they did not believe him. Little Phil was becoming redder in the face with frustration, and I could see that his Irish blood was about to boil. Then he told me to tell them sternly that the white man has the talking wire and that he had in his possession a little black box that enabled him to speak with the great white father in Washington anytime he wanted, day or night. When he told me *that*, I had to think for a moment. I then told him with great reluctance. 'General! Now, *I* don't believe you.' " Nate and Wild Bill roared with laughter, their voices carrying throughout the ravines, breaking the wintry silence.

"Blizzard comin', looks like it might be a northerner," observed the plainsman as he gazed at the menacing low, gray sky. "I don't like all these signs, I hate to say it, but it sure seems like it's the quiet before the storm."

"I don't think we can make it back to the bivouac site 'fore nightfall," responded Nate as he glanced at the dark canopy. He was prepared to spend the night with Wild Bill out in the open, away from the campsite, rather than risk traveling in the dark and getting lost.

"I think we can retrace our tracks before the snow and winds come." Unlike Nate, Wild Bill did not relish the prospect of spending a night away from the camp if there was a chance they might make it back before the blizzard hit.

The men proceeded to retrace their steps through the snow, encouraging their horses to tread in the tracks that they had made earlier, hoping to reduce stress and fatigue. Their mounts, already weakened by the lack of forage since being marooned at Palo Duro Creek, were now truly exhausted and famished as their chests heaved, and their weakened legs stumbled in the broken snow. As the sun quickly descended in the west, Nate was becoming increasingly concerned about Frederick's ability to go much farther, but he knew his mount had heart and would go as far as he could. Since Wild Bill's horse was in slightly better condition, the plainsman led the way, Nate following closely behind.

It started to snow and Nate could feel the rapid drop of temperature on his face. He removed the yellow leather gauntlet from his right hand and touched the scar on his face with his fingers. It surprised him that his cheek felt like a hard block of ice. He then touched his ear but could only feel it with his hand and became astonished that there was no sensation because it had become completely numb.

"I can probably *flick* the damn thing right off my head with my finger," he whispered loudly.

His body, hands, and feet were warm, however, because the temperature during the day had been relatively mild and there was no wind. Also, his army greatcoat was sufficient to protect him from the elements, and as long as he was riding Frederick, his blood circulation kept his feet and hands from freezing.

Nate had been staring at the ground guiding Frederick through the snow, but when the big flakes started to descend he looked up at the back of Wild Bill's buckskin coat and perceived that the snow on the plainsman's shoulders and broad-brimmed hat was accumulating quickly. Although Nate fully realized that the weather was now their immediate concern, he thought that the way the snowflakes were thinly distributed and the slowness of their descent from the menacing dark clouds seemed to him as if the white flakes were dancing toward the ground. The flakes were large, and when he was not looking at the ground, he enjoyed observing each one and identifying its particular characteristics.

After a while, the volume of snowflakes increased with great fury and the snow became like sand, rendering visibility difficult and painful for both the two men and their mounts. About two hours after Wild Bill and Nate started to retrace their steps back to the bivouac site, the falling snow became so intense with violent bursts of winds that the sound reminded Nate of a freight train. The men were blinded and had to partially shut their eyes and Nate finally succumbed to the elements and removed the scarf around his neck and wrapped the article around his head. Their horses slowed and Frederick in particular started to flounder as the winds increased and slammed into them, throwing their mounts out of balance and disorientating the beasts. Although Nate was only a few feet away from Wild Bill, the raging snow and swirling winds obliterated his visibility. Nate was about to call out to Hickok to slow down so he could catch up but was hit with a fatal bluster that knocked over Frederick and pinned Nate to the ground. He cried out Hickok's name several times, beckoning for assistance, but his words became lost in the tempest of wailing winds and spiraling snow.

Six

Cougar Eyes' tipi was located at the far end of Black Kettle's Cheyenne encampment along the western end of the Washita River where the Dog Soldiers had pitched their lodges. All along the Washita, the Cheyennes, Kiowas, Arapahoes, and even some Apaches had come to spend the winter in the valley.

Cougar Eyes' squaw, Willow Branch, was roasting some venison steaks over a slow-burning cook fire located in the center of the tipi. Her husband had brought back a young mule deer from a hunting trip, and she had spent the later half of the afternoon skinning, dressing, and butchering the meat by carefully following the natural contours of the animal. Because it was exceedingly cold and windy, Willow Branch also made a soup from dried turnips, squash, and corn and soon the interior of the tipi became filled with this aroma, blending with the burning of dried sage and sweet grass.

Although Willow Branch could hear the winds of the blizzard mercilessly pounding the buffalo hides of the tipi, she was warm and the lodge's anchor pegs and ropes remained taut. She was expecting Cougar Eyes to appear at any moment because she made it clear to him that dinner was going to be ready soon, and that she did not want to wait for him and have the venison steaks cool down. She gazed around the interior of the lodge to make sure that everything was in order because her husband preferred that all of their possessions be in their proper place. She looked over to where the bedding was located and nodded to herself in approval, satisfied that the winter buffalo robes were neatly covered over the soft inner hair of muskrat hides. Next to their bedding were Cougar Eyes' weapons for hunting and making war. Several bow-lances, quivers filled with arrows, war clubs, and lances were displayed against the painted inner lining of the lodge. To the right of the door flap was a pile of neatly stacked parfleches filled with jerky and dried fruits, nuts, and vegetables.

Willow Branch was becoming impatient waiting for her husband because the meat was almost ready and she wanted to serve the soup. She squatted on the ground near the cook fire and was about to take the U-shaped tongs made from a willow sapling to turn over the venison steaks when she felt a gust of cold air mixed with snow breeze past her body. The sudden cold draft indicated to her that the door flap had been abruptly opened. She looked up as she held the tongs and was glad that her husband had returned.

"The winds are shifting. I will have to adjust the smoke flaps," declared Cougar Eyes as he glared at the smoke hole while he removed his winter buffalo robe that was almost entirely covered in fresh snow. He wore no hat and his long braids, wrapped in mink, were heavily speckled with fresh snowflakes that had fallen on his hair. Willow Branch saw that the flakes had started to melt and drip in tiny beads of water on his doeskin shirt.

"That can wait. The soup is ready and I don't want the meat to burn," insisted Willow Branch as she handed Cougar Eyes a wooden bowl that contained a turnip, corn, and squash soup. At first, Cougar Eyes placed the rim of the steaming bowl gently to his lips and sipped slowly to avoid being burned. He felt the warmth of the liquid go down his throat and into his stomach and became glad that he had returned to his tipi after visiting with Turkey Legs and some of the Dog Men in his Red Lance warrior society.

"How was your visit?" inquired Willow Branch after she had sat down next to her husband.

"Some of the scouts have reported seeing many bluecoats and their tracks." Cougar Eyes took another sip of the soup and looked up at the smoke hole.

"Do you think that the *Ve' ho' e* are coming?" Willow Branch, like her husband, was a survivor of the Sand Creek Massacre, and she lived in fear that their camp would be attacked.

"Black Kettle has made peace with the *Ve' ho' e,*" responded Cougar Eyes cynically. "It is as if he had learned nothing from what happened at Sand Creek!" He shook his head bitterly. "The old man thinks that the *ho' nehe* will not harm him or the people again. He is a fool." Cougar Eyes took another sip of the soup and felt its warmth. "That is why we, the *Hotame Ho' nehe* are camped separately from the main village so we can be ready to repel any attack on the people."

They could hear the wind blow outside but the conical shape of the tipi held up superbly against the forces of the blizzard.

"Besides, the snow is deep and we know that many of the *Ve' ho' e* and the *Mo' ohtae-Ve' ho' e ho' nehe* are starving and are eating their *mo'ehno'ha*.

Willow Branch was not reassured. She had lost many relatives at Sand Creek and at night she often experienced nightmares, reliving the horrors of what Chivington and his savage bluecoats did to the squaws and papooses. She slowly raised herself from her squatting position on the tipi floor and went over to the cook fire and reached for the U-shaped tongs. She then elegantly removed the steaks and placed them on a small slab of polished stone.

"After I eat, I must adjust the smoke-hole flap," declared Cougar Eyes, grabbing a piece of buffalo steak with his hands.

Willow Branch took her place near her husband again. "And tomorrow?"

"I will leave at dawn, if the blizzard has stopped. We will need more fresh game."

II.

When Cougar Eyes awoke the next morning, the first thing he noticed was the calmness of the new day. The winds had died and Willow Branch was already awake, stoking the fire and fanning the embers with the wing of a bird. He gazed at the smoke hole and became momentarily blinded by the yellow light that poured down on his face. He shielded his face with his hand and then noticed that each of the three supporting lodge poles had become a stripe of turquoise, reflecting the sky. He then glared at the painted interior lining and could tell by where the light beamed on the wall that the sun had been up for quite some time.

He rubbed his eyes, stretched, and scratched his crotch to remove some horsehair that had gotten caught in between his legs. As he lay under his buffalo robe in a fetal position, he held his hard organ in his hand and stared at the backside of his squaw. For a moment he regretted that he had refused her advances the previous evening but then he became reassured when he thought about one of the golden postulates of the *Tsitsitas*: Abstinence is essential to conserving male energy for war. The sun was already high in the sky, motivating Cougar Eyes to unfurl the heavy bison hide that covered his body and crawl to the flap door. He pushed the painted rawhide slightly aside and peered out and smiled. It gave him pleasure to see that the sky was a deep blue and the freshly fallen snow sparkled in the bright sun.

"I will leave after I have had some pemmican and sage tea," he announced, closing the door flap.

Willow Branch nodded and went over to the buffalo paunch that was suspended from a tripod made from ash branches and used the buffalo horn ladle to pour the sage tea into a crude wooden bowl. She handed him the container and looked at his long dark unbraided hair, and thought to herself. *He's so handsome and strong.*

"Will you be gone long?" she asked.

"As long as it takes for me to bring back food," he responded directly, taking a sip of the hot sage tea.

Willow Branch placed her warm body against Cougar Eyes' chest and wrapped her arms around his waist. She could feel his organ and felt that it was still firm.

"Hurry back."

III.

Cougar Eyes had spotted some antelope tracks that led away from the Washita. Game had been scarce lately because so many of the Northern and Southern Cheyennes and Arapahoes had come to winter along the Washita. He was mounted on his favorite hunting pony and armed with his bow and a quiver filled with arrows in case he ran into any *ho' nehe*.

The crown of his head was covered with a mink turban that coordinated with his sheathed braids. He was dressed in a heavy dark trade-cloth tunic with matching leggings and a winter buffalo robe was draped over his lap for additional protection against the wind.

Cougar Eyes' well-fed chestnut pony's unshod hooves confidently broke the fresh snow crystals that glittered in the brilliant sunlight. The Dog Soldier noticed that the antelope tracks were becoming closer together, indicating that the animal was slowing due to fatigue, or because of the deep snow or weakness for lack of food. He was hoping that he was closing in on his prey as his strong chestnut moved swiftly through the drifts. Near a creek that fed into the Washita, Cougar Eyes saw the tan coat of the antelope nibbling at some chockberry bushes. Although he was upwind, the hunter gazed at the animal for a moment to see if he had been detected, but the antelope was so busy eating some of the dried fruit to satiate his hunger that he did not hear Cougar Eyes' horse move through the snow. Satisfied that he still retained the element of surprise, Cougar Eyes removed an arrow from his quiver and fastened the end to his bowstring and placed his index and middle finger of his left hand at the base of the arrow head. He was about to pull back on the string and take aim at his prey when his attention was drawn toward a strange heap that did not resemble anything that he would ordinarily find among the landscape. The object, partially covered in a snowdrift, was a short distance away from the antelope and Cougar Eyes was convinced that it was neither a fallen tree, a large rock, nor an earthen mound because of its out-of-place coloring and alien shape. His hunting pony sneezed, alerting the antelope of his presence. The animal gave a startled look at the Dog Man and bolted through the drifts and out of reach from Cougar Eyes' arrows. Cougar Eyes became disappointed but he knew that he had been distracted and had lost the element of surprise. He decided to investigate the strange object that had caused him to lose the opportunity for fresh meat.

He gently tapped his heels to the pony's flanks and headed for the foreign object. He approached cautiously and squinted his eyes to focus and cut through the glare that the sun and snow crystals made on the snow and drifts. Cougar Eyes' mount snorted several times, billowing large clouds of his breath in the crisp air. When the animal got within a few feet of the alien object he hesitated, refusing to advance. Cougar Eyes kicked harder but the beast just snorted and pawed at the snow. This alarmed the Dog Man. His experienced hunting pony rarely ever shied away from uncertainty due to his master's prowess as a horseman and the effort that went into training. Taking his mount's cautious behavior seriously, however, he decided to dismount and approach on foot. Cougar Eyes patted his pony on the neck as a sign of reassurance, and moved gingerly forward, holding his bow at the ready. A sudden but gentle gust of wind removed the top layer of the new snow and revealed the face of a black man with closed eyes, his head resting on an expired cavalry horse's stomach.

"Mo' ohtae-Ve' ho' e!" observed the Dog Soldier with satisfaction. Cougar Eyes always enjoyed seeing the enemies of the people dead. He was not entirely surprised, however, because he knew that there were hundreds of the *Mo' ohtae-Ve' ho' e* soldiers stranded within a day's ride, and assumed that this one probably became separated and overwhelmed by the blizzard. Cougar Eyes walked a little closer to the body and examined it carefully. He noticed the kepi's brass military insignia pulled down over the man's forehead and army blue greatcoat. He then scrutinized the black man's ice-crusted eyebrows and beard stubble.

"Hotoa' e Gordon," he exclaimed in astonishment. For a moment Cougar Eyes remained motionless as he gazed into the face of his nemesis. *Was he dead?* he wondered. Nate's face was completely motionless, and Cougar Eyes knew that last night's temperatures and blizzard conditions would normally kill a man who was unfortunate to be caught unprepared. He reached into his beaded deerskin pouch and removed a small finely polished river stone and placed it under Nate's nose. Cougar Eyes watched closely

to see if the surface of the stone's gloss face would fog up, indicating that Nate was still breathing. He waited for what he thought was sufficient time and was about to remove the stone thinking that *Hotoa' e Gordon* had finally met his fate, when he detected a faint cloud on the stone's surface.

Cougar Eyes became astonished. *"Hotoa' e Gordon* is still alive." *"Epeva'e!"*

IV.

"You *macarra!"* screamed Cara, shielding her head from Antonio Vasco's blows with her arms and hands. The Creole pimp had been slapping her around in his tent for several minutes in one of his tirades and Cara could do nothing except try to protect her delicate head and face from her tormentor's corpulent hands and sharp nails. Vasco would chase her around the tent, forcing Cara to seek refuge behind pieces of furniture to escape his poundings.

"You will obey me, wench, or get more of the same," screamed back Vasco, standing over Cara who was now cowering in one of the corners of the tent. Although the temperature inside the canvas structure was sufficient to render standing water into a block of ice, the flesh peddler was perspiring profusely because he had overexerted himself. His face was marked by rivers of perspiration, and his face, neck, armpits, and belly were wet, soaking his white evening ruffled linen shirt.

After Vasco had abducted Cara from Fort Wallace, the next morning he ordered Miguelito to strike the tents and prepare the train to move out and proceed east, on the Smoky Hill Trail toward Fort Hays. Cara was now a prisoner of her former master. He had threatened her that if she refused to comply with his every wish, he would beat her and break the bones in her face. It was now several days that she had been kidnapped, and she felt her will to resist Vasco's demands waiver. The pimp had relentlessly bullied Cara into servicing him as if he were a pasha and to submit to his sexual needs. Every evening Vasco would order Miguelito to untie Cara and bring her to him at his tent. At first, Vasco attempted to be verbally persuasive, telling Cara that he really cared for her and that he would no longer be abusive.

Cara cynically defied Vasco and demanded that he bring her back to Fort Wallace and that she belonged to Nate. This enraged and insulted the pimp and he quickly forgot his empty promises and started to beat her into submission. At night, after the beatings, she would lie awake in Miguelito's tent on the floor, her hands and feet tied, and under the watchful eye of Vasco's henchman. In an effort to break her will, Vasco had instructed that she was only allowed one wool blanket. She would lie awake, hungry and in pain, staring at the tent's ceiling, thinking about Nate and hoping that he would soon return from the field and discover what Vasco had done, and come to her rescue. She feared that the procurer's relentless brutality would eventually break her resolve and that she would be forced to submit to his conditions.

V.

Cougar Eyes decided to save *Hotoa' e Gordon*'s life. Although Nate was a bluecoat and the enemy of the people, the Dog Soldier possessed a deep respect for his nemesis's fearless prowess in battle, and unlike the behavior of white soldiers, the Dog Man recognized Nate's past honorable and brave comportment. Cougar Eyes also remembered how this black *ho' nehe* stopped his men from destroying and pilfering the burial scaffolds of dead warriors from the fight at Beecher Island.

Cougar Eyes knew that Nate was suffering from hypothermia and was in shock. The Dog Soldier had to work quickly, for he knew that the longer Nate remained exposed to the elements, his chances for losing some of his limbs would increase. He cleared Nate's body from all the snow and covered him with his buffalo robe, and then proceeded to cut down two straight willow branches to make a travois. He then took his long rawhide lariat and weaved and lashed it in between the two poles, creating a crude net that would hold and carry a man's body. Cougar Eyes then dragged the structure to the rear of his pony and attached the travois to the beast's withers, using a rope to secure the two poles over the pony's rump. The hardest task was loading Nate's huge body onto the travois. Although the Dog Soldier was strong and was accustomed to lifting heavy items, Nate's dead-body weight proved too much. So he had to untie the travois from his pony and use the last bit of the rawhide lariat that he had left and lashed the cord around Nate's torso. He then wrapped the other end of the rope around his pony's chest and urged the animal forward, dragging Nate's body onto the travois. Accomplishing that, he reattached the travois to his pony and slapped the beast's backside for him to start moving.

The journey back to camp took nearly three times longer for Cougar Eyes than when he was mounted. Even though he walked in the snow and drifts alongside his hunting pony, Nate's weight sank the willow poles deeply into the fresh snow, rendering the task of transporting him burdensome and slow. When they finally reached the camp and approached Cougar Eyes' tipi, the Dog Man cried out for Willow Branch to help him unload Nate.

At first, Willow Branch was astonished that her husband had brought back the *Mo' ohtae-Ve' ho' e ho' nehe*.

"Why do you bring the enemy to our camp?" she berated.

"He is an honorable warrior. I will not see him die in the snow and cold," he insisted. "Now, go and prepare hot stones for him."

With the help of two other Dog Soldiers, Cougar Eyes managed to carry Nate's body inside the tipi and onto a pallet of buffalo robes.

One of the Dog Soldiers, after carrying Nate by his feet, felt the softness of the *ho' nehe* high-top boots.

"I want the leather of his boots," he demanded.

"*Hova'ahane.**" You will take nothing that belongs to *Hotoa' e Gordon* while he is a guest in my lodge," barked Cougar Eyes.

"*Henova'e?*† He is not a hostage or a prisoner?" replied the astonished Dog Man.

"He is our enemy, this is true. But he is a worthy and fair opponent. He is not like the *Ve' ho' e.*" Cougar Eyes looked into the other Dog Man's face and saw that he lusted for Nate's boots. "I had a dream several nights ago. I dreamed that I was riding among thick white clouds and in the distance I saw *Hotoa' e Gordon* and his horse fall."

The Dog Man looked at Cougar Eyes skeptically. "So you believe that fate led you to save him?

"*Heehe'e!*"‡

"I don't want any men in the tipi!" commanded Willow Branch sternly as she started to undress Nate.

"*Epeva'e!*§ We will go to Turkey Leg's lodge," replied her husband. "*Noheto.*" He gestured to the other two Dog Soldiers that they had to leave. He had done his part. Now it was up to the squaws to nurse *Hotoa' e Gordon* back to health.

Willow Branch worked quickly. With the help of Turkey Leg's wife, who had come to assist her after she had learned that a big *Mo' ohtae-Ve' ho' e* had been brought in suffering from hy-

---

*No!
†What?
‡Yes!
§It's good.

pothermia, the squaws had removed his army greatcoat and un-buckled the saber belt. They then stripped Nate of his uniform but left his undergarments on. The squaws had difficulty in re-moving his boots, however, and Turkey Leg's wife had to take a skinning knife and slit the leather above the foot to remove them. When Willow Branch gently peeled back the wool socks on Nate's feet, she immediately perceived that the three middle toes on Nate's right foot were dangerously close to frostbite.

"We must get his body temperature up. Place the stones of the fire around him," she commanded. Willow Branch then loosened the strings of her doeskin shirt and placed Nate's injured foot in between her round breasts and started to gently rub them against his damaged toes.

Turkey Leg's squaw completed placing the hot round river stones around Nate, each stone only a half inch away from him, creating a ring of heat. Since hypothermia attacks the body's ex-tremities first, she started to massage his hands, arms, and legs to quicken the blood circulation.

"He will need fluids and much sugar," clamored Willow Branch.

"He feels very stiff. A few more hours in the cold, and he would have been a dead *ho' nehe!*" responded Turkey Leg's wife, straining her arms, hands, and fingers to massage Nate's rigid mus-cles.

VI.

The first thing that Nate saw when he awoke in Cougar Eyes' lodge were drawings on the tipi's smoke-stained lining depicting a brave's exploits as a warrior and hunter. One scene that drew his immediate attention was an incident regarding a Dog Man dressed in full battle regalia mounted on a fine painted war pony with notched ears, armed with a lance piercing what appeared to be a soldier who was shooting at him on foot. Nate felt very tired and disoriented, and for a moment thought he was dreaming.

"Lawd! Where am I?" he whispered to himself, half realizing that he was in an Indian tipi. He examined his person and saw that his greatcoat, uniform, and accoutrements had been removed, and he only wore his underwear. He tried to think. He remembered Frederick's fatal collapse in the blizzard and his cries for help as Wild Bill Hickok disappeared in the tempest. After that, his memory was a haze. He felt weak and he could not feel the toes in his right foot. He unfurled the buffalo blanket to see his foot and saw that his toes were wrapped in beaver pelts. He gazed toward the center of the lodge and could hear the crackling of a fire that was dug deeply into the ground and surrounded by round river stones. Nate could feel its warmth on his face while its light reflected on the lining, causing him to focus on another scene. In this picture, the brave, again mounted on another pony, was shooting at a mountain lion. Nate started to move his head about and noticed that his body was elevated from the ground by a pallet of buffalo hides. A heavy winter buffalo robe covered him and his head rested on several pillows made from buckskin, embroidered with porcupine quills. He looked around the tipi and observed that the lodge had an array of skins arranged on the floor: mountain lion, grizzly, deer, wolverine, possum, elk, and moose. He also noticed a neatly stacked pile of painted parfleches at the opposite end of the room, and several beaded bags hanging from the smooth pine lodge poles. Shields, quivers, and headgear made from eagle and hawk feathers festooned from a rawhide rope halfway up the lining. Nate was about to rise up from his horizontal position when the tipi's willow frame bearskin door swung open. A brave entered, his head bowed as a result of stooping into the lodge. Nate stared at him intensely and felt that he was at this man's mercy. The Indian raised his head and smiled smugly.

"Haaahe! Hotoa' e Gordon!"* greeted Cougar Eyes as he hung his bow and quiver on the rawhide rope.

Nate did not recognize the Dog Soldier when he entered the tipi. But when he called him by his Cheyenne name, he knew it was Cougar Eyes.

"How did I get here?" inquired Nate, trying to lift his torso with his elbows.

"My squaw, Willow Branch, speaks your tongue." Cougar Eyes' wife pulled back the bearskin door flap and gracefully stepped into the lodge. She carried a basket filled with buffalo chips. She went over to the fire and fell to her knees looking at Nate's face across the small flames.

"I learned the white man's talk when I was child at Bent's Fort," she said proudly. "There, I met many white traders and trappers. Most were good, but some had bad hearts," she sighed deeply but then strategically placed several buffalo chips on the fire, just enough to keep the flames from becoming too large while generating as much heat as possible. If the interior became too warm, Willow Branch would raise the flaps at the base of the canvas and ventilate the lodge. Cougar Eyes quietly sat down next to Nate on his willow-rod backrest.

"My husband." Willow Branch pointed to the Dog Soldier. "I try to teach, but he stubborn. He no like to make the talk of the whites."

"How long have I been here?" Nate had lost all sense of time. He had no idea how long he had slept.

"You sleep long time," she replied.

---

*Greetings!

With great effort, Nate managed to lift his torso into a sitting position.

"Please, tell your husband, that the w'ite man talk was not the talk of my ancestors, long time ago. I was forced to talk like them to survive." Nate looked at Cougar Eyes. He felt weak and stiff at the same time, but recognized that he was in no danger and that he was certainly not a prisoner. Willow Branch translated, and Cougar Eyes listened and nodded. The Dog Soldier was curious. He had been intrigued with Nate ever since he first saw him, so he was prepared to listen and talk.

"Why did he save me?" asked Nate, looking at Cougar Eyes who still bore an air of smugness. Nate wondered, Was he going to try and win him over to his side?

"My husband not wish you to die in snow and cold." Willow Branch squeezed hot water from the buffalo pouch that hung over the fire into a wooden bowl that carried a tuft of sweet sage. She carefully brought the bowl over to Nate and handed it to her guest. "You drink! You need much water and need . . ." For a moment, she had forgotten the word, but then it came back to her. "Sugar!"

"But I am bluecoat," responded Nate as he took a sip of the hot sage tea. "Why he save life of bluecoat?"

"My husband believes in his heart that you are good and truthful man," she replied.

Cougar Eyes spoke to his wife while looking at Nate from his willow-rod backrest. "Tell *Hotoa' e Gordon* about my vision."

"My husband had dream and you appeared in his vision. He saw you and your fine horse in clouds, and fall from horse. He then say that spirit of meadowlark spoke to him and told him to save you."

Willow Branch started to prepare for the evening repast. She opened a parfleche that was painted in red and yellow geometrical patterns, and removed several handfuls of dried plums. She usually served them at breakfast, but considering that the *Mo' ohtae-Ve' ho' e* had not eaten since he was brought in yesterday, and that he needed as much sugar as possible, decided to give him a bowl of the sweet fruit while she prepared to roast a rack of buffalo ribs.

Nate thought about Frederick. He was saddened by the loss and felt responsible. The beast had been faithful, obedient, and unwavering, even in the face of starvation. He thought that maybe it was a mistake to venture so far from the bivouac site, hence exposing his horse to danger. He knew that it would be a long time before he would find such a fine mount again.

"You rest, *Hotoa' e Gordon*. Squaw make food. We talk later," commanded Cougar Eyes as he underscored his broken English with sign language.

Nate suddenly felt very drained. He slid back into his warm and luxuriant buffalo robe, resting his head on the buckskin pillows. He took a deep breath and could smell the scent of burning sweet grass and sage as he drifted back to sleep.

VII.

Nate woke up in the middle of the night, sweating. Another nightmare regarding Jacques Napoleon Gaches, the Creole gambler from Natchitoches, had once again intruded into his sleep. This time he saw his octoroon friend fall backward from the stern of the paddle steamer onto the giant, revolving wheel while the whistle blew a deafening blast of steam, drowning Jacques Napoleon Gaches's scream.

With the exception of the light glow coming from the slow-burning buffalo chips, the interior of the lodge was dark and still warm. He gawked at the lining and at the painted figures that decorated the walls of the tipi. The low light from the chips had deformed the figures and rendered them ghostlike and much larger and Nate felt a little uncomfortable. He had slept for another two hours before Willow Branch had gently awoken him to eat some broiled buffalo meat, pemmican, and wild turnip soup. Nate remembered eating like a starved dog, but could not recall how many helpings he had of the meat and pemmican. He looked to his left and saw that both his hosts were asleep, snug in their buffalo robes.

He decided that he was strong enough to crawl toward the willow-frame door flap and get some air. The lodge felt stuffy with leftover cook smoke that still smelled of meat and stale tobacco. He crawled to the entranceway and pulled back the bearskin that covered the frame and felt the cold clean air on his face. He breathed deeply and felt almost intoxicated by its freshness. Nate closed his eyes and took several more deep breaths as if he were going to spend time underwater. The air cleared his head but his thoughts returned to his escape with the Creole gambler, on the big stern-wheeler *Belle de Jour* on the Red River.

After Jacques Napoleon Gaches and Nate had introduced themselves, they remained silent for the entire morning, fearing that any sounds coming from their secluded hiding place among the cotton bales would reveal their existence. Only at lunch, with the sounds of the galley drowning out their voices, did they dare to whisper.

"Whut you runnin' frum?" asked Nate.

"Oh, the usual." The octoroon smiled, elegantly removing his black leather gloves and glancing at his manicured nails.

"Us'al whut?" Nate was curious. Here was this dapper, seemingly articulate, light-skinned Colored man with him in the hole on the run. He could not help but be amused by the contrast between them. Nate had not washed in days and he knew he reeked. His clothes were also dirty and well worn, and his skin was black as coal. His guest on the other hand smelled of cologne, dressed in silk and linens, and his boots were polished to perfection. The only thing they had in common was that they were both fugitives.

"Let us say, dear sir, that I am being pursued by ungrateful philistines who are not gentlemen."

"You mean you owe them *money*," scoffed Nate.

"Oh, my dear sir, that is a rather crude way of putting it," responded Gaches in flamboyant denial. "These desperate men called in their note, sir, violating a long-standing agreement." Gaches pointed his finger at Nate accusingly. "And you, sir, you are a runaway slave, going north, perhaps even seeking to join the Union Army," declared Gaches with a smile. The gambler enjoyed getting the jump on people by accurately guessing their backgrounds and status.

Nate smiled back but remained silent. He thought it was best that he neither confirm nor deny his situation.

The Creole had a plan but needed Nate's help. "I am not ungrateful for your assistance in secluding me among these lovely bales of cotton, kind sir, so allow me to repay my debt to you by providing a way out of this hole to become passengers."

"How you goin' to do that?" Nate was skeptical at the dandy's plan. The fast-talking octoroon was on the run, just like him, how could he provide a way out of the hole to mingle with the passengers and crew?

Jacques Napoleon Gaches reached into his vest and pulled out a huge wad of *Dix* notes and held them triumphantly in the air.

"With *these,* my good man, with *these!*" The octoroon smiled broadly, as if he held a full flush of cards at a gambling table. "These bills are printed by the *Banque des Citoyens de la Louisiane de la Nouvelle Orleans*," he explained. Although Nate knew only a few words in French, he noticed that this man's pronunciation and accent sounded more sophisticated and learned than Jean le Fou's Cajun bayou twang.

"These bills are recognized as legal tender *all over* the South and even among the Yankees! We will bribe a member of the crew and have him steal some decent clothes for you and I will purchase our passages for us, and you will act as my servant. That way we can travel in style and comfort."

Nate was amazed at the man's hubris. It was a bold plan that would demand nerve and guile. "I admit, I want to get out of this stinkin' hole real bad, but I can't see us bullshittin' our way past the w'ite folk . . ."

"Not to worry," interrupted Gaches, raising his hand and exposing its smooth palm and delicate fingers. Nate could see the polished fingernails of the gambler's hand when he held it near the crack in between the bales. "I can pass for white, I have money and style and I was educated in England. When the sun goes down, I will leave here and return with your clothes." He looked at Nate's huge frame and gave him a bemused smile. "Although, I must confess, it might be difficult to find garments that will fit you."

True to his boast, Jacques Napoleon Gaches proved reliable. At dusk, they removed the bale that entombed them and the gambler sneaked out from the hiding place within the mountain of cotton bales and found the steward. He greased the man's palm with a small pile of *Dix* notes to procure a cabin and some clothes for Nate. He then returned to the hiding place and handed Nate a pair of black trousers, shoes, wool socks, a simple white linen shirt, and a black waistcoat.

"We were fortunate, my good man, the headwaiter had some clothes left from a recently deceased passenger who happened to be a gentleman of some size. I regret to say though that there was no hat big enough to fit your rather large cranium."

Surprised at his new friend's resourcefulness and recognizing an opportunity, Nate dressed, and stepped quickly but cautiously out of the hole, keeping a sharp eye for the Confederate soldiers who were still on board.

"Now, where do we go?" inquired Nate awkwardly. The clothes were tight and made him feel uncomfortable but he was glad to be out of the worn-out duds that Jean le Fou had given him.

"I will take my supper in the dining room while you, my friend, will go to the cabin where I have made arrangements to have food brought to you." The octoroon placed his hand gently on his new friend's shoulder. "Do not be concerned, my good man. I have made all arrangements necessary to travel in comfort."

The gambler had to bribe the steward again to secure a place at a dining table that had several single men who looked like they had money. They did not resemble planters or tradesmen, but rather individuals who had acquired money easily through deal making or engaging in some form of black marketing. They were ostentatiously attired in silk and velvet clothes and cravats, ruffled shirts, and wore more jewelry than was necessary. Gaches could spot a man of chance from a distance. He possessed a keen scent for recognizing opportunity when it came to identifying prospective cardplayers. He planned to befriend the gentlemen during the repast and as they sipped cordials lure them into a friendly game.

Meanwhile, Nate was now snug in the cabin that Gaches had procured. The accommodations were simple but comfortable. There were two built-in beds on opposite sides, two chairs, and a matching divan covered with horsehair. Nate sat on one of two ladder-back chairs with rush seats at a solid oak table that was in the middle of the cabin. About twenty minutes after he made himself cozy, and was about to doze off in his chair to the sounds of the rhythm of the steamboat, a black cook dressed in a full-body white apron carrying two trays of food kicked the door open and bellowed. "You must be *one special nigger!* You to gettin' yo'r suppa in a cabin, 'stead of eatin' with the rest of us in the galley." The cook was irate because the steward had ordered him to bring Nate his meal. He knew that the steward had been bribed and resented that he was not compensated for his effort.

Nate watched in embarrassed silence as the cook placed the heavy trays on the table, then marveled at the sight of boiled ham and potatoes, oysters, bread, butter, and pie.

"What's the ma'ter? You *dumb* as well as *spoilt?*"

Nate glared into the cook's eyes. "I'm much obliged fo' the food, sir, but I ain't *no shirker.*"

The cook looked into Nate's eyes and saw that although his tone was defensive, the voice was strong, and he sensed that this young buck possessed determination. Nate, for his part, could smell the aroma of the river and the fumes of the galley on the man's clothes. He noticed that the cook's skin and face, weathered by the sun and hard work, made him look much older than he probably was and Nate thought that he resembled an old black leather bag.

"I hear ya, I hear ya," he responded, somewhat taken aback by Nate's baritone voice. "Mean no harm, son. You sit now, and have your suppa."

Nate was ravenous. The smell of boiled ham and potatoes reached his nostrils and his mouth started to water up.

"Go on, boy. Take a load off," beckoned the cook as he removed a white porcelain dish, and spoon and fork that were rolled into a linen napkin. He neatly arranged them on the table while Nate moved the ladder-back chair closer to the table.

"You runaway, ain't you, boy?" asked the cook, placing a huge piece of sliced ham on Nate's plate.

Nate felt the blood in his head flush his cheeks and thought:

How did this old man know? Did Gaches tell him? He continued to stare at the beautiful slice of juicy ham on his plate, but hesitated in stabbing it with his knife and fork.

"Don't you fret none, son. Ah knows how to keeps my mouth *shut* tighter than an oak barrel," reassured the cook.

"How you knows?" asked Nate calmly.

"You gots that *same* look 'fore m'ah boy ran off. Ah a *freedman* m'ah self, an' I was fixin' to buy m'ah son's freedom frum his mas'a, but he wanted to join Abe Lincoln's army."

"He up North?" inquired Nate, stabbing the piece of ham with his knife and fork.

"He was headin' for Kansas." The old cook bowed his head and scratched the stubble on his face in uncertainty. "Ah don't knows if he made it."

"That's where I'm headin', I'm headin' north to enlist."

The cook moved his head again in bewilderment. "You gots a *long way* to go."

" 'Bowt five hundred miles!" boasted Nate, chewing on some of the boiled potatoes.

"You got that right." The cook extended his right hand. He liked what he saw in Nate and wanted to help. "My name's *Sam*. Sam Garland. But jest call me whut folks long de river call me. An' that's *Red* Sam, 'cause I've spent most of m'ah *whole life* on the Red." Nate stood up from his chair and clasped the old man's hand.

"Yes, sir, thank you."

"Sit down, boy, eat yo'r suppa," ordered Red Sam, placing his hand on Nate's shoulder.

"I hear that!" Nate threw his backside back into the ladder-back chair and continued to eat.

Meanwhile, Jacques Napoleon Gaches was winning at cards in the salon. He had been successful in luring his dinner companions into playing poker and was slightly ahead in chips. It was his turn to deal out the cards when the steam boilers and the rhythm of the paddle wheeler slowed.

"I believe we are puttin' to shore," commented one of the players dryly.

"Probably pickin' up more passengers," responded another.

"At this time of night? I do not see any lights or indications of a town." Gaches was concerned. Suppose the henchmen that his creditors had sent to find him had caught up with the boat and forced the craft to berth on the shoreline? "Excuse me, gentlemen, but I think I will take some air and have a look." He got up from his chair and headed for the door that led to the port side and the narrow gangway.

"You comin' back so we can win some of our money back?" laughed one of the players nervously.

"I would not *dream* of leaving you gentlemen," gibed Gaches as he opened the door and stepped outside.

It took a few moments for Gaches's eyes to adjust to the darkness of the night and to see the bank of the river. There were only a few lanterns on shore illuminating the mountains of cordwood, and a small number of lanterns that were hung along the gangway. After his vision had been fully acclimated, he saw that *Belle de Jour* had berthed at a crude wooden dock. Dozens of black men had formed a human chain from the piles of cordwood on the river's edge all the way to the engine room of the steam wheeler, and started to pass down the logs.

Gaches pulled out a miniature cigar and ignited it as he slowly rotated the tip of the stogie with his nimble fingers so it would burn evenly. He watched the men work and took a few deep breaths of river air in between pulling on his cigar. He was about to return to the gambling table when he heard some voices coming from the dock. He turned his gaze toward the structure and noticed two men, dressed entirely in black, the sounds of their boots stomping down the boat landing toward *Belle de Jour*.

"We want to see the pilot!" demanded one of the men, who was carrying a cane and tapping the silver tip on one of the hog chains.

"Yes, suh, right way, suh," jumped one of the crew members.

Gaches's heart started to beat rapidly, and he suddenly felt very warm. He had recognized the man's voice immediately, and knew why he wanted to see the pilot.

VIII.

Nate was putting on his uniform that had been nicely folded by Willow Branch. It had been two days since he was rescued by Cougar Eyes, and although he still felt exhausted, he wanted to get up and start rebuilding his strength. He had no idea what time it was, but knew that he had overslept because the occupants were not present and the light from the smoke hole revealed that the sun was already high in the sky.

He was surprised to find his knee-top boots, brass spurs, trousers, blouse, leather accoutrements, gauntlets, greatcoat, and kepi placed in a pile near his buffalo pallet bed. Even his beloved red bandanna was properly folded on top of the kepi, and he thought that he could not have done a better job himself. He became a little concerned, however, but was not anxious, that he did not see his trusty Walker-Colt horse pistol and holster on or near his effects. Although Nate was tired and weak, he felt at ease and out of danger, almost as if he were home.

He also noticed that his McClellan saddle, army horse blanket, bedroll, poncho, saddlebags, canteen, tin cup, and horse picket rope and spike were arranged near Cougar Eyes' war clubs and lances. He took note that his carbine sling was draped over the saddle but the Spencer was not anywhere in view. Nate stumbled and almost fell to the floor as he attempted to pull on his wool cavalry trousers, and had to brace himself against one of the tipi poles to prevent himself from falling into some parfleches. *"Neva' felt so weak an' helpless. I feels like a* baby," scoffed Nate to himself, scornfully. He resented feeling feeble and fatigued.

"Where you go, *Hotoa' e Gordon?*" demanded Willow Branch as she stepped into the lodge carrying a pile of buffalo chips in a basket. The squaw noticed that Nate was in the process of getting dressed. She was about to rest the willow basket on the ground to close the bearskin tipi door when Nate limped over and tried to close the flap himself. She smiled at this act of consideration and watched Nate tie the flap, securing the entrance from the cold.

Nate smiled and started to reach for his greatcoat. "I need to take a walk." Nate slapped his legs and smiled. "Need to stretch."

"You too weak to walk. You need more food and . . ." Willow Branch could not remember what the term in English was for water. So she picked up the buffalo horn ladle and scooped some water from the pouch that was suspended from the tripod and handed it to Nate.

Nate took the ladle and drank while Willow Branch prepared a dish of crushed dried turnips, corn, and squash vegetables and stirred in some water. Nate watched her as he scooped up some more water from the pouch.

*"Haaahe! Hotoa' e Gordon! Nepevomohtahehe?"** Cougar Eyes stepped into the lodge carrying a large albino jackrabbit. Its winter fur was perfectly white except for a crimson spot in the chest where Cougar Eyes had shot the hare with an arrow. The Dog Man was wearing his buffalo robe, black and red trade-cloth leggings, and dearhide beaded moccasins. He handed Willow Branch

----
*Are you feeling good?

the hare and removed his buffalo robe, revealing a quilted blouse made from deerskin. *"Etoneto!* It is . . . cold."

*"Heehe'e, etoneto!"** replied Nate, agreeing with his host that it must be cold outside, and he did feel a crisp draft when Cougar Eyes had unflapped the tipi door to enter. Nate was happy that he knew those few words in Cheyenne.

"You eat; we go," insisted the Dog Soldier, using the palm of his hand to press against his stomach and point to his mouth. Willow Branch handed Nate the bowl of soup.

Nate placed it against his lips and breathed in the vapors of the turnip, corn, and squash soup. He first took a tiny sip. The broth tasted good and wholesome, and he realized that he was quite famished. He started to take big gulps of the heated brew and feel his body warm up and his face become flushed. "It tastes good," remarked Nate.

"Epeveeno'e!" translated Willow Branch to her husband who did not completely understand Nate's comment.

Nate finished draining the bowl while Cougar Eyes was putting on his buffalo robe.

"Noheto!" he commanded.

Nate understood. He seized his army greatcoat with cape and hurriedly put it on. He then placed his kepi on his head and slipped the gauntlets onto his hands.

"Noheto! Let's go."

Cougar Eyes wanted to show Nate the camp and visit with Turkey Legs in his lodge at the other end of the Dog Soldier encampment. Nate followed his host out of the tipi and into the bright wintry day. The sun was strong and a slight breeze made the top layer of white flakes blow off the snowbanks into the sky. Nate breathed deeply to fill his lungs with the invigorating air and

---

*It's cold.

140

pointed his head toward the sun to feel its rays. As they walked on the crisp snow, Nate became astonished to see so many lodges pitched along the banks of the Washita and the degree of human activity in the village. The men were coming and going on their well-fed hunting ponies, either going out to find game or bringing in fresh kill for their families.

He also marveled at the organized foraging parties of squaws that occupied themselves by searching and collecting dried wood from the riverbank, while some of them transported their thickly bundled papooses on their backs in frames made from willow branches. He saw several women using their buffalo bone scraping tools to work on fresh hides in the snow near their lodges, while others were busy dressing game for the cook fire. He also noticed young children assisting their mothers while dozens of canines roamed the camp at will. These activities and menial but vital tasks reminded Nate of the days when he was a slave and lived in the "quarter." The time when everyone—man, woman, child, and animal—had to participate in chores for the good of the community in order to survive the hardships of subsistence living.

Nate was surprised that he did not attract much attention. Compared to the last time he was in a Cheyenne village, when it seemed that the entire population of the encampment turned out to gawk at him, this time, with the exception of some of the children, he barely drew a passing gaze from the women and men.

Nate followed Cougar Eyes to the huge corral. Seeing hundreds of well-fed ponies of every color and breed astounded him.

"How many horses are yours?" queried Nate, pointing to the herd and then to Cougar Eyes.

Cougar Eyes did not understand his guest's words, but the Dog Man's keen sense of human nature enabled him to decipher Nate's question. He held out his right hand and made a fist, and stretched all of his fingers slowly and then closing them, ten times, at the same rhythm as a beating heart.

"Fifty?" exclaimed Nate.

Cougar Eyes smiled and nodded, satisfied that he had made the impression he wanted to make. He wanted to demonstrate to *Hotoa' e Gordon* the strength of the people and illustrate for the *Mo' ohtae-Ve' ho' e* his personal wealth.

"You like?" asked Willow Branch. She had rejoined her husband because she was curious about Nate's reaction to the pony herd and to offer herself to facilitate communication between the two men.

"I like very much." Nate smiled, looking at a sleek black mare.

"The spotted ones"—Willow Branch pointed to several painted horses with large markings on their coats—"are the favorites among the people."

"They sure are beautiful," acknowledged Nate as his eyes kept turning back to the sleek black mare with a very long mane and notched ears.

Cougar Eyes spoke to his wife who in turn translated for Nate. "He knows that you like the black one."

"He's a fine-lookin' animal."

"He know that you know," riposted Willow Branch with a gentle smile.

Nate laughed at his hostess's retort, and soon Cougar Eyes and Willow Branch joined in.

Nate and Cougar Eyes were sitting in Turkey Leg's lodge. The Dog Man was in the middle of recounting the details of the fight against the Pawnees two years ago. Turkey Leg explained to his listeners how surprised his large band of Dog Soldiers became when they had engaged a smaller party of Pawnee army scouts armed with Spencer repeaters and dressed in the clothes of the bluecoats.

"It was a sharp fight and we lost many Dog Men," he emphasized. "We were not aware that the *Ho'nehetane'o** were armed by the *Ve' ho' e* with fire sticks that shoot many bullets while we had only our bows and lances!" Turkey Leg passed his most prized possession to Cougar Eyes, a pipe tomahawk. The instrument had a shaped metal trade blade that incorporated a pipe bowl on one side, and on the other side of the hollow shaft was a medium-size ax. The triple purpose item could chop wood, be wielded in battle in close combat, or utilized as a pipe.

Nate was sitting to the left of Cougar Eyes. He had removed his kepi from his head when he had entered the tipi as a sign of respect and placed the hat on his lap when he took his place at the circle. He knew he was in the tipi of Turkey Leg, the warrior who had given his friend Medicine Bill Comstock safe passage through their lands, but whose warriors violated the promise by ambushing the plainsman and Sharp Grover. When Cougar Eyes handed the pipe to Nate, he hesitated to draw on the pipe tomahawk because he still felt weak from the effects of hypothermia. As he stared at the item, he realized that all of Turkey Leg's visitors who were sitting around the fire in a circle were leering at him. He knew that he was expected to take a toke from the pipe or risk insulting his hosts.

"Perhaps, *Hotoa' e Gordon* is still not strong enough to smoke tobacco," explained Cougar Eyes. He wanted to reassure Turkey Leg that Nate was not going to deliberately insult him by passing up the pipe.

"*Noxa'e!*"† barked Nate. He placed the stem to his lips and

---

*Pawnee
†Wait!

pulled hard on the shaft. He then released a large cloud of the tobacco smoke from his lungs into the air toward the fire.

"*Epeva'e!*"* exclaimed Turkey Leg.

"*Heehe'e!*"† clamored some of the other guests as they nodded in approval.

Nate passed the bowl to his neighbor, a warrior named Big Foot. The Dog Man took a hit off the pipe and slowly released the tobacco toward the smoke hole.

"I am reminded of the time"—Big Foot was speaking in English, and Nate assumed that it was for his benefit so he would understand—"when Bobtailed Porcupine, Red Wolf, Spotted Wolf, Wolf Tooth, Yellow Bull, and I removed one of the two iron paths of the *Mo'ehno'ha*,‡ causing it to fall onto the grass."

Big Foot used his hands to illustrate how the locomotive skidded off the tracks as if it were a huge buffalo bull, shot by a powerful rifle.

"We then killed *all* of the *Ve' ho' e,* and took coals from the belly of the *Mo'ehno'ha* and placed them in the wooden wagons." Big Foot took another hit from the pipe, and added with an air of reflection, "It was like killing a snake. It was good to see them burn."

"*Heehe'e!*" replied most of the Dog Soldiers in the lodge as they nodded to each other in approval.

Nate remembered hearing talk among the officers and reading the newspaper accounts of the derailing and burning of the Union Pacific freight train, and how the engineers were all slaughtered and found stripped and scalped.

"How did you learn to speak the tongue of the *Ve' ho' e?*" asked Nate. He was eager to learn more about his hosts, and Big

---

*It's good.
†Yes!
‡Iron Horse

Foot's command of the English language relaxed Nate because he spoke softly, and the words possessed a simple but pointed rhythmic melody to them, inviting conversation.

"Many of the *Tsitsitas* have been to Bent's fort to trade with the Bent family. Over years, many of us have learned to make the *Ve' ho' e* talk."

Nate had heard about old man George Bent, his trading post, and his half-breed Cheyenne family, and how the trader was revered among the Cheyennes as a white man who treated the Indians fairly, and had shown respect.

"Is it true that *Hotoa' e Gordon* was a slave of the *Ve' ho' e*, and fought in the *Ve' ho' e* war?" inquired Big Foot, passing the pipe to his neighbor.

"*Heehe'e!*" confirmed Nate, who was feeling a little dizzy from the tobacco smoke that was beginning to fill Turkey Leg's lodge. "*My people* were held as slaves for hun'reds of years. Mos' of the time, we were treated *badly* by the *Ve' ho' e!*"

"*Heehe'e,*" acknowledged all of the Dog Men loudly, concurring with Nate that the *Ve' ho' e* treated everybody badly.

Nate felt comfortable speaking the few words of Cheyenne that he had learned over the past year, and desired to learn more. It also gratified him when he perceived that the faces of the warriors in the tipi would brighten when he spoke them.

"Why did your people . . . accept to be slaves of the *Ve' ho' e?* Were you too *few* and they too *many?*" emphasized Big Foot, his eyes widening. He was curious about this *Mo' ohtae-Ve' ho' e* and why a whole people would submit to be slaves rather than fight to be free.

Nate became stunned by this question, but his face was void of any expression. At first his mind remained blank. Then his thoughts raced back into the past and strangely, only minute, obscure details came to mind such as being *whupped* by the overseer for not moving fast enough, or for stealing hams at night from Mas'a Hammond's smokehouse. *Where should I begin?* he asked himself. *These people could never, ever, understand what it was like to be* born *a slave on a plantation. How could they? These Indians were free as birds while most of his life was spent under the threat of the lash, and the abuse of the patrollers, working in the blistering sun and always feeling the hunger pains in your belly?*

"My people . . ." commenced Nate slowly and deliberately, as if he was about to tell his captive audience a long, sad story. *"Neva* ax'cepted bein' slaves. The Southern tribe of the *Ve' ho' e* had all the power an' my people had none."

Cougar Eyes, Turkey Leg, and Big Foot as well as the other guests were listening intently to Nate. They relished the prospect of hearing what the *Mo' ohtae Ve' ho' e* had to tell them regarding his experiences as a man who was once in bondage, and who had intimate knowledge of the alien ways of the white man.

"We, the *Mo' ohtae-Ve' ho' e,* long ago were *stolen* from our lands and brought here to this world by bad men. They shackled us in iron chains and whupped us ev'ry time they felt like it. They sold us like cattle to other *Ve' ho' e* men who forced us to work the land from sunup till sundown."

Nate halted his narration, and with the exception of the crackling fire in the pit, the lodge became very quiet. He bowed his head slightly in deep reflection and took a deep breath. The pain of slavery days was too deeply embedded in his soul for him to distance himself from the recent past. Flashes of thought were passing through his mind about his mother, and how she had been raped and his half sister sent away. He felt anguish in his heart when he reflected about her lonely death in the wretched slave shack while he was away fighting for the Union. The hideous murder of his father by Bloodhound Jack, who hunted him down and dragged his bleeding and broken body through the quarter. The drunken overseers and their toadying nigger drivers, who enjoyed and engaged in petty mental cruelty and physical abuse as ol' Mas'a Hammond, the oblivious overlord of this earthly hell, rode around his kingdom on his fine steed. How could he explain to a people who had no concept what it was like to be totally owned by another human being?

"Perhaps *Hotoa' e Gordon* is hungry and thirsty," commented Big Foot softly. The Dog Man realized that Nate had become tired in his effort to speak, and was lost in painful contemplation.

"Heehe'e!" replied Cougar Eyes. He also saw that Nate was tired, and was still suffering from the effects of almost freezing to death. *"Epeva'e.* We talk later. Now we go back to my lodge. *Noheto!"*

Cougar stood up and Nate followed. They left Turkey Leg's tipi and as their footsteps crushed the snow beneath their feet, Nate was hoping that Willow Branch would make him some sage tea when they returned home.

IX.

FORT DODGE, KANSAS.

Cara de Quervo Zarata was clutching her wool blanket next to her chin as she lay shivering on the ground and listened to the howling winter winds outside her tent slam against the canvas roof of her crude shelter. Although there was a potbelly stove in the center of the room, the cast-iron heater was cold due to the shortage of fuel. The only source of real warmth came from the tiny flame on the wick of the oil lamp that stood on a table at the right side of her skimpy bedding. She would occasionally remove her hands from under the blankets and place them near the lamp's hot glass shade to feel the heat.

Antonio Vasco had brought his little train of whores to Dodge City, a major terminus for the Union Pacific Railroad, to shelter his party of concubines from the harsh winter on the plains. Vasco also wanted to get a head start to establish his bordello as the best one in Dodge when the spring brought the cash-rich cowboys from Texas herding huge droves of longhorns. The pimp also needed to recruit more hookers in anticipation of satisfying the insatiable appetite of the cowboys for carnal gratification after spending weeks on the cattle trails. Vasco had learned that although Dodge City was a small town, it was poised to generate great financial activity due to the recently built stockyards next to the rails of the expanding Union Pacific. The yards were hastily constructed to accommodate the herds of longhorns from Texas and to meet the demands for beef in the East.

Vasco had Cara placed in her own tent. He had ordered Miguelito to construct all the structures of his little camp of debauchery with crude, disgarded planks abandoned by the railroad. Due to the overall shortage of lumber, however, only the walls were made from wood while the roofs were covered with the canvas covers from the wagons or the tents that were in Vasco's possession.

Vasco had been wooing Cara for days, only to have his advances rebuked and insulted by the half-breed. He had tried to change his normally brutish behavior by exempting her from all manual work and stopped slapping and kicking her. He had also hoped that by giving Cara her own tent and furnishing it with some modest items such as a bed, vanity, table, and lounge chair that it would soften her opinion of him and facilitate his passage to her bed.

Cara, however, remained obstinate in defying her tormentor.

Her actions and thoughts were concentrated on keeping her unborn child safe and waiting for Nate and her deliverance.

While Cara shivered in bed, Vasco was on his way to pay her a visit. He had decided that he had been patient and considerate long enough, and now wanted her to submit to his carnal demands, and was determined not to be rejected or insulted. As he tromped through the snow, his mind conspired on how he would achieve domination over her and decided that he was going to be brutal.

Cara's eyes were closed and she was about to fall asleep when she felt a cold burst of air on her cheeks, forcing her eyes to open suddenly. She saw the flame in the lantern flicker slightly, caused by the draft when Vasco opened the flap of the tent. Her next vision saw the towering and obese figure of her tormentor leaning over her bed. He had already thrown his coat and hat off and Cara could see the gloss of his heavily pomaded black hair.

"Tonight, you will do what I command! *Comprendez?*" snarled Vasco as he lustily leered at her.

"Go to hell, you fat alcahuete!" retorted Cara, clutching the blankets more firmly with her tiny hands. Although Vasco had recently shown restraint and tried to be polite, Cara knew that it was simply a change of tactics on his part and she fully anticipated that he was going to resort to his physically abusive ways again.

"I have been decent to you, half-breed! And this is how you repay my kindness?"

"Kindness? *Kindness?* I am here against my will, you beat me, and want to rape me."

"Because that is the only way you understand! You are *half-breed*—half Comanche, half Mexican—and should be treated us such."

"Cochino! You will never have me again!"

"I have been patient long enough. Now, I will take what is

mine! *Miguelito! Ven aquí,*" yelled the Creole pimp, summoning his lackey.

The Mexican entered the tent holding a lariat and a black rawhide whip. Miguelito was smiling, his gold teeth shining in the oil lamplight. His master had instructed him earlier to enter the tent if he thought that he would be needed, and be prepared to assist him in tying Cara's hands and feet and, if necessary, take the whip to her backside.

Cara started to breathe heavily, her chest heaving with fear. She knew that this time, it was going to be impossible to resist. Her thoughts turned to the baby that was in her womb, and when she saw Miguelito's gold teeth, filthy long hair, and Vasco's leering corpulent face, she became very fearful. Vasco waved his arm and pointed to Cara, signaling to his peon to proceed as planned. Miguelito started to advance toward her, still grinning, his gold teeth becoming brighter as he came closer to Cara and the oil lamplight.

"*Ya no . . . más!*" Cara swung at the burning oil lamp and sent the object flying toward Miguelito. The glass shade bounced off his face and crashed into one of the corners of the hut.

"*E yii! Coño!*" screamed Miguelito as he felt his flesh burn on his face from the hot glass. He released the lariat and whip and placed his hands against his face. He then started to uncontrollably run around the room, knocking himself against the furniture as if he were a blind man.

The burning oil lamp broke apart against the dry wood floor planking, splattering the walls with oil and spreading flames that started to lick at the timber and reached for the canvas roof. Cara grabbed her blanket and bolted for the flap doors, pushing Vasco aside with her right elbow while Miguelito screamed in horror from pain. Her thoughts were to make her way toward where the horses were kept and ride out of harm's way. As she ran outside, stumbling and slipping on the wet snow, she could hear the sounds of flames devouring the wood planking and setting the canvas roof ablaze.

Cara had the livery in view. Vasco had made arrangements to board his horse and mules at the stables and it was her intention to grab one of the mules and ride out of town. She did not care that it was the middle of winter and that she had no supplies. The temptation and opportunity to take flight was too great to pass up. All that she wanted was to flee and escape her predicament, and decided that she would worry about food and shelter later on.

When she entered the livery it was pitch-black and she was forced to pause for a moment. Being half Comanche, however, and living all her life on the frontier, most of the time in the open, her senses were sensitive and her ability to adjust to a change of lighting was highly flexible. The livery was warm and smelled of straw and animals. Her eyes were now acclimated to the lighting of the interior of the stables and she could see the outlines of the stalls and the backsides and tails of mules and horses. She knew that the owner kept Vasco's mules in a very large box stall in the rear of the livery. Most of the stock were kept outside during the day but were brought in at night for warmth and protection against thieves and wolves. She approached the box stall carefully, trying not to startle the mules that were crammed tightly in the small area. She seized a lead rope that hung near the door of the stall, and entered the small area where the mules were kept. She grabbed the halter on one beast and attached the lead rope, which she planned to use as a means for controlling the animal once mounted, and led the mule out of the box stall. She then mounted him Indian style and dug her deerskin moccasins into the animal's flanks. The mule, however, refused to move and decided to be obstinate. The animal was not accustomed to being mounted because he was primarily used for pulling wagons, and he particularly disliked being mounted in the barn. Cara kicked harder but still the beast refused to advance.

By now Antonio Vasco had caught up with Cara. The pimp and Miguelito had escaped the burning tent structure and while his Mexican servant plunged his singed face in the snow, Vasco shuffled his great weight through the slush, huffing and puffing in a rage. He had lost his beloved fur coat and hat in the tent and was outraged that Cara had burned his property and run off. He assumed that she had made her way to the livery since it was the closest building near the bordello tent village and that Cara would either seek to hide in the stables or steal a mount.

Cara saw Vasco's silhouette in the doorway; the huge contours of his obese body blocked her way. Cara started to frantically kick the mule and hollered for the beast to move, but it remained inflexible. Cara could see that Vasco had commenced to slowly advance toward her and she started to breathe heavily in anticipation of what his rage might lead him to do. When Vasco was only a few paces away from her, he raised his arms to seize Cara but spooked the mule instead. The animal jerked, kicked, and then bolted for the door, knocking Vasco to the ground in the process. Cara was almost at the threshold of the livery doorway when she felt a terrible blow to her face, forcing her body to fall off the back of the mule and tumble to the ground.

"*Puta . . . Bastarda! Para qué esarmientas,*" cursed Miguelito, holding a manure shovel near his head as if it were a trophy. He gawked triumphantly at Cara's limp body that lay stretched out on old manure and urine-soaked straw.

X.

Cougar Eyes, Big Foot, Turkey Leg, and Nate were sitting around a fire that flickered brightly in the pit at the center of the lodge.

They were having their evening meal that consisted of broiled buffalo meat ribs, dried red turnips, and thistle. Nate was in the process of polishing off a rib when a man shouted outside the tipi flap door. *"Haaahe!"* he clamored, waiting for a reply to his request to enter.

*"Ne'estsehnestse!"** responded Cougar Eyes, acknowledging his request as he sipped on some sage tea.

"It is Man Who Walks On The Clouds, of the *hemanhe*. I have been expecting him. He asked me if he could listen to *Hotoa' e Gordon*'s tales of the war between the white tribes."

Man Who Walks On The Clouds entered the lodge. The tall transvestite was wearing a magnificent white buffalo robe that fell to his quilted moccasins and his head was snugly buried within the hide of the head of the beast, its protruding horns resembling menacing hooks of prey. The half man-half woman looked into the eyes of his host and nodded to him as a sign of thanks for being invited to his lodge. He then acknowledged Big Foot's and Turkey Leg's presence and slowly and elegantly lifted the hide from his shoulders and placed the article on a pallet of buffalo robes. He then quietly sat at the spot opposite from Nate. Under his snow-white buffalo robe, Man Who Walks On The Clouds wore a silver pectoral with *najas* hanging down from his neck, matching eardrops, and German silver armbands that hugged the sleeves of his beautifully quilted doeskin shirt that Nate thought was more suitable for a squaw than for a brave.

"Man Who Walks On The Clouds is here to listen to your stories about the great war between the whites," explained Big Foot.

"Why does he wish to know?" inquired Nate as he munched on some thistle and dried berries.

*Come in.

153

"Man Who Walks On The Clouds is a spiritual leader in war, and all things about war, he wants to know." Big Foot gently rested the palms of his hands on his chest. "And he also *Medicine Man*, who has knowledge of the heart when young braves and girls seek to marry. We, the *Tsitsitas*, respect his loneliness, manhood, bravery in battle and taking coup against our enemies." Big Foot's eyes looked momentarily about the lining of the tipi wall, searchingly. He was seeking the word to describe celibacy. "The *hemanhe* do not go with squaws," he finally said with great seriousness in his voice. "So they have more *strength* in battle." Big Foot's eyes locked on to Nate's to give his statement emphasis.

Nate believed what Big Foot was trying to explain to him was that this man and his kind preferred the company of men and apparently did not sleep with women in order to preserve the potency of their semen for war. He nodded to Big Foot and Cougar Eyes to indicate that he understood, but his mind had already turned to the war and he felt lost in where or how to begin. Should he speak about the reasons for the war, or the nature of modern battle? Or should he express how it felt to be a black man fighting a ruthless foe, bent on keeping his people in bondage?

Big Foot noticed that Nate was contemplative, and deduced that maybe he should be more specific. "Perhaps *Hotoa' e Gordon* can tell us of his *most dangerous* moment in battle . . . fighting the Southern *Ve' ho' e* tribe." Big Foot then quickly interpreted his question into Cheyenne for the others.

"*Heeh'e!*" cried out Cougar Eyes and Turkey Leg after they had listened to Big Foot's translation. Although Man Who Walks On The Clouds remained silent, he was very eager for Nate to recount his experiences as a soldier in the war of the whites. True, he was a *Mo' ohtae-Ve' ho' e* and fought with the pony soldiers against the *Tsitsitas*, but he had also fought against the whites in battle and might shed light on their behavior as warriors.

Nate's eyes widened. His thoughts became aflame with two images that immediately appeared in his mind: William Clarke Quantrill and "Bloody Bill" Anderson! A chill ran down his spine whenever he thought about the two Missourian border miscreants, or when their names were mentioned in conversation. He had to shake his head in horror, as he usually did, whenever the visions of Quantrill's guerrillas mutilating dead Colored infantrymen appeared in his mind. The massacre of Negro troops of the First Kansas Infantry at Sherwood Springs, Missouri, and at the battle of Baxter Springs, Kansas, still left his heart heavy with rancor and anguish.

"When I was a young bluecoat, after I had fled my life as a slave, I fought against two very evil *Ve' ho' e* men who had no honor."

"Heeh'e!" repeated Cougar Eyes and Turkey Leg enthusiastically, supporting Nate's assertion that the *Ve' ho' e* have no honor.

"These men—members of the Southern tribe of the *Ve' ho' e*—hated men who were black and who fought for the Northern tribe because they wanted to be free."

"Who were these men?" inquired Bull Bear.

"The chief of the band was named William Quantrill, and the other chief was called Anderson! *'Bloody Bill'* Anderson," responded Nate as he bowed his head and stared at the flickering blue flames that protruded from the fire pit.

The lodge became silent, and while Willow Branch gathered up the eating utensils and made order in the tipi, Cougar Eyes took the opportunity to load the bowl of his polished stone pipe for the ritualistic evening smoke after the last meal of the day. He removed some tobacco from a buffalo scrotum pouch that was snugly placed in a parfleche that Willow Branch had brought him, and gently stuffed the bowl.

"I have heard of these men," stated Big Foot, slowly nodding his head in reflection. "George Bent told us that a band of *Ve' ho' e* men from the Southern tribe attacked a Northern tribe settlement, and"—Big Foot made a quick sweeping horizontal movement with his right arm for accentuation—"nearly *rubbed out* all of them."

"The same as was done to Black Kettle and the *Tsitsitas* at Sand Creek!" added Cougar Eyes bitterly, thinking about the cruel deaths of his relatives at the hands of Colonel Chivington and the Colorado Volunteers. The lodge again became quiet as the Dog Men reflected on their losses at the hands of the bluecoats. Cougar Eyes fired up the pipe and took several deep hits, igniting the tobacco and releasing the exhaled fumes toward the fire pit where it would ascend toward the smoke hole and dissipate in the still, frigid night air.

Nate decided that Old Man Bent must be very communicative with his Cheyenne brothers and sisters when it came to the white man's world. Therefore, he was not completely surprised that the Dog Men had heard about Quantrill's bushwhackers massacring over a hundred Yankee civilians in Lawrence, Kansas. The trader, George Bent, certainly had read old newspaper accounts or was verbally told by travelers going west that Southern guerrillas from Missouri under Quantrill and "Bloody Bill" had been ravaging pro-Union Kansas settlements.

Man Who Walks On The Clouds went over to Big Foot and softly whispered into his ear. The transvestite had been carefully listening to Nate when he spoke and wanted to know more.

Nate looked at the *hemanhe* who was gawking at him while Big Foot translated. "Man Who Walks On The Clouds wants to know in *what way* were these *Ve' ho' e* men bad?"

"They treated us like runaway slaves rather than warriors! They denied us the honor and respect as soldiers by removing our uniforms and chopping up our bodies as if we were *Hotoa' e*."

Nate wanted to explain to his listeners how he had to watch help-lessly as he observed Confederate bushwhackers strip the Colored men's uniforms and bash in their heads with rifle butts and rocks. Or how some of the guerrillas decapitated dead men and used their Bowie knives to slice off limbs, but he was afraid that the Dog Soldiers would not understand. Or would they? Nate had seen the handiwork of Cheyenne depredations against innocent civilians and knew the reality of what burning malevolence against people of different races is capable of inflicting upon each other.

"Did they treat you like we treat the *Ho'nehetane'o?*" inquired Turkey Leg as he lifted his right hand and placed the palm near the top of his head to indicate that the tribe in question, the Paw-nee, arranged their hair in a roach and scalp-lock fashion.

"I do not think that the *Hotame Ho' nehe* treats the *Ho'nehetane'o* or any other of their Indian enemies the same way you treat the *Ve' ho' e,*" replied Nate, realizing that he might be insulting his hosts by implying that they were no different than Quantrill and his guerrillas. There was an awkward silence within the lodge. The Dog Men seemed to be reflecting on what Nate had said. They respected *Hotoa' e Gordon* because he spoke only after he had given thought to his statements, and possessed a mod-est and direct demeanor that closely resembled their own com-portment.

"It is true that we are harsh with the *Ve' ho' e*. It is because they come to steal our land and murder our families and break their promises as so many rains in the spring," responded Cougar Eyes. His chest was heaving but his voice remained calm and strong. Nate was surprised that his host's English seemed to be improving so rapidly. He speculated that maybe anger and outrage augmented his host's English vocabulary whenever his heart pained him.

XI.

Nate woke up in a cold sweat. He had been dreaming about William Quantrill. The pit fire had died and only some embers remained burning, shedding its red glow on the tipi's lining. Nate could hear heavy breathing and panting from where Cougar Eyes and Willow Branch slept. The breathing and panting intensified, drawing Nate's attention momentarily away from his nightmare. He turned over in his buffalo robe blankets and looked toward his host's bed area and saw that Cougar Eyes was mounting Willow Branch from the rear. Their half-naked figures glowed from the light of the dying buffalo chips as they moved gracefully together, perfectly following a slow and deliberate rhythm that made them look like one. He gawked at the two lovers for a moment, then turned his body back to where it faced the tipi's wall and crouched his huge frame into a fetal position. He sighed and muttered to himself in self-pity, *"Oh, Cara, how I miss you."* Although Cougar Eyes, Willow Branch, and all the Cheyennes he had met at the camp had been very hospitable and courteous toward him, and shown genuine concern regarding his recovery from hypothermia, he felt lonely and homesick. He thought about the last time he made love to Cara, and felt his organ growing harder and longer as he listened to the sounds of panting and groans from Willow Branch's and Cougar Eyes' physical efforts as the aroma of copulation, perspiration, and body essence filled his nostrils.

To free the mind from his longing for Cara, and the sounds of lovemaking from Cougar Eyes and Willow Branch, Nate focused on William Quantrill's face. The face still haunted him. His mind focused on his cold, cruel steel-blue eyes, thick and wavy reddish hair, and pale, sickly complexion. When it came to Quantrill, most of the reminiscing focused on the man's slight frame sitting on his horse yelling orders to his howling murderers: *"Leave no survivors,"* as he cocked and fired his Colt .44-caliber revolver at the wounded or already dead Union soldiers.

The other face he envisioned when he thought about Quantrill, and the days when he was fighting Confederate guerrillas, was "Bloody Bill" Anderson. Nate decided that if Lucifer had human features, he would resemble the bushwhacker lieutenant who smiled every time he pulled the trigger, usually at very close range because he enjoyed looking into the eyes of his *"Damn Yankee Dog"* victims. Nate mumbled to himself, "Them two bastards were hell worse den any pissed-off Dog Man!" It was becoming increasingly difficult for Nate to think because the breathing and moaning from the couple's sexual exertions seemed to be getting louder with every passing moment. He closed his eyes and concentrated his mind to increase the focus on the days when he was an anxious enlisted infantryman with the First Kansas Colored Infantry at Fort Scott. *"Gawd* Almighty!" he whispered. *"Wuz only five years ago that those two bastards* tried to kill me."

Nate shook his head to chase the bad thoughts away and in its place he pondered on perhaps what was his greatest day as a United States soldier. On that January 1, 1863, gray morning, Nate and his companions were assembled on the Parade Ground at Fort Scott to hear the Emancipation Proclamation read to the First Kansas Colored Volunteer Infantry. It was a day for great speeches made by fiery abolitionist officers against the background of sterling martial music as hundreds of black and white soldiers sang.

"John Brown's body lies a-moldering in the grave;
John Brown's body lies a-moldering in the grave;
John Brown's body lies a-moldering in the grave;
His soul is marching on.
Glory halle—hallelujah, Glory halle—hallelujah!

Glory halle—hallelujah.
His soul is marching on."

Nate took a deep breath as he remembered the stirring words and verbal bravado spoken by zealous officers to rally the troops against the Secesh. The hairs on the back of his neck would always rise as he recalled his commanding officer, Colonel James M. Williams's striking words.

"Now, boys!" shouted the abolitionist colonel as he pointed to Old Glory with his sword. "Do you understand what the stars-and-stripes means to *you now?*" There was a great silence among the ranks as the men pondered his words that poured out of his mouth with great exultation. "It means, *boys* ..." he continued, "that you may *hunt, shoot,* and *destroy* every Rebel slaveholder in the land, and that *this flag* ... and all who serve under it, shall not hinder, but *aid* you in such *righteous retribution!*"

The roar of jubilation and tumultuous cheering among the Colored volunteers, men who were mostly escaped slaves from Missouri and Arkansas, and who had risked everything to join the regiment, was overwhelming. Nate stood at attention as tears poured from his eyes, soaking the collar as other men sobbed openly and gave thanks to the Lord and Father Abraham.

Nate had memorized the second paragraph in the Proclamation, and frequently repeated it to himself as a tonic whenever he felt uncertainty as to why he wore the blue uniform of the United States Army.

"That on the first day of January, in the year of our Lord one thousand eight hundred and sixty-three, all persons held as slaves within any State, or any designated part of a State, the people whereof shall be in rebellion against the United States, shall be then and thence, forever free; and the Executive government of the United States, including the military and naval authority thereof, will recognize and maintain the freedom of such persons, and will do no act or acts to repress such persons, or any of them, in any efforts they make for their actual freedom."

Nate's mind, however, shifted back again to the horrors that he had witnessed five months later, in May 1863, and how he was almost killed by Confederate guerrillas led by Quantrill and "Bloody Bill."

He sighed as he thought about the day when twenty-five men from his regiment and the twenty men from the white Second Kansas Battery were detailed to forage for feed for the horses and mules that were kept at Fort Scott. The Colored regiment was assigned the task of cutting grass and loading the wagons while the Second Kansas watched lazily among their caissons and six-pound cannon for any trouble. If the foraging party was attacked, the battery would blast away at the Confederates and give time for the black infantrymen to form up and repel the assault.

"We will proceed in the usual fashion. Ride hard and pitch into them as if we were locusts devouring a cornfield," instructed Captain William Quantrill. He was speaking to two of his bushwhacker lieutenants, "Bloody Bill" Anderson and Frank James.

"What the hell are we waiting for, *damn it?*" demanded Bloody Bill as he mounted his Thoroughbred. He was beginning to froth at the mouth as he usually did in anticipation of attacking Yankees, and the fermentation was slowly covering the thin black hairs of his mustache and beard.

"I give the command when to mount," insisted Quantrill. He

was irritated that Bloody Bill had mounted his horse without waiting for his orders. Ever since he had come up from Texas to join his guerrilla band, Anderson had been insolent or indifferent to his commands.

"What's the difference? We all here to kill Yankees and not waste time listenin' to the same ol' orders," riposted Bloody Bill. He removed one of the .44-caliber Colt revolvers from his holster that was attached to a Federal cavalry officer's saber belt and half cocked the weapon so he could rotate the cylinder slowly in front of his right eye. He smirked to himself and grunted. "Goin' kill me some *dog meat* today."

"Half them Yankees are darkies," said Frank James. "They the ones cuttin' grass in the fields and loadin' the wagons."

"Godless bluebellies got the niggers doin' their dirty work now. I got something *real special* for those black turncoat sons of bitches," raved Bloody Bill. He violently dug his stolen Union officer eagle spurs into his excited steed's flanks and yanked the reins to take his place at the middle of the column where the other well-mounted Missouri guerrillas had formed a long line.

The bushwhackers were all checking their Colt revolvers. Some of the men carried four six-shooters stuffed into their belts and high-top boots. No man carried less than two revolvers at any time. With the exception of Quantrill, who was clean-shaven and kept his hair trimmed, because he wanted to maintain all pretenses that he was the officially sanctioned leader of the band, most of the guerrillas were rough and dirty-looking. The men were mounted on big, swift Missouri horses and traveled light except when transporting looted property. Although the Missourians all bore the manifestations of hard-boiled ruthless veterans of many skirmishes, such as shoulder-length locks that they called "bushwhacker's hair," and long scraggly facial hairs, they retained a certain style. Their clothes, light-colored frock coats and trousers, silk vests and cravats and colorful shirts, though soiled, made the bushwhackers look like filthy dandies. Their headwear was often decorated with ostrich plumes or a home-sewn patch, resembling a star, would decorate the brims of their hats. Some of the older guerrillas, however, such as "Bloody Bill" Anderson, Frank James, and Coleman Younger, had long wild-looking beards that made them look like demented pirates.

"All right, boys, put on the uniforms," ordered Quantrill. The Missourians quietly removed from saddlebags, plundered Union cavalry shell jackets, trousers, hats, and other Yankee accoutrements and placed them over their clothes.

All the bushwhackers knew that the usual plan of attack was to advance as close as possible at a walk against their target without raising the alarm. By wearing Federal uniforms or dark coats and jackets, they had the advantage of hoodwinking their foes into believing that they were approaching Union cavalry. Then, when the order was given, when they were within effective range of their Colt revolvers, gallop into their enemies' center and flanks, working their six-shooters in rapid-fire fashion.

Private Nate Gordon and his companion, Private Randall Garland, were wielding their sharp scythes with great speed, cutting large swaths of spring grass that covered the prairie. Nate had reached Fort Scott in September 1862, after traveling as a runaway through Louisiana and Arkansas to reach the post that was on the south fork of the Little Osage River in Kansas near the Missouri border.

Fort Scott was the recruitment site for escaped slaves to enlist in the Union Army. Nate had learned while he was on the move within the underground railroad in Arkansas that the great abolitionist, James Lane, the leader of the righteous Redlegs, was forming an infantry regiment called the First Kansas Volunteers, made up from escaped slaves. The regiment was under the control of the state of Kansas, and yet to be sanctioned by Washington.

Although Nate had been with the outfit for only nine months, he was already a veteran. His regiment had participated in the first battle of the war by black troops, the fight at Island Mound. The escaped slaves fought bravely and learned quickly how to fight and stay alive. Fighting guerrillas and gruff Confederates in the traitorous and inhospitable environment along the Missouri–Kansas border taught a man how to survive. They had to learn how to fight against an enemy that knew the country and who attacked their enemies without warning or mercy.

"Man! Sure is hot!" complained Private Randall Garland as he stopped his cutting to wipe his forehead and face with the sleeve of his blue tunic.

"Least we don't got *the man* sittin' on some horse carryin' a whip waitin' to lay rawhide or cattails on our backs," responded Nate as he continued to wield his scythe back and forth, cutting great tufts of green grass.

"I *tired* bein' treated like a slave," whined Garland. "Doin' field work, diggin' ditches and latrines, drivin' mules, haulin' heavy shit on my back . . . Dis ain't the reason I escaped the South to fight."

"Boy! You sure do a lot a complainin'," interrupted Nate as he paused and pulled out a small sharpening stone and spat on it. "I didn't think that ol' man Red River Sam's boy would be a shirker." Nate proceeded to run the gray stone along the edge of the long curved scythe blade. "Tell me, Garland, I forget. You an ol' man or an ol' woman?"

"Neither. An' don't you mention my pa again! What do he know? He just a cook on a boat. I just one unhappy nigger that came here to fight, and whut do we gets instead?" Private Garland stared at Nate, daring his companion to tell him what they possessed that made them soldiers. "I tell you whut we don't gots. We got no real un'forms, or good guns, an' food *wurse* at the fort than on the *plantation*. *Baa*—We do mo' heavy *liftin'* than *fightin'*."

"Your pa is a good man. I wouldn't have made it up the Red River if it wasn't for your ol' man's help. As fo' the army, you made the choice, same as me." Nate ceased running the stone against the edge of the scythe and returned the object to his trousers' pocket. He then rested his enormous arms on the dull side of the curved blade while balancing the bottom of the shaft on the ground. "We soldiers now. We take orders and we obey them 'cause the uniform is the *instrument* of our freedom."

"Whut uniform?" exclaimed Garland, pointing to his clothes with his left hand while he held his scythe in the other. "We ain't got the same digs as the w'ite boys, an' you *knows* that."

Nate knew that his companion had a point. All of the volunteers in the regiment were clad in nonregulation uniforms that came from white outfits when they discarded their old uniforms and accoutrements for new ones. The state of Kansas could not supply the volunteers with new uniforms, so many of the men also wore a variety of dark frock coats and pants, homespun shirts and wool vests. The diversity of hats, however, revealed the cold fact that the regiment resembled a mélange of individuals rather than a military unit. There were many old Hardee hats worn by the men, but others still wore the same headwear that they had on their heads when they enlisted. The only piece of clothing that the regiment possessed that at least made them look like a cohesive force was the pale blue Union overcoat. Most of the brass buttons, however, had disappeared and the men had to replace them with what was available.

"I knows that we a poor regiment. But I have faith that we will git through this by winnin' our freedom and our people's freedom! I has to believe that better times are a-comin', 'cause so much blood has already been spilt." Nate repositioned the scythe so the implement's handle was firmly held in his hands and recommenced cutting grass. Other infantrymen were busy gathering the grass into bundles and placing them in the wagons where the drivers waited with their mule teams smoking pipes and gossiping under a warm May sun. "As for the uniforms, I don't care whut we wear, long as we git the opportunity to fight. Hell! Them Mis'ouri bushwhackers don't wear Secesh uniforms an' don't seem to boder them none."

"Ain't the same 'ting!" scoffed Garland. He had grudgingly resumed his cutting. "The bushwhackers are murderin' thieves, we soldiers."

There were no officers present to supervise the foraging party. The highest-ranking soldier among the First Kansas was a corporal who had a gray beard and wore spectacles, revealing his advanced years. Nate thought he was a little old to be in the army, but he had enlisted like everyone else in order to serve the Union and he was the only man in the regiment, excluding Nate, who could read and write.

The foragers and the white Second Kansas Battery Regiment were becoming too spread out for the cannons to offer any protection against a sudden attack. The men of the Second Kansas were also smoking pipes and talking as they soaked up the warm spring rays of the sun. They also had no officer in charge so the detachment was led by a first sergeant who was fast asleep in the grass near one of the caissons.

Nate heard several of the mules that were hauling the hay wagons bray loudly. He abruptly halted his cutting and looked at the long-eared animals who had their heads turned toward the northwest. In the distance, Nate discerned a thin dark line of mounted men approaching at a trot.

"Cavalry a-comin'," commented Garland as he also took the

moment to cease his cutting and gawk at the approaching riders who were about a half mile away.

"Yeah. But whose cavalry?" wondered Nate. "Corporal! Do you see what we see?" shouted Nate.

"I see 'em!" responded the corporal, squinting his eyes and scratching his gray beard. He stared at the approaching mounted men and then gazed toward the white troops to gauge their reaction, noticing that they were completely oblivious to the dark line of horsemen descending upon them at a rapid gait. "Looks like Union cavalry to me," decided the corporal.

"I see no flag, no colors," protested Nate. He had made up his mind that they were Confederate guerrillas. He had heard how they wore Yankee clothes to fool their prey, and he knew enough about cavalry procedures that if they were Union soldiers, they would approach in columns of twos or fours, not in one long line, unless they were advancing to attack. "Corporal, I swear they bushwhackers, probably Quantrill and his bunch that burned Lawrence."

"Them w'ite boys don't seem to pay them no mind," dismissed the corporal, continuing to gawk at the men of the Second Kansas who were still chatting among themselves while the first sergeant snored.

Bloody Bill was in the middle of the line with Quantrill closely at his left and Frank James to his right. Although the long line of Missouri guerrillas stretched for nearly an eighth of a mile, they led their horses, first at a rapid trot, then slowly urging them to a canter, all the while keeping the swift animals perfectly in line. Bloody Bill as always was anxious to get off the first shot. His eagerness to kill the first and last Yankee in a fight was very important to him. That was the price every Yankee he came upon would pay for the death of his sister. The loss of his beloved sister haunted him. Yankees had arrested and imprisoned her because of her anti-abolitionist sentiments, and then allowed her to be burned alive when the jail caught fire. This had ignited a blazing longing for vengeance within his dark soul. He removed one of his Colts from the holster and fully cocked the piece in his hand and was about to aim and fire the weapon when Quantrill, noticing that his lieutenant was about to open fire before he gave the order, wanted to stop him.

"Wait for the order to fire, damn you! Wait for my order, *Lieutenant.*"

Bloody Bill was frothing at the mouth as if he were a rabid dog. His lust to kill and the anticipation of blowing away Yankee bluebellies always overwhelmed him. He turned to Quantrill and saw that his commanding officer was glaring at him in a disapproving manner. By now most of the men, taking their cue from Bloody Bill, had also drawn their revolvers and held them in the air at the ready.

"To hell with your orders," sneered Bloody Bill. The bearded guerrilla, his dark hairs now covered with the white froth from his mouth, grinned hideously and intimidated Quantrill who frowned in disgust. He started to laugh uncontrollably as he pointed the Colt at one of the bluecoats of the Second Kansas Battery who was sitting on a caisson sipping on a canteen. Bloody Bill fired the Colt and watched the man's body arch forward and fall off the caisson. He howled with laughter and this encouraged some of the younger guerrillas to bellow the Rebel yell. Encouraged, more guerrillas yanked their revolvers from their belts and holsters and took aim at the cannoneers of the Second Kansas and at the infantrymen who were cutting and collecting hay.

Realizing that his orders had been usurped by a subordinate, and fearing that he was going to lose control over his command, Quantrill gave in to the growing fanaticism among his men and shouted the order to charge and commence fire.

The first sergeant of the Second Kansas Battery had been awakened by the crack of gunfire and by the thump that the shot soldier made when he tumbled off the caisson and fell to the ground. The first sergeant looked into the dead man's face and saw a bullet hole in the middle of the forehead. He recoiled in horror and stood up. Some of his men were gawking at the on-coming horde of approaching Confederate guerrillas, paralyzed with fear and uncertainty, while others were desperately trying to turn around their field pieces to train on the bushwhackers.

Panic-stricken, the first sergeant raised his arms wildly in the air and started hollering: *"Hitch up the guns and move out. Hitch up the guns and move out."*

As the soldiers frantically moved about to comply with his orders, several of the men and mules of the detachment were hit by gunfire, creating more pandemonium among the cannoneers as they tried to control their horses and mules.

The corporal of the First Kansas bellowed for the infantrymen to grab their converted percussion altered muskets and cartridge belts and form a line to repel the attacking Confederate guerrillas. Nate and Private Garland dropped their scythes and seized their muskets and stood side by side. They formed the anchor of the line at the left flank while other men of the First Kansas hurriedly formed up next to them as the corporal nervously stole glances to see how far the Missouri riders were.

"Whut you say 'bout not bein' soldier 'nough?" gibed Nate with great satisfaction, watching Garland nervously fasten his belt buckle that held his cartridge box, cap pouch, and bayonet scab-bard. "Well, boy! Now's the time to put yo'r mouth to rest and *kill* the enemy!"

The twenty-five men of the First Kansas that composed the foraging party had quickly created a skirmish line and held their muskets at the ready, waiting for the corporal to give the order to fire a volley. Nate became appalled as he watched the batteries of the Second Kansas flee without even firing off a shot from one of the batteries. The drivers of the caissons furiously lashed their whips against the haunches of their mules while the cannoneers struggled to hang on as the wheels of the cannons, caissons, and limbers bounced and twisted in the air.

"Prepare to fire!" commanded the corporal, still squinting through his spectacles at the horde of galloping bushwhackers who were screaming at the tops of their lungs, firing their army Colts. He was about to shout the order to fire a volley when a .44-caliber bullet penetrated his neck, severing the main artery. He frantically tried to stop the jet of blood that poured from his cut vein, but gagged hideously and fell to the ground. The infantrymen became stunned at the sight of the old corporal getting hit and falling dead in front of them. The twenty-five men were now leaderless and the bushwhackers were only about fifty yards away. Bullets either rained by their heads or found their mark among the men on the line. One man was hit twice in the chest and fell face first, while another was hit in the knee and started to howl in agony. One infantryman was shot through the face and started to wander about in the field in a state of deranged hysteria.

Nate looked about and saw that the skirmish line of infantrymen was wavering and that the line was in jeopardy of collapsing in confusion if someone did not give the order to fire. He stepped out and placed himself in front of his companions on the left flank so his comrades could see him and bellowed, "Fire, boys, fire!" Those men who were not wounded or killed fired smartly at the attacking bushwhackers, but the volley went over the charging guerrillas' heads, and within seconds the horde of bloodthirsty Missourian miscreants were among them, firing their Colts with deadly accuracy at point-blank range.

"Kill them all. Kill them all," ordered Quantrill as he coolly and methodically fired his revolver at the heads of black infantry-men. He was sitting calmly and perfectly erect in the saddle and seemed impervious to danger.

The hastily formed skirmish line began to crack. Realizing that the guerrillas were about to run them down with their horses or shoot them to death with their Colts, Private Garland was the first to cut and run, dropping his weapon and belt to gain more speed as he fled away. Taking their cue from Garland, several other soldiers dropped their weapons and broke ranks. Nate saw that their faces showed signs of fear at the prospect of falling into the hands of the guerrillas.

Hoping to instill what discipline the line still possessed, Nate pulled out his socket bayonet from the scabbard and bellowed. *"Stand your ground, men . . . Fix bayonets!"* For the men of the First Kansas, however, it was too late. A hail of Colt gunfire decimated them and there was no time to fix bayonets. Those who were still alive and not wounded and able to defend themselves were too preoccupied with swinging their rifles as clubs at their attackers.

Nate was about to attach the bayonet to the musket when a guerrilla, holding the reins in his teeth and wielding two Army Colts, halted his agitated horse a few feet from him. He lowered his pistols at Nate and pointed both six-shooters at him. Though his face was dirty and stained with black powder smoke, Nate could not help notice that the lad's face revealed that he was very young, perhaps fourteen or fifteen years old. His pink cheeks were also marred with several large ripe pimples protruding from his flesh and chin. Although Nate's eyes were full of outrage from the heat of battle, he simply stared at the Rebel youth who was about to shoot him. Nate held the bayonet in his right hand and carried his empty musket in the other. There was no time to react because the guerrilla was about to pull the trigger, so Nate stood motionless and prepared himself to be shot at point-blank range. The bushwhacker pulled the trigger, but Nate could not hear the action over the excited, yelling Confederates, the moans and cries of the wounded, neighing horses, and the deafening explosive crack of revolver fire. The Missourian cursed and pulled the trigger on his second Colt, but again, no shot came from the barrel. The guerrilla cursed, and refusing to believe that he was out of ammunition, recocked the hammer to fire one of his empty Colts when Nate saw an opportunity. Yelling at the top of his lungs as if to defy death, he charged the Confederate holding and pointing the bayonet as a sword.

The young guerrilla became stupefied and suddenly fearful. He was out of ammunition and here was this huge, angry black man coming for him with a bayonet. He wanted to spur his horse and ride away, but Nate had already grabbed the bushwhacker's stirrup and plunged the bayonet through his stomach and left it there as he quickly stepped back. The Rebel dropped his Colts and Nate jumped from the horse's neck, breathing heavily. The youth moaned a sickening sound and fell off the saddle, pressing his hands against his mortal gut wound as he gawked in horror- at the steel rod that protruded from his belly.

Nate saw that all of his comrades were either dead or in the process of fleeing for their lives as the Missourians rode their lathered horses to knock them down or emptied their six-shooters at any blue uniform that still moved. Nate saw one infantryman, a young man whom he had known since he had enlisted, fall to the ground on his knees and lift his clasped hands toward the sky in prayer, begging for mercy. He was pleading for his life with Bloody Bill. The crazed zealot was laughing hysterically and urging his horse to run over the hapless soldier, but the excitable beast refused to obey. Tiring of trying to get his mount to walk over the begging black infantryman, Bloody Bill yanked a fresh pair of Colt revolvers from his belt and fully cocked both weapons simultaneously. Still laughing rapturously as froth from his mouth spattered his scraggly black beard, Bloody Bill fired several shots from both revolvers at the begging bluecoat. Nate saw his comrade's body twitch violently from the impact of the bullets, then collapse to the ground.

Nate decided to seize the dead bushwhacker's mount and ride toward Fort Scott to sound the alarm. He seized the reins of the horse that took to grazing on the lush grass by the side of his mortally wounded master, and swung his body into the saddle. He was about to touch heel to flank when Captain William Quantrill cut him off with his large stallion. He was completely calm, his cruel mouth showed anger and his droopy blue eyes sneered at Nate from under his broad-brimmed green-gray slouch hat that had a thin cord wrapped around the crown with acorn ends. He was the only guerrilla in the command that wore any vestige of a Confederate uniform. He wore a light gray single-breasted wool shell jacket with yellow trim, but there were no markings to indicate his rank. He looked at the youth's lifeless body whom Nate had just bayoneted to death and leered at Nate. "You godless nigger! I'll cut your foul black head off!" Quantrill pulled from his scabbard the largest Bowie knife that Nate had ever seen. The blade was over a foot long and had a large D-shaped guard at the hilt. The guerrilla chieftain cocked back his arm that held the enormous blade all the way behind his back as if he was prepared to chop up a carcass, and dug his spurs into the stallion's flanks.

Nate leaped from the saddle as the edge of Quantrill's Bowie knife cut past his head, and landed on his feet. He turned to look at Quantrill who was only a few feet away and snarling at him. Nate turned on his heels and started to run in the direction of Fort Scott. Like most of his henchmen, Quantrill had exhausted the ammunition in his six-shooters and decided to run Nate down with his stallion. He lashed the beast with his whip and the animal went into an immediate gallop, catching up with Nate within a few dozen yards. Although he did not look back, Nate knew the guerrilla leader was pursuing him, because he heard the snorting and thumping of the stallion's approach. He also assumed that Quantrill was going to use his Bowie knife to cut him down, so he increased his speed, but Quantrill's swift horse was only a few feet away and he held the long, hooked knife behind his back, ready to hack.

Nate knew that he was losing the race and that he had to do something to avoid being cut down. Turning his head from the corner of his right eye, he saw that the horse was almost even with him and in another moment he would face the sharp curved edge of the long Bowie if he did not move. He decided to abruptly turn to the right and pass in front of the galloping horse's head. The stallion became unnerved by this unexpected move and suddenly shifted his gait to the left to avoid Nate, sending Quantrill past him. The guerrilla chieftain was unable to turn his horse or slow the crazed beast down and dropped the Bowie knife in the grass. Quantrill quickly recovered, however, but had to use both hands to rein in his horse and maneuver the animal into small circles where he eventually came to a halt.

As Nate was running, he heard Quantrill curse the stallion. He turned his back to see how much distance he had gained on his pursuer, and saw that the guerrilla had dismounted and held the reins in one hand while lashing the hapless beast in the face with his whip. He was so enraged at his horse that he had forgotten all about Nate. Quantrill hated being defied by either man or beast, and frequently vented his frustrations by whipping horses, beating dogs, or torturing cats.

Nate continued to run as fast as he could and did not look back. He hoped that Quantrill would forget about him and that the other Missouri bushwhackers were too busy dispatching the wounded and looting the dead to notice him. The grass became higher among the ravines and Nate was becoming exhausted from his flight. He decided that he would lie down and hide among the tall green blades and rest until dusk, when it would be safer to return to Fort Scott.

Seven

The gold miner Silas Quinn wanted a woman. He had traveled on foot with his mule and burro from one of the gold-mining camps located at South Pass, Wyoming, to Dodge City, Kansas, in search of a wife. He made the six-hundred-mile trip from South Pass during the fall and arrived at Dodge in time to avoid the heavy snows. Quinn's plan was to return to his claim when he had achieved his objective.

Silas Quinn was a middle-aged man with very few teeth and a long flowing salt-and-pepper beard that fell to his belt buckle. He was short in stature and the most distinguishing physical features he possessed was a worn leather patch over his right eye and two crimson birthmarks on his bald head. Quinn also stuttered his speech, which made him frequently the focus of ridicule among his fellow miners, causing the one-eyed man to react violently.

Joining the thousands of other hopefuls, he had gone to South Pass in 1867 to dig and pan for gold. He hit a moderate strike of the precious metal and decided that he would use his modest proceeds to purchase a woman. Although there were some prostitutes at the mining camp, Silas Quinn did not want to have anything to do with them because they were too old, too fat, or too ugly. The prostitutes were also in constant demand by the miners, and

Quinn was fed up with *"old meat that had been chewed by every ditch-digging and pan-wielding prospector for a hundred miles."*

He had noticed the half-breed Cara de Quervo Zarata when he saw her at the livery stable, escorted by a Mexican, and immediately coveted what he saw. Silas Quinn had made some inquiries and was told that the breed was part of Antonio Vasco's troupe of whores. He decided to seek out the Creole pimp and make him an offer.

II.

It did not take Silas Quinn long to locate Antonio Vasco. Dodge was a small town and considering that it was winter, most of the inhabitants or visitors were killing time indoors, preferably next to a potbelly stove. The miner found his man at one of the many wretched saloons that plied their trade along Dodge's main thoroughfare. Vasco was playing cards with some professional gamblers.

"Mmm-Mm-M-Mr. Va-Va-*Vasco*?" stammered Silas Quinn when he approached the Creole from behind. The miner smelled the pimp's perfume, and recoiled from the strong scent.

Vasco slowly turned his corpulent body around in the chair and faced the miner. He gently placed his cards facedown, over his huge paunch, and glared at him, scrutinizing Quinn's appearance.

"Yes, *monsieur*?" queried Vasco. The Creole flesh peddler liked to use what little French he knew to impress strangers.

"You—you the ow-*owner* of that Co-Co-Comanche *half-breed*?" blurted the grizzly miner.

"Please, *monsieur*. Keep your voice lowered," responded Vasco, embarrassed that this crude individual was talking too loudly about Cara.

"I—I ne-needs me a *woman* t-te-*to buy*."

"*Très bien!* Let us talk, but at another table." Vasco excused himself to the other players and rose from the chair holding his cigar in between his fleshy fingers while he held his beer glass in the other. As the two men made their way through the crowded saloon to another table that was free, Vasco thought about Cara and pondered if he was really prepared to sell her. He sighed as he decided that all of his efforts to seduce the half-breed had failed to lure her back to his bed. He had become weary of her obstinacy and hostile demeanor and, most importantly, she was five months' pregnant and her belly started to grow. This disgusted Vasco because he did not like pregnant women and the fact that she was carrying Nate's child made the matter worse.

"Here is good." Vasco pointed to an empty chair at a table that still had dirty shot glasses, beer mugs, and cigar ashes on the surface.

"Li-li-like I sa-said. I wants to buy your bre-*breed* bitch."

"She is my prize possession, *monsieur*. I will not let her go for cheap. If at all." Vasco shrugged as he took a long puff on his cigar and through the smoke gazed into the eyes of Silas Quinn, looking for a reaction. He thought to himself, *If this filthy miner is prepared to pay, so be it*.

"I—I—I can *pay*," stammered Quinn. "I ga-ga-*got* gold. How much?"

Vasco's attention was piqued. He felt the tiny hairs on the back of his neck rise, and decided that if he could take all of the eager miner's gold, it might be worth it for him to sell to Cara.

"*Five hundred in gold,*" responded the Creole pimp coolly as he downed the last bit of beer in his mug and took another puff from the stogie.

Silas Quinn's eyes narrowed, but other than that, his face remained void of expression. He was shocked by Vasco's outrageous price to purchase Cara, but not intimidated by the pimp's shoddy sense of his self-importance. Silas Quinn was a seasoned miner and had killed to protect his claim from interlopers.

"Da-dats a lot of money. I—I ain't sur' n-n-no mo' dat she worth it," he stuttered as spit sprayed from his mouth, splattering Vasco's white silk cravat and crimson vest.

"Porco miseravel," cursed Vasco in Portuguese, aghast that he had been drizzled upon by this uncouth miner's saliva. He quickly removed a white linen handkerchief from the bottom of his right sleeve and spot dried his cravat and vest. Although appalled and insulted by Quinn's behavior, he controlled his anger because he wanted the miner's gold and to be rid of the half-breed. Vasco regained his composure.

"You will not find one like her for a thousand miles in each direction. I could sell her to *half a dozen* miners who have more gold than you," bluffed the pimp, forcing a smile.

Silas Quinn rapidly stroked his beard, then wiped his hands on his oily pants. He wanted to have the girl, but five hundred dollars was all he had brought with him, and he had not planned to pay more than two or three hundred for a woman. The gold digger's one good eye rotated in thought. He knew that he wanted Cara badly, and he had not seen a comparable substitute in town. He also was not willing to return to his lonely shack in the Antelope Hills without a bitch to cook, clean, wash, and service him. For a moment he lamented his failure to purchase a squaw from the local tribe near the mining camps, the Shoshoni, and how it would have been much cheaper. The Shoshoni, however, had refused to bargain their women for the yellow metal.

"Three hundred and fifty!" replied the miner, proud that he did not stutter his words. He decided that he would try and negotiate to see if the pimp would come down on the price.

"My price or nothing," scoffed Vasco, still using his handkerchief to spot dry Quinn's saliva stains. He had considered coming down a little on the price but he was so revolted by Quinn's presence that he decided to hold firm.

Quinn was disappointed that the flesh peddler rejected his counteroffer. Five hundred dollars was about all the money he had on his person and he needed to purchase supplies before returning to his camp.

"Four hundred, mister. Da-dats all I got," pleaded Quinn, hoping that Vasco would believe him.

Vasco pulled on his cigar and eyed Quinn suspiciously as he released the smoke slowly into the air. The Creole knew that the miner was lying, but also knew that he was close to getting his gold and did not want this fish to get away.

"Four hundred and fifty, and you can have her tonight," Vasco replied, believing that his tantalizing counteroffer would convince the miner to pay.

"Mister, you got yourself a deal." For the second time in one day, he did not stutter his words.

III.

Cougar Eyes had chosen a big buckskin gelding from his herd to give to Nate. The Dog Man had stolen the horse during a raid from a trooper who belonged to the Seventh Cavalry. The animal had the "U.S." brand on its thigh so Cougar Eyes thought it would be appropriate to give his guest this particular mount. He placed one of his better horse blankets on the animal's back and slipped a handsome *vaquero* bridle decorated with silver medallions that he had traded an Apache for over its head. He then led the beast from the enormous pony herd and headed back to his lodge.

Nate was sitting near the fire pit eating some leftover antelope meat that Willow Branch had cooked the night before. Nate also took large gulps of hot sage tea from a deep wooden bowl in anticipation of his departure and return to the harsh winter elements. He had decided that it was time to leave his host's hospitality and return to his regiment. He glanced over to where Willow Branch was stirring a cauldron of buffalo stew over the pit fire and felt a sense of deep gratitude and affection for this woman. Thanks to Willow Branch's care, his recovery from hypothermia was complete, and he had regained his strength, and Nate was grateful. Although his time with his Cheyenne hosts had been restful and stimulating, he was eager to find General Carr's command and feel Cara's tiny, but firm arms around his waist upon his return to Fort Wallace. Turkey Leg had told him that his scouts were still observing the regiment's movements and assured him that the pony soldiers were only a two-day ride away toward the northeast.

Nate had put on his army greatcoat when Cougar Eyes stepped through the tipi flap door. *"Nox'a!"* Cougar Eyes went over to where a pallet of buffalo robes was located and looked through the pile. He selected the biggest one out of the lot and walked over to Nate and handed a beautiful winter hide to his guest.

"For you, *Hotoa' e Gordon*." Nate was stunned by Cougar Eyes' gesture. He had never received such a gift, and felt awkward as his host held out the heavy robe. "You need! Outside . . ." Cougar Eyes glanced toward the tipi's door. *"Etoneto."*

"Hahoo!" replied Nate, taking the buffalo robe from his host. He looked it over carefully and felt humbled that Cougar Eyes had honored him with such a present.

"Put on," commanded Willow Branch, leaving her cauldron by the fire to stand next to her husband.

Nate quickly removed his army greatcoat and wrapped the huge hide around his body. It felt warm and comfortable and he was glad to have it considering that he was about to set out into possibly adverse weather. *"Napevomohtahehe,"* remarked Nate with a huge grin.

"Hotoa' e Gordon has learned some of the talk of the *Tsitsitas*. *Epeva'e!* . . . It is good." Cougar Eyes nodded in approval as he crossed his arms against his chest.

"Heehe'e. Epeva'e," acknowledged Nate.

"Come!" Cougar Eyes turned to exit the lodge and Nate followed him outside.

When he stepped outside, Nate had to squint his eyes to adjust to the bright mid-November sun. With the exception of the low flames that burned in the fire pit, the interior light of the tipi was always dim, so when Nate emerged from the lodge, the strong light from the sun that reflected on the patches of fresh snow blinded him. He reached for his kepi that was lodged within his shell jacket and adjusted the hat on his head and pulled the visor down on his forehead so it would shade the eyes from the brilliant morning light.

The buckskin horse that Cougar Eyes had given him was preoccupied with pulling on some dried grass that protruded at the bottom of the tipi. The hay was wedged in between the lining and outer wall that served as insulation for the lodge. Nate did not see immediately the gelding because the coruscating sun momentarily blinded him. Only when the beast snorted and tugged at the hay did Nate turn his head toward the sounds and notice him. Cougar Eyes went up to the horse and pulled the beast's head away from the tipi and stroked his neck.

*"Mo'ehno'ha."** Cougar Eyes smiled, gesturing to the horse. "For you, *Hotoa 'e Gordon*."

Nate knew that Cougar Eyes was going to give him a mount for his trip back to the regiment because his host had mentioned

*Horse

183

it the night before, but he had expected a small spent Indian pony who would be expendable. When he saw the large army mount with the "U.S." brand burned on its thigh he became surprised. The horse appeared to be in excellent condition and Nate was convinced that the animal probably once belonged to an officer. He was well fed and his coat was thick and shiny.

*"Hahoo! Nesene!"** Nate smiled, his face showing an expression of gratitude. He was touched by this generous gesture but felt self-conscious that he had nothing worthy to give in return. He approached the horse and patted the animal on the neck and examined the hooves, chest, eyes, and teeth and determined that the horse was about four years old. *"Epeva'e,"*† acknowledged Nate, nodding his head in approval.

Willow Branch emerged from the flap door of the lodge carrying a bulging parfleche bag. She approached Nate, her tiny moccasin feet carefully trudging in the melting snow and soft ground. "For you, *Hotoa' e Gordon*." She raised the parfleche bag almost over her head so Nate could take the article from her.

"Thank you, thank you. *Hahoo!*" exclaimed Nate, feeling a little overwhelmed by his hosts' generosity. Not only did Cougar Eyes give him a fine buffalo robe to protect him from the elements and a healthy horse so he could travel without fear that the animal would go lame or soon die of starvation, but food for himself for at least several days.

Cougar Eyes felt a gust of wind and noticed the buffalo hairs on Nate's robe move with the wind. He looked at the sky and saw dark clouds moving in from the west. "You go now, *Hotoa' e Gordon*. Soon, *hesta'se*."

Nate did not understand what *hesta'se* meant, and his face twitched in incertitude.

---

*Thank you.
†My friend

"Snow!" said Willow Branch, noticing that Nate did not understand.

"Heehe'e," agreed Nate, looking at the black clouds that were moving toward their direction. He seized the buckskin's mane near its withers with his left hand while holding Willow Branch's parfleche bag under his right arm and effortlessly leaped onto the horse's back. He looked at Cougar Eyes and Willow Branch and smiled. "You"—Nate pointed to Cougar Eyes and then to Willow Branch—"my friends! My heart is warm and at peace because of the kindness you have shown me."

Willow Branch translated for her husband and Cougar Eyes replied, *"Epeva'e.* It is good."

"Ni'ifos-ho'ihneyo ... Come again." Willow Branch smiled as she shrugged from the cold. She was only dressed lightly in a deerskin dress and the temperature was dropping quickly. Nate turned the buckskin toward the northeast where Turkey Leg's scouts had last seen the pony soldiers. *"Hahoo ... Nesene."* Nate saluted Cougar Eyes and gently tapped his heels to the horse's flanks.

The Cheyenne couple watched Nate ride off, his big buckskin firmly negotiating the wet ground. They waited for him to disappear over some ravines and Cougar Eyes turned to his squaw. *"Hotoa' e Gordon ... Nahevesenehenostse."*

IV.

First Sergeant Jesse Randolph was searching the ground for tracks. He had been out for two days riding Cailloux, searching for Nate. After much badgering, permission was granted for him to search for his companion. When Wild Bill Hickok returned to the bivouac site where elements of the Tenth Cavalry and Fifth Infantry were camped, he reported that Nate and he had become separated during the blizzard. Hickok's horse was too spent to return to the area where they had been separated but he was able to give Jesse the distance and general direction where they had been foraging for food when the snow and howling winds hit them.

Jesse had been out for a day and a half looking for any signs that might reveal Nate's whereabouts but was becoming increasingly frustrated due to his lack of experience in tracking. What's more, most of the snow that had fallen during the blizzard had melted due to a thaw, making tracking Nate more difficult. He had seen some tracks, but recognized them as being either coyote, jackrabbit, or whitetail deer. His heart raced several times when he identified unshod Indian pony tracks in the snow and soft ground. He was not overly concerned for himself because he was well armed and brought extra ammunition for his Spencer. It was Nate who he feared might have had a run-in with hostiles, and Jesse knew what possible hell that could be based on his own personal experience not too long ago when he was trapped in a railroad cut and tormented with lances by Cheyenne Dog Soldiers. *"God, I hope the boy didn't fall into the hands of them Dog Men,"* whispered Jesse to Cailloux. He spoke softly to his mount, encouraging him to plod on in his weakened condition.

Jesse knew that Nate was probably riderless because many of the horses in the command had perished during the storm. He half expected to find Nate either walking or perhaps holed up in some makeshift shelter because he was too injured to walk or he didn't wish to be caught out in the open when the country was crawling with hostiles. He refused to believe as some of the officers had insisted that he had perished. Even if that was the most extreme case, Jesse was determined not to leave his friend's body to the wolves and coyotes.

Time was running out though. Although Cailloux had managed to graze a little on some brown grass, his weight was steadily declining and he was becoming weaker by the hour. Jesse was beginning to fear that his life would be in serious jeopardy if his mount collapsed from hunger and fatigue. He looked at the sky and saw dark clouds approaching and felt the temperature drop.

"Don't want to be caught out here in another storm," he whispered to himself as he patted his horse's neck. He adjusted his collar and tightened the wool scarf around his head. Like many of the men in the command, he had grown a beard for protection to shield against the freezing winds.

In the distance near a clump of piñon trees, Jesse saw a rider approaching on a large horse. The rider was too far to identify, so Jesse swung his Spencer into his hands and moved the lever so a round would enter the chamber. He held off cocking back the hammer until he could get a closer look at the man who was riding toward him.

"Must be a Dog Man scout or hunter," he told Cailloux. The beast snorted and actually picked up speed when he saw the other horse in the distance. Jesse had to pull on his reins to control him because he wanted the unknown rider to come to him. He was also concerned that there might be other Dog Men nearby, hunting for food, who could, if he was spotted, cut him off or chase him, neither prospect Jesse looked favorably upon.

Jesse started to look for cover if the unknown rider, who appeared mounted on a horse in very good condition, started to gallop toward him or commenced shooting. He decided that it would be futile for him to try to outrun a well-mounted Dog Soldier in Cailloux's exhausted and famished condition. The rider was fast approaching and still the man remained silent, but Jesse could see that he was bundled in a huge buffalo robe and decided that he was a possible hostile. His eyes searched the terrain for any natural cover but he was too far from the clump of piñon trees that he saw grew nearby and the ravines were too shallow to offer any protection from bullets and arrows. He made up his mind that if he was going to be attacked he would have to shoot Cailloux and use the animal for a breastwork. Jesse reined in his mount and dismounted. He firmly held the reins in his right hand and knelt in the soft ground. The rider was still coming at a consistent pace and Jesse cocked back the hammer on his Spencer.

He held the weapon close to his chest, and rubbed his cold trigger finger in between the reins and trigger rim of the Spencer to increase circulation.

"Why don't the bastard stop, or holler or do som'tin'. He knows I'm goddamn army, and he *knows* that I don't know who in the hell he is," bitched Jesse as the unidentified rider kept coming closer. "Damn if I'm goin' let you git any closer." Jesse raised the stock of the Spencer to his right cheek and prepared himself to shoot. "You ain't goin' use your coup stick on my ass!

"Hold it right there, mister," warned Jesse firmly. "Don't come any farther till you *identify* yourself."

The rider coughed a little but kept coming and was only about a hundred feet away.

"I'm telling you, mister! I swear I'll shoot you if you comes any closer." Jesse was about to squeeze the trigger when the rider shouted.

"You always get on your knees when you shoot, boy?" mocked Nate as he reined in his buckskin to a halt. He glared at Jesse with so much amusement and satisfaction that he had scared his friend into nearly shooting him.

"By Jezuz! You son of a bitch, Nate! I damn nearly put a bullet into you," yelled Jesse as he stood up and brushed off some of the mud and snow from his trousers.

"So?" gibed Nate as he urged the buckskin to advance toward his friend. "You're a sorry ass shot and prob'ly would hav' missed."

"Nice coat! Bet your black hide is warm," retorted Jesse.

Both men gawked at each other for a moment and then broke into a boisterous laugh as they fell into each other's arms.

V.

Nate and Jesse decided to bed down for the night and return to the bivouac site the following day. The two men pitched their modest camp at dusk along the bank of a creek and found enough buffalo chips to make a fire. As they were preparing their camp, the sky became very dark and hung low in the sky and the temperature suddenly dropped. The menacing canopy, however, only yielded a brief but furious dusting, and the sky was now only slightly overcast and the wind had completely died down.

Nate revealed the contents of Willow Branch's bulging parfleche bag to Jesse, and his friend became amazed by its contents. Dried buffalo jerky and antelope meat, dried wild vegetables and berries, and a generous assortment of nuts. What pleased Jesse most though was that Nate also carried some forage for his buckskin that he shared with Jesse so Cailloux could have a hearty feed. Jesse had brought some ground coffee and made a pot that Nate savored with gusto. If there was one thing he missed most during his stay with the Cheyennes, it was the smell and taste of boiling hot coffee.

"You goin' to tell me whut went on back there at that Cheyenne village?"

Nate puffed on his pipe in thought. His tobacco pouch was refilled, again thanks to Cougar Eyes' benevolence, and he gave some to Jesse who also filled his pipe bowl.

"I lost Frederick," lamented Nate.

"I figured that," responded Jesse, sipping on some old watered-down coffee that he had made. "I knew that when I saw you on a dif'ent horse. How you come by that army horse anyways, an' why does he look so *good*?"

"My Cheyenne friend, Cougar Eyes, gave him to me. He stole him from the army an' I figure he didn't want the animal no mo' 'cause he eats way mo' than Indian ponies," replied Nate dryly.

Jesse became astonished. "Friend? That murderin' Dog Man your friend, now?"

"Can't say he's my enemy, that's fo' sure." Nate took a deep breath and peered into the tiny fire. "Jess, the man found me near dead an' could hav' just left me for the coyotes an' the buzzards, like I was carrion." Nate took another sip of the bad but hot coffee. "But he took me in, me, the enemy, into his camp and had his squaw nurse my strength back an' cared for me as if I was *family*." Nate shook his head. "I can't forget that kind of kindness, like I can't forget the kindness some w'ite folk shown me when I was on the run."

"Well, I can see that he was mighty generous an' all. He givin' you a fine horse, a warm buffalo robe, food and tobacco an' whut not." Jesse was a little envious that his friend appeared to be in better condition and equipped than he was. "But I feel dat . . ."

"*Shhh!* Listen!" whispered Nate, placing his index finger to his lips.

"I don't hear nuthin'," responded Jesse, straining to listen for any unusual sounds.

"Look at the horses," Nate said, gesturing.

Jesse turned his head to where their mounts were hobbled and noticed that both animals were behaving nervously and twitching their ears back and forth, indicating that they too had heard something.

"Wolves? Coyotes?" whispered Jesse, seizing his Spencer.

"Don't think so. Wolves and coyotes don't like fires, only man is drawn to fire," responded Nate, raising his head in the direction of where he heard some noise, but was unable to discern what it could be. Both men remained motionless and stared into the dark void of the prairie. The sound of a horse sneezing in the distance pierced the silence.

"Dog Men?" Jesse gently pulled down on the lever of his repeater to enter a round in the breech.

Nate went for his Walker-Colt and half cocked the hammer on the piece. He held the weapon in his lap, the barrel resting on his left arm, pointing toward the ground. He reminded himself that just because he had been a guest of Cougar Eyes for several days did not make him immune from possible attack. He thought about his friend "Medicine Bill" Comstock, and what the scout Sharp Grover had told him. How the plainsman, and Nate knew that "Medicine Bill" was a friend of the Cheyennes, was ambushed and killed by Turkey Leg's Dog Soldiers after he had been received as a guest in their camp under a pledge of truce. Nate remained doubtful, however, that Cheyenne raiding parties were riding about during a cold winter night seeking mischief when they could be snug in their warm lodges eating grilled buffalo meat and sipping hot sage tea.

The two hobbled horses started to snicker and shake their heads and manes, and Nate knew that an individual or a small party of riders was out there in the dark watching them. Both men glared into the night trying to detect the faintest sound or discern if it was man or beast that was lurking nearby.

Nate could see the faint figure of a horse's head and tail coming toward them. The animal was walking at a leisurely pace and Nate saw that the rider, a tall man wearing a large broad-brimmed hat, was coming right for their campfire.

"Evening! I've been smelling your bad coffee for miles." The rider smiled as he came within the full light of the campfire. He was riding a large gelding that was in good condition and Nate noticed that the stranger held a .52-caliber Sharps New Model rifle across his saddle.

Although relieved that the rider proved to be friendly, Nate felt embarrassed that their unannounced guest had smelled the aroma of the coffee from a distance. He wondered if he was becoming careless and complacent after spending a relaxed time as Cougar Eyes' guest.

"You men with the Tenth?" queried the rider as he dismounted from his gelding. The stranger's voice was calm and reassuring and Nate thought that it possessed a magnetic quality. There was sufficient light from the flames of the fire that Nate could see that he was wearing high-top boots that came up to his thighs, the kind that he saw high-ranking officers wear during the war. The stranger also wore a long-fringed buckskin coat lined with fleece of bighorn sheep with matching gauntlets.

"Yes, sir, we part of the Tenth," replied Jesse eagerly as he gently released the hammer on his Spencer. He was glad that he was out of danger and that the stranger seemed sociable.

Nate had returned the Walker-Colt to its holster but kept smoking his pipe as he gazed at the stranger who had emerged from the dark and cold prairie night to appear in their camp as if he had an appointment. The unexpected guest was well over six feet and Nate thought he looked familiar but could not place the man's handsome face. His thick wavy blond hair fell gently on his shoulders, and although he had several days' growth of beard stubble on his cheeks, his manicured goatee and mustache gave his face a strong sense of masculine beauty. Nate guessed that he was about the same age as himself and Jesse, and became convinced he was a scout for the army, but could not recall where he might have seen him.

"Mind if I have some of your coffee?" The stranger's hawklike eyes leered at the steaming kettle that belched its weak, but inviting aroma as it precariously rested on some dying buffalo chip embers.

"Help yourself," offered Nate, pointing to the kettle with his pipe.

"Thank you." The man looked at Nate's buffalo coat with envy. "Nice hide . . . Mr.?"

"Sergeant Major," stated Nate crisply. "Sergeant Major Nate Gordon of the Tenth Cavalry." Nate then pointed to Jesse with his pipe. "And this is First Sergeant Jesse Randolph."

The man nodded and walked with great agility toward the saddle and loosened the cinch of his saddle so the animal would be more comfortable. Nate then watched him remove a tin cup from one of his saddlebags.

"Haven't I seen you somewheres befo'?" asked Nate as he downed the last bit of the coffee in his tin. He was a little put off that the man had not yet introduced himself, after he had identified who they were. "You scoutin' for the Seventh?"

"Nope, I'm scoutin' for the *Fifth* under General Carr lookin' for Penrose's command." The unexpected guest sipped some of the coffee in the tin and savored its warmth down his throat. "And from what I see here, I reckon I'm close, 'cause your outfit is probably bivouacked not far from here."

"We bivouacked at Palo Duro Creek, 'bout half day's ride from here." Jesse was in a chatty mood. He was pleased to have someone to converse with other than his taciturn friend.

"You seem to know a lot 'bout us," commented Nate dryly. "And who are we addressing?"

"Oh, didn't I say?" responded the stranger, knowing full well that he had deliberately omitted introducing himself. "The name's *Cody. William F. Cody."* He smiled and took another sip of coffee. But you can call me 'Buffalo Bill' like everyone else."

"You 'Buffalo Bill'?" fawned Jesse.

"Yes, sir."

"Now I know where I've seen you," added Nate. "I've seen your picture in the newspapers."

"Think they do a good likeness?" Cody stood up straight and placed his head near the fire so Nate and Jesse could see his handsome facial features.

"Oh, the newspapers do you justice, all right." Nate was willing to accommodate Buffalo Bill's vanity. He was curious about this man who shared the same name title, only he was the one with a growing reputation as a great hunter and scout. Nate had read about the man's extraordinary exploits in the press and wondered if they were true.

"I heard you was in the Pony Express," exclaimed Jesse enthusiastically.

"I held the record for the longest run!" responded Cody unabashedly.

"Why, why don't you have a seat—I'll take your mount fo' you," offered Jesse, walking toward Cody's gelding.

"Thanks, Sergeant, but I'll take care of my horse. But I will finish my coffee and spend the night here, if you all don't mind?" Cody handed the tin cup to Jesse and removed the saddle but left the blanket on the animal's back. He placed the saddle on the ground and untied a bedroll from it and spread the article on the damp surface. Jesse then handed the tin cup back to Buffalo Bill as the great scout and hunter lay down on the blanket and leaned his back against the saddle seat and arranged his body in a lounge-like fashion. Nate thought that his pose resembled his old master's wife when she would lounge on the day couch in the parlor to hold court. The plainsman then pulled his long buckskin coat tightly around his legs and crossed his high-top boots as if posing to be photographed.

"Whut 'bout the Pony Express, Mr. Bill? They say that you

were just a young-in when you signed up?" inquired Jesse eagerly.

"I was fourteen years old when I signed on to the outfit," responded Cody. He then chuckled. "Had to lie 'bout my age though."

"Oh, that young?" replied Jesse, wide-eyed.

Nate was not impressed. He had been riding horses since he could walk and was behind the plow driving a mule team in the broiling sun when he was nine. He continued to let Jesse do the talking, however, since he seemed so agog at Cody's presence.

"They say that one time you rode three hundred miles in a day, to deliver the mail, that be true?"

"Well, actually it was three hundred and twenty-two miles in twenty-one hours and forty minutes," corrected Cody as he took another sip of coffee.

Jesse's eyes widened even farther. "Not with the same horse though," jested Nate, finally breaking his silence and joining in the conversation.

"Took twenty-one horses to do it," replied Cody proudly. "You see, when I arrived at Red Buttes Station in Wyoming after ridin' 'bout a hundred and fifty miles, the relief rider had been killed by hostiles and there was no one else to take his place! Well, the mail had to be delivered, so I mounted a fresh horse and completed his run to Rock Ridge Station, changing horses on the way."

"Whut's the distance 'tween stations?" inquired Nate, genuinely curious.

"It depends. If the country is hard on the horses, stations are sometimes as close as five miles apart. But if a rider is on the prairie, stations could be as far apart as twenty miles."

"Run into any Indians?" snapped Jesse, always obsessed with the prospect of running into hostiles.

Cody nodded his head slightly. "Not many. Oh, sure, I've been chased, shot at, and couple times nearly got my hair lifted, but the biggest problems are gopher holes and the weather. Nothing worse than a horse breakin' a leg in a hole or gettin' trapped by a storm that can beat down man and beast."

Jesse was listening attentively, but Nate preferred to stare in contemplation into the dying buffalo chip fire. He had lost interest in Buffalo Bill's tales and was thinking about Cara. A flame shot up from one of the chips and Nate saw the outline of Cara's face within the flame. Her image in the fire scared him, and he considered it as a bad sign.

Jesse felt the hairs on the back of his neck stand up when Cody mentioned the prospect of being scalped on the trail. As Cody sipped his coffee, he carefully observed his two hosts in order to gauge their reactions. He noticed that Jesse's face revealed anxiousness and apprehension while Nate's appeared to be reflective and possessed a more self-assured manner than his companion's.

"What kinda horses did the riders mount in the Pony Express?" Nate wanted to know if they used Indian ponies because they were hardy and efficient.

"The outfit used Morgans and Thoroughbreds for the eastern stations, pintos in the middle, and mustangs for the western half," answered Cody.

Nate nodded and thought about the Morgans. During the war, he once saw an entire Vermont cavalry regiment mounted on powerful Morgans. He remembered vividly how impressed he was with the breed's compact muscles, gleaming rust coats, and sparkling intelligent eyes. At the time, he promised himself that he would one day own a full-bloodied Morgan. He reminisced how his former commanding line officer, Lieutenant Zachary Hennessy, the Vermonter, had told him that the original breeder, Justin Morgan, had come to Woodstock, Vermont, to breed the first Morgan. He remembered that Hennessy had told him how the animal was so versatile that it could also pull a plow and wagon and be hitched to a buggy and trot for hours.

"Ride any Morgans?" queried Nate.

"Many Morgans," acknowledged Cody.

"How they fare compared to the others?"

"They were by far the *best*," stated the scout without hesitation. Hell! The whole outfit should have been mounted on nothing but Morgans, 'cause they strong, fast, and don't eat and drink water as much as those damn stupid Thoroughbreds!

"I 'gree," concurred Nate, nodding his head gently.

"Whut 'bout the pintos?" asked Jesse hurriedly, fearing that Cody was paying more attention to his friend than to him.

"I know the Indians favor them for huntin' and at times fightin' 'cause of their black and white spot coats. For them, it's good medicine to possess one." Cody got up from his lounging posture and went over to the fire and took a stick to poke at the glowing buffalo chips, trying to stir up more flames. "Ownin' a pinto gives the buck prestige among the warriors, and gets attention from the young squaws." Cody failed to arouse any more flames from the dying chips, so he turned his backside to the expiring fire and faced his two hosts who were listening as if they were an audience at a theater. "But I didn't think they were as good as Morgans." Buffalo Bill reflected for a moment as if he was trying to make up his mind on some important issue. "No! The only horse that comes close to a Morgan is a *mustang*. Problem, though, is you gots to be a hell of a rider, 'cause they wild and we rode 'em when they not even green broke. Can't control the animal! Best you can do"—Cody lifted his right hand and pointed—"is point the horse in the right direction and hold on for dear life, 'cause the bastard won't stop till you get to the next station." Buffalo Bill grinned and gazed at the ground. "Fact is, the couple of times that I had to outrun Shoshoni and Cheyennes, I was mounted on mustangs." Cody looked at the partially covered sky and acknowledged as an afterthought. "Them wild horses probably saved my hide and hair."

Nate thought about Frederick and how the horse had plodded on during the blizzard and finally collapsed from exhaustion and starvation.

"Is it true what the newspapers say 'bout how you gots your name?" asked Nate, stuffing his pipe with some fresh tobacco. He had felt drowsy earlier and was ready to bed down for the night, but the theatrical entrance made by William Cody had given the camp's atmosphere a lively mood. Although Nate thought that Cody was a bit of a show-off, he had to acknowledge that the scout possessed genuine charisma, mixed with natural charm. Nate also had to admit that his beautiful blue eyes glowed with verve when he spoke and his voice possessed gravitas.

"Newspapers say a lot of things 'bout a lot of people, half of them don't come near the truth and the other half are lies to get people all worked up," lambasted Cody, still standing with his back to the glowing chips, warming his backside.

"I read that you won the name in a shootin' contest." Nate took a puff from his pipe and wondered what tall tale Cody would recount now.

"Well, there was a shootin' contest, and I did win it but that event was not where I got the name. You see, 'bout a year ago, I was employed by the Kansas Pacific Railroad to feed their line crews with buffalo meat. The railroad had a voracious appetite for meat, so I was out for seventeen months shootin' them. Well, I managed to kill 4,280 bulls and cows and the papers started calling me 'Buffalo Bill.' "

"Oooh wee! Over four thousand head?" exclaimed Jesse, highly impressed with Cody's buffalo carcass count.

Nate was less dazzled, however. To kill so many buffalo was a feat to be sure, but more of marksmanship than a demonstration of a hunter's cunning and guile. Nate also knew that killing buffalo was not like killing any other animal. Buffalo did not have the same instincts for survival as deer or elk, and would gather in huge, crowded herds, facilitating a hunter's work. He remembered talking with buffalo hunters at Forts Lyon and Wallace and what they had told him. As long as the hunter was upwind from the beasts and shot the biggest bull in the herd first, he could spend hours shooting the hapless animals one by one as they grazed, oblivious that they were being systematically slaughtered.

"How many did you kill in a single stand?"

"Oh, I would say that I had quite a few stands where I killed at least a hundred in an afternoon," responded the plainsman dryly. "There were occasions"—Cody smiled and Nate thought that he looked rather smug—"when the barrel of my Sharps would become so hot that I had to stop shooting. Or I would kill so many of them that the skinners begged me to stop 'cause they couldn't keep up with the butcherin'. Fact is, I killed so many that most of the time we would have to leave them on the prairie for the buzzards and coyotes, 'cause nightfall would come or we be so tired of shootin' and butcherin'."

Nate thought about Cougar Eyes and what he had told him while he was a guest at the Cheyenne camp. "The *Ye' ho' e* kill too many *hotoa' e*. One day soon, if this continues, there will be no more *hotoa' e* and my people will starve!"

At the time, Nate belittled his host's assertion that the buffalo would disappear from the plains. Nate had seen so many of the beasts in enormous herds, moving among the ravines like a gigantic brown carpet. At the time, he asked himself, *How can an animal that is so numerous be wiped out?* Now, however, after what Buffalo Bill had just told him, Nate thought that if there were a couple of thousand buffalo hunters, killing hundreds of the animals a day, then in twenty or so years, they might be wiped out.

"That don't bother you? You killin' so many of them? What 'bout the Indians, won't they starve?"

Cody shrugged his shoulders at Nate's comment. "The way I look at it, this land is going to be settled by farmers, ranchers, and townsfolk, no matter what." Cody's eyes sharpened as he focused his gaze at Nate. "The railroad will see to that! So, being that this is a fact, there's no room for the settlers with the Indians and the buffalo roamin' around. One or the other will have to give way to make room."

Nate appreciated Buffalo Bill's point, but was disturbed by his cold assessment. He contemplated how the white man, through his control of the food supply, once used against slaves, was now being practiced upon Indians.

"You got no sympathy for the Indian?" he retorted, hoping that Cody would express a little empathy for the redman.

"The most honest people I have ever met are Indians!" snapped back Buffalo Bill, irritated that Nate had questioned his genuine fondness for the Indian way of life. "An Indian would just as soon cut off his leg than lie!" insisted Cody. "A white man on the other hand will lie at a drop of a hat if he smells opportunity. Hell! I don't have to tell *you boys* that. But change is comin'. Just as fast as the railroad"—Cody stretched out his right arm and hand and moved it from left to right, Indian style—"is laying track across the prairie." Cody then returned to the spot where his saddle rested on the ground and placed his head on the saddle seat and wrapped his wool bedroll tightly around himself. "And the Indian? Well, he's goin' to have to change to survive."

"Maybe so, but not 'fore he puts up a hell of a *long* fight," riposted Nate as he also placed his head against his saddle and wrapped the buffalo robe around his frame and pulled the hide up to his neck. He gazed at the horses to make sure that they were fine, and then looked at Jesse who was already fast asleep and snoring, his breath making huge clouds in the cold November air. Nate listened for a few moments at Jesse's snoring and then his mind again turned to thoughts about Cara. He longed to be with her, and wanted to get back to the post as fast as possible, but he knew that the campaign against the hostiles was not yet over and it could be weeks before he would see her. To give himself comfort, he whispered slowly, *"I am a soldier! I must do my duty, I must do my duty! I have a responsibility toward my men and this uniform. I must be patient."*

VI.

Silas Quinn had untied the ropes that had bound Cara's hands together, and after extracting a promise from her that she would not scream, removed the rag in her mouth that he had stuffed down her throat.

When he had placed her on the back of his mule at Dodge City, Cara had resisted so vehemently to being tied that he had to ask Miguelito to assist him in subduing her. When a gloating Vasco told Cara that she had been sold to the miner, her first thoughts were of Nate and her unborn child and how he would never find her if she went with her new master to some distant mining camp.

Now, they were on the trail toward the gold fields at South Pass, Wyoming, and had paused on the trail for lunch. It was a bright day and the snow was melting. Quinn ordered her to make a fire and prepare a pot of coffee while he pulled out some buffalo jerky from a bulging sack that hung on the right side of the mule.

"W-w-we goin' gi-git long jes-jest fine, little darlin'. M-m-me an' you, you'll see." Quinn handed some of the jerky to Cara and she reluctantly accepted the piece of dried meat only because she was so famished and was beginning to feel dizzy.

She had not spoken a single word to him since Dodge, preferring instead to occupy her mind with thoughts of escape. Unlike Vasco, the miner did not have a brawny lackey to assist him, but Cara knew that Quinn was very strong because she felt his powerful arms when he placed her on the back of the mule. After she had chewed a few pieces of the jerky, she went about the business of making a fire by collecting some dried twigs that she had found near a small oak tree, and Quinn lit the delicate pile with a match. She was then handed a coffee grinder by the miner and told to grind the beans and place them in the pot. Cara silently complied with her new master's commands as the miner squatted on his haunches staring at his new possession with his one good eye as if he were a predator with a captive prey.

"I—I know dat you scared of me, but you—you—you'll see— you goin' be nice to me," blurted Quinn as he grinned hideously and stroked his beard with his greasy hands.

Cara was aware that the grizzled miner was gawking at her and she knew she would have to fight him off too.

"Mi Dios! Donde está Nate?" she whispered to herself as she cast a melancholy gaze toward the prairie and stared at the endless horizon of partially snow-covered ravines and brown grass.

Part Two

DEATH ALONG THE BANKS OF THE WASHITA

One

WOLF CREEK VALLEY, INDIAN TERRITORY
NOVEMBER 25.

General George Armstrong Custer was chafing as he always did when he feared that the Indians would escape his reach. The boy general was impatient to get his beloved Seventh moving out from its bivouac site along the banks of Wolf Creek to locate the hostiles. The winter campaign against the Cheyennes, Arapahoes, Comanches, and Kiowas was not going according to plan and Custer had to leave Camp Supply during a raging winter storm with over a foot of snow already on the ground. The storm had been so severe that he had to use a compass to guide the regiment through the howling winds and snow because visibility was reduced to a few feet. Now the fresh snow was impeding the march of his column of over eight hundred men and a large wagon train. He was frustrated that they were only able to travel an average of fifteen miles a day because the troops had to wait for the army wagons to catch up. The cumbersome and heavily laden vehicles transported all of the regiment's forage for the horses and mules, tents, blankets, cots, stoves, ammunition, extra firearms, food, cooking utensils, medical supplies, extra clothing, and all of the officers' personal baggage.

The original plan was for General Penrose's Tenth Cavalry and General Carr's Fifth Cavalry to act as pincers and sweep down upon the hostiles that were believed to be camped in the vicinity of the North Canadian River near the Antelope Mountains and Washita River Valley. General Sheridan had placed all of his confidence in his protégé's ability to find the hostiles and engage them before they could flee. So Custer was anxious not to disappoint his mentor's belief in him and wanted a fight to punish the Indians and especially the Dog Men who were committing depredations against settlers in Kansas.

The whole objective of the winter campaign, the brainchild of General Sheridan, was for the separate columns to surround the tribes and defeat them in detail at their vulnerable winter camps. "Little Phil" relied on stealth, rapidity of movement, and overwhelming firepower to crush the enemy. He told Custer to kill as many braves as possible and destroy their lodges, hides, supplies, and dispose of the enormous pony herds. He had also given orders that all survivors were to be escorted back to Camp Supply for confinement.

Custer had given orders to the bugler to sound "To Horse" and the cavalrymen moved smartly to execute the boy general's command. The fear of a brutal tongue-lashing or worse from the man who once commanded the men who shot down Confederate General Jeb Stuart from his horse kept the cavalrymen alert. Two days ago, the general had disciplined several of the wagon masters and teamsters for their slow response in loading wagons when he gave the order to decamp. He had made them get off of their vehicles and walk in the snow at the rear of the column as punishment. He was pleased that within a few hours of this castigation, they were pleading with him to return to their wagons while promising to be more diligent in loading and unloading the supplies.

Custer was conversing with the Osage scouts Little Beaver and

Hard Rope about the prospects for locating the winter villages of the hostiles.

"Do you think that they could be near the Antelope Hills?" queried the general. Custer respected Indians and usually treated his Indian scouts with reverence because he considered their powers of smell, sight, and hearing superior to the average white man's.

"Me think *close*," responded Little Beaver who was a chief of his tribe.

The response disappointed the general. He wanted more precise information. The command had been out for three days in inclement weather without sighting any Indian activity, and he had no reliable information on the whereabouts of General Penrose's Tenth Cavalry or where Eugene Carr's column was. Not that he was concerned that they were out of reach in terms of supporting the Seventh. Custer was determined that his regiment would do the real fighting and that the other regiments would serve as mere "beaters" in corralling the hostiles from flight.

Custer then went over to where the white scouts had gathered and went up to California Joe who was standing with his mule and faithful dog with another scout by the name of Romero who everybody in the command called Romeo. He was a short and heavyset half-Mexican half-black breed who spoke Cheyenne and who had once lived among the *Tsitsitas*.

"Well, California?" asked Custer eagerly. He was wearing a buffalo coat over his buckskin-fringed jacket and matching trousers. He breathed in the crisp cold morning air and felt vigorous. "What do you think about the weather?" Custer was concerned that there might be another storm, which would further delay his progress toward the Antelope Mountains and Washita Valley.

"A-up! Looks like the travelin' is good ahead," stated the scout as he scratched his thick curly brown beard and looked at the sky.

"You think we can catch the hostiles in about a day or so?" asked Custer anxiously. It was six o'clock in the morning and although the uncouth scout was smoking his briarwood pipe full blast, Custer could smell alcohol on California Joe's breath, but for the moment chose to ignore the infraction. California's incessant drinking had forced Custer to relieve him of his position as chief of scouts on the second day of the campaign but the boy general still valued his experience and bluntness.

"Find them in a day or so? Hell, Jineral! I'm still thinkin' that supposin' we run into more villages than we bargain fur?" replied California as he removed a hoof pick from his pocket and started to check his mule's hooves to make sure there was no ice buildup.

Custer's eyes showed his disappointment with California's cryptic response. The boy general was genuinely fond of the scout and considered him a colorful frontier figure but he missed the clarity of the now departed Medicine Bill Comstock's answers to his questions.

"Do you think it is *possible* that we might find their villages within forty-eight hours?" pushed Custer, hoping for some kind of positive input from the scout.

"Oh, I think it's possible, Jineral," blurted California, stomping his feet on the ground to increase the circulation in his feet. The scout was wearing long boots, and while they were ideal footwear for most of the year on the plains, they were ill suited for cold and prolonged dampness. "But what I can't figur' is how many tribes we goin' run into and how many lodges for each of them camps. Shit, Jineral, I figur' dat we kin run into Kiowas an' Comanches 'sides them Dawg Men."

"The Seventh will be able to defeat any force that we surprise!" flouted the boy general.

Custer had worked hard in organizing the regiment's companies and training. Fresh horses were provided and the men underwent a thorough drilling in marksmanship. Custer was especially proud of his personal touch on the regiment. Inspired by his hero, the great Napoleonic cavalry commander Marshal Joachim Murat, the King of Naples, he had ordered the "coloring of horses." A cavalry term used to describe how different squadrons and troops are to be divided by horse color, giving the companies more visibility during the confusion of battle.

"If youz saize so, Jineral." California Joe pocketed his hoof pick and then checked his long breech-loading Springfield musket.

"I want you and Romeo to ride way in front, California," instructed Custer. "I'm giving you the privilege to scout on ahead and I'm placing the Osage scouts on the flanks."

"Yes, sir, Jineral." California Joe adjusted his floppy black hat and placed the toe of his boot in the stirrup to mount his mule. He then placed his Springfield musket against the pommel of his saddle and tapped his heels to his mule's flanks.

Custer watched California Joe and his mule trot off in the snow and marveled how the big equine hybrid shifted its hind hooves with such grace on the blanket of white ice that it reminded him of a ballerina. His attention was quickly broken, however, when he heard the movements of his crack regiment behind him. He became reassured upon hearing the sounds of hundreds of cavalry horses and mules neighing, snorting, whinnying, and their shod hooves trampling in the snow as dozens of heavily laden army wagons creaked and tossed and dipped on slippery ruts.

The boy general felt intoxicated with power for he knew that his force of over eight hundred men and a huge wagon train were lined up in column of twos and awaited his instructions. He took a deep breath and yelled for his orderly to bring him his horse. As he waited for his mount, his back still turned toward the column, he gazed at a small herd of buffalo in the distance. Most of the huge beasts were huddled together near a creek seeking shelter at the edge of the timber, but some of the larger bulls were plunging their giant heads from side to side into the fresh snow, creating immense clouds of white ice, to get to the grass. As Custer watched the bisons, his two young staghounds, Blucher and Maida, rushed past him, nearly knocking him over. The hounds were rough-housing in the snow and Custer decided that the two big pups needed experience hunting buffalo.

II.

Nate and Jesse were riding toward Custer's column. General Penrose, exasperated that his weakened force was marooned at Palo Dura Creek, wanted to make contact with Custer's column to alert him of his situation. The arrival of General Carr's scout, Buffalo Bill Cody, along with Nate and Jesse's return, had been greeted by much enthusiasm by the men and signified that Carr's Fifth Cavalry would soon link up with the Tenth. Penrose, however, still needed to alert Custer that his movement toward the North Canadian had come to a halt, but planned to at least provide a screen to prevent any of the hostile tribes from fleeing north.

Therefore, he decided to send Sergeant Major Nate Gordon and First Sergeant Jesse Randolph to find General Custer and the Seventh Cavalry and inform him of his situation. Penrose's initial instinct was to send Wild Bill Hickok to look for Custer, but the scout's horse was too spent to engage in such a task, and he did not trust anybody else in the regiment to act as couriers in this type of weather in hostile country. Penrose knew he was taking a risk by sending two valuable noncoms and using them as couriers. The general, however, felt that he had no choice considering that the column's mobility had been reduced, and its fighting capacity limited due to the condition of his troopers' mounts.

The commander was also impressed with Nate's sense of survivability and that Jesse had successfully tracked Nate in the snow. In addition, Sergeant Major Gordon's horse was in excellent condition for the task and First Sergeant Jesse Randolph's mount still possessed sufficient strength to accompany Nate.

Nate thought about what Penrose told Jesse and him before they departed: "And besides, Sergeant Major, if one of you perishes en route, the other might reach the Seventh."

"Didn't Penrose say nuthin' to *you* 'bout your *horse*?" inquired Jesse as he spurred Cailloux to keep up with Nate's frisky mount.

"Oh, he gawked at my animal for a *long* time, all right." Nate patted his new mount on the neck with satisfaction. He felt good about the stolen U.S. Army horse that Cougar Eyes had given him. "But he didn't say a *word* to me 'bout that."

Nate watched as his horse's legs broke through the fresh snow with vigor. "But I *knew* he was wonderin' how come my buckskin was fat an' ornery while ev'ry other man's horse under his command is nuthin' but skin an' bones or *dead!*" responded Nate, reflecting for a moment on his commanding officer's puzzlement. "All the man was concerned 'bout was that my animal was fit fo' the task at hand."

"You goin' give this *fine* animal a name?" teased Jesse.

"Yes, sir. I'm fixin' to call him . . . John Brown." Nate patted the horse's neck again to christen the mount with his new name.

Jesse paused for a moment and acknowledged, "That's a good name."

"I though you'd approve," mocked Nate, forcing a smile on his face for Jesse's benefit.

At around midday, Custer's Seventh Cavalry came into view. The cavalrymen were moving in column of twos and the procession was so long that they could not see the wagon train that was in the rear. The two noncoms saw the column at a distance and Nate thought that the regiment resembled a giant snake moving across the snow-covered landscape. Although the air was very cold, the day was bright with sunshine, enabling Nate and Jesse to see great distances. Nate reckoned that the regiment was about two miles away and suggested to Jesse that they proceed toward the head of the column at a trot.

III.

General Custer was accompanying his two staghounds, Blucher and Maida, in hunting down a yearling buffalo bull. The general had noticed a small herd of the bisons and decided to separate himself from the command to give his dogs some needed experience in running down the beasts. He successfully cut out one of the bulls from the rest of the herd and was encouraging his dogs to attack the beast. The snow and drifts in particular were very deep and the general's horse as well as the hounds and fleeing buffalo were exerting much effort. Custer had drawn his revolver and half cocked the piece but could not get a clear shot at the yearling bull because his dogs were too close to the animal and he was afraid that he might shoot one of his darling pets instead of the buffalo.

As Nate and Jesse approached, they came upon Custer and his dogs chasing the yearling bull. At first, Nate did not recognize the general because he was too far away and had not expected him to be dressed in buckskin. Only when he heard the man shout, "Go, Blucher, go, Maida—*attack*," did he recognize Custer's voice. Nate motioned to Jesse to rein in their mounts so they could watch him and the hounds struggle in the deep drifts trying to run down the hapless animal.

The scene seemed incredulous to Nate and in a way strangely comical. It was a usual practice to grant permission for officers and noncoms to stray from a column to engage in hunting for fresh meat. It was an excellent way for supplementing the men's food with fresh game and it allowed for the other supplies to be stretched while they were campaigning. What bothered Nate was that Custer was engaged in allowing his staghounds to snap and bite at the bison's legs, neck, face, and shoulders rather than simply shooting the fleeing and terrified animal.

There was a group of mounted officers standing about a hundred yards or so away and Nate and Jesse could hear them laugh and joke in amusement as they watched their leader and his pets plunge into the snow and at times almost disappear in the drifts.

The yearling bull was bellowing in anger and desperation as the dogs barked, bit, and snapped at him while Custer tried to maneuver his horse to get close enough to get off a shot. The yearling, however, kept cutting away from the general's horse even though the dogs were wearing him down. As the chase continued, Nate could not help remember his own flight from the patrollers' dogs when he escaped Mas'a Hammond's plantation. He felt sympathetic toward the buffalo, and disgusted that the officers were laughing and joking as if the spectacle was for their personal amusement. Nate was reminded of the pandemonium that was generated by the cockfights in the quarter during slavery time, and the level of excitement demonstrated by gambling Mexicans when he saw brutal cockfights in San Antonio. More poignantly though, he remembered that he too was also very young and afraid when he thought about Bloodhound Jack and how his trained slave-catching hounds had almost run him down. He wished that Custer would shoot the poor bastard and get it over with rather than letting his dogs' jaws rip and tear at the beast's flesh.

One of the staghounds had seized the yearling bull by the throat while the other had sunk his teeth into the buffalo's shoulder as Custer reined in his horse to watch his pets try and pull the buffalo down. The dogs were snarling and tugging furiously, but the exhausted bull, its body radiating clouds of steam from its hide, managed to remain on his feet and tried to shake off the hound that held his throat. The yearling plunged its head repeatedly into the snow in an effort to either smother his tormentor in the drifts or crush him. Nate saw that Custer's smiling face suddenly turned serious, as if realizing that a situation he had initiated was now getting out of control. The general feared that his hounds were losing the initiative and were in danger of becoming injured or killed by the frantic yearling.

Custer finally leaped from his horse and pulled out a hunting knife. He ran clumsily in the snow toward where his dogs and the buffalo were struggling. When he arrived at the melee he quickly slashed the animal's hamstrings, forcing the beast to tumble into the snow. He then removed his revolver and shot the yearling in the head at point-blank range as his excited dogs tore at the carcass.

The spectacle over, the group of officers that were watching now turned their gaze toward Nate and Jesse who were standing still and mounted on their horses, a hundred yards away. One officer who had very long whiskers that fell past his shoulders beckoned them to approach. The two noncoms urged their horses forward and Nate felt relieved that he did not have to face the boy general, who at their last meeting looked at him and Jesse with contempt.

"You men with Penrose?" asked the officer with the long whiskers.

"Yes, sir!" Nate and Jesse saluted smartly and for a moment forgot how cold their feet were. "I am Sergeant Major Nate Gordon and this is First Sergeant Jesse Randolph, *Tenth Cavalry.*" Nate reached into his army greatcoat and retrieved an envelope. "I have dispatches for General Custer."

"I am Colonel William Cooke, commander of the Seventh

Cavalry's sharpshooters," he responded, taking the envelope.

A slight winter breeze blew by, lifting Cooke's long whiskers from his youthful cheeks and Nate was suddenly reminded of the Spanish moss hanging from thick oak branches blowing in the stagnant Louisiana air that he had seen for most of his life when he was a slave. Nate deduced that this officer, who was about the same age as him, and introduced himself as "Colonel," must have earned his brevet rank during the war because he wore lieutenant bars on his shoulders. He knew that those officers, who had served in the war and had attained high rank, were allowed to be addressed by their former titles. He also knew that promotion came quickly during the war, but was achieved at a price. Only through bravery and proven leadership could a soldier excel to high rank, and only through luck in not being killed was he able to keep it.

"Well, I think 'Ringlets' is too busy right now killing buffalo to read dispatches," quipped another officer wearing captain bars. Nate thought that this officer looked elderly and rather portly.

"I will remind you, Captain Benteen," snapped Cooke, giving him a scornful gaze, "that the commander of this expedition will be called by his wartime rank of general."

Captain Benteen was holding a curved pipe that had gone dead in his hand. He snickered at Cooke's comment and placed the pipe in his mouth.

"I will take the dispatches to the general, Sergeant Major." Cooke placed the envelope inside his greatcoat. He was about to spur his horse toward Custer when he saw that the general was making his way back to them at a canter. He had remounted his horse and his staghounds were following closely behind their master's horse's hooves. Nate noticed that they were panting heavily, exhausted by their efforts. One of the hounds, though, held a piece of meat in his mouth and as he came closer, Nate noticed that it was the yearling bull's liver.

"These men from the Tenth?" demanded Custer as he reined in his horse. The commanding officer's mount was a big black gelding in fine condition, and Nate noticed that all of the horses in the command appeared to be well fed and recently shod.

"Yes, General," replied Cooke as he handed the article to Custer. The general opened the envelope and removed the piece of paper. His pale blue eyes rapidly read what Penrose had written as the officers watched him in anticipation.

"Penrose is marooned at Palo Duro Creek," stated Custer dryly. He then turned to Nate. "Is it true that the Tenth is facing these dire circumstances as General Penrose describes in his dispatch?"

"Yes, General, the horses are dyin' like flies in a frost," replied Jesse, irritating Nate who resented that his friend had usurped the answer.

"What the first sergeant is trying to say, General, is that the com'and is in no condition to pursue the hostiles in an a'gressive way," explained Nate. He wanted to speak as clearly as possible but without divulging too many details of his regiment's sorry state.

"Have I not seen you before, Sergeant Major?" Custer looked into Nate's eyes searchingly. Nate's face was bearded as was his own, but it was not Nate's face or eyes that reminded the boy general that he had seen this big black sergeant major before. It was Nate's tall and athletic physique that forced Custer to search his memory.

"Yes, General. Last ye'r on the Fort Hays road," responded Nate smartly, looking straight into Custer's face. "You was with the scout, Medicine Bill Comstock." Nate paused and then looking at the hound that still carried the liver of the buffalo in his mouth, "An' with all du' respect, General, I bel'eve you had the same dawgs with you."

"Yes, yes, I recall. I remember that you knew Comstock and that I asked you about your fight with the Dog Men along the Saline," replied Custer, pleased with himself that he had remembered Nate in spite of his beard and that he was a man of color. The hero of Yellow Tavern was not an abolitionist but he prided himself in treating the Negro fairly, although he did not feel comfortable commanding them.

"Sir! This means that the Seventh will be alone in attacking the hostiles," cautioned Captain Benteen. "And we still do not know the size of their encampments, nor how many tribes are wintering in the Washita Valley."

"More glory for the Seventh then!" boasted Cooke as he turned his gaze toward Custer. The general smiled, and felt proud that the commander of his sharpshooters was confident of success.

"Indeed, Cooke!" acknowledged Custer. "It appears that we are to engage the enemy without the support of Penrose's Tenth." Custer was pleased with the news, and his face showed it. Nate noticed that several other officers were smiling as well. The general had secretly feared that either Carr's or Penrose's columns might strike a hot trail that led to the hostiles and engage them without the participation of the Seventh. Or, just as bad, he was concerned that his Seventh would have to share the glory of a victory with the participating regiments if they also engaged the enemy in the same battle. Now, with Carr's Fifth Cavalry roaming about aimlessly somewhere along the North Canadian, and Penrose's *"brunettes"* mangled because of the weather and a shortage of food and forage, Custer was reassured that his regiment alone would now locate the Cheyennes and surprise them.

Nate and Jesse felt a little humiliated by this overt display of enthusiasm shown by the officers of the Seventh. It was not their fault that the boys of the Tenth were stranded in deep snow with starving horses. All the men in his regiment had performed well under adverse conditions and were eager for a fight. What really vexed Nate, however, was that all of the Seventh Cavalry's horses appeared to be in excellent shape while their own mounts, with a few exceptions, were in poor condition when they had departed from Fort Lyon and were then hit by blizzards that crippled the column.

"Penrose does say that he will provide a screen against the hostiles if they should flee toward his direction," added Custer with some amusement. He folded the letter back into the envelope and placed the article in his inside pocket of his buckskin coat. "From now on, officers are forbidden to separate themselves from their commands to hunt game, and I want the column to move faster!"

"And the supply wagons? Shouldn't we wait for them, considering that we can't afford to be without forage for the horses?" asked Benteen. The question irritated Custer. He disliked Benteen's constant preaching of caution and regarded him as an obstacle to the regiment's esprit de corps.

"Order those lazy and overpaid teamsters to keep up with the command or I'll make them walk again!" Nate saw that Custer's face was animated with energy and impatience. "For the Seventh, gentlemen, will *press on*, with all haste." Custer yanked his reins to turn his animal toward the van of the column. He then spurred his black gelding to catch up with his Osage scouts, Little Beaver and Hard Rope.

IV.

Nate and Jesse shared a tent that was provided for them through the quartermaster sergeant. Custer did not wish to reply to Penrose's dispatches and decided that he would keep the two noncoms

Date due

December 19

Hudson Public Library

Please leave card as placed in item
for correct due date

50¢ fine if card is lost or defaced

568-9644

568-9644

50¢ fine if card is lost or defaced
for correct due date
Please leave card as placed in item

Hudson Public Library

June 21

Date due

Date due

September 20

Hudson Public Library

Please leave card as placed in item
for correct due date

50¢ fine if card is lost or defaced

568-9644

568-9644

50¢ fine if card is lost or defaced

for correct due date
Please leave card as placed in item

Hudson Public Library

March 23

Date due

for the duration of the expedition. He ordered that they attach themselves to Major Joel Elliott and make themselves useful. Nate wanted to return to the Tenth but Jesse was delighted at the prospect of accompanying the boy general and his well-supplied regiment. Although Jesse knew that Custer would most likely encounter the hostiles and that there was to be heavy fighting ahead, he decided it would be much better to be with Custer's well-fed outfit than return to his impoverished regiment where victuals were almost exhausted and forage nonexistent.

Nate wanted to make an entry into his journal but Custer had forbidden the troops to light any fires for fear of attracting attention to their location and alerting the hostiles. As he stared at the tent's ceiling he thought about Cara and felt depressed that he did not know when he would be reunited with her. As usual when he could not sleep and to avoid thinking about his beloved, he pondered about the past and the events that surrounded his escape from slavery and the perilous trip toward Kansas and freedom. He could still hear the deafening blare of the steam whistle from the paddle wheeler *Belle de Jour*, as if it were yesterday.

It was one of those sounds that had become part of him. The strain of the steam whistle represented his relationship with the octoroon gambler, Jacques Napoleon Gaches, and his escape on the Red River. Like the soothing words that his mother articulated when she spoke to him when he was young and in pain, or the bellowing of the nigger drivers to get to work in the fields, certain sounds would remind him of situations and events that had occurred during his life. The crack of the whip of the overseers was another sound that still made him jump when he would hear it used by teamsters or the rhythm and musical melodies of banjos and fiddles and twang of Jew's harps in the quarter on Saturday nights and Sundays.

Nate thought about the dramatic moment when Gaches returned back to his cabin and told him that his pursuers had caught up with him.

"They found me!" he exclaimed. Nate remembered that the gambler was sweating and his face showed great anxiety when he burst through the cabin door. The Creole's chest was heaving with effort, which explained the hurried footsteps that he had heard running down the upper cabin deck moments before.

"Who found you?" Nate had become so relaxed after his big supper that he had forgotten that his host was on the run from henchmen sent by creditors.

Gaches walked around the cabin as if he were a caged animal. His head was bowed in reflection and he was rubbing his hands as if they were cold. "I better tell you the whole story." The gambler halted his pacing and faced Nate. "I borrowed a rather large sum of cash from some unsavory individuals back in Natchitoches."

"Why you do that?" probed Nate. He did not understand the word "unsavory" but assumed that it meant that the individuals in question were bad men.

"I had an arrangement with some people who loaned me a rather large sum of greenbacks interest free!" Gaches raised his arm as if he were a preacher referring to the Almighty. "On condition that I would repay them in gold and silver."

"How was you goin' do that?"

"At the gambling table, my good man," responded the gambler as if surprised by Nate's question. "You see, I would enter card games where the players possessed gold and silver and who were willing to gamble with the metals."

"Why would these players risk losing their gold and silver in exchange for greenbacks?" Nate was puzzled by why an individual would gamble with precious metals while the other players would only risk losing currency.

"Because not everyone has gold or silver." Gaches's eyes were wild with anxiety because he was trying to think how he could lose his pursuers, and he was also growing impatient with Nate's simplistic questions. He was still pacing around the room, rubbing his hands in thought. "And cocky men with gold and silver," he continued, "*fresh from the mining fields in Colorado, are full of themselves,* and prefer to gamble with their precious metals. Other men gamble with gold and silver because they are paid that way, such as merchants and suppliers, and they like to gamble just like everyone else."

"Why don't you pay them with that pile of *Dix* notes you got?"

"They don't want *Dix* notes!" snapped Gaches.

"Why not, you tol' me that *Dix* notes are . . ."

"Not in New York!" stammered the Creole. "You see . . ." Gaches took a deep breath to calm down. He needed Nate's help with the tormentors that had boarded *Belle de Jour,* and becoming impatient was not going to solve his problems. "The men who loaned me the money want to leave the South and move to New York to escape the war and start new enterprises in the city. And they prefer to do this with gold."

"Why would you do that?" Nate thought that this arrangement sounded very risky for a loan that was only interest free.

"I stood to make a very tidy profit." Gaches's seductive smile had returned to his face and Nate could tell that the Creole had anticipated a hefty payoff at the gambling table. "The terms of the loan was that I would return the original loan amount in gold or silver and I would be free to take all of the profits above and beyond the original amount, as well as acquiring precious metals of my own." Gaches finally halted his frantic pacing and stood at the end of the table that occupied the center of the room. Nate watched him place his hands on the wooden surface, stretching his fingers. He then sighed and bowed his head for a moment, as if he were in prayer, and then raised it, looking into Nate's eyes. "For a while, my luck held and I not only covered my winnings into the metals but was making a handsome profit. The winnings were so good that I just kept playing and playing more and more games and making a killing."

"Well then? What happened?" inquired Nate, spellbound by Jacques Napoleon's story.

"I got into a poker game with an astute player. A rich gent from Vicksburg." Gaches shook his head in disbelief. "He took it all, and I never saw it coming."

"How could he have taken all of your gold and silver in one game?" Nate knew very little about professional high-stakes gambling. He had seen older men in the quarter gamble when he was a slave, but the stakes were modest and the men played for amusement rather than for material gain because everybody was poor.

"We sat down at the table at eight o'clock at night and there was five of us," explained Gaches. "We played for over twenty-four hours and consumed enough brandy and whiskey to float a horse! By noon the next day, there was only two of us remaining at the table, the other players had either lost their purses to us or did not have the stomach to continue. The remaining player besides myself was an elderly gentleman with fine manners. He was reserved and at first made basic mistakes and lost a lot of money. I thought he was not a professional like myself. But I was dead wrong." Gaches paused for a moment and grinned ruefully. "Appearances and first impressions can be deceiving." The Creole removed himself from the edge of the table and resumed his pacing.

Only he was more relaxed now, finding that confessing to Nate about how he had lost all of his winnings tranquilized him.

"Go on, whut happened?" urged Nate, who wanted to hear the end of the story.

"Well, there's not much more to tell, he baited me and I took the hook. At a little past noon, every single hand he had was better than mine. I kept hoping that my luck would turn, but it was not in the cards, so to speak."

"You think he was cheatin'?"

"If he was, I couldn't tell. He was good!" Gaches raised his eyebrows and nodded. "He was *real* good."

"Couldn't you get mo' time to pay off the loan?" asked Nate naively.

"I didn't even inquire. Word got out that I had lost most of my winnings, and the next thing I knew, my creditors hired a couple of brutes to either get it out of me—or kill me."

"Well, we could go back to the hole an' hide till dey get off de boat," offered Nate, although he was saddened that they would lose the comfortable cabin.

"And surrender our accommodations to hide like river rats?" Gaches also did not wish to return to the hot and crowded hole among the cotton bales near the bow of the boat. "Absolutely not, my friend. No, no. There must be another way."

"Whut else is there?" wondered Nate aloud. He thought that remaining in the cabin would only increase the chances of being discovered and Nate did not wish to tangle with these dangerous men. By returning to their previous hiding place, they could at least buy time while remaining secluded.

"No! I have a superior alternative." The gambler's face lit up as if he saw a revelation. "I will *disguise* myself and we will be able to go about our business, unmolested by those brutes."

"Disguise?" Nate thought it was not a bad idea, considering that he also had used various mild forms of physical deception to mask his fugitive state.

"Yes, my good man. I will alter my appearance and throw off my pursuers." Gaches paused for a moment and bit his lip. "The problem is what mode of deception should I adapt to conceal my true identity?"

"How 'bout some crutches and peelin' one of your legs behind the other so you only have one leg?" suggested Nate half seriously.

"Sounds too painful, my good man. And besides, I still intend to travel up the river in some kind of style. I am not going to let these two boors hound me." Gaches resumed his pacing around the cabin, circling the central table. "No! If I must be a cripple in order to appear convincing and throw the scent off those two dogs, I must be comfortable, and besides"—the gambler turned to face Nate—"we need to find a role for you to play, my good man. Like actors on a stage." Gaches raised his hand as if he were already performing. "We will perform convincingly and beguile the audience!" Gaches paused and suddenly snapped his fingers. His eyes showed that he was a man who appeared to have experienced an epiphany. "A wheelchair. Yes, of course, of course." He turned to Nate eagerly. "And you will be my servant, bodyguard, and companion who wheels me about." He placed his hand on Nate's forearm and smiled. "Yes, that is the perfect role for you, my good man. Why, with your bulk and brute strength, coal-black skin, and huge hands, you fit the role ideally."

Nate was trying to digest this plan. It was bold, yet simple, and he agreed with the octoroon's idea that he should have a role to play to cover his own fugitive condition.

When Red River Sam entered the cabin to collect the eating utensils that he had left earlier, and the remains of Nate's repast, Gaches instructed him to bring him the following items: some white hair powder, base for the face, eye shadow sticks, and a wheelchair.

"How I's goin' git me some of dese female t'ings?" asked Red River Sam. The sultry old river hand was irritated that Jacques Napoleon Gaches was now making fresh demands on his services. "And wher' in Gawd's name is I goin' fin' me a *wheelchair*?"

The Creole gambler removed his huge wad of elaborately designed *Dix* notes and peeled several of the bills and handed them to Red River Sam. The old man stared at the big bills, admiring the intricate detail on the front face of the note. The top half had a picture of a oceangoing steamer that pleased him very much. When the old Negro went to take the two notes, however, Gaches held on to them and looked him in the eyes and smiled. "Steal those articles, old man, steal them and bring them to me and I will further reward your efforts."

"We'll find that goddamn octoroon on this floating tub, or my name is not Simon Fury," boasted the man with the cane to his associate, Vincent Clemente.

"My money is that he's playing possum," responded Clemente, downing a shot of rye. The hired henchmen were standing at the bar drinking. Earlier in the evening, when they had boarded *Belle de Jour* they had visited the captain and his apprentice in the pilothouse.

The river pilot, a big man with a long waxed dark mustache, possessed a no-nonsense type of attitude. The master of the vessel was in the middle of barking orders to his intimidated hands for the steamer to move away from the landing as beads of sweat poured down from the inside rim of his dirty white cap. The perspiration formed rivers of water against his forehead that trickled down his face and onto his long waxed mustache that dripped beads of water onto the floorboards. He wore his blue linen frock coat loosely and kept the garment open; the article was heavily stained around the armpits and collar with old salt crystals.

His apprentice, a young lad wearing a cap and who had blond curly hair and gentle eyes, appeared intimidated by his master's loud voice and gruff manner. He was gripping the immense wheel with great effort because he was short and could barely look out of the open window of the pilothouse.

"You there!" bellowed the master of *Belle de Jour* to one of the hands. "Push that buoy on the starboard side before I tan your hide!" he commanded, pointing to the object in question. He then looked at his young novice and commented contemptuously, "I swear that boy was born to hang."

The two henchmen stood at the entrance of the pilothouse waiting for the river man to finish giving orders. They saw that he was very occupied with his responsibilities and even Simon Fury saw that he was not a man to trifle with while performing his duties. Satisfied that the paddle wheeler was moving away from the landing nicely, the pilot turned to the novice.

"Boy! Let the bastard blow." The apprentice smiled delightfully as though he were a child that was just offered a peppermint stick. The gleeful lad pulled the cord that released the steam from the whistle, startling the two henchmen and causing them to jump. Both the pilot and the novice roared with laughter, amused that the blast had frightened the uninvited visitors out of their wits.

"You know you're not supposed to be here," bristled the pilot, taking a handkerchief from his waistcoat pocket to wipe the perspiration that still poured from his scalp from his face. He was incensed that these two uninvited individuals had the audacity to linger about while he was trying to get the steamer on its way upriver.

Simon Fury took a step forward toward the entranceway of

the pilothouse. "We apologize for the intrusion, Captain, but we are searching for a fugitive."

"Y'all the law?" interrupted the pilot, irritated at the insolence of these two men.

"Well, no, sir, we have been hired to find an octoroon who owes our employers a great deal of money," responded Vincent Clemente with a sense of righteousness.

"If you ain't the law, 'tis none of my concern," retorted the pilot. He then turned his attention to his apprentice who was striving to hold the giant wheel and peer out of the visor. "Look for the safe water, boy!" he ordered. "Look for the safe water. And for God's sake watch out for river debris." He further instructed the novice, concerned that the apprentice would either run aground on the treacherous Red River or damage the vessel if he failed to see floating trees and branches that lurked just beneath the surface of the water.

The pilot leered at the two men with contempt. "If ya'll ain't the law, then you gots no bizness standing here, and I consider your presence here as an in-trusion."

"Captain, if you help us find this man of color"—Simon Fury nervously turned the silver handle of his cane in the palm of his hand causing the sharp tip to rotate against the floorboards—"my employers would be generous in compensating you for your efforts."

The pilot gaped in horror at the cane's rotating silver tip that was digging into the deck boards of his beloved *Belle de Jour*. It was not so much that this act was unusual, lots of passengers possessed walking canes and frequently used them to dig into the deck boards or bang on the hog chains or pound on the bar for service, what infuriated him was the man's unabashed rudeness.

"How dare you offer me money to assist you in your sordid task!" scorned the pilot. "And kindly remove your backsides from these premises immediately, before I have my boys throw you in the river and you can hitch a ride with the gators, as far as I'm concerned."

The two henchmen stared at the pilot in disbelief. They were under the impression that with an offer to compensate the master of the boat that they would get all the assistance they needed in locating Jacques Napoleon Gaches. Without his cooperation, finding the octoroon gambler would be more difficult and they would have to proceed with caution if they wished to avoid irritating the pilot.

"Well then, sir," said Simon Fury humbly, trying to soothe the pilot's attitude. Although thoroughly rebuked by the master of *Belle de Jour,* he needed to make amends if they were going to find their fugitive on his boat. "We apologize for disturbing you, sir." Clemente bit his lip. "We only desire passage on your boat and we will abide by the rules as passengers."

"You think I'm a goddamn fool?" roared the pilot, his face reddening with anger. "I know the type of men you are . . . *bunch of shit beetles,* that's what you all are!"

"Captain, I protest!" snapped Simon Fury who was also becoming mad at the man's insults and uncooperative behavior. They had been polite and had offered compensation. There was no reason why he should be rude, even if he was the master of the sternwheeler.

"Don't call me captain, sir. I will be addressed as pilot," chastised the river man as he waved his index finger at them. "And if you wish to make arrangements for your passage, you will have to see the purser." The pilot cast one eye on the novice's tiny hands that held the big steering wheel as he nervously peered out of the open window at the river. "Watch out for that barge up ahead, boy. Only a drunk would steer like that." He stuck his head out of the door and hollered, "Goddamn river hog!"

"Yes, Pilot," responded the novice softly.

"Good, boy. Good!" complimented the pilot, gently placing his large weathered hand on the boy's shoulder.

Castigated and humbled, the two henchmen left the doorway of the pilothouse and made their way toward the passenger deck in search of the purser to secure accommodations on *Belle de Jour*.

Nate was watching Jacques Napoleon Gaches apply makeup on his head and face. They were seated at the central table and the gambler was working on his disguise with the expertise of a seasoned actor. First, he rubbed his face with base and added some soot that Red River Sam had brought him from the boiler room to darken his face. He then put a thin layer of soot to his face, making him look blacker but at the same time ashen. Satisfied that his face was properly disguised, he liberally poured white powder on his scalp, eyebrows, and side facial hairs and worked the ingredient into the hairs to make him look decades older. To add detail to his face, Gaches delicately used a grease pencil to draw several thin but pronounced lines across his forehead and shaded the area beneath his eyes with more soot. He also added half a dozen moles on his cheeks, forehead, and neck, giving his head an unsightly appearance, so people would not stare at him except, perhaps, nosy children. This particular process made Nate's face cringe. He watched the gambler lie down on the bed and coolly hold a match to the wax stick and melt away globs of the hot material onto his smooth skin to form tiny mountains. Gaches would then color them with soot to darken the wax. The effect had the desired results. The man looked a half century older with bad skin.

"Well? Do you think that I look like an old decrepit black man?" asked Gaches as he looked into a shaving mirror admiring his handiwork.

"You sure look old, that's for sure," confirmed Nate.

Red River Sam entered the cabin pushing a deep-seated wicker chair with rickety wheels. "Don't axs where I found this t'ing, 'cause whut I done was not Christian."

Jacques Napoleon Gaches gazed at the contraption and although he was disappointed that the chair was not more elegant, he smiled at the prospect of being wheeled around on the boat by Nate, saluting passengers.

"Well, this will just have to do." He looked at Nate and added in his typical theatrical manner, "I look forward to you wheeling me around in comfort among the gambling tables."

Nate winced. Being this man's servant was not what bothered him, but he was a little put off by the gambler's ceaseless sense of self-importance.

"Now, there is one small detail that we must attend to in order to complete this little masquerade."

Nate rolled his eyes and wondered, *Whut could he want now?*

Gaches pulled a thick envelope from inside his breast pocket and removed some papers that were attached together. "These documents, my friend, are almost better than money. Do you know what they might be?"

"May I read them?"

Gaches was surprised by this request. "Certainly." He handed the documents over to Nate. "Be my guest, but I don't think you will get very far."

Nate spread the documents on the table and glanced at the forms. "Why, these are manumission papers. I neva seen these before."

"I am in awe, my good man. I did not know you could read."

"I can write too," Nate added with gusto. He loved to tell people that he could read and write.

Gaches was genuinely impressed. It was the last thing he had expected considering that he knew that Nate was a runaway field slave and not a house nigger. His curiosity was now stimulated and he became interested on how this coal-black giant, although handsome and possessing intelligence and quickness of mind, could be literate. Nevertheless, he was reassured that his decision to include Nate as part of his plot to elude his pursuers was a smart move and that this man had many talents that could be of use to him.

"Now, do you know what manumission means?" Gaches felt as if he was the teacher educating the student.

"Means freedom!" retorted Nate. "My mother, she tol' me that it means freedom from bondage."

"Your mother?" Gaches hesitated for a moment. He did not want to make a faux pas regarding Nate's mother. "Is she the one who taught you how to read and write?"

"Yes," responded Nate demurely.

"Manumission does mean freedom, my good man, but based on Southern slavery law there are many interpretations regarding what the word really means for the particular individual. In my individual case, for example, I was released upon the death of my master who was also my father."

Nate was reminded of his half sister, the child that his mother was forced to give birth to because she was raped by Bloodhound Jack. *Well,* he thought, *we share something in common after all— Mister Ruffled Shirt.*

"You the house boy? That's where you got all of your fancy manners and high talk?"

"In a way, yes," Gaches responded calmly as looked in the mirror and added a few more touches of grease pencil to his face and around the eyes. "But I was much, much more than just a *house nigger*, my good man. Oh, much more than that. You see, my mother was a mulatto and my father, the great master of this plantation, loved her dearly because his first wife died from yellow fever and his only white son was killed in the war with Mexico. So I became his son and heir."

"If you is heir why you on the run?"

"It's called Southern justice and let us leave it at that." Gaches wanted to terminate this line of discussion and regretted that maybe he had revealed too much of himself to Nate. He preferred to be incognito and retain an aura of mystery about himself. "*Now*. Regarding that last detail that needs to be done. See the date on the document where it says when I was born and when I was manumissioned?"

Nate's eyes searched the text for the dates and located them near the top of the page. "Says here that you were born in 1840 and that you were manumissioned in 1859."

"In order to give credence to our little masquerade in case we are questioned, I will have to show that I was born at least in 1790 and manumissioned—oh, let us say, no later than 1830," explained Gaches. "So, place the documents on the table and I will show you something."

Nate compiled and Gaches melted a tiny bit of wax on the dates and waited until it was dry. He then took a quill pen and slowly rewrote the dates of his birth and manumission. He held the papers in the air and examined his forgery. Pleased that the dates looked authentic enough, he theatrically pronounced to Nate, "Now, my good man, my disguise is complete."

Two

NORTH BANK OF THE CANADIAN RIVER
NOVEMBER 26.

Jesse was sitting on a hardtack crate munching on a frozen biscuit and on some cold salt pork while Nate was checking the cinch of his saddle as he watched John Brown draw straw to his hungry mouth. The early morning air was very cold and every time man and beast breathed, huge clouds of hot air would emerge from their nostrils and mouths. Custer had ordered no campfires so there was no coffee or anything warm to put in the troopers' bellies.

All the cavalrymen spent the days obsessing with keeping warm. The soldiers stomped their feet and rubbed their hands to keep from getting frostbite. Nate saw one officer remove his gauntlets and cup his hands around his stallion's scrotum. The huge beast neighed and recoiled in shock because his master's hands were so cold. The officer managed to quiet the stallion sufficiently for him to resume warming his hands on his horse's balls.

"Now, I've seen ever'thin'," commented Nate under his breath as he watched the officer's face crack a gratifying grin as he felt the heat of his stallion's privates on his palms and fingers.

A young lieutenant was walking toward Nate and Jesse in a hurry. He was breathing heavily and huge clouds of his breath filled the area in front of him.

"You men are to go with us," he instructed. "Major Elliott has been ordered to take three troops and march up the Canadian to see if we can strike a trail that will lead us to the hostile camps. You are to draw from the quartermaster sergeant one hundred rounds of ammunition and forage and food for one day."

"Beggin' the lootenant's pardon—is the jineral goin' to divide the column?" inquired Jesse nervously.

The young officer glared at Jesse and Nate knew what the man was thinking. "Sergeant, I am trying to give you the benefit of the doubt that you earned those stripes. Don't make me question your rank by asking questions that do not concern you! You are to follow orders. Is that clear, First Sergeant?"

"Suh! Yes, suh," replied Jesse, coming to attention as his face became flush with embarrassment. "The first sergeant understands."

"I want you men to ride in the rear where you will be less conspicuous. Is that clear?" The brash young officer briefly looked at Jesse and Nate with contempt, then turned on his heels and marched off to where Major Elliott's three companies were forming up in column of twos.

Nate gave Jesse a disapproving look. "Should have held your tongue, boy, 'stead of workin' it so now we's at the tail end of this column where we can be picked off by Dog Men."

It did not really bother Nate that they were now placed in the rear. He had half expected it anyway. *Where else would a white regiment place two uninvited black soldiers even if they were in the same army?* he asked himself. Nate just wanted to remind Jesse not to ask stupid questions or speak when not spoken to if you wanted to stay out of trouble.

As Nate and Jesse took their places at the rear of Elliott's small flying column, the major, the scout Corbin, and the brash lieutenant trotted past them. When Major Elliott saw that the two men at the tail end of the column were black, he halted his horse.

"Were you men with Colonel Armes at the Battle of the Beaver last year?" Elliott's horse's right hoof was digging at the snow anxiously and pulling down on the bit.

"Yes, sir, Major," replied Nate sharply, pleased that the commanding officer would pay them the time of day.

Nate briefly glanced at Jesse who remained very quiet, still reeling from the earlier chastisement he had received from the young lieutenant.

"I heard that was a damn good fight!" Elliott's horse continued to be unruly and he had to smack the animal along the side of its head and tell the brute to behave.

"Yes, sir, the boys showed real promise, sir."

"I also heard that if it wasn't for you boys from the Tenth, those Kansas Volunteers would have been *wiped out.*"

"Yes, sir. The boys fought well, sir." Nate liked this officer. His face was handsome and his eyes sharp. His dirty blond hair protruded from the crown of his kepi, and he wore a pair of groomed lambchops and mustache whiskers. Nate sensed that Elliott possessed an aggressive air about him and perhaps he might be a reckless sort, but his tone of voice, however, was not boisterous or patronizing like Custer's. He also noticed that the man had an amiable temperament and seemed popular among the men of the Seventh.

"Well, nothing like real soldiers, eh, Sergeant Major?" boasted Elliott with a smile.

"No, sir, not like real cavalry, sir," replied Nate enthusiastically, enjoying the moment with a senior officer in front of white troops. He noticed that some of them turned in their saddles to see who their commanding officer was talking to, and several troopers' faces revealed astonished expressions upon seeing their commanding officer chitchatting with a Negro.

Elliott became silent for a moment as his horse continued to prance around in the snow and exhale great clouds of hot air.

"I want you two noncoms up front with the scout. Most of my boys never seen Indians before and I need experienced men in the van of the column where you can be of use to me."

"Yes, sir," replied Nate and Jesse simultaneously. Nate was pleased with this show of confidence in front of the white troops and certainly in front of the young lieutenant who had chastised Jesse earlier and who now shifted anxiously in his McClellan.

Major Elliott's command of three companies started to move and Nate thought that the sounds of the shod horses' hooves against the snow was so loud that if there were hostile scouts nearby, they could certainly pick their movements.

As they advanced along the Canadian, the day became increasingly cloudy and made the grim landscape even more foreboding. There were many tracks in the snow: small game, bison, deer, and elk but no signs of any pony tracks. All the men were suffering from the cold and many of the troopers would place one foot at a time on the saddle and try to rub their toes through the cold leather. Others would remove their gauntlets and place their freezing fingers in their mouths to warm them. The column halted for their noon repast of hardtack and Elliott ordered that the men give their horses a good feed but no fires were permitted so the men had nothing warm in their bellies, much to Jesse's consternation.

Shortly after Elliott had ordered the three companies to mount and advance did the scout Corbin come trotting back. He had exempted himself from eating or resting his horse and had proceeded ahead of the troopers, hoping to locate pony tracks. He was successful.

"I figur' dare's 'bout a hundred to hundred fifty warriors frum the tracks I saw, Major. And not twenty-four hours old!" Nate overheard Corbin explain to Elliott.

"What makes you think that it was a war party?" asked Elliott skeptically. The major found it hard to believe that a hostile warrior party would be out in this kind of weather.

" 'Cause, Major"—the scout hurriedly looked about for a moment and saw a small patch of snow to his right. Satisfied on the location, he then hurled a dark wad of spent tobacco that was lodged in his right cheek into the patch of virgin snow—"no dawgs. I didn't see any tracks in the snow or mud that tol' me that this party of bucks had dawgs."

"What in creation does that mean?" scoffed Elliott, perplexed at the scout's assessment. He reasoned that if the regiment had many dogs following the column including Custer's two hounds, why not the Indians?

"It means, Major"—Corbin bowed his head and picked at his front tooth with the thumbnail of his right hand to dislodge a piece of tobacco that was caught in between two front teeth—"that dogs don't run with no war party."

Major Elliott reflected for a moment and concurred that the scout's observations made perfect sense.

"How far do you think their camp is?" he asked eagerly. His orders from Custer were to strike the trail and pursue with all haste while sending word back to Custer as to the nature of the trail. The general would then catch up with Elliott and intercept the hostiles.

"Corbin," beckoned Elliott, straightening his frame in the saddle, "you are to inform the general that we have located the trail, inform him of its nature and how many warriors you think are in advance of us. Tell Custer that I await his orders." The scout listened attentively as Elliott spoke, and the major thought that he might not be digesting all of his instructions. "Are you clear on all of this, Corbin?"

"Yes, sir, Major. I'll tell him." he replied, taking a fresh pinch of tobacco and placing it to the side of his mouth. He tipped his hat and turned his horse around and moved at a fast canter toward Custer and the bulk of the regiment.

Major Elliott ordered his three companies to dismount and await the orders from Custer. Nate saw this as an opportunity to make an entry in his journal.

> Jesse and me are bivouacked on the upper banks of the Canadian River with three companies of the Seventh Cavalry. We are waiting orders from General Custer as to if we should pursue the trail that the scout Corbin located, or remain here until the general arrives with the rest of the Seventh.
>
> We are with Major Joel Elliott in pursuit of hostiles and my impressions of this man are that he is a good officer and a gentleman and seems to care about his men.
>
> I expect that we will run into hostiles tomorrow. I feel that we are close to their camps and I pray I do not run into Cougar Eyes or we attack his village. The Seventh is a good regiment. Far better equipped than we are. They have better horses, clothes, forage, and food for themselves. But I have seen nothing in these white men that would make them any better than the boys from the Tenth. Fact, I feel that these boys from the Seventh are young, inexperienced, and surly! Think I rather be with the "brunettes" instead of riding with greenhorns. Maybe Cook's sharpshooters are worth

something, but the rest of the regiment sure seems to be average.

I think of Cara most of the day when I am in the saddle. Nothing has changed in my heart and I hope all is well with her and our unborn child.

II.

"Half-breed bitch! I—I—I ow-owe-*own you*, damn it!" bellowed Silas Quinn as he threw a small cast-iron skillet at Cara who was cowering in the corner of the wretched one-room mining shack. "You—you—you had e-e-enough time. I—I—I be-been go-goo-*good* to you!"

They had arrived at the South Pass, Wyoming, mining camps a few days earlier after the long and arduous trip from Dodge. Fortunately, the weather had been mild in southern Wyoming for this time of year making the voyage tolerable. Quinn had not really spoken to Cara during the trip except when he gave orders to prepare meals or help arrange the camp in the evening. Even at night when they were together in his tiny makeshift canvas tent, he left her alone while he snored loudly. He did, however, upon Vasco's advice, tie her hands and feet with strips of leather with a harness bell around her neck, so if she moved about too much he would hear it.

Quinn's shack was located at the base of a large hill near a stream where miners panned for gold. His claim was upstream and quite isolated from the other mining shacks, tents, and dugouts that scarred the landscape. Cara was one of the few women in camp and probably the only one who was not a whore. Consequently, Quinn wanted to keep her presence a secret from the other miners who if they discovered her existence would pose a threat.

Now Quinn was coming for her to satisfy his lust. He believed that he really owned her and that he had given her sufficient time to become adjusted to his presence. As far as the grizzled miner was concerned, he had been courteous and patient. Now, he wanted what was his, and he wanted it now. He removed his mud-caked boots and filthy overalls and was in the process of unbuttoning his long underwear when Cara seized a small kitchen knife that was resting on a small table where some dead birds were bunched together.

"Animal! No te acerques!" Her eyes had become aflame with hate and fear. *"Eres un cerdo miserable!"* she threatened, holding the blade toward her antagonist. "I'll cut you, I swear it!" she added, in her thick half-Mexican half-Comanche accent.

"Wi-with th-th-that?" scoffed Quinn as he hideously grinned at Cara, her back against the corner holding the tiny kitchen knife.

"Yo pertenezco a otro! I belong to another," she pleaded. "I am with child!"

"To hell you do! And the hell with your bastard child! I—I bought you! In gold—*d'Oro, sabes*?"

The miner, his buttons undone past his navel, lunged at Cara and attempted to seize the knife, but she moved quickly and as he flew by her, she slashed his face and ran toward the front door. Silas Quinn felt the blood run down his face and became enraged. He ran toward the door where Cara had opened it and was about to bolt for the outside when Quinn grabbed one of her ponytails and slammed her onto the hard dirt floor of the cabin. She still held the knife but had hit her head so violently on the surface that she blacked out and Quinn easily pried her fingers loose, one at a time, and retrieved the blade.

He then started to beat her. First slapping her face, and then after he felt the cut on his face and realized that it was deep and needed stitching, resorted to using his fists to punch her arms and kick her legs.

"You ga-ga-got to-to learn to *mind* me!" he kept hollering in between striking Cara's tiny body.

Cara managed to place her body in a fetal position so she could at least reduce the impact of the blows and protect her womb. After a few minutes, Quinn became exhausted and had to rest. His sexual urge, however, was increased by the thrill of the beating. He felt that he now showed her who was the master and that the slave should obey. He pulled down his long johns and went over to Cara. Quinn thought she looked lifeless and kicked her to see if she would move. She groaned and moved her left leg a little and that made the miner smile.

"Go-goo-good. I—I—I was ho-ho-hopin' da-dat I did—did— didn't damage the goods. He then took the kitchen knife and placed the blade at the hem of Cara's doeskin dress and starting cutting the soft hide as if it were a burlap bag. "Yo'r—you're goin' like it, girlie, ju-ju-just *you* wait!"

III.

Nate had just given John Brown some hay when the scout Corbin rode up at a gallop, his horse kicking up dirt and snow. He galloped right up to Major Elliott who was standing near his horse talking with some young officers. The commander's eyes were filled with anticipation. He was pretty sure what the boy general was going to order him to do. Elliott believed that there was never very much imagination in Custer's plan of attack. His strategy usually entailed speed, surprise, and luck.

Corbin reined in his mustang and reached for the dispatch within his coat and handed it over to Elliott.

Elliott read the instructions carefully and then looked at his officers. "It is what I had expected. Gentlemen, we are to pursue the trail until eight o'clock this evening and await his arrival with the rest of the regiment unless he catches up with us."

"Sir, suppose we run into hostiles and Custer has not caught up?" asked a shavetail lieutenant nervously. This was the same officer who had chastised Jesse earlier, and he was still rubbing his hands and stomping his feet to keep his fingers and toes from freezing.

"Well, I certainly do not intend to attack the hostiles without orders or support, Lieutenant. If we run into hostiles we will seek a holding action." Elliott folded the dispatch and gave it to his adjutant.

"Have the men mount up, Lieutenant, and let's move before we freeze to death here."

The order was quietly given to the companies and the troopers quickly got on their mounts and formed a column of twos. The order was for the three troops to walk their horses to allow Custer time to link up and also spare the animals undue exertion. They followed the trail that was made by unshod Indian ponies, and Elliott increasingly believed that the trail must lead to the hostile village. Although daylight was rapidly disappearing, the late November evening gave way to a rather effulgent dusk, and soon the moon came out, enabling the scout Corbin to continue his tracking. At eight o'clock sharp, Major Elliott ordered the command to halt and bivouac. The major knew that the Washita River was nearby and assumed that if there were hostiles located in the valley it would be along the banks of the river and decided to wait for Custer.

Nate and Jesse were near their horses as they watched them eat what was left of the forage that had been allocated to them. Nate had his pipe in between his teeth but the bowl was not lit.

No fires were permitted and that also included pipes and cigars. They spoke in a whisper as most of the men did.

"I'm so damn cold," complained Jesse as he stomped his feet in the crusty snow.

"You makin' a lot of noise by stompin' 'round," admonished Nate. "You likely to bring that lootenant ov'r here an' git 'nother tongue-lashin'."

"Damn his white hide," cursed Jesse, raising his voice a little. "He makin' mo' racket with his stompin' an' clappin' hands to keep frum freezin' than I."

"Here comes the *boy wonder* now," whispered Nate as he slipped the reins of the bridle in between his hands back and forth to create friction to keep his fingers from becoming incapacitated by the cold. With the exception of the general himself and some of the senior officers, he was the warmest man in the outfit. Thanks to Cougar Eyes' generous gift, he perspired when he had the buffalo robe tightly wrapped around his body. His feet and hands, however, remained clad in regulation cavalry boots and gauntlets, and as a result, his extremities were threatened by frostbite.

Custer was at the head of the column with his Osage scouts Hard Rope and Little Beaver. The column moved at a canter and in good order. Nate noticed that regardless of the adverse ground conditions, the troopers moved at an orderly clip, and there were no stragglers. Nate took note that the wagon train was still very much in the rear, and thought that was where California Joe must be.

Nate and Jesse had distanced themselves from Elliott and his officers after the major had ordered a halt. With the arrival of Custer and the rest of the Seventh, Nate wanted to be close by to hear the conversation among the officers.

"Let's git a little closer in." Nate led John Brown by his reins and Jesse followed with his mount Cailloux. They were within ear range and Nate told Jesse to look busy.

Major Elliott pulled out his pocket watch and clicked the lid of the timepiece open and became dismayed to see the glass surface had frosted over. He breathed some warm air over the glass and rubbed the surface, clearing away the frost.

"Almost nine o'clock," he remarked to his junior officers who were milling around him and wanted to be present when Custer appeared. "Looks like he made good time."

The boy general was chafing. "Have you seen the hostiles?"

"No, sir. We proceeded to track the Indian pony trail, but we found no signs of any hostiles."

"Why did you order a halt at this location?" he demanded.

Elliott snapped back, "General, your orders were to halt by eight o'clock if you did not catch up with us."

Custer looked into his eyes. "Well! We would have caught up with you but the melting snow slowed the column." He then dismounted and started to look about. He was about to tell something to Major Elliott when Hard Rope came up. His blanket was wrapped tightly against his body while cradling his army-issued Sharps carbine. He was wearing a well-worn silk top hat that Nate thought looked ridiculous and out of place. Nate was coming around to believe that the Osage scouts had none of the dignity or fighting prowess of the Cheyennes and he was disturbed that a red brother would so readily sell out his brethren to the white man. He was reminded of those freed blacks in Louisiana who owned slaves of their own, or those who worked with the slave catchers to bring in runaways.

"Me smell fire," said Hard Rope, raising his head.

Custer and some of the officers started to sniff the air as if they were hounds seeking a scent. "I don't smell anything," said the general, dismissing Hard Rope's instincts.

"Nor do I, General," said another officer. W. W. Cook had just come onto the scene and Nate noticed that his long whiskers were caked with ice.

"No! Me right. Me smell fire," insisted Hard Rope. "Camp not far." Custer's eyes lit up as if he were a little boy that was given permission to go to the state fair.

"How far?" he demanded.

"Not far," replied Hard Rope.

"Can you find the camp?" Custer was becoming impatient with the Osage's cryptic replies. Hard Rope then motioned for the general to follow him. Custer obliged him and told the rest of his staff and the other scouts to remain behind. They wandered off in silence together for some distance in the moonlight toward the Washita and after a while Custer was beginning to become tired of walking. He was about to make a comment about returning to the column when Hard Rope stopped suddenly and pointed to the earth. Custer gazed at the ground and noticed that a fire had been made. "Me told you so!" quipped the Osage scout smugly.

Custer squatted on his haunches and touched one of the two remaining pieces of burnt wood. "Still warm," he commented. He then looked around and saw that the ground was heavily marked with signs that a sizable Indian pony herd had been recently grazing, and that the fire must have been made to keep the boys that looked after the pony herd warm. All of a sudden, Custer heard a dog bark in the near distance and then a bell jingle that he knew was probably attached to the neck of a wandering Indian pony.

"We've found them!" he whispered, looking at the Osage scout for confirmation.

Hard Rope nodded, and then the sounds of a baby crying in the direction of where they heard the barking dog and the pony with the jingling bell could be discerned. Custer's mind was made up.

"Return to the column."

When Custer returned to the regiment, the wagon train had just caught up and as Nate suspected, California Joe and Romeo were bringing up the rear. The old scout was cursing at the livestock that had problems moving in the snow as his dog nipped and growled at some of the steers.

All of the senior officers were present waiting for their leader to return from reconnoitering with the Osage scout. The officers were huddled together to ward off the cold, watching Custer walk back as wind gusts blew the little capes on their army greatcoats revealing the yellow lining.

Present were Colonels Myers and Thompson, Major Elliott, Captains Weir, Barnitz, and Benteen, and the general's brother, Captain Tom Custer, a professional soldier and Civil War veteran who held more decorations for bravery than his brother. Also present were Lieutenants W. W. Cook and Louis Hamilton. As he walked back, the general's head was bowed as if in thought.

"The hostiles are about a mile or so away, toward the Washita," he explained as he approached the group. His full beard had streaks of frost, but he seemed to be impervious to the cold. He was never seen stomping his feet or rubbing his hands to keep warm. The general's baby-blue eyes were alive with excitement.

"I have decided to divide the regiment into four attacking columns and surround the village at dawn."

"Do we know their strength and the number of villages?" inquired Captain Benteen, removing his cold clay pipe from his mouth. Benteen's tone of voice sounded as if he was questioning his commanding officer's intelligence and W. W. Cook cringed when he heard Benteen's patronizing question. He knew that Custer would view this as a challenge to his authority and judgment.

"The Seventh Cavalry is eight hundred strong, Mr. Benteen. We can handle anything," retorted the general as his blue eyes leered at Benteen who finally lowered his gaze and placed his pipe back into his mouth.

"The regiment will deploy in three separate detachments. Major Elliott will take Companies G, H, and M and swing to the far left of the village as far to the rear as possible. Colonel Thompson, you will take Companies B and K and swing to the right and you, Colonel Myers, will take E and I and support Major Elliott toward the center of the village on the left. I will take Companies A, C, D, and the remaining troopers from Company K, as well as Cook's forty sharpshooters, the Osage scouts, and Lieutenant Hamilton, and make the initial frontal attack. Gentlemen, we attack the hostiles at dawn and we will catch them asleep in their warm lodges. Major Elliott, Colonel Myers! I suggest that you move out immediately, so you can be in place at first light. You, Colonel Thompson, I suggest you move out in two hours."

Nate saw that the hero of Yellow Tavern's eyes were alive with excitement at the prospect of the attack. Nate remembered seeing eyes like that before, during the war, when young officers, especially the ones filled with noble ideals, would be overjoyed in learning that they were going to enter a fight! They would lead the charge and usually were the first ones killed.

"Oh, gentlemen!" The officers had started to disperse to return to their respective commands when Custer called them back. "Spare the women and children if possible, I don't want atrocities committed here. Is that understood? This is a *United States Army* operation. We are not undisciplined militia rabble."

Some of the officers nodded affirmatively while others remained indifferent in their expressions. Nate knew that this last order could not be enforced. Restraining men whose hearts were filled with rage in the heat of battle was almost impossible, unless you start shooting them on the spot. During the war, he had seen many of his brethren murdered and mutilated because of the color of their skin after they had surrendered to the Rebs. Nate's beliefs were also supported by the discussions he had with Cougar Eyes, and he remembered what the Dog Man had told him regarding the murder of most of his family at Sand Creek four years earlier. As recently as last year, Nate had seen with his own eyes the ghoulish plundering of Indian burial scaffolding by white troopers and officers and the lifting of scalps by some of his own men.

"General?" asked Major Elliott. "What is the signal for the attack to commence?"

Custer smiled and was delighted that the major had asked this particular question. "I will order the band to strike up "Garry Owen," and charge the village."

Several of the officers, such as the general's brother, Captain Tom Custer and Captain Thomas Weir and Lieutenants Louis Hamilton and W. W. Cook, smiled with delight at the prospect of assaulting the village to the tune of the regimental song. Other officers, however, such as Captains Benteen and Barnitz, and even Major Elliott, remained silent. Benteen's face more than the others revealed an expression of distaste at such hubris.

IV.

Nate and Jesse were ordered to accompany Major Elliott in his attack at the end of the village. Before they had mounted, however, they were close enough to overhear Custer and California Joe who was with the Osage scouts and Romeo converse. Custer went up to the group and addressed them. The commanding officer wanted to be reassured by the seasoned scouts that the upcoming battle would be successful. He had heard that the Osage scouts had no confidence in the Seventh's ability to attack an unreconnoitered village, and some of them voiced concern that if the regiment should face imminent disaster they would sacrifice them without hesitation.

"So? Any thoughts on tomorrow's fight?" asked the boy general. Nate sensed that Custer, although oozing exuberance and confidence, had the tone of a man who was unsure of his next move.

"Fight?" bellowed California Joe. He was sober although his clothes and body still reeked. His dog was by his side and his mule was nudging him from behind, demanding to be fed. "Hell, Jineral! Ther's no doubt concernin' dat bit of the bizness!" The grizzled scout scratched his beard and Nate could hear his filthy fingers run through the thick facial hair. "Whut I've been tryin' to figur' out is like whut I said before, Jineral, supposin' we run into more than we bargain fur?"

"Then you do not think the hostiles will flee, Joe?" Custer was still obsessing that the Indians might "skedaddle."

"Skedaddle?" California Joe stopped scratching at his beard and gawked at Custer in amazement. "How in God's creation can Injuns fly the coop when we gots dem surrounded 'fore dawn?"

"Well then," Custer wanted to pursue another line of questioning, "suppose we are successful in surrounding the hostiles— do you think we can hold our own?" Nate was surprised to hear this question. *What happened to the boy wonder's confidence in his lucky star?* he pondered.

"Ifs we gets the jump on these Injuns at dawn, we're goin' make a spoon or spile a horn, an' dates fer sur'." California Joe chuckled and resumed scratching his beard as his dog placed his left leg over his head to assume the position to lick clean his genitalia. The hound was making loud licking sounds that annoyed Custer, whose own dogs were tethered in the rear. "One thing's certain, Jineral, ef the hostiles don't har nuthin' uv us till we open up at first light, then they'll be the most powerfully 'stonished

249

Injuns dat dese parts hav' ever seen." California Joe nodded. "Yes, sir! That's fur sur'." The scout went to his grain sack that was attached to his McClellan and took a handful of oats and fed it to his mule. The big animal ravenously devoured the food from his master's palm. "On the other hand, Jineral. If dare's a whole bunch of hostile Injun villages upstream on the Washita, then we could be in a heap a trouble."

Custer remained quiet. He looked at the Osage scouts who still looked skeptical about the white man's successful ability to attack a village without knowing how many of the enemy they would face.

V.

Major Elliott's three companies arrived at their designated spot which the major assumed was near the rear of the village. This was difficult to ascertain because with the exception of the moon, there was no light coming from the encampment. Although he was uncertain that he was at the tail end of the village, he was certain that he was near the hostile encampment because he also heard dogs barking and children crying in the near distance. He ordered the troopers to dismount and stand near their horses and await first light.

Nate and Jesse were near Elliott, and like everyone else suffered greatly from the night's cold temperatures. They were denied permission to move about or even stomp their feet loudly, thus making the cold even more unbearable. To escape the frigid air, Nate's mind kept returning to what Custer said regarding the women and children and how they should not be harmed. "Spare the women and children if possible . . ." Nate scoffed at the order; a demand he knew would not be obeyed or enforced. He dreaded the prospect of witnessing senseless killings and mutilations by the troops against the redskins. He knew that innocent women and children would surely be killed, so he just hoped it was not going to be Cougar Eyes' village. Nate's mind began to think about the vicious Missouri bushwhackers and how they had executed and butchered the men in his regiment when the guerrillas near Sherwood, Missouri, ambushed them.

He thought about how he had awoken in the tall green grass where he had hidden and fallen asleep after he had escaped Quantrill and his fast horse. He remembered making his way back to Fort Scott in the dead of night and reaching the camp just before daylight where he found Colonel James Williams, the abolitionist officer, had organized a relief force and was prepared to move out at all speed. Nate was informed that when the white troops from the Second Kansas Battery had returned to the post after they had fled from the bushwhackers' onslaught they had informed Colonel Williams of the ambush. The abolitionist became outraged when he learned that his men were left alone on foot, without the protection of cavalry or field guns at the mercy of well-mounted guerrillas. He tongue-lashed the sergeant of the Second Kansas for cowardice and gave orders to move out at first light hoping to find some survivors.

Nate volunteered and received permission to accompany the relief force and was brought a mount. An old wind-blown nag but he didn't care. It was the first time he had ridden a horse since he had escaped from the plantation, and although he felt tired and worn from his ordeal, he became revived by feeling the power of a horse in between his legs once again.

As the relief force approached the site where the men of the First Kansas had cut grass for forage the day before, they discovered the area was littered with abandoned rifles, cap pouches, cartridge boxes, canteens, haversacks, forage caps, saber belts, and pieces of uniform. The men's personal items that were in their haversacks and backpacks were also pilfered by the Missourians and Nate remembered the first mutilated body he had ever seen.

The infantryman's uniform and underwear had been completely stripped from his body and his face was bashed into a pulp, rendering him unrecognizable. A bloody club, used to beat the hapless soldier, rested near his body. Nate became shocked at this sight. It was one thing to die a brutal death in a fight but not even during his days as a slave did he see such butchery against helpless men. As the relief force covered the area, more men were found in hideous states of death. Some men had been stabbed to death repeatedly after they had been wounded, while others had their brains beaten out with clubs. Other signs of mutilation were just as ghoulish. Ears, noses, and fingers were cut off and some of the men's privates were hacked from their bodies. All the men were stripped of their uniforms and those articles of clothing that were not taken by the bushwhackers were scattered about the field.

Colonel James Williams was in a state of rage. As he came upon one dead and horribly mutilated body after another, his blood boiled with outrage. At one point Nate overheard him loudly cry out to himself. *"Demons. Barbarians. Rebel fiends!"* He then looked toward the heavens and bellowed as if he were a preacher. "We will seek righteous retribution for these cowardly acts!"

Some of the troopers from the relief party had entered a nearby house and Nate saw a corporal calling for Colonel Williams.

"Kernel, better come and take a look at this, sir."

Williams galloped over to the structure, dismounted, and entered the house. There was a brief silence and then Nate heard the colonel's voice cry out in outrage.

"My God. They are going to pay for this barbarism."

Nate had led his horse toward the cabin and dismounted. Some of the troopers from the relief party started to ransack the house and Nate took the opportunity to enter the dwelling. In the parlor were eleven black soldiers lying dead on the floor, shot execution style. The bodies were also stripped and mutilated and Nate recognized all of the dead men, some of them he had known fairly well. He was staring at the bodies, and although his face was void of expression, he felt deep rage within his heart, and desired vengeance.

Nate's attention was diverted by some pandemonium that was occurring outside the house. Men were yelling and Nate could hear Colonel Williams shouting orders. He went back outside and saw a civilian being held in custody by some infantrymen with fixed bayonets.

"Bring me that man," demanded Williams. A Federal patrol had found the civilian in the vicinity whom they suspected of aiding the guerrillas and had brought him in. One of the men in the patrol told Williams that he recognized him from when he was a Confederate prisoner at Fort Scott. The colonel looked him over carefully and when his eyes fell on the man's feet, he noticed that he was wearing a pair of newly issued U.S. government shoes.

"I am a released prisoner, sir. And I have papers," he protested vehemently. "I have not committed any unlawful acts."

The abolitionist colonel was unconvinced. "Where did you get those government shoes, sir?"

The man's face became flush and he stammered, "I found them in the field."

"No, sir! You stole them, sir," accused Williams, pointing a finger at him. Nate saw that the colonel's facial expression showed contempt and disgust toward this individual.

"Take this swine into the house and shoot him," ordered Williams coldly. He knew that he had a guilty man in his hands and most certainly a Rebel sympathizer. The opportunity for retribution had arrived, and the abolitionist leader wanted it to start immediately.

The sergeant of the patrol marched the man into the house as he pleaded his innocence and demanded a trial. Williams remained unmoved and simply responded, "There are no trials for those who are in league with Lucifer and savageness!" He then gave further instructions to the sergeant. "Shoot him in the same room where our brothers lie murdered and throw his body on the pile, and *burn the house.*"

A moment later a shot rang from inside the structure and Nate's face twitched. Shortly after the shot, several infantrymen carrying torches fired the house. As Williams watched the structure burn, he swore an oath to his officers.

"I will devastate the land for five miles around," he promised, raising a clenched fist in the air. "And show these *damned* Rebels that we will not tolerate such atrocities."

VI.

Major Elliott's detachment included Captain Benteen's G Company and Captain Barnitz's H Company. Benteen's company was to be in the rear, following Major Elliott and Barnitz's troops that led the advance. Nate and Jesse were ordered by Elliott to accompany Barnitz at the head of the attacking detachment. The men had moved out immediately after Custer had given the order, and time was precious since daybreak was only a few hours away.

Nate was troubled by what he saw earlier and could not purge the visions in his mind. When Major Elliott's detachment departed from the main body, most of the regiment's dogs followed. The officers instructed several troopers to dismount and catch the animals so they could be dispatched with a lariat or by cutting their throats. It was feared that they would bark and jeopardize the detachment's movements, so orders were to kill the animals immediately. Nate was glad that he was not ordered to execute the hapless pets, who trusted the troopers and stared at their murderers as they were strangled with the lariat or had their throats slit. Some of the poor beasts yelped and gagged in fear and pain as they were garroted and Nate could not help but be reminded of the time when he had to flee Bloodhound Jack and the patrollers through the bayous and where the hounds had met their horrible fate with the alligators. One particular execution disturbed Nate more than the others. One dog, a mongrel named Bob, had a horse picket pin driven through his skull by a trooper who thrust the spike as he held the regiment's mascot pinned to the ground by his neck.

Major Elliott's detachment made their way toward the bluffs where they thought the Indian village would be. En route, Nate saw that the trail was crossed with many pony tracks and lodge pole markings, all indicating that a big village was nearby. When Elliott and Barnitz reached the tall bluffs, the major called for a halt and spoke with Barnitz.

"I think we are too close to the village," Nate heard him say.

"Well, if they are down by the river, they can hear our horses or make us out in the moonlight," responded Barnitz. He was a big, tall man and despite the fact that Elliott's horse was taller than Barnitz's the captain towered over the major.

Elliott thought for a moment and then decided. "We will countermarch and hide behind those bluffs to our right."

Just then a sergeant came up and informed Elliott that the regimental band had been following his detachment by mistake.

"Idiots!" whispered the major loudly. "They're supposed to be with Custer, damn it."

"They were misinformed, sir."

"Send them back, now," ordered Elliott. "And where is Captain Benteen and his squad?"

"I believe he is still in the rear," explained Barnitz.

"All right, then. We will move toward those bluffs to our right, and use low voices and hand signals only."

"Yes, sir," responded Barnitz.

"Take the lead, Captain."

"Sir." Barnitz nodded and turned his horse.

Nate and Jesse were in front with Barnitz when they came to an imposing canyon that barred the way. After some searching, Jesse found a narrow path that led through the canyon. Barnitz ordered that the men pass through single file and keep quiet. When the troopers had left the canyon, they were faced with a steep incline that had to be ascended. Barnitz's mount hesitated, and to encourage the unsure animal, Nate forged ahead, spurring John Brown and leaning forward, holding on to his mane. The captain followed and the rest of the men proceeded up the incline to where they came upon some ponies and mules that were tethered with lariats. The hungry animals paid no attention to the cavalrymen as they poked at the ground with their hooves for grass underneath the snow. The area was scattered second growth white oak, and Nate noticed that many of the leaves, although dry, still clung to the branches.

Major Elliott ordered a halt and had the troopers dismount at a stream. He again called for Barnitz.

"I think that we should reconnoiter and see if we can see other villages downstream." Major Elliott was concerned that there were other encampments and that he did not want his back to be exposed. Barnitz nodded and the men proceeded downstream on foot. As Nate watched the two officers he heard some noise behind him, forcing him to turn his head. It was Captain Benteen and H Company that had finally joined the detachment.

Elliott and Barnitz could not see any other villages downstream so they had returned and the men were ordered to cross the stream on foot, to avoid making noise.

"*Man*. Look at that!" exclaimed Jesse to Nate. He was looking toward the horizon and observed what he swore was a rocket or at the very least a long flaming arrow that had been shot into the air. The night was crystal clear with a full moon, so the trajectory looked very bright.

"Must be some kind of signal," remarked one trooper as he stared at the luminous object in the sky. By now most of the men in Elliott's command saw the trajectory and gaped in wonderment. Most of the troopers were convinced that it was a flaming arrow that was meant to signal other hostiles. Nate knew that it was not a flaming arrow, and certainly not a signal rocket. During the war he had seen rockets deployed against entrenched Confederates and this object was too high in the sky to be a rocket. He looked at Major Elliott who was conversing with Benteen and Barnitz and overheard Benteen say that it was a shooting star. Barnitz and the major concurred and Nate nodded his head. He knew it was a shooting star because when he was a slave in Louisiana, he had seen a few of them fly in the sky with his father and mother when he was very young. He thought about how it was one of the few times that they were together as a family and happy; sitting on the stoop of their cabin in the quarter watching the stars dance in the sky. He smiled at these past memories as he thought about his dead parents and then sighed as the pain of personal loss crept into his heart.

Major Elliott ordered Captain Barnitz to take his company and ford the stream and take up position on the right bank while moving toward where they suspected the pony herd was kept. Captain Benteen was ordered to accompany Elliott and move along the left bank and advance toward the village. Barnitz ordered ten men to remain mounted to protect the squad's crossing, but Nate and Jesse had to dismount with the other cavalrymen and plunge into the cold water. Due to the crooked nature of how the Washita flowed, the troopers had to cross the knee-deep ice-cold water several times. Nate felt the freezing water fill up in his boots, and he had to bite his lip from crying out in pain. When all of the men had reached the right bank, Barnitz ordered the men to remount and proceed toward where he heard the tiny bells of the pony herd. As they proceeded cautiously Nate saw several ponies and mules eating some branches underneath some cottonwood trees.

Suddenly a pony guard who had been sleeping under a red blanket leaped from his sitting position and bolted for the village. Several of the men were equally startled and raised their carbines to shoot at the fleeing Cheyennes but Barnitz ordered them to refrain from firing. The pony herd guard was not alone, however; several other Indian sentries stood up and started running in the same direction but again Barnitz ordered the men to hold their fire for fear of alerting the village.

It was only a half hour or so before daylight and Barnitz was gazing at his pocket watch. His company was hidden behind a shallow ravine and he was concerned that the command might lose its striking cohesion and timing if the men were slowed down by the cottonwood trees and brush that sheltered the village before they had penetrated and surprised their part of the encampment.

Nate and Jesse and some of the more seasoned troopers were rubbing down their mounts' legs to make sure they were not going to be stiff when they charged the village. Anticipating that an attack was imminent, the cavalrymen removed the stoppers of the muzzles of the carbines, loaded magazines, tested levers to verify that they were not frozen. Others verified saddle cinches and bridles and made sure that their canteens, pickets, blankets, and saddlebags were securely fastened to the rings of their McClellans.

Some dogs were barking in the village as the troopers made their way through the timber and Nate hoped that the canine guards would not alert their owners. A few minutes passed and the dogs still continued to bark, causing nervousness among the men, fearing that the element of total surprise was now placed in jeopardy. All of a sudden, a shot rang out and Jesse felt the round pass by his cheek. The bullet landed harmlessly in the side of a sand hill that stood behind him but spooked the horses.

Major Elliott was becoming concerned that their presence had been detected by the hostiles. He was about to order the men to proceed cautiously toward the village, when the faint rollicking sounds of "Garry Owen" could be heard. The sun had just appeared over the horizon and Custer had ordered that the band strike up the tune for the attack to begin. The regimental band, who had worked their way back to Custer during the night, now stood on top of a bluff, playing their instruments and watching the boy general charge the village as the regiment's standard, guidons, and Old Glory followed the leader into battle.

Elliott ordered all of the men who were on foot to mount and form a line. Some of the cavalrymen in Elliott's command, however, became excited by the lively sounds and quick pace of the regiment's song and ignored their officers' commands to await the order to charge the village en masse. The Irish drinking tune of singing flutes and clarions rejuvenated the freezing troopers and made the men forget about the cold and their weariness. They also knew that Custer was charging the village in full force and they wanted to join their comrades in the fray. When the cavalrymen saw the outline of tipis, they broke into cheering and yelling, spurring their mounts toward the encampment, discharging their Colts and Spencers at rapid fire at the lodges.

When Nate came out of the ravine, he was gratified that it was not Cougar Eyes' village. Although the white tipis were arranged in their usual irregular manner among the timber, Nate knew it was not the village where he had spent several days recovering from near hypothermia. Satisfied that it was not his friend's encampment, Nate leaned forward in the saddle and unflapped the cover of his holster and pulled his Walker-Colt. He then spurred John Brown forward and joined the charge, with Jesse and Cailloux next to him. They could see the smoke of the feeble cook fires that streamed from the smoke hole flaps, and knew that most of the Cheyennes were asleep in their buffalo blankets. Both Nate and Jesse refrained from firing their weapons. They held their revolvers at the ready, and half cocked, but did not want to waste cartridges firing blindly at the lodges where they might hit women and children, and partially out of habit in conserving ammunition until they identified the target, because Colored troops were always short of ammunition.

As the assault got under way, many of the Cheyenne warriors came toward Elliott's squadrons downstream, to avoid Custer's frontal attack. Most of them were trying to go downstream to escape the onslaught of the *Ve' ho' e*. Barnitz did not want any of the Indians to escape, so he ordered his line to concentrate their fire on the fleeing hostiles. The Cheyennes crashed into the skirmish line and were checked, but withdrew to a ravine and started to return a hot fire.

Barnitz sighted another group of fleeing hostiles on his left, running over some sand hills, making for the pony herd. The captain ordered Jesse to fire on the group but they were too far and moved very quickly among the cottonwood trees. He then ordered Jesse along with some other mounted men under a sergeant, to either cut the hostiles off or drive them toward where Barnitz thought Colonel Thompson was to appear with his squadrons.

Barnitz ordered Nate to accompany him in dashing toward the center of the village where Custer's four-pronged attack was slowly weaving its way through the encampment. The troopers discharged their weapons, cheered and cursed at the Cheyennes as the scantily clad Indians emerged from their tipis to face their attackers with what weapons they could readily seize. Warriors emerged from door flaps shooting rifles, pistols, and arrows at the troopers. Some of the braves, armed with war clubs and toma-hawks, leaped at the mounted cavalrymen and pulled them from their mounts to engage them in hand-to-hand combat.

Nate was riding behind Barnitz when they came upon three fleeing braves. Nate was about to shoot the one closest to the cap-tain and had him in his sights, but Barnitz shot first, hitting the first one in the chest. The brave howled and threw up his arms. Barnitz then spurred his mount to catch up with the second brave who had turned around and launched an arrow at the officer, singeing his neck. Nate shot his Walker-Colt but missed the war-rior. Barnitz, however, got off another round from his Army Colt and also shot this brave near the heart.

The third Cheyenne brave, whom Nate noticed carried a Lan-caster rifle, stopped to confront Barnitz who charged the warrior as he leaned forward behind the right side of his horse's neck. He was about to shoot when the Indian moved to the left. Barnitz skillfully reined in his animal and charged the Cheyenne again but the brave just moved to the right side to escape the pony soldier's aim. Both antagonists were so close together, each trying to shoot the other, that Nate was afraid to fire, fearing that he might hit Barnitz in lieu of the hostile. Nate tried to maneuver John Brown to render assistance, but the human obstructions of wailing squaws, crying papooses, running warriors, and zealous cavalrymen who were shooting at anything that was not blue slowed his progress in getting any closer to Barnitz.

The Cheyenne brave meanwhile had suddenly removed his dressed buffalo skin from his back and started to wave it at Bar-nitz's horse's face, attempting to spook the beast. The captain's horse bolted slightly, distracting his rider while enabling the brave to aim his Lancaster at the *Ve' ho' e*'s torso. Barnitz quickly recovered though, and aimed his Colt. Both men fired at the same time at point-blank range. Nate saw that the blast from the big Lancaster rifle had occurred at the left side of the captain's rib cage, penetrating his body at that location and exiting at his lower back, sending pieces of flesh, muscle, and fragments of wool from the uniform and greatcoat into the air.

The warrior had been hit as well. He had dropped the rifle in his left hand and placed his right into his deerskin blouse as if he were clutching the wound. The Cheyenne brave grimaced horribly at Barnitz, and when Nate finally got close enough to the officer to render assistance, the hostile sneered at him with contempt as well. Nate thought that maybe he was not covering the bullet hole with his hand after all, but rather preparing to reach for a scalping knife and go after Barnitz's hair. Nate spurred John Brown forward, but a squaw and her papoose ran in front of his horse, causing him to rear up, nearly throwing Nate. Although gravely wounded, Barnitz managed to turn his mount to the left and cock his revolver. He weakly leaned his body forward, using his horse's neck for support, aimed, and fired another round into the Indian's torso, causing the wounded brave to fall over his rifle and collapse.

"Sir? You all right?" yelled Nate, approaching Barnitz.

Barnitz was speechless. He tried to open his mouth but no words came forth. It was clear to Nate that he had been very badly wounded and that he needed attention.

"We've gots to git you to the surgeon." Nate brought his arms to bear around Barnitz in order to support him in the saddle.

Barnitz nodded his head in disapproval and lamely waved his Army Colt for Nate to go on without him. He was breathing heavily and his eyes were half shut. Nate was hesitant to leave him. He knew that the officer was gravely wounded but Barnitz appeared to realize that he was not going to make it at all, and did not want Nate to bother, preferring to die on his own.

"Go, Sergeant," he heard Barnitz whisper meekly. "Go, now."

"Sir, I will get help." Nate turned John Brown toward the left and spurred him toward the center of the village.

Nate saw that most of the braves were still making for the timber and the riverbank, where they took cover and returned fire. Most of the squaws and children hid in their lodges, but quite a few of them were also still fleeing toward the river, some clutching screaming infants in their arms, while others ran with wailing papooses strapped to their backs.

The four separate detachments had now successfully converged within the village and squadrons swarmed among the tipis, firing at defending warriors and squaws alike. Nate saw several women get shot as they fled for the river, and became appalled to see one squaw, who got caught in a cross fire, shot several times in the back and head before falling onto the frozen ground. Nate had hardly fired his Walker-Colt because he could not get a clear shot at any of the fast-moving Cheyenne warriors who ran among the women and children. As he made his way to the center of the village, to his astonishment he saw an American flag attached at the top of a lodge pole near a big tipi, which he suspected belonged to an important man of the tribe. The flag was motionless because there was no breeze, and difficult to see because of the clouds of smoke from gunfire, but he was sure that it was the stars and stripes.

Near the lodge pole that flew the flag, Nate noticed an old but distinguished Cheyenne man emerge from the big tipi. His body was wrapped in a modest trader's blanket, and he was unarmed, but the way he held his head and stood his ground amid the confusion, terror, and killing that was occurring all around him convinced Nate that the old brave was a chief. The man looked around in complete disbelief at what was happening to his village, and Nate saw that his face was wet from tears that poured from his eyes. The old man looked up at the sagging American flag and sat down next to the door flap of his tipi and started to sing his death song. The monotonous melancholy rhythm of the man's song disturbed Nate. It reminded him of Isaac Moore's voodoo preaching and hexing when he was training recruits in New Orleans and San Antonio. Although mayhem was occurring all around him, the elderly brave remained calm and his weeping ceased as he held his head high and sang to himself. Nate was about to turn John Brown around and leave this place of sorrow when a sergeant from the Seventh galloped up to him hollering and waving his Army Colt.

"What's the matter with you?" The noncom was wild with rage and his horse was foaming at the bit. "Shoot the son-of-a-bitch. Shoot him, *damn you.*"

"He's unarmed!" protested Nate.

"You'r a damn fool, *black* man," scoffed the sergeant. He then aimed his Army Colt at the old man and shot him in the head. Nate grimaced as he watched the elderly brave's torso collapse to the ground as if he were a kicked-over sack of flour. The sergeant then turned to Nate before galloping off.

"Better get your mind right, or you'll be dead."

Nate raised his head high in the air and yelled in frustration, "Gawd Almighty, I swear!"

"You all right?" asked Jesse as he pulled up next to Nate with Cailloux. The barrel of Jesse's Army Colt was hot, and Nate could see the fumes pouring out of the bore. Jesse's mount, Cailloux, also showed signs of heavy use. His chest heaved from exertion and Nate could see that the horse's nostrils were red from broken blood vessels.

"Yeah, I—I'm all right," responded Nate, as if he were coming out of a trance. The sight of seeing the elderly chief shot to death while Old Glory stood on a pole in the middle of the village as U.S. cavalrymen killed and wounded its occupants bewildered Nate. Not even during his fighting days on the Missouri–Kansas border and subsequent combat in the East had he seen such indiscriminate killing. Not even during the past year of Indian fighting and engaging ruthless Dog Men in battle had he witnessed such infamy. This was a different kind of warfare and Nate had no taste for it. There was no glory or even purpose in killing women, children, and the old.

Jesse was about to suggest that they move toward the other end of the village where some of the braves had taken refuge behind a deep depression when a warrior charged them, discharging his pistol at rapid fire. He was running toward them so his accuracy from his pistol was poor, the bullets falling short and hitting the frozen ground near the horse's hooves, frightening the animals. The brave was only a few feet away, still firing his weapon, when Nate and Jesse brought their pistols to bear on the attacker. Nate was faster though, he quickly lowered his Walker-Colt and took aim at the man's chest and fired the big horse pistol at the charging warrior. The bullet found its target and the Cheyenne man's head snapped back, throwing him off his feet.

"Let's get out of here." Nate yanked the reins on John Brown and led him in the direction to where the heaviest concentration of fire was taking place. By now most of the troopers were fighting on foot, going from tipi to tipi to root out holdouts and to round up those squaws and their children who had not fled for the river.

As they made their way through the village while troopers searched the tipis and kept shooting at anything that was Indian, a screaming squaw ran past them, making her way toward the riverbank. Nate saw that she was transporting a half-naked child in her arms.

"Jezus Crist," yelled Jesse in astonishment. "Is that chil' white?"

Nate was also surprised; not so much that the fleeing squaw was carrying a white toddler boy, but more shocked that the lad was in such wretched physical condition, and the revealing expression of terror that his sunken eyes conveyed. His blond hair was long, filthy, and savage-looking. His skin, jaundiced and bruised, was caked with dirt. He looked sickly and frail; resembling someone who was suffering from starvation, disease, and physical abuse. His face, legs, arms, and buttocks were skin and bones, and exposed to the elements, with only an old Indian blanket wrapped around his torso. The white adolescent also seemed to be only semiconscious, his mouth was open, and his eyes partially drooped. His face remained motionless as chaos and mayhem reigned all around him.

When some of the cavalrymen noticed that the squaw was transporting a white child who was most certainly a captive of the Cheyennes, they surrounded the tiny woman and hollered at the squaw to release the young boy who was now shivering from the cold. The squaw, who was already hysterical with excitement, looked at the troopers with a combination of fear, loathing, and desperation, knowing that her escape was cut off and that capture or death at the hands of the pony soldiers was at hand.

The soldiers were yelling and cursing at her to disengage herself from the lad, but she refused. She then suddenly removed a large knife from its place of concealment under her blanket and held it high in the air. Nate and the troopers were taken by surprise by this act and did not know how to proceed. She still held the hapless boy in one arm so the cavalrymen hesitated to shoot her, fearing that they might hit the captive, and reluctant to rush her as she was prepared to use the knife. As the soldiers watched anxiously, she yelled a war whoop and plunged the big blade into the boy's chest dropping his half-naked body on a snowdrift. Enraged by the squaw's merciless killing of the white boy, all the troopers opened fire on her, riddling her body with bullets. She stood there briefly, rotating her tiny body as she took the lead in her chest, legs, arms, and head before falling on top of the miserable body of the white boy in the snowdrift.

"By Gawd, I swear!" exclaimed Nate, shaking his head in confusion and woe. He had held his fire as he watched the outraged men of the Seventh shoot the squaw to death. Jesse as well blasted away with zeal, cocking back his hammer and firing his Army Colt at her, placing a round in the squaw's chest.

Disgusted and without saying a word, Nate turned his horse toward the Washita to get away from the dreadful scene that he had just witnessed. Jesse called out and beckoned Nate to stay with him and with the other men from the Seventh who were milling around the corpses of the pathetic white captive and bullet-riddled squaw. Nate, however, remained silent, and just kept moving toward the river where he could hear disciplined volleys of Spencer repeating rifles mixed with irregular though intense Indian fire. He assumed that those warriors who had not been killed or wounded in the initial assault or had managed to flee downstream had taken cover and were resisting Custer's men.

As soon as he reached the proximity of the river, Nate saw Lieutenant W. W. Cook and his forty sharpshooters through the thick gunfire smoke. They had taken cover behind rocks and hardwood trees, and were firing rapidly at about two dozen Cheyennes who had found cover behind a deep depression near the Washita. Lieutenant Cook was standing behind a line of kneeling men who were firing at the warriors behind the depression.

Cook was shouting orders to his men to maintain a hot fire while reminding them to carefully pick their targets. Nate believed that these last holdouts were Dog Soldiers. Although Cook's sharp-shooters fired every time a brave would briefly expose himself to get off a round, the braves would yell a war whoop and aim their guns at the pony soldiers and fire rapidly. Several of the troopers fell with wounds and Nate overheard Cook order some of the sharpshooters to disperse and try to flank the well-concealed hold-outs.

"Move among the rocks and trees!" ordered Cook, waving his Colt toward the nearby bluffs that hovered over the Washita. "Sweep 'em, men! Get behind 'em!"

"Sergeant Major," clamored Major Elliott. Nate turned in his saddle to face the officer and saw that the major was leading a squad of about fifteen enlisted men.

"The general has ordered me to round up those fleeing women and children." He pointed to a nearby small bluff that was toward the south, downstream, where Nate could see a large party of women and children with three men, one of them carrying a rifle and powder horn. They were in the process of escaping down-stream, making their way along the steep banks. Major Elliott was excited and breathing heavily. His face was also sweating and he had abandoned his army greatcoat.

"I need a noncom to come with me to capture those Indians." Elliott's horse was chopping on his bit and panting heavily as the major shifted his gaze from the hostiles on the bluff near the river and Nate.

"Sir. I'm at your service," responded Nate. He desperately wanted to go with Elliott and depart from this place of infamy. Elliott at least preferred to fight warriors and not shoot women and children.

"Take the rear and let's go then." Elliott spurred his mount and his squad followed quickly. Nate waited until the troopers passed him and then quickly maneuvered John Brown at the rear of the galloping squad.

As the squad galloped out of the village, Elliott crossed paths with a junior officer. The major flamboyantly lifted his kepi in the air and Nate could not help overhearing Elliott's loud boast to the lieutenant, *"I'm going for a brevet or a coffin!"* Nate cringed at such bravado. During the war, he frequently had the misfortune to hear similar braggadocio from officers who were prepared to sacrifice their lives and often those of the men who served under them for the sake of gaining higher rank.

Elliott pushed his men hard. He wanted to catch those Indians before they could escape. His men were beating their rifle barrels on their mounts' rumps in an effort to keep the tiny column together.

Nate knew as they closed in that the three warriors that were covering the retreat of this large party of women and children would turn and fight. As he approached and got closer to the group, he became astonished. He recognized one of the fleeing braves with the rifle and powder horn. It was Little Rock, from Cougar Eyes' village. They had met during the meeting at Turkey Leg's lodge. Nate assumed that he must have been an overnight guest at this village when the Seventh had attacked it. Nate also recognized the other fleeing male Indian, a Kiowa who had been visiting Cougar Eyes' camp when he was recuperating.

The squad was closing in on their quarry. The Indians' progress was hampered by the rough terrain and the difficulties the squaws were experiencing transporting children. Little Rock, the brave with the rifle and powder horn, turned to confront Elliott's pursuing men. He raised the rifle, aimed, and fired, hitting the horse of a trooper who was riding next to Elliott. The beast wailed in agony and collapsed to the ground, propelling the rider into the air and sending him crashing to the ground. He then started to curse the Indian for shooting his horse. Several of the troopers returned fire, killing Little Rock instantly. Little Rock had gained precious time for the fleeing squaws and children though, and Nate respected the fact that he had sacrificed his life to protect them from the bluecoats.

The Kiowa, however, ran over to Little Rock's body and seized the rifle and powder horn and started to load the weapon as Elliott's troopers blasted away at him, the bullets whizzing by his body and sending mud and snow into the air. He got off a shot but did not hit anything. He then rejoined the Indian civilians and yelled for them to move faster as he loaded his rifle while running.

Elliott's men managed to catch up with one exhausted squaw with three terrified children. As the troopers pointed their Colts and Spencers at her, she begged them not to shoot her and the children. Nate became aghast when he realized who it was. It was Buffalo Woman, Willow Branch's best friend, and one of the squaws who had spent that first night nursing him after Cougar Eyes had found him half frozen in the snowdrift.

"Major, sir, I know this squaw," pleaded Nate. He hoped that his interference on her behalf would prevent the troopers from shooting her.

"Hold your fire! Hold your fire!" ordered Elliott.

"Sergeant Major. You know this squaw?"

"Yes, sir, I do," reaffirmed Nate.

"Very well then. You there . . . Private," beckoned Elliott, pointing to the enlisted man who had his horse shot from beneath him by Little Rock.

"Yes, Major?"

"Escort the squaw and the brats back to the command."

"Sir? Permission to accompany the group back to the command," asked Nate desperately. He wanted to make sure that no harm would come to Buffalo Woman when she returned to the village where fighting was still going on.

Elliott looked at Nate and took a deep breath. "Permission *granted*, Sergeant Major." Elliott then pumped his right arm several times in the air, ordering the command to proceed downstream to root out any other holdouts. The troopers rode off and Nate was left with Buffalo Woman and her charges, and the dismounted cavalryman.

As the group made their way back, sporadic gunfire could be heard in the direction of the village, responded to by Cook's sharp-shooters firing on concealed warriors bent on selling their lives as dearly as possible.

"*Etoneto!*" complained Buffalo Woman, pointing to a young girl who was barefoot. The child was shivering from the cold and her feet were cut and blue from walking on the frozen ground.

"*Etoneto!*" she repeated as she stopped and started to tear pieces of clothing to make rags for the child to bind her feet. Nate nodded and ordered the enlisted man to halt to give the squaw some time to wrap the child's freezing feet.

"We gotta git back. Place is still crawlin' with *Injuns*," whined the trooper, casting anxious eyes downstream and toward the south bank of the river.

"Give 'em a moment. This child's feet are freezen," insisted Nate.

"Yeah, well, we goin' be losin' our hair if we stay here any longer," he replied contemptuously, resenting taking orders from a black man. He glanced longingly at Elliott's departing squad as the cavalrymen cantered southward, seeking more Indians.

Nate now was becoming impatient with the squaw as she took her time binding the child's feet. He now agreed with the enlisted man that it was best to get moving and return to the command.

"*Neheto!*" ordered Nate, gesturing with his hand.

"Shit!" exclaimed the enlisted man.

"Now what?"

"Indians! That's what, God damn it!" bawled the private, pointing to oncoming savages who had emerged from their hiding places.

About half a dozen Indians who were on foot, which Nate recognized as Arapaho, had appeared from some of the nearby low ravines and were in the process of cutting off their retreat from Elliott's now departed squad and from Custer's command.

The enlisted man saw an approaching brave who was running toward him and wielding a hatchet and yelling war whoops. He raised his Spencer and fired at the warrior but missed. The squaw, seizing the opportunity to profit from the situation, suddenly removed her blanket and started to wave the article furiously in John Brown's face, spooking the horse and causing him to abruptly bolt. Nate had his finger on the trigger of his Walker-Colt and the sudden jerk from his mount caused him to fire the piece into the air. The trooper tried to fire his Spencer again at the charging hostile, but discovered that he was out of ammunition. Panic-stricken, and realizing there was no time to clear his Army Colt from its holster, he decided to run. He threw the repeater away and started to run toward the village. The Arapaho, who was wielding the hatchet, was only a dozen yards or so away, followed by other braves wielding war clubs, tomahawks, and bows. The trooper saw that the Indians were gaining on him so he tried to accelerate his step but the leather soles of his cavalry boots made him slip and slide on the frozen ground and the hatchet-wielding Arapaho was soon within striking range. The warrior yelled a war cry and expertly swung the weapon across the back of the fleeing *Ve' ho'e*'s head, sending him tumbling to the ground. Nate heard the hideous sound of the hatchet splitting the skull of the cavalryman but did not see the act itself because he was too preoccupied in quieting his startled horse.

By now, the hostiles were closing in on Nate, and rather than try to hold his ground against superior numerical odds, he turned John Brown around and jabbed his spurs into the animal's flanks and took flight, heading for Elliott's squad that was closer than trying to make it back to the village. He barely managed to elude several braves who tried to block his way and had to run down one of them in order to escape the closing circle of screaming hostiles who were competing to take coup on his person while hurling arrows and war clubs at him.

Nate found Elliott within a few minutes; he had followed the shod horse tracks on the ground and reached the squad that had run into other well-armed Indians as well. These hostiles, however, were mounted on unshod ponies and possessed greater control over the rough, frozen, and partially covered snowy ground.

Elliott's little command had chased this fleeing band of Indians for about a mile or so, when the hostiles abruptly halted, turned, and faced the troopers.

"Sir, beg to report. Numerous hostiles in our rear." Nate was not panicked, but he wanted to acquaint the major with this intelligence.

"How many?" asked Elliott, surprised to see Nate. He then turned toward the warriors and leered at the hostiles who were shouting taunts and insults.

Suddenly dozens of other warriors appeared from the south joining the ones that had stopped. Nate saw that they were well armed and wearing war paint, indicating that they had had time to prepare to meet their antagonists. Nate recognized that those approaching were not Cheyennes, but a mix of Arapaho, Kiowa, and Comanche. They shouted war whoops and brandished their shields, lances, and rifles at the pony soldiers.

"*Sir*. We outnumbered, we gots to git back to the village!"

"Too late! *They're boxing us in.*" Elliott saw that his retreat had now been cut off and he faced encirclement by a superior force.

"Sir, I suggest we move the squad and make for that nearby ravine and take the *high* ground." Nate pointed toward the east and Elliott nodded his head in agreement.

"Left oblique," ordered the major. He yanked his reins and turned his horse around and led the squad at a gallop, heading toward the nearby ravine to seize the high ground.

When Custer's Seventh Cavalry suddenly attacked Black Kettle's village, Cougar Eyes and Willow Branch, as well as most of the Cheyennes, Arapahoes, Kiowa, Comanches, and Apaches camped along the banks of the Washita, were still asleep. When gunfire broke out and refugees from Black Kettle's beleaguered encampment started to appear at the other villages, crying out the alarm that the *Ve' ho' e* had struck, Cougar Eyes and the other Dog Soldiers of his warrior society moved quickly. They grabbed their weapons and shields and scampered to their war ponies to render assistance to their besieged brothers. They were enthusiastically joined by warriors of the other tribes and proceeded to move upstream. Most of the warriors were mounted, but many were also on foot, because of the weakened condition of their mounts due to limited supply of forage.

The Dog Soldiers' camp was situated near the Arapaho and Kiowa villages. Consequently, the different tribes were mixed together.

"We will kill them all," swore Cougar Eyes as he left his squaw to join his fellow *Hotame Ho' nehe* to do battle with the hated *ho' nehe*.

Willow Branch wanted to tell her husband to be careful, but she knew better. She could only remain silent and watch her man and Turkey Leg ride off as other warriors ran or rode past her, heading for Black Kettle's village.

Cougar Eyes was in a rage. He grew up with Black Kettle's band and was barely inducted into one of the Dog Soldier societies when the butcher Chivington and the Colorado Militia slaughtered many of his friends and family members. Now, other pony soldiers were repeating the same treacherous task! He was also mad that Black Kettle, the peace chief, who had adhered to the belief that it was possible for the *Tsitsitas* and the *Ve' ho' e* to live in harmony, was once again reaping the whirlwind of his preaching. Blinded by wrath, Cougar Eyes was determined to kill as many of the *Ve' ho' e* as possible, or die in the process.

"Sir, we're not going to make it." Nate could see that their path toward the ravine where Elliott sought to gain the high ground was now cut off and the hostiles were gushing forth from all sides, rapidly encircling the squad.

"Dismount!" bellowed the major, leaping from his saddle and slapping his horse's runt to get rid of the animal. *"Abandon your horses,"* he further ordered. "Abandon your horses."

"Sir, we will need the horses to ride out!" cautioned Nate, alarmed at such a dangerous order.

"Abandon your horses! Turn 'em loose!" insisted Elliott firmly. "Can't spare any men to hold them," barked back Elliott to Nate while using both hands to work his Army Colt to shoot at a Comanche who hurled a long lance at him. His troopers looked at their commanding officer anxiously and Nate saw that they all had the expression of fear marked on their faces. As the Indians shouted *"Hi-hi-hi,"* and blew on their bone war whistles, the enraged warriors started pouring a heavy fire at them and one trooper was first hit in the kneecap and then almost immediately shot through his left armpit. Elliott and Nate remained cool, however, as the rest of the squad frantically removed their saddlebags and canteens from their saddles before releasing their mounts.

One enlisted man that had just set his mount free received an arrow in his stomach and hollered in pain and horror at the sight of the shaft protruding from his gut. He collapsed to his knees and received another arrow through the throat, finishing him. Another trooper who was kneeling and struggling to load a Blakeslee tube into his Spencer got shot in the face by a bullet. He dropped his repeater and cupped his hands onto his face before falling flat onto the ground.

"Have the men lie on the ground and form a circular skirmish line. *Now*," ordered Elliott unwaveringly. His years as a professional soldier and experiences during the war had taught the major that panic only met with disaster.

"Aye, sir!" responded Nate without saluting. He pulled his saddlebags off of the McClellan and slapped John Brown's rump and told the beast to beat it.

"Fire at will. Fire at will," commanded Elliott as he took his position in the center of the circle.

Nate used his huge frame to physically position several of the remaining fifteen troopers in a circle in the tall grass. *"Get on your bellies and mark your targets. Keep your legs apart,"* he exhorted, kicking one trooper's legs farther apart.

The troopers, however, were too panicked to render disciplined fire and most of them turned around on their backs to avoid the hail of arrows. They discharged their Spencers wildly through the tall grass at the hostiles who were crawling on their bellies toward the circle or using the surrounding high ground to fire and send hundreds of arrows at the bluecoats.

Cougar Eyes and Turkey Leg were observing the fight from a nearby small bluff that gave them a good overall view. They saw that there was much firing on the part of the white soldiers but that they were few and that they could not escape.

"They are afraid," remarked Cougar Eyes with contempt. "They fire on their backs at nothing."

"The *Ve' ho' e* will last as long as the sun takes to travel in between two lodges," observed Turkey Leg dryly.

"The pony soldiers attack our people and willingly kill the squaws and young. Yet when they face our warriors they cower in fear like rabbits."

Cougar Eyes was momentarily distracted by the sight of some braves riding captured cavalry horses that they had caught when Elliott ordered his troopers to let go of their mounts. He saw an Arapaho brave smiling with glee as he rode off on a big buckskin gelding. He immediately recognized the beast as the one he gave to *Hotoa' e Gordon*. There was no doubt about it, he thought to himself. Every horse was different, and Cougar Eyes knew that Nate was probably among the besieged bluecoats.

Cougar Eyes was close enough to see his friend, Roman Nose Thunder, a member of his Dog Soldier society, ride near and around the circle as the bluecoats fired at him. A great cheer went up as dozens of warriors chanted war whoops and encouragement at their fellow brave who wanted to take the first coup. He urged his pony to break through the skirmish line but the animal refused and Roman Nose Thunder had to turn back.

"*Neheto!* Let us join in the fight," invited Cougar Eyes. He wanted to kill pony soldiers and he also wanted to see if *Hotoa'e Gordon* was among the group that was surrounded and was certainly going to be annihilated.

"*Heehe'e!*" responded Turkey Leg. "I don't want our Arapahoe, Kiowa, and Comanche brothers to take all the coups."

"*Heehe'e*," acknowledged Cougar Eyes. "They have already taken most of the best horses."

While the two Dog Men went over to join the fight, an Arapaho named Tobacco stood up from his place of concealment and charged Elliott's circular skirmish line. Tobacco had no trouble penetrating the perimeter because most of the soldiers were lying on their backs and firing wildly into the air, without looking or aiming.

Due to the huge clouds of gun smoke, Nate only saw the brave when he jumped into the circle. He trained his Walker-Colt on the attacking warrior and pulled the trigger. The hammer struck the nipple but the cap was defective. Tobacco carried a flat war club that was meant to be used in great feats such as counting coup. He yelled a war cry in Nate's face and took a swipe at his head with the war club. Nate ducked in time to avoid being struck and tried to pistol whip the Arapaho with the long barrel of his revolver, but Tobacco moved too quickly and was finally shot in the chest by Major Elliott.

Nate looked at Elliott and was about to nod in gratitude when the major took a bullet in the right cheek, shattering his jaw. He groaned in agony but remained on his feet, clutching the wound with his left hand. Nate quickly made Elliott lie down in the middle of the circle to avoid being further exposed to gunfire. Nate saw that the heavy caliber lead ball had ripped open the skin on his right side just slightly above the major's whiskers and had exited through the other cheek. At the place of entry, Major Elliott's jawbone was exposed and the bullet had smashed into his teeth, leaving a hideous gap. The major was in so much pain and reeling from shock that Nate knew that he could no longer dictate orders. He also realized that he was next in line in the chain of command.

———

"Pull down all the lodges and make a pile," instructed Custer to Lieutenant Godfrey. Custer had established regimental headquarters at the proximity of Black Kettle's tipi where the American flag still hung on a lodge pole. The boy general thought it would be appropriate to direct all military activities from this location. A field hospital was also established at this spot and about a dozen wounded men were being treated for arrow and gunshot wounds.

"Romeo, tell the squaws to come out of their lodges," directed Custer. "Tell them we will not harm them or their children and that they are our prisoners and in our protection."

"Sí, General," responded the scout with his heavy Spanish accent.

Jesse was looking for Nate among the wounded and dead. He had not seen his friend depart with Elliott and had not seen him since he rode away when the squaw with the white captive was killed. Consequently, he thought that maybe his friend was among the casualties. Earlier, Jesse had been with W. W. Cook and his sharpshooters, picking off Dog Men who were hiding along the banks waist-deep in freezing water. As he walked searching among the wounded, he was in earshot to hear Custer bark orders at his scouts and officers as teams of troopers carried the dead and placed the bodies on the ground in a straight line. Army blankets were placed over their bodies and Jesse had to go up to each one of the corpses to see if Nate might be underneath the cover. Jesse counted four dead men, and was a little surprised to discover that three of the dead cavalrymen died from gunfire. One had been struck in the face with a bullet, while the other two were shot through the body. The last victim was a man killed by a lance that had pierced his back and came out of his stomach; the iron lance tip was long and protruded grotesquely from the dead man's belly. Jesse was reminded of the time not too long ago when he was trapped in the railroad cutting as Dog Men jabbed their lance tips at him, wounding him in almost every part of the body.

"Put all the lodges, hides, food, and weapons in a pile and set the whole lot ablaze," shouted Custer to Lieutenant Godfrey.

It was about ten o'clock in the morning, and with the exception of several Cheyenne holdouts, most of the fighting had stopped and Custer was now issuing instructions to his officers to destroy all property belonging to the former occupants.

Jesse saw California Joe leisurely ride up to Custer on his mule, the scout's faithful dog at his side. Evidently, the plainsman's mutt had escaped execution when the order was given to kill all of the dogs that had accompanied the regiment. California was puffing on his briarwood pipe and looking as filthy as ever. Jesse had not seen the grizzled scout during the battle and assumed that he played only a minor role in the flight. The barrel of his Springfield rifle looked cold and he appeared to be completely oblivious to the destruction and slaughter that was occurring all around him. Jesse watched as California Joe's mutt sniffed at the elderly corpse of Black Kettle who was lying nearby. The dog inhaled the dead chief's body aroma intensely, as if he was searching for the source of a particular scent. After a few moments of smelling, the hound lifted his left leg and urinated on the cadaver.

"Jineral, dare's a whole herd of Injun ponies yonder, an' I wants to git 'em," solicited the scout. He then took his bandanna that Jesse thought looked like an Indian breechcloth from around his neck and loudly blew his nose with the rag.

"I can't spare any men for that," responded Custer curtly.

"Hell, Jineral, I don't need no help," responded California, puffing on his pipe with vigor. Jesse could see the blue smoke pour from the scout's bowl.

"Very well then. Bring them in . . . if you are able."

California Joe touched the brim of his huge well-worn sombrero with the wet stem of his briarwood pipe and gently tapped the heels of his boots to his mule's flanks. Jesse saw the hinny and the dirty scout trot off in the direction of the Cheyenne pony herd, his devoted dog keeping close to the mule's quick-moving hooves.

Lieutenant W. W. Cook appeared with Captain Weir and Tom Custer and approached Custer. The general's brother had been wounded slightly in the neck by an arrow and the regimental surgeon made him stand still while he examined the nasty gash. As the surgeon's fingers probed the wound, Jesse saw that Tom Custer bit on his lip to avoid flinching. Nearby, Captain Barnitz was propped up against a stump. He was covered in blankets and unconscious.

"General, hordes of hostiles are forming on a knoll downstream from here," informed Captain Weir, pointing to mounted warriors in the distance.

Custer trained his field glasses to where Weir had indicated and saw that several hundred warriors had assembled, some of them firing into the village at the soldiers who were in the process of tearing down lodges and collecting hides and weapons for the bonfire.

"Romeo, bring me that squaw," demanded Custer. The scout had brought all of the surviving women and children to regimental headquarters near Black Kettle's lodge. The squaws and their charges shivered from the cold and fear, and some of the women, with the memory of the Sand Creek massacre still fresh in their minds, started to sing their death songs in anticipation of being executed.

"*Ninaasts!*" commanded Romeo, beckoning a squaw to approach him. The tiny woman walked slowly over to him, her head bowed. Romeo asked in rapid Cheyenne where the hostiles were coming from. The squaw was reluctant to speak, but Romeo was persistent and told the tiny woman that if she did not tell him, he would see to it that she and the other women would be shot.

Fearing for her life, the squaw told the scout that the warriors belonged to many different villages downstream. The scout turned to his commander and translated what she had told him. Custer became astonished at this news and leered into Romeo's face.

"General, we are running out of ammunition, and Major Bell and the ammunition train is nowhere in sight," cautioned Cook.

"Have the men secure a perimeter around the village, and pick their targets. Don't waste any ammunition!" Custer thought for a moment, his eyes moved about as if searching for an answer. "Major Bell will be up shortly, so we will just have to wait."

The general looked toward the nearby knoll and noticed that there were already more hostiles now than there had been a minute ago. He suspected that the reason why they had not counterattacked yet was because the braves were waiting for their chiefs. He saw Lieutenant Godfrey in the distance and ordered the officer to his side.

"Report, Lieutenant? Why is the destruction of the village taking so long?"

"There's so much stuff, General," pleaded Godfrey. "About seventy-five lodges, hundreds of buffalo robes and other hides, breechclouts, leggings, bonnets, saddles, tobacco, tons of jerky, Indian personal items . . . eh, cooking utensils, clothes, meat, weapons of every description . . ."

"Enough, sir. Just get on with it," interrupted the general, showing visible irritation at the officer's droning.

"Aye, General, but before destroying the village, I request permission to take a few men with me to round up the pony herd that the Osage scouts had seen south of the village."

"Permission granted, Lieutenant, but do it quickly," Custer said with a nod.

Lieutenant Godfrey asked Jesse to come with him along with

a platoon from his own Company K to round up the ponies at the southern end of the village. When the group came upon a relatively high hill that blocked the view from downstream, Godfrey ordered Jesse to accompany him up the crest to verify that the pony herd was below the ridge. The two men scaled the muddy side of the hill and arrived at the crest to behold a sight that made their hearts jump.

"Jezus Crist. Look at that!" exclaimed Jesse in astonishment pointing his index finger to indicate his disbelief. Lieutenant Godfrey was equally astounded. His mouth popped open in shock as he gawked at the sight of hundreds and hundreds of lodges below them with thousands of hostiles running madly about.

"There must be at least five thousand Indians down there," guessed Jesse, feeling a little weak-kneed.

"More like six or seven thousand," corrected Godfrey. "There must be half a dozen villages in this valley! That means about fifteen hundred warriors are going to come our way."

"Shit, Lootentant, wez gots to get outta here! That's a hornet's nest down there, fo' sure an' they are amassin' to attack us!"

Godfrey saw that several hundred riders, painted for war and mounted on their strongest ponies, had spotted them and were now galloping in their direction.

"Return to the command!" ordered Godfrey as he scampered down the hill with Jesse following at his heels.

The two men quickly mounted their horses and the platoon galloped to avoid a collision with hundreds of mounted outraged hostiles coming to the aid of Black Kettle's village. Godfrey's men fired their Army Colts at the pursuing hostiles in a running fight. Only when the platoon reached the safety of the skirmish line that the Seventh had formed around the village were they safe. The pursuing Indians drew off and joined their brothers on the knoll that overlooked the village.

"Stop firing in the air, damn it. Mark your targets!" roared Nate.

He turned to see if Major Elliott was still lying on the ground, and became surprised to see him wandering about aimlessly within the skirmish circle.

"Major, get down," pleaded Nate. Elliott turned to look at him and Nate saw him get shot in the back of the head, sending fragments of bone, brain, and blood into the air. The major's head snapped forward, and several of the troopers watched in abhorrence as their commanding officer's body tumbled to the ground. Nate ran over to see if there was still some life left within Elliott but when he knelt down and turned the major's body over, he knew that the wound was lethal. He then cupped his right hand and lowered Major Elliott's eyelids over his lifeless blue eyeballs.

Nate looked at the Indians on the high ground and knew that the ground that Elliott had selected was untenable. It was one thing to defend a position against besiegers who were on the same level ground, but the odds and the advantage tilts fatally against the defenders when the attackers are able to shoot down at you. He cursed Elliott's decision to dismount and abandon the horses. He thought that at the very least, if they still had their mounts, they could attempt a breakout rather than hold a hopeless position against overwhelming odds. Nate looked around and saw that several other cavalrymen from the squad also lay dead.

Most of the panic-stricken men of Elliott's squad were now firing their Spencers on their backs despite Nate's admonishment to get them to fire their weapons at least on their bellies, so they could see their targets. Ever since they saw their beloved commanding officer shot dead, the men became so horrified at the prospect of being killed or taken captive at the hands of the savages that they had forgotten all of their training and discipline.

The hostiles, however were fastidious in proceeding at a slow pace, creeping through the grass toward them, taking their time and shooting at the pony soldiers only when they had a bluecoat in view.

Nate was firing his Spencer in a kneeling position at any object that he saw moving in the tall brown grass, but it was becoming increasingly difficult to see the attackers because of the clouds of gun smoke that stagnated in the air all around them, obscuring vision. One trooper, who Nate saw had a crazed look in his eyes, suddenly got up from his back and bolted from the skirmish line.

"Come back here, damn you!" hollered Nate to no avail. The man ran for dear life, screaming in fear at the top of his lungs.

Cougar Eyes, armed with a bow-lance, descended upon him from his left side. The Dog Man urged his favorite war pony forward, anticipating counting coup and screaming "*Hi-hi-hi.*" The trooper turned to avoid being run down but slipped in the snow and landed on his side. As he tried to get up, Cougar Eyes rammed the tip of his bow-lance into the cavalryman's throat. Nate saw the hapless man's head tilt violently toward the ground as his mouth opened, gasping for breath, but the sounds of the battle prohibited Nate from hearing the ghastly gurgling of blood pouring from the mortal wound.

Nate was too preoccupied to care. As the hostiles crawled and maneuvered on their bellies to get closer to the pony soldiers, the fire from their rifles became more deadly, and the incoming arrows more accurate. Nate was now on his stomach shooting his Spencer at the encroaching Indians but he was not sure if he was hitting anything. The lingering gun smoke and tall grass was making it extremely difficult to see.

Three men had been wounded and another four lay dead including Major Elliott. That only left six able-bodied troopers in addition to himself to ward off the attack until help arrived. Two of the wounded troopers, though, were able to discharge their Army Colts at the encroaching hostiles but were firing so wildly that their shots were ineffectual.

Nate moved about on his stomach within the shrinking circular skirmish line to try to cover the spots where soldiers now lay dead.

A young cavalryman with several ripe pimples on his face looked at Nate and yelled, *"They goin' to murder us all."* His countenance exhibited all the signs of terror. Nate was quick to see that although the youngster's face was smeared with dirt, perspiration, and gun smoke, his eyes bulged clearly from their sockets, while his mouth quivered as if he was about to cry. "You—you—you think . . . Custer will come and save us?" he added, his voice filled with consternation.

"Keep firing and mark your man," retorted Nate, pushing back the lever on his Spencer and cocking back the hammer to shoot off another round.

"I—I am out of ammunition."

Nate fired a round at a big fat buck who ran across his line of fire and dropped him. "Here." Nate threw his saddlebag in front of the youth's chest. "Get some frum my bag." The lad's hands trembled as he struggled to unflap the lid when a shower of arrows came from the sky, descending upon the remaining survivors of the squad. Two of the lethally pointed shafts plunged into the young soldier's rib cage. The pimpled youth grunted and his body contorted from the blows. He turned to Nate to beg for help, but Nate could do nothing except watch him die as the soldier's young anguished eyes gaped at him.

Two other men also received mortal arrow wounds. One received an arrow in the groin as he lay on his back while loading the last few shells in his Blakleslee tube. The arrowhead had sliced his penis off, pierced his scrotum, and entered into his abdomen.

The soldier howled in pain as he withered on the ground, blood gushing from his wound. The other trooper, a corporal, and one of the few cavalrymen who was on his belly trying to carefully pick targets, was more fortunate. He caught two arrowheads deep in his back, puncturing his lungs and liver. He tried to raise himself from his horizontal position, but he hacked blood from his mouth and collapsed to the ground. He died quickly.

Effective fire from the skirmish line was being decimated due to growing casualties. Several bullets had pierced Nate's buffalo coat but had avoided hitting him directly, only ripping his skin in several spots. One shell had, however, taken a piece of flesh off his left foot. Besides Nate, the eight survivors were too few and too far apart to cover all of the approaches of the skirmish line. Aware of this situation, the emboldened hostiles were maneuvering closer; popping up from their places of concealment to take shots at the surviving and terrified bluecoats.

"Gawddamn Elliott," growled Nate as he shot off his last round that he had for his Spencer repeater. "Givin' up the horses an' makin' us lie here like trapped rats!" He threw the repeater down and pulled his trusty Walker-Colt from the holster. He knew, however, that he only had about a dozen rounds left for his Walker-Colt and after that he would have to search among the dead for ammunition. Nate fully expected the Indians who were creeping toward them in front, flanks, and rear to rise up from the grass and charge them to count coup and finish the fight. His experience had taught him that Indians competed with one another to count coup and take scalps from the enemy, and this was especially true when they sensed that the end was near for their opponents.

"Come on, you bastards. Come and get it!" he yelled defiantly. Nate was determined that if he was going to be killed, he was going to take a few bucks with him.

Cougar Eyes had spotted Nate. It was not too difficult, considering that his figure was familiar to the Dog Man and he was the biggest bluecoat among the pony soldiers. He also observed that he was the only one who was putting up an honorable fight. He had one knee planted firmly in the ground and used the other one to support his right elbow when firing the Spencer.

Cougar Eyes knew that all of the trapped bluecoats were going to die. The Arapahoes and the Kiowas had already taken the first coups and the soldiers had many dead. In a few minutes, the Comanches and even the Apaches would be descending on this place on their way to attack the soldiers at Black Kettle's village. Cougar Eyes did not want his friend to die at the hands of the Arapahoes, Kiowas, or Comanches. True, they were brothers and eager to engage the hated mutual enemy, but it troubled Cougar Eyes that his friend might fall to a member of a different tribe. *Hotoa' e Gordon* was fighting with honor and he was not in the village killing women and children.

"Hova'ahane!" exclaimed the Dog Soldier. "No, if *Hotoa' e Gordon* is going to die, it will be at the hands of the *Tsitsitas."*

Nate had managed to get the survivors into a tighter circle to cover the front, back, and flanks, but that had the disadvantage of allowing the hostiles to concentrate their fire at a smaller, more compact target. Two of the wounded were killed by another arrow barrage as they lay helplessly in the grass.

The Arapaho, Kiowa, and Comanche warriors sensed triumph. They were excited at the prospect of annihilating this party of invading pony soldiers and capturing all of their possessions.

Realizing that all of the pony soldiers were going to be rubbed out within a few minutes, Cougar Eyes tapped his moccasin-clad heels to his horse's flanks and charged at the dwindling party of defenders. He raised his war club high in the air in readiness to take coup.

Nate saw Cougar Eyes coming toward him but did not recognize the Dog Man because his face was smeared with smoke and war paint. Nate had exhausted all of the ammunition for his Spencer and was now firing the last few balls he had in the cylinder of his Walker-Colt. He still had his Bowie knife and was prepared to defend himself with the huge blade until he was cut down. He fired at Cougar Eyes but the Dog Man zig-zagged his pony skillfully, avoiding Nate's bullets. Seeing Cougar Eyes rush the surviving bluecoats, and not willing to let the Dog Man take all the honor, some of the Arapahoes and Comanches decided to follow the Dog Soldier.

Only Nate and six troopers were left, and as some of the Arapahoes and Comanches hurled lances and shot their revolvers at them, one trooper received a lance in the shoulder, severing his arm from its socket. Another trooper was shot in the face and was screaming and swearing as he kicked his feet in the air.

Cougar Eyes was fast approaching and Nate was out of ammunition for his Walker-Colt. He quickly holstered the big horse pistol and removed the Bowie knife from its sheath. He gripped the pommel firmly, and held the weapon in front of him, the edge facing outward at an angle. Cougar Eyes saw that Nate was ready to use his knife but was not concerned. He knew *Hotoa' e Gordon* and his fighting abilities, so he was prepared. As his war pony galloped forward, the Dog Soldier pulled his war club from his belt and held the lethal weapon where he could swing the club with efficiency. Cougar Eyes was only a few feet away from Nate when he noticed an Arapaho warrior had maneuvered his pony to within the skirmish line slightly ahead of him. The Arapaho dismounted from his excited war pony as he screeched "*Hi-hi-hi*" and drew his knife. He leaped upon the belly of a terrified trooper who was lying on his backside. The pony soldier stared in horror at his assailant and froze in fright, his hands clutching the empty Spencer repeater. The Arapaho leered at his victim and gave a quick, repulsive grin, and then slashed the trooper's throat. He then removed the cavalryman's forage cap and seized the dying man's hair with his left hand and lifted his scalp with his bloodied knife.

Cougar Eyes' pony came up to Nate and both men looked at each other. Nate finally recognized the Dog Soldier and became confounded. He slowly lowered his knife while Cougar Eyes' pony pranced excitedly around him. Cougar Eyes' face remained firm, his lips were tight, and his gaze possessed a determined look. Nate was breathing heavily and his face was grimy with perspiration, dirt, and gun smoke. He was still uncertain what to do because he had not expected to encounter his onetime nemesis, and the last time they saw each other the Dog Man had saved his life.

Cougar Eyes touched his moccasins to his pony's flanks, commanding the animal to rear on his hind hooves and move forward. The beast responded instantly, and the pony's left hoof hit Nate on the right side of his face with great force, knocking him over on his side. Nate felt the blow to his temple and ear but then immediately blacked out as he was thrown to the ground.

The three remaining troopers were rapidly dispatched. One trooper started to weep and beg for mercy as arrows pierced his torso, buttocks, arms, legs, neck, and face, as several outraged braves methodically fixed arrow after arrow to their bowstrings and sent them hurling into the cavalryman's body.

Another trooper, lying on his back, became locked into hand-to-hand combat with a Cheyenne Dog Man who carried a Lancaster rifle. The warrior was on foot and the combatants were fighting with empty weapons. The Dog Man held the Lancaster by the barrel and was attempting to bash in the trooper's head with his rifle butt, but the pony soldier kept moving his head away and for a while successfully beat off the warrior's blows with his own empty Spencer rifle. The stock of the Cheyenne's Lancaster, however, unexpectedly snapped off at the rear end of the trigger guard when the warrior inadvertently hit the frozen ground. This so infuriated the Dog Man that he took the jagged end of the stock and thrust the splintered object into the trooper's rib cage with such force that the wooden piece protruded from the man's side as if it were a tree branch.

The last trooper in Major Elliott's command who had earlier been wounded in the hip by a bullet kept firing his Army Colt at the Indians who were swarming all around him. The cavalryman, however, was too terrified to aim accurately and quickly ran out of ammunition. Seizing the opportunity, Turkey Leg rode up to the trooper and lanced him in the chest.

General Armstrong Custer was looking through his field glasses at the mounting presence of hostiles that occupied the high ground overlooking Black Kettle's ravished village. Some of the other officers such as Benteen and W. W. Cook were also viewing the heights with great interest. The officers noticed that the Indians were circling wildly and were dressed in bright warbonnets as they taunted the soldiers to come out and fight while they provokingly brandished lances and rifles.

Jesse was standing next to Lieutenant Godfrey thinking about Nate. He had a bad feeling that his friend was in trouble. It was increasingly obvious that thousands of warriors were descending upon the command from the villages downstream, and that Custer would have to do something. Jesse became relieved when he saw that the ammunition train and supplies had now caught up with the command. The quartermaster sergeant and his men were in the process of issuing more ammo to the troopers in anticipation of a second fight with the hostiles. Only these Indians, however, unlike Black Kettle's sleeping tribesmen, were prepared to do battle and outnumbered Custer's Seventh by at least two to one.

"Those hostiles are riding like devils incarnate," remarked Benteen as he peered through his field glasses.

"Yes, I am surprised to see that their steeds are in such good condition," added Custer coolly.

Benteen lowered his field glasses from his eyes and turned to Custer. "Sir, should we not send out a party to search for Major Elliott? I fear that his prolonged absence from the command . . ."

"I am sure Major Elliott will be returning soon," interrupted the general. "I want to take inventory of all the hostiles' property, and continue to burn their lodges and all of their means to make war!"

"Sir, we have gathered the pony herd together," reported Lieutenant Godfrey.

"Excellent. What's the count?"

"We've counted eight hundred and forty ponies and mules, General."

Custer's eyes lit up in wonderment. "That many?"

"Yes, sir, General."

"Well, at that number it will be impossible to bring back the herd to Camp Supply," commented Tom Custer who had joined his brother and the other officers only moments before.

"Kill all the ponies, but no ammunition will be used for the task," ordered the general as he placed his field glasses back into its case.

Jesse was shocked at the order. Kill over eight hundred horses by hand? Godfrey was also surprised at the order, but knew better than to question the impatient general.

Custer saw an Indian dog licking at a pool of blood. The general removed the .44-caliber revolver from his holster and quickly aimed and fired at the dog, hitting the mutt in the head. He then turned and leered at Godfrey. "Move on it, man! We don't have time to waste. I don't care how you do it," he snipped. "Cut their throats, use axes and sledgehammers for all I care. But no ammunition is to be wasted. Are you clear on that, Lieutenant?"

"Aye, sir." Godfrey saluted and went off to collect additional men to assist him in executing the appalling order.

Not willing to be involved in such a horrendous enterprise, Jesse left to help burn the tipis and collect saddles, weapons, and buffalo robes. Before placing the articles on the enormous heap of burning Cheyenne property, each trooper had to stop and wait for a corporal to meticulously enter each item into a ledger that was divided by columns.

A corpulent trooper with a thick neck approached Jesse. He was carrying an ax and his hands and arms were stained in blood. He had removed his army greatcoat because he had exerted himself to such a point that he was sweating and breathing with effort.

"Goddamn Indian horses won't stay still long 'nough to kill, 'cause dey can't stand the smell of a white man," he complained. "I did kilt a couple though, but it took a couple hits to the head 'for' they go down." The trooper grinned and held out the ax for Jesse. "Here, boy! Maybe they'll stand still for a darkie." The coarse trooper laughed heartily, as if he were telling a preferred joke and looked at Jesse with a daring look in his eye.

"You call me Sergeant, Private!" retorted Jesse defensively. He felt insulted that this white enlisted man had failed to address him by his rank and called him boy. "I'm not in yo'r damn regiment, boy! But as long as I wear these stripes, you call me Sergeant." Jesse turned away from the crude trooper and headed for the burning heap of Indian accoutrements.

Although Jesse had managed to exempt himself from taking part in the killing of the horses and mules, he quickly discovered much to his disgust that his current task, to go about the village and gather Indian belongings for the bonfire, was equally repulsive. Dead, half-naked bodies of Cheyenne women, children, and old men and some warriors were scattered about the ground everywhere. Their corpses were heavily caked with mud and blood and many of the dead lay in hideous contorted positions, their faces staring into oblivion. Most of the bodies, men and women alike, shared the same fate of being mutilated and showed signs of pilfering by Custer's men. Jesse noticed that many scalps had been lifted and he witnessed cavalrymen taking jewelry from the squaws, using their knives to cut off fingers.

Jesse thought about the bloody battle of Milliken's Bend during the war. The surrounding carnage reminded him of his regiment, the Ninth Louisiana Guard, and when they had to fight the Rebels under savage close-in combat where the wounds and means of death were horrendous. On that occasion, however, it was fighting man against fighting man, Bluecoat versus Secesh, and not soldiers slaughtering civilians. Although Jesse had taken part in the killing at Black Kettle's village and participated in shooting at the squaw who murdered the white captive boy, he now felt disgusted. The frigid and lifeless landscape was dotted with dozens of burning tipis, mixed with the stench of burning buffalo robes, dried meat, and the wailing of squaws and sobbing of papooses.

"Jezus! Hell must be like this!" he whispered to himself, shaking his head in disbelief. He feared slipping and falling into blood. As he transported Indian saddles and weapons to the central burning pile, he constantly had to watch where he stepped because of the large pools of steaming gore that oozed from the heaps of Cheyenne corpses that were thrown on top of each other.

The process of killing all of the Indian ponies and mules proved to be extremely arduous and lengthy. With the exception of those animals fortunate enough to be taken by the officers and the scouts and about fifty ponies that the captured squaws were told to select for their trip to Camp Supply, the men were slow in capturing the beasts for slaying. Jesse overheard Lieutenant Godfrey plead with Custer to grant him permission to shoot the animals to death because even with four companies of men, mostly armed with knives, axes, and sledgehammers, the soldiers barely made a dent in the enormous herd. Custer grudgingly gave permission but ordered Godfrey to make haste as he was preparing to re-form the command and descend upon the other hostile camps downstream. Within a few moments Godfrey had given the order to surround the herd and commence firing at the ponies. Jesse could hear the report of dozens of Spencer repeaters. The Indian ponies started to neigh in fright and groan in pain as they were shot to death by the cavalrymen. The hapless beasts would try to flee in one direction only to be met with a hail of gunfire so they would turn in another direction but again meet the same rain of lead. Jesse cringed as he was forced to listen to the hellish sounds of hundreds of dying horses breathe their last breaths as they collapsed on their forelegs and rolled over dead, or simply plunged their long necks and heads into the ground while their asses remained in the air. Jesse again whispered to himself, only this time more loudly, "Damn place! Wez butchers in a slaughter yard gon' mad!"

The systematic annihilation of the pony herd enraged the Indians who were congregating on the bluffs. Seeing and hearing the ponies being shot to death filled them with dread and increased their anger at the pony soldiers. Many of the braves started to increase their fire at the bluecoats but their shots fell short and were more irritating to the troopers than effectual.

Most of the braves wanted to charge the pony soldiers but the lessons of the Beecher Island fight were still fresh in the minds of the chiefs and they restrained their hot-blooded warriors because they feared that the disciplined fire from the Bluecoats would only decimate their numbers.

When Custer ordered that the Seventh re-form and prepare to descend in force toward the lower villages, most of the officers became astonished that he should command such a maneuver when the regiment had many wounded and most of the men were exhausted. The irascible Benteen voiced his concerns, but the general dismissed his objections and told the officer that it was his intention to march on the other villages with the band playing "Garry Owen" and all the flags and guidons flying high.

"Sir, what about Major Elliott?" asked Captain Thomas Weir.

"Take two squads and search for him, but do not lose sight of the village and you must report back by the time the regiment moves on downstream," ordered Custer. The general felt that he had to compromise. Custer had been told by some of his officers that the enlisted men were starting to grumble that they were leaving their comrades behind. So the general felt that he had to at least make a search for the missing troopers in order to stop the griping.

"Captain, sir," pleaded Jesse to Weir. "Permission to accompany you, sir."

"Why do you wish to come?" Thomas Weir's eyes sized up Jesse. He wondered why this black noncom would bother to volunteer to search for white soldiers.

"Sir, my friend, Sergeant Major Nate Gordon, went with Major Elliott, sir.

"Very well, Sergeant, permission granted."

"Sir, the first sergeant thanks the captain."

"Mount your animal, First Sergeant."

"Sir," replied Jesse, giving a crisp salute.

Captain Weir and Jesse, along with the two squads, trotted in the direction of where Major Elliott, Nate, and eighteen troopers had been last seen. Because of Custer's orders that they remain in sight of the village and the growing number of hostiles, Captain Weir was limited in his search for Major Elliott. Jesse was in front of the two squads with Weir when he spotted a dark item resting on a patch of snow directly in front of him. He indicated his curiosity to the captain and Weir told him to investigate. Jesse cantered Cailloux over to the patch of snow and Jesse identified the item as a kepi, like the one Nate wore. He dismounted and picked up the item and saw that the brass crossed sabers and regiment insignia had been removed. He then looked at the inside of the headgear and saw a yellow label in the back with someone's name written in dark print. The ink was very much faded due to time and wear, but Jesse examined each letter carefully and made out the first initial of the name, which was capitalized.

"N," he said aloud. His heart then jumped when he identified the second capital letter of the last name and then the next five letters. "G, o, r, d, o, n. N. Gordon!" Jesse stared at the label and then looked up, his eyes searching the landscape. "Damn!" Jesse shook his head in dread and whispered aloud to himself, "I knew it. I got a bad feelin'."

"What is it, Sergeant?" demanded Captain Weir as he came up with his men.

"A kepi, Captain." He handed the article over to Weir. Weir looked over the article carefully. "Only officers wear kepis, and this could belong to Major Elliott."

"Beggin' the captain's pardon, sir. But if you look inside on the sweatband you'll see that it belongs to Sergeant Major Nate Gordon of the Tenth Cavalry, sir." Jesse paused as if he lamented telling Weir the bad news. "He was with Major Elliott, sir."

"N. Gordon," confirmed Weir, reading the label. He handed Nate's headgear back to Jesse and smirked with apprehension. "This does not look promising."

"No, sir," agreed Jesse, gently turning Nate's kepi in his hands as he stared at the inside of his friend's hat.

Several dozen mounted Indians appeared within sight of Weir's detachment. They were yelping insults and beckoning the pony soldiers to attack them as several fired their guns hitting the ground and frightening the cavalry horses.

Weir decided to return to the command immediately. He was not going to be lured into a trap as Major Elliott had apparently done, and he was convinced more hostiles were coming his way. He motioned with his right hand to turn his tiny column around and return to Black Kettle's scorched encampment.

Although Jesse felt remorse and anxious regarding Nate's fate, he knew that they could no longer search for him. He cursed Custer for only giving Weir a few men for the search, hence hampering their efforts. Uncharacteristically, Jesse was the last trooper to leave the area. The squad galloped past him and he had to firmly hold the reins on Cailloux because the animal wanted to follow the other horses. Only when several bullets zipped past his head did he turn Cailloux round and dig his spurs into his mount's flanks to take flight.

Part Three

THE SEARCH

Silas Quinn was snoring heavily through his mouth. He lay on his backside on a straw mattress bed that was slightly elevated by rows of ash wood stumps. The miner's feet stuck out from under a heavy soiled patch quilt, and Cara could smell the foulness of his foot odor. Quinn had drunk himself to sleep the night before and his hands still clutched the empty bottle of rye next to his chest as if he were a baby holding a spent milk bottle. He wore a pair of white stained long johns that had yellowed over time and had big holes at the toes. Both his big toes had overgrown nails and protruded from the wretched garment as if they were mushrooms.

The sun had just appeared over the horizon and Cara was watching the big bright ball rise out of Quinn's only window that had a burlap bag over the opening. One of the few pleasures she now enjoyed was to watch the sun rise and set because she knew Nate was doing the same somewhere, and this connection gave her hope that her man would come.

She felt a slight movement within her stomach, signaling that the child was growing within her womb. She placed her hand on her belly and smiled.

"Mio bebe," she whispered softly to herself with satisfaction. She had successfully fought Quinn off the day when he forced

himself on her and the miner was only able to ejaculate on her leg. He had become so humiliated by this mishap and horrified that Cara had giggled when he had come onto her buckskin leggings that for the moment he did not have the courage to sexually attack her.

Unable to sleep, Cara had been awake for several hours and used the time to do some sewing repair work on her Mexican blanket that she used to keep her body warm and repair her Comanche moccasins as well as preparing Quinn's breakfast.

A blast of cold air entered the room from the window and breezed past Silas Quinn's face, waking him from his drink-induced slumber. He moaned in discomfort and felt sick. He had barely devoured the food that Cara had prepared for him, preferring instead to consume liquor.

"Sh-sh-shuu-shut th-the damn window, will ya," he commanded with great irritation. The miner did not like being rudely awoken especially when he was hungover. Although he felt sexually humiliated, he had intensified his verbal and physical abuse toward Cara in part to retain control and partially to compensate for his inadequacy. Cara quickly rolled the burlap bag over the opening and fastened it with some hooks.

"I have breakfast," she retorted defiantly, wrapping her Mexican blanket over herself. Ever since Quinn had forced himself on her she had felt nothing but abhorrence for the miner. She had continued to do her chores, however, such as fixing his meals, sweeping the cabin, and doing laundry as a means for keeping herself occupied.

"Fuck breakfast," snipped Quinn as he tossed the empty bottle and turned on his side. The bed was large enough for two but Cara refused to join him even at the expense of keeping warm and instead slept in the corner on the floor.

"*Perezoso!* You lazy," she replied in disgust.

"I—I ain't lazy, da-da-damn you," bristled the miner defensively. Cara's insult motivated Quinn to raise himself from his fetal position and sit at the edge of the bed. He stared aimlessly with his one good eye for a moment and then his face suddenly became contorted as he gave a great yawn. He then vigorously scratched his beard and then his rectum before standing up. He stretched his body and felt the pain in his lower back. Squatting and panning for gold by the creek for hours on end day after day, had given the miner flashes of pain through his left buttocks that traveled down the back of his left leg. He sat back down on the bed and dragged his mud-caked boots across the crude wooden floor. He winced in discomfort as he placed each foot in a boot and pulled the straps over his feet. Completing this essential taks, he rose again from the bed and bowed his head in reflection. He mumbled something incoherently and then proceeded to slowly walk over toward Cara, who was carefully watching all of his moves. Quinn halted when he was about a foot away from her and raised his enormous right hand, the palm wide open. Cara felt the sting of the miner's smack on her left cheek. The blow forced her body to slam up against the cabin wall.

"Dh, dh, don't yu, you say that I'm lazy. You ain't my mother."

Cara touched her face and felt that it was hot from the impact. She felt stung, but had received harder hits from Vasco when he used to beat her.

"Where's my coffee?" demanded Quinn. He was proud that he did not stutter the sentence.

"On the table." Cara nodded her head toward the tin cup and a plate that held some biscuits and bacon. Silas Quinn was a boorish brute, but he believed in being well supplied with victuals.

The miner took the cup of coffee and sipped carefully. Cara deliberately made the brew very hot, hoping that her jailer would burn his lip on the liquid. Quinn had learned over the past few weeks after he had purchased Cara from Vasco that the half-breed was a pugnacious individual. Quinn sat down at the table and Cara went over to the fireplace to fetch some biscuits and salt pork from the cast-iron pot.

"Hh, hh, hurry up with that grub, will ya." Quinn was hungry. He had had no dinner the night before and the smell of the biscuits and bacon had now given him an appetite.

In silence, Cara placed the tin plate in front of him but quickly turned away to return to her corner that had a stool to finish her sewing. As she maneuvered her bone needle through the antelope hide on one of her moccasins, she heard the uncouth miner slurp down the strips of bacon one by one.

"D-d-*did* you fix my britches?" snarled Quinn, struggling with his tongue to maneuver a piece of hot bacon fat in his mouth.

Cara remained silent, her delicate hands working her bone needle through the sole of her beaded moccasin.

"D-d-did you hear me, woman? Are m-m-my br-br-britches sewed up?" he demanded to know as he grabbed a biscuit and started to tear it apart.

"Sí. Acabado," she retorted coldly. She suddenly rose from her stool and picked up Quinn's britches from the floor and threw them on the table near his plate of food.

There was a loud knock on Quinn's cabin door that startled both the miner and Cara.

"What the hell?" growled Quinn. He was still hungover and did not wish to see anybody until he had at least completed his breakfast. In addition, he had been careful in keeping Cara hidden from the other miners who lived along the creeks and streams of South Pass, and was not eager to let the word out that he had a woman.

Hiram Mackenzie stood outside the door waiting to enter. The middle-aged mountain man was a big and stocky individual with a long unkempt gray beard. His equally lengthy hair protruded from under his round beaver hat, and with the exception of a vest made from the hide of a mountain lion, was entirely clad in buckskin, decorated with colorful Shoshone beaded trimmings on his breast and shoulders.

"Open up the goddamn door, Quinn. I know you got a breed woman in there and I want to have a looksee." Mackenzie was a very determined fellow, and when he wanted to find out about something, he never took no for an answer. He carried a Hawken rifle and was never seen without it. He held the weapon easily and cradled it in his arms as if the long-barreled gun were a child. He had spent over forty years as a trapper and hunter, traveling throughout the Missouri River basin and knew many of the original mountain men who were already legends. Mackenzie had been told by the Shoshone that they had seen a half-breed woman traveling with Silas Quinn and Mackenzie was interested to know more. Women, whether they were Indian, white, or half-breed, were rare in southeastern Wyoming, consequently they were eagerly coveted.

"Da-*damn* him, tha-that *nosy* mountain man pesterin' me all the time." Quinn was so irritated at this intrusion that spit sprayed from his mouth. He quickly rose, violently shoving the chair that he was sitting on backward. He then wiped his greasy hands on his long johns before he unbolted the door and swung it open.

"Mornin', Quinn. I smelled your bacon a mile away." Mackenzie smiled mischievously. The big mountain man entered the cabin, his beaver-clad head nearly touching the ceiling. He searched the premises with his sharp eyes and immediately noticed Cara sitting on her stool sewing. She suddenly raised her head to look at Mackenzie and the mountain man caught her eyes gazing at him. Feeling self-conscious, she immediately lowered her head and returned to her needle and thread. The seasoned trapper and hunter marveled at her brilliant eyes and delicate bronzed visage. Over the decades, Mackenzie had seen many half-breeds in the mountains and on the plains, but none that possessed such exquisite features.

"Wh-wh-wha-what you want?" replied Quinn as he scratched his ass.

"Some coffee would be nice," responded Mackenzie with a wide grin as he advanced away from the doorway and made for the chair that was facing Quinn's plate of food. He gently placed his Hawken rifle against the edge of the table and looked at Cara.

"You her-*heard* the ma-man. Git him some coffee so he'll leave me in peace," ordered Quinn as he positioned his chair back at the table, facing his uninvited guest.

Cara rose from her corner and went over to the tin coffee kettle and poured the brew into another cup. She then went over to Mackenzie and handed it to the mountain man who took the opportunity to gaze into her face. His huge and powerful hands gently took the cup of steaming coffee from Cara's delicate grasp and placed it on the table without tasting it. Cara was in the process of turning away and returning to her corner when Mackenzie lightly seized Cara's arm.

"What's your name, *señorita?*" he inquired softly. He knew that part of her was Mexican but he was eager to find out what tribe was her other half.

She raised her head up proudly and looked deeply into the mountain man's gray eyes. "Cara de Quervo Zarata," she stated loudly and clearly.

Hiram Mackenzie was impressed by her confidence. This woman sounded intelligent and strong as well as beautiful. He liked what he saw and thought that Quinn did not deserve to have such a woman.

"Are you half Apache? White Mountain tribe perhaps?" he

asked casually, taking a sip of the coffee. Mackenzie had spent some time with that tribe, twenty years ago, and thought that she resembled them.

"*No, señor. Comancheria!*" she proclaimed, lifting her head proudly.

"*Ah, bueno. Es de grande raza!*" replied Mackenzie, who enjoyed practicing his Spanish that he had learned from Mexicans. "*De dónde viene?*" pressed Mackenzie. He wanted to know where this woman came from.

"*Yo soy de Tejas,*" she replied.

"*Yo he estado en Tejas. Buena Tierra,*" responded the trapper.

"St-st-stop that damn Mexican lingo," stammered Quinn, irritated that he could not understand what they were talking about. "Mackenzie!" Quinn pointed his finger at the mountain man. "U-u-you sp-spoilin' my wo-wo-*woman.*"

"Why? By being polite to her, you ol' coot?" ridiculed the trapper.

"Who—who you callin' a coot? I'll remind ya th-tha-that you in *my* cabin."

Hiram Mackenzie remained silent. The uncouth miner was correct nevertheless, but the mountain man had become intrigued and desired to talk more with his host's half-breed woman.

Two

Nate woke up with a burning fever and he felt his head throbbing in pain. He was flat on his back and his eyes had trouble focusing at the beamed cottonwood and adobe ceiling. A lantern flickered on a table near his bed at low flame, and since he could not detect any natural daylight in the room, he assumed that it was evening. He went to touch the side of his head and felt a damp, cool cloth at the spot where Cougar Eyes' war pony had kicked him. He tried to open his mouth but it was painful because his jaw and cheekbone were very sore from the blow.

Nate forced his eyes to focus on the room and decided that he was in a small chamber with adobe walls with no windows. He saw a closed heavy wooden door with Mexican wrought-iron hardware to his left and wondered if it was locked. After a few moments, he also noticed that some areas on the walls had minor scorch marks from a fire, but there was no lingering smell of smoke. He tried to raise his head and sit up, but found that it was impossible because of the pain in his head. He moaned and decided that not since he was hit by sunstroke when he was a child had he felt such pain. Nate tried to remember what had happened and past events. His mind returned to Major Elliott's death and the annihilation of his men. He suddenly recalled how Cougar

Eyes came up to him and how they briefly stared at each other, and that the Dog Man's face was void of any real emotion but Nate retained the image of his determined gaze.

"His goddamn horse! He—he knocked me over," he groaned, recalling the moment when the beast reared up and hit him in the head with his hooves.

Nate heard the iron door latch move followed by a long creak made by the rusty hinges of the door and saw that it was slowly opening. He first saw a lit lantern and then the hand that held it. He then heard a man's voice say something in Cheyenne that caused him to feel some anxiety. *Am I captive?* he wondered. The individual slowly entered the chamber. Nate could see that the individual was a tall and burly man, but because of the pain in his head and the bright light from the flame in his lantern, he was unable to see his facial features.

"How are you feeling?" asked the man as he raised his lantern to flood the chamber with light. Nate could see his face now and immediately decided that the man was a breed. His skin was bronze in color, like Cara's, and his eyes were dark. His face was very large and oval in shape. His thick, pitch-black hair rested on his broad shoulders and he had dark eyebrows that matched the thin Mexican mustache that covered most of his upper lip. His manner of dress was all Indian except for his blue silk shirt and wool pants that was beaded on the outside seams of the legs with matching elegant moccasins.

"Can you hear me? How are you feeling, *Hotoa' e Gordon?*" inquired the man again.

Nate became stunned when he heard his name spoken by the man who appeared to be a breed but he looked genuinely concerned and his voice was soft and controlled, sounding as if he was a caring friend.

"Like hell," cursed Nate. He placed his right hand on his fore-

head as a means to try to slow the throbbing discomfort. "Wher'—wher' am I? How did you know my name?"

The tall and burly man took the only chair in the room that was against the far wall of the chamber and placed it near Nate's bed. He lowered his lantern and placed it on the adobe floor.

"Let me look at your head," asked the man who gently removed the damp cloth from Nate's forehead. He placed his right hand on Nate's forehead to verify the temperature and to look at Nate's swollen cheek. Although the stranger was a big man who looked very fit, Nate could feel the gentleness of his hands. "You are at my father's old fort."

"What fort?" Nate became perplexed. He was already at a loss to explain how he arrived at this strange place, when he should have been killed with Elliott, and now he wondered about the identity of this caring man who was dressed in Indian clothing and who spoke perfect English.

"You are at Old Bent's fort, and I am George Bent," he replied.

"You Colonel William Bent's son?" Medicine Bill Comstock and Sharp Grover had told Nate about Old Bent's fort and its founder, the trader and friend of the Indians, William Bent. The two scouts had told him that the fort was at one time considered the castle of the plains and during its heyday was the center of trade west of the Missouri River.

"But Bent's fort is 'bout two hundred and fifty miles from . . ."

"The Washita," interrupted George Bent.

"How in hell did I get here?"

"By travois, pulled by a mule. I see that your wound is much improved."

"Who brought me here?"

"A friend, who did not wish to see you rubbed out with Elliott. At least not yet." Bent smiled sardonically.

"Which friend? An' how you know Major Elliott?" Nate

thought he was dreaming. His situation did not seem real. The last event he remembered was Cougar Eyes staring at him as his war pony reared in front of him while hostiles swarmed all about killing off the surviving troopers. Now, he was at Old Bent's fort two hundred fifty miles away from the Washita, talking with the half-breed George Bent.

"Cougar Eyes brought you here, and asked me to take care of you."

"Cougar Eyes? He dragged me here?" Nate was not entirely surprised by this information.

"Cougar Eyes wanted to spare your life and get you out of there. His pony knocked you over and he and another warrior then placed your body on his horse and led the animal away from the fight. He then transferred you to a travois to bring you here." Bent suddenly turned to the door and shouted some words in Cheyenne that Nate did not recognize. A fine-looking squaw wearing an elegantly embroidered full body length deerskin dress entered the room carrying a wooden bowl of steaming turnip broth and some bread. "This is my wife, Magpie," introduced Bent. "She has brought you food, so now you must eat."

The smell of the steaming broth had stimulated Nate's appetite, and the pounding in his head subsided a little.

George Bent helped Nate to sit up in his bed so he could consume the liquid in the bowl. Magpie carried the soup carefully as she walked toward Nate's bed while George Bent got up from the chair so his wife could take his place to feed Nate. The squaw delicately sat at the edge of the chair and dipped the buffalo horn spoon into the broth and held it in front of her patient.

"*Meseestse!*" she commanded. "Eat."

"*Hahoo,*" replied Nate willingly. He opened his mouth and Magpie feed him a spoonful of soup. He swallowed the liquid and felt its warmth down his throat.

"Epeveeno'e." He nodded in approval. Magpie was about to serve him another spoonful when Nate stopped her by placing the palm of his right hand in front of the spoon. *"Noxa'e."* Nate did not want to be fed as if he were a helpless infant. He felt better now and wanted to feed himself. He gestured that he wanted to take the bowl and spoon. Magpie nodded and obliged him. She then raised herself from the chair, and her husband then took over the seat.

"Cougar Eyes told me that you spoke some of the people's language," commented George Bent, watching his guest spoon-feed himself.

"Just some words," he responded modestly. Nate thought that the broth tasted so good that he wanted to abandon the spoon and simply gulp the soup directly from the bowl. His sense of propriety, however, prevented him from submitting to his impulses.

As a compromise though, Nate placed the wooden bowl next to his mouth and used the spoon to quickly drain the basin. Magpie took back the container and spoon and handed Nate the piece of fried bread.

Bent told her in Cheyenne to bring another helping of broth and Magpie left the chamber.

"Mr. Bent, sir. How you know Major Elliott?" queried Nate as he broke the piece of bread in two.

"Oh, I know many of the officers among the soldiers who attacked Black Kettle; my wife's uncle's village," replied Bent caustically.

Nate thought about the old chief whom he saw shot to death in front of his tipi that had the American flag hanging from a lodge pole. He assumed that this was Black Kettle.

"I met Major Elliott at the Medicine Lodge Creek Treaty Ceremony last year. He was not a bad man but he was a bluecoat. He used to come every evening to our camp when the soldiers were bivouacked nearby. At the time, I was translating for the Cheyennes during the treaty negotiations and while we were all camped around Medicine Lodge Creek, I also met Lieutenant Louis Hamilton, Custer, and General Sherman."

"You know Custer?" Nate was feeling much better now. The turnip soup and bread were lifting his spirits and his host's agreeable demeanor invited conversation.

"He is like a coyote." Bent smirked as soon as he heard the general's name. "The man is a liar and has no honor."

Nate broke off another piece of the fried bread and placed it in his mouth. Magpie had returned with another bowl of soup and placed the vessel on the night table where it was near Nate.

"Hahoo." Nate nodded, grateful that she had brought him another serving. He thought about Custer and how he felt that "Ringlets" had abandoned Elliott and his men to their fate.

"Did Cougar Eyes say anything when he brought me here?" Nate was curious about what the Dog Man might have told George Bent.

"He did not say much. He simply told me that he had saved you from the other Indians and that Custer had attacked the peaceful village of Black Kettle on the Washita."

"Does he hold me responsible for the killing of the women and children?"

"Cougar Eyes is very angry but he does not hold you accountable for the slaughter of the innocent squaws and children. He knows that you are a man of honor and a warrior, not some crazy *Ve' ho' e* looking to kill and destroy anything that they do not understand."

Bent paused for a moment and called for Magpie again. Nate's presence made Bent think about the slave that his father had at the fort when he was a boy. He remembered warmly how the Cheyennes became very fond of this black man and one of his uncles became so enchanted with him that he renamed himself Black-White Man. Magpie appeared at the doorway and looked at her husband, waiting for instructions. Bent smiled at her.

"Bring me some coffee, please," he asked. She bowed her head in obedience and departed. Bent then turned to Nate who was chewing on some of the bread. "I am trying to teach my wife proper English, as I was taught when my father sent me away to St. Louis for my schooling." Bent stared at Nate for a moment as if he had something on his mind. "Were you a slave, *Hotoa' e Gordon?*"

Nate finished chewing on the piece of bread and swallowed it. "Yes. Yes, I was a slave," he responded, lowering his eyes in reflection.

"Where?" pressed Bent.

"In Louisiana, St. Charles parish." Nate thought for a moment and then added, "But it was a long time ago."

"Were you set free by the army?"

"No." Nate nodded firmly. "I ran and joined up with the army in Kansas." Nate looked into Bent's face and squinted his eyes. "I fought for my freedom."

"How did you escape?" Bent was drawn to Nate. With the exception of seeing slaves in St. Louis when he was attending school, the half-breed had only known one other black man, the slave that his father had once kept during the 1840s. Nate, however, seemed different from the ones he saw back East or at the fort. This man's tone of voice was confident and displayed inner strength in his facial expressions.

"I ran, I walked, I hid in the swamps and in the woods. I traveled hidin' in a wagon for a week, stayed at Underground Railroad safe houses, and stowed away on a steamer up the Red River."

Although George Bent was interested in what Nate had to

say, his mind was elsewhere. He was thinking about the friends and relatives he had lost at Black Kettle's village, and wondered when the state of mindless warfare that existed between the Indians and the white man would cease.

"I will leave you now. Finish your food and sleep. Tomorrow we will talk more."

"Yes, I do feel tired now," acknowledged Nate. He polished off the last of the broth and placed the bowl on the night table. George Bent went over and picked up the lantern that he had brought with him earlier and turned toward the door and was about to leave the chamber when Nate called out to him. "Mr. Bent, sir!" His host stopped and turned to face Nate. "I would like to thank you and your wife for yo'r hospitality."

George Bent bowed his head slightly and nodded.

"You seem like a good man, *Hotoa' e Gordon*." Bent stroked his thin mustache in contemplation and stretched his lips. "Perhaps Cougar Eyes was right in saving your life," he remarked dryly. "I look forward to talking with you some more."

Nate nodded and as he moved his body down on the mattress, he heard the heavy iron hinges squeal and the door latch close behind him.

II.

As soon as George Bent had departed from the adobe chamber, Nate blew out the wick in his lantern and placed his head on the pillow. The head cushion was soft and very comfortable, filled with goose feathers. Nate was glad that the pounding in his head had greatly subsided, enabling him to think. He wished that he had his precious journal with him and lamented the loss. The book was in his saddlebag strapped to the McClellan on John Brown's back. "I guess some hostile found it," he whispered to himself with resignation. Nate hoped, however, that the book would at least be used wisely and not used to wipe some buck's or squaw's ass or start a cook fire.

He liked George Bent. He seemed kind and thoughtful and in a certain way reminded him a little of Jacques Napoleon Gaches. Although the two men were very different; Gaches was a flamboyant dandy and a huckster, while Bent was serious, thoughtful, and physically powerful. Both men, however, were half-breeds and spoke the English language in an educated manner.

As he thought about the Creole gambler, his thoughts turned to *Belle de Jour* and his escape on the Red River, disguised as Gaches's body servant and companion while the gambler pretended to be an elderly rich invalid in a wheelchair.

His thoughts turned to when they first ventured out from their cabin in their disguises and proceeded toward the dining room. Nate was pushing Gaches in the wheelchair along the passenger deck, carefully avoiding the brass cuspidors that were set on the deck for tobacco-spitting passengers. Red River Sam was successful in procuring a wheelchair. The wicker chair had belonged to a former passenger who had passed away on the previous trip down the river and Red River Sam found it in the storage room. He also managed to acquire all of the makeup items that Gaches had requested and some dark clothes for Nate that were suitable to his new position.

It was suppertime and Nate could smell the cooking of food coming from the galley. The aroma of boiled ham, fried oysters, and steamed vegetables permeated the air and Nate pushed the chair faster toward the dining room. The chair picked up so much speed that Gaches, fearing that Nate might stop suddenly and that he would be propelled into the air and over the railing into the river, had to tell him to slow down.

Nate did slow down, though it was not because Gaches told him to. Coming toward them was the Confederate officer that was in charge of the company of soldiers that were billeted on the paddle wheeler. When Nate saw him approaching, his polished high-top boots gleaming from the glow of the lanterns that hung on the side of the walls of the cabin deck, he quickly bowed his head. Nate tried to avoid eye contact with any white person, fearing that they could tell that he was a runaway and that they would call the authorities or the patrollers on him. He was especially careful to stay out of harm's way from any Confederate officer who might ask him for papers or force him to do manual work for the Confederate Army. Before he had escaped the plantation it was not unusual for Confederate officers to come to Mas'a Hammond's estate and request slaves to dig ditches and build fortifications around New Orleans. The officer, however, paid no attention to Nate and Gaches, he was too much in a hurry to get back to his men after he had spent too much time at the bar.

Nate had to stop at the base of the stairwell and carry Gaches and the wheelchair down the stairs to reach the lower deck. He wheeled Gaches past the stacked piles of cotton bales and past their old hiding place to the dining-room entrance where Gaches instructed him to halt.

"Remember, my good man, you are my servant and companion, so you must listen attentively to everything I say."

"I understand." Nate nodded as he wheeled him in.

The dining area was a simple and pleasant room designed for hot weather. Numerous large square windows with blue curtains were on the port and starboard sides to create a draft in the room and the ceiling was higher on the main deck than the passenger deck above. The furnishings were basic. Simple wooden chairs and tables were arranged in rows with glass oil lamps on each table. The dishes and pewter utensils lay on top of white tablecloths.

The dining room was almost full and Gaches saw that Vincent Clemente and Simon Fury were eating at a table near a window. He looked at them briefly but they did not notice him. There was a free table next to them but Gaches did not wish to be seated next to his pursuers. When the head steward came to them, Gaches reached inside his slit pocket of his vest and placed a *Dix* note in the steward's hand. He then altered his voice to sound like an old man.

"Give us that table over there at the other end of the room."

"Yes, suh." The steward bowed as he accepted the money. "Please fol'ow me, suh."

Nate followed the steward past the tables that were filled with passengers eating their suppers as black waiters dressed in white hustled to accommodate their demands. He maneuvered the wheelchair up to the table and the steward handed Gaches a menu of what was being offered for dinner. "Please let me know if dare is an'thing mo' I can do fo' you, suh."

"Yes. Thank you. I will," replied Gaches, taking the menu with aplomb.

Nate felt awkward sitting at the table. His hands hung at his sides and he sat stiffly in his wooden chair.

"Relax and place your hands on the table," instructed Gaches, reading the list of items to eat on the menu.

"Put my hands where?" asked Nate, looking perplexed.

"Place them at each end of the place serving."

Nate did not know the term "place serving" but assumed that it meant the dish and the eating utensils, so he gently place his hands on each side but clenched his fists.

"Open your hands and place your palms on the tablecloth." Gaches was clearly enjoying his role as teacher. He wanted to instruct Nate on some basic table manners, so it would not be obvious that he was a primitive field slave. Gaches turned for a moment and glanced at Vincent Clemente and Simon Fury who were eating their dessert of lemon pie. Satisfied that his two pursuers had not noticed him because they appeared too preoccupied devouring the pie, Gaches turned to Nate. "I must say for such a plebeian tub as this, the menu is not bad."

"What does plebeian mean?" Nate wanted to keep the conversation going as a means to release his anxiety and keep to his role as a "companion" to Gaches.

"A peasant, a worker, a member of the lower classes."

"Well, that means I'm a plebeian," observed Nate proudly.

"That is true, my good man," acknowledged the Creole gambler. "But I will teach you how to behave as a patrician. Now, allow me to acquaint you with some of the items on the menu. We have soup, fish, roast, relishes, and entrées."

"What's an entrée?"

"The main dish of a meal or one served just before the main course," enlightened Gaches. "Allow me to read to you some of the entrées they have listed. We have *Pieds de Veau à la Puceline* or *Filets de Poulets aux Truffes.*" Although the menu listed the items in both French and English, Gaches wanted to impress Nate with his fluency and command of the French language.

"I don't understand nuthin'." Nate became a little irritated at his host's patronizing manner. He did not like being at the mercy of this man's antics and he felt like bolting the table and returning to his hiding place among the bales of cotton.

"Patience, my good man, patience," cautioned Gaches soothingly. "I will translate. We have calves' feet or chicken. Now, what would you prefer?"

"I'll take the chicken," decided Nate with exasperation.

"An excellent choice," praised the gambler as if he were the maître d'hôtel. "Oh, *waiter.*" Gaches raised his arm in the air and snapped his fingers at a nearby attendant.

"Yes, suh. Comin' right 'way, suh," he replied as he hastened to clear a nearby table. He returned promptly and stood at attention, waiting for Gaches's order.

"My companion and I will start with some boiled ham with some cabbage and hominy and as for the entrées, I will have the *Pieds de Veau à la Puceline,* while my companion will have the *Filets de Poulets aux Truffes.*"

"Yes, suh! Very good, suh," replied the waiter, bowing in obedience.

"Now, I would like to see the wine list," ordered Gaches.

"Sor'y, suh. We got no wine 'cause of the Yankee blockade," replied the waiter apologetically.

"What? No vino? This is an outrage! *Damn those Yankees! How dare they steal our wine."* Gaches's loud theatrical expression of disappointment did not go unnoticed by the other guests in the dining room. Several of the men looked up from their plates and some of the women became aghast at the sudden verbal outburst. Both Vincent Clemente and Simon Fury stopped eating their pieces of lemon pie and now turned their gaze toward Gaches and Nate's table. One patron, however, shared Jacques Napoleon Gaches's sentiment. A well-groomed and elegantly dressed elderly gentleman rose from his chair and held a shot glass of bourbon in the air.

"Well said, sir. You are quite right. Send the thieving Federal rascals straight to Hades!" he clamored, as he nearly lost his balance and had to support himself with his left hand on the table. "Drink good Southern liquor, sir. Consume bourbon."

"An excellent suggestion, sir," confirmed the gambler, raising his hand high in the air from his wheelchair. *"Waiter.* Bring me a bottle of your best bourbon."

"Yes, suh. Right 'way, suh."

His host's ostentatious performance and public display of bravado embarrassed Nate. He felt that not only did Gaches needlessly attract attention to himself and therefore to him, but risked being recognized by Gaches's enemies. Nate could see out of the corner of his eyes that Vincent Clemente and Simon Fury were gawking at them and it made him uncomfortable.

All of a sudden the steam whistle blew twice, startling the passengers and propelling several of them out of their seats.

"What the hell?" shouted the elderly gentleman who had advised Gaches to consume bourbon.

The engines of *Belle de Jour* suddenly changed rhythm and Nate could feel the paddle wheeler slow down and come to a halt in the river. At first, Nate was relieved because all of the dining patrons stopped staring at them and shifted their gaze into the air or looked at the waiters for answers why the steamer had suddenly halted. After a few moments of silence, which seemed to Nate to be much longer, he became concerned that the steamer might be experiencing boiler problems.

"Must be debris in the water," speculated one passenger.

"Maybe it's the Yankees comin' to steal our bourbon," shouted another dinner patron jokingly.

"Yankees? Here? That will never happen!" scoffed the elderly gentleman as he emptied his shot glass of bourbon.

"Go and investigate," whispered Gaches to Nate. "And be discreet about it."

Nate slowly got up from his chair and left the table to go out on deck. He kept his head bowed in order to avoid eye contact with any of the passengers. He thought to himself how ironic Gaches's instructions to him were regarding being cautious while the gambler had almost jeopardized their cover by his verbal indiscretion.

Nate walked onto the deck on the port bow and peered over the railing and saw nothing. The night was cool and the murky water of the Red River was speckled with spots of light, reflecting the star-filled sky. He looked toward the bank and only saw the outline of trees and brush. He then made his way toward the starboard side of *Belle de Jour*, passing the engine room, and made his way toward the huge stern wheel that was rotating very slowly, just enough for the craft not to drift. Nate heard a gruff man's voice hollering from the pilothouse.

"Watch it, boys. Careful, don't let that monster hit my boat, damn it! Attach those bales smartly."

Nate saw a man holding a lantern peering out from the entrance of the pilothouse and assumed that it was the captain of *Belle de Jour*.

Nate turned his gaze toward starboard and saw a huge ironclad vessel floating in the water. He had never seen such a craft, and he thought that the boat looked ghostly and foreboding. On closer examination, however, he observed that the craft looked like a giant rectangular box floating on a thin slab. Several of the crew from *Belle de Jour* were lowering bales of cotton along the starboard side of the steamer to cushion the boat from rubbing against the ironclad.

He noticed that the vessel was entirely encased in iron plating and that her bow resembled a digging shovel. Her length was equal to that of *Belle de Jour*, with a long centrally located smokestack protruding from its roof, bellowing black smoke. The stern paddle wheel was only partially visible because the bottom half was covered in the boxlike structure. As was the case with *Belle de Jour*, the wheel was slowly turning to maintain its stationary position. Nate looked toward the stern and saw a tall flagpole leaning away from the vessel and noticed the Stars and Bars hanging from the pole. Nate bit his lower lip and cursed, *"Shit! Mo' soldiers comin' on board?"* His eyes searched the bow for the name of the ironclad and saw some lettering on the side but he was too far away to decipher the lettering. He moved cautiously toward the bow of *Belle de Jour* where there were more lanterns to get a better view, walking past some harried members of the crew who were hustling to fulfill their duties and avoid the wrath of the captain. Nate got as far as he dared to venture forward, but close enough to where the light from the lanterns lit up the writing on the ironclad's bow. He strained his eyes and whispered to himself slowly. "C.S.S. *Missouri*." He also noticed that the cannon doors were open revealing the heavy guns. Nate could see that there were two in front and three on the port bow, and he assumed that the C.S.S. *Missouri* was carrying another three on the starboard side, totaling eight cannons.

"Permission to come aboard, Captain," shouted a man who was standing on the bow of the ironclad with his right hand in the saluting position. Nate could not see the facial features of the man, but noticed that he was wearing a Confederate infantry uniform because he wore a straight sword on his left side and his brass buttons were double-breasted.

"Permission granted, Major, I have been expecting you. But you are tardy, sir!" yelled the captain of *Belle de Jour*, irritated that the rendezvous with the C.S.S. *Missouri* was past schedule.

Nate watched the Confederate officer leap elegantly from the ironclad onto the steamer. By now, quite a few passengers had either left their cabins and the dining room to investigate, and most of them were leaning on the railing observing events.

"Major Prescott, sir." The officer snapped off a salute. "Confederate Army, Corps of Engineers."

The captain of *Belle de Jour* did not return the salute. He did not care for the military very much and knew that any day now the Confederacy was going to impress his steamer and incorporate the vessel into the Red River defense system.

"My steward will show you to your quarters, Major. I must

return to my duties as captain of this boat," he replied gruffly, turning his back to the major.

"Thank you, sir," replied the officer, bowing his head in gratitude. "But before you go, sir." The officer raised his voice suddenly, startling the captain who turned to face him. "Would you kindly tell me where I can find Lieutenants Wilson and Seay?"

"They share a cabin next to yours, but you might want to check the dining room first," suggested the captain, returning to the pilothouse.

Nate returned to the dining room and informed Gaches that a senior Confederate officer had boarded *Belle de Jour* from an ironclad.

"Hmm, wonder what he is up to?" pondered the gambler, devouring his boiled ham and hominy. The waiter had brought them their food while Nate was observing the events on deck and the aroma from the boiled ham and steamed cabbage made his mouth water. He quickly sat down and seized the knife and fork and dove into his plate.

Major Prescott stood in the doorway of the dining room, his eyes searching the room and among the tables for the two lieutenants.

Gaches noticed him but was discreet. "Yes, I see. He has an aura of importance about him, as if he were on a mission." Gaches then turned and watched in horror at Nate crudely slicing the boiled ham. The gambler smirked in disapproval and commented in his patronizing manner: "If you are going to continue to eat like a starving field hand, someone will surely notice that you might be an escaped slave."

The remark startled Nate and he became self-conscious of his primitive table manners. "What shall I do?" he whispered to Gaches.

"Follow my lead." The gambler slowly picked up his knife

and fork and held them in the correct manner for Nate to see. Nate followed his example and Gaches proceeded to maneuver the utensils to eat the food in a refined manner.

Major Prescott had left the entrance of the dining room only to return within a few minutes with the other two Confederate officers whom he had found in their cabin. He insisted that they return to the dining room and have a brandy, and much to Gaches's and Nate's dismay, they were seated two tables away from them.

"What's the situation in the Gulf?" asked Lieutenant Wilson.

The major sighed and nodded his head in trepidation. "Admiral Farragut is amassing a powerful fleet to attack New Orleans and move up the Mississippi." Prescott took a sip of brandy and turned the snifter in between his fingers. "If he succeeds, the Yankees will split the Confederacy."

"Surely, Governor Moore and Major General Lovell will not allow that and defend the city to the last man," protested Lieutenant Seay.

"I am afraid, gentlemen," replied Prescott with resignation, "that the queen will fall within a few months."

The two lieutenants gawked at each other and Nate saw from the corner of his eye that their expressions were that of gloom.

The major sighed, then changed the subject. "That is why I am here, to go north, to Shreveport, and help organize the defense of the upper part of the Red River and then travel overland to assist building the coastal defense for Vicksburg."

"You believe that Vicksburg is threatened?" gasped Lieutenant Seay. It was bad enough that New Orleans was in danger of falling, but if Vicksburg was taken, then the South would be cut off from its supplies of raw materials from Texas.

"*Please,* Lieutenant. Keep your voice down," rebuked the major gently, looking about to see if any of the passengers might have overheard the indiscreet junior officer. "Since the outbreak of the war," he explained, "the Crescent City, as well as the whole state of Louisiana for that matter, has been stripped of men and matériel by Richmond to fight the Federals in Tennessee and Virginia. We simply do not have the resources to defend New Orleans against a determined assault by the Yankee navy."

A sense of despondency descended upon their table. The two lieutenants concentrated their gaze at their brandy snifters and remained silent, while the major stared through the glass at the flickering flame of the table lantern.

"Surely, Major, General Lovell, the commander of New Orleans, can defend the city with twenty-five thousand men?" pleaded Lieutenant Wilson.

"Twenty-five thousand men, yes. Are they trained soldiers? No!" scoffed the major, raising his voice. Major Prescott was feeling his brandy and now he was the one who was speaking too loudly. "Governor Moore ordered General Lovell to hold a review of the troops, and I did not see more than six thousand men that were armed." Prescott pulled on his brandy snifter and gulped the remaining liquid. "And those men were armed with the most miserable and unserviceable of weapons known in the civilized world. Rather than reassuring the population, the parade only demonstrated how unprepared we are."

"But I heard that there were over ten thousand Europeans forming brigades and regiments for the defense of the city. Outfits such as the European Brigade, the Spanish Cazadores, and the French Guards," insisted Wilson.

"Oh, they mean well, but they are not fully trained." The major looked at his empty brandy snifter and became irritated that the glass was empty. "The Europeans, and especially the French, are armed only with shotguns and swords from the Napoleonic wars!"

"What about the great raft between the islands to keep the

Yankee fleet from approaching the city?" inquired Seay.

"It's sagging. The barrier is full of debris because we do not have the ability to keep it clear." Prescott was eager for another round of alcohol. "Where's that waiter? I need another brandy." Prescott anxiously looked about for the attendant. By now, most of the passengers had left the dining room to either stroll out on deck or return to their cabins for the night. Prescott saw one waiter who was clearing a table and beckoned him with his right arm. "You there, boy! Get me another brandy."

"Yes, suh, right way, sir," responded the man, kowtowing.

"With all due respect, sir, you have a defeatist attitude," accused Lieutenant Wilson.

"I will not take offense to your remark, young sir. You are passionate in your beliefs, and clearly you are a patriot and I appreciate that, but it will serve you no purpose to dwell in happy ignorance of the facts and the perilous circumstances our country faces, Lieutenant." The waiter returned with Prescott's brandy and the major immediately lifted the snifter to his lips. He took a sip and then looked at the lieutenant slyly. "Do you know what that ironclad was carrying to New Orleans?"

"No, sir," he responded, somewhat irritated that the major would ask him a question that he obviously would not know the answer to.

"Bells, sir, hundreds of bells. From all over Louisiana. You see, General Beauregard requested that he needed bells to melt into cannon balls for the defense of New Orleans." The major took another sip of brandy and savored the undivided attention that the two young officers were paying to him. "So, bells of every kind of description and size poured forth from plantations, schools, government buildings, and churches."

"I find that admirable. A symbol of patriotic duty," exclaimed

Wilson, his chest heaving with pride. He looked at his companion, and Seay nodded in approval.

Prescott leered into the eyes of the brash lieutenant as if he was a teacher questioning a surly student. "It is certainly admirable, young sirs, but what else does this tell you?"

Although the major and the lieutenants spoke softly, trying not to be overheard, Nate and Gaches still managed to catch most of what the major had said. Nate was surprised to hear this information. A Yankee fleet poised to attack New Orleans? For a moment Nate thought how maybe it was a mistake to have fled the plantation and live in fear as a runaway. Maybe he should have waited for the Yankees to come and invade Louisiana and then join up.

Besides the Confederate officers and Gaches and Nate, the only other patrons that remained in the dining room were the two henchmen sent by Gaches's creditors. They had also ordered brandies and were taking their time sipping the liquid and occasionally taking glances at the officers and at Gaches.

Simon Fury polished off his snifter and rose from his chair. He decided that he wanted to speak with the officers. Vincent Clemente followed and Gaches could hear them approaching the officers' table.

"They are coming our way," cautioned Gaches, blinking his eyes at Nate.

"I know, I can hear 'em."

"Good evening, gentlemen." Simon Fury tipped the brim of his planter's hat, while Vincent Clemente nodded cunningly as he worked a toothpick to pry loose a piece of crust that had lodged in the back of his front gum. "My associate and I wanted to pay our respects to you officers and render praise and gratitude for your patriotism."

"Yeah, we want to express our gratitude," whispered Vincent Clemente, still working the toothpick in his mouth, much to the major's annoyance and growing disgust.

"Thank you, gentlemen," replied the major, trying to be polite. "I'm Major Prescott, Confederate Engineers, and this is Lieutenant Seay and Lieutenant Wilson, these gentlemen are in the infantry," said Prescott, gesturing. "May I inquire, sirs, why you are not in uniform and serving in the Confederate Army?"

"Oh, we in the militia, Major, in our home parish of Caddo," responded Fury unconvincingly.

"Why are you not with them now?" inquired the major provocatively, feeling his brandy.

"Our positions in private life are deemed as 'essential' by the state," replied Clemente, taking his toothpick out of his mouth.

"Oh? What 'essential' positions are those?" Prescott glanced at the two junior officers and winked.

"We slave catchers mostly, though sometimes we hire out for other, more complicated matters." Clemente's mouth became crooked and the major did not like his expression or his response.

Nate felt the hairs of his neck rise up and Gaches gave a slight nervous cough and placed his hand on his breast.

"A noble profession, I'm sure," exclaimed the major sarcastically, raising his snifter into the air in tribute. Both lieutenants howled with laughter and Gaches could not contain his own loud sniggering. The octoroon was so amused with the major's comment that his voice slipped out of character and Simon Fury abruptly turned around. The henchman looked long and hard at Gaches and then at Nate but then turned back to Gaches.

"We met before, old man?"

Gaches coughed again, trying to break the sudden tension in the air. "No, I don't think so," he responded feebly, trying to get back into his old man character.

"You sure look familiar, somehow." Fury's eyes scrutinized Gaches's face and then stared at the wheelchair. "How long have you been in that contraption?"

"Since my accident," responded Gaches with a sense of outrage, trying to bluff Simon Fury.

The henchman scratched the slight stumble on his face. "When was that?"

"I beg your pardon, sir. That is none of your business, and I take great offense that you ask such insulting questions," retorted Gaches indignantly. Nate was breathing very slowly and keeping his head bowed, eyes fixed on the table. He wanted to stay as uninvolved as possible.

"Sir, I also *protest.*" Major Prescott slapped his linen napkin on the table and suddenly raised himself from his chair and stood at attention directly in front of Fury.

The major had had enough of the two henchmen. He thought that Vincent Clemente was uncouth and sly and he recognized Fury as an opportunist and a liar. He finally snapped when Fury's contemptuous behavior toward the elderly cripple proved too much to bear. Appalled by Fury's actions, Prescott's sense of propriety and patience for such ill conduct had vanished with every sip of brandy.

"Your presence here offends me, sir! Please leave." Prescott tapped his hand on the top of the handle guard of his sword and smiled. "And I am certain that Lieutenants Seay and Wilson will support me if I require their assistance."

"Sir, we are at your service," shouted Lieutenant Seay as he also rose from his chair and stood at attention. Lieutenant Wilson followed his comrade and all three faced Fury and Clemente.

"We jest want to ask this man a few questions, that's all, Major. I don't see no harm," replied Clemente; his face drew an obnoxious smirk and his toothpick was still stuck in his mouth.

"No, sir," taunted the major, peering into Fury's eyes and glancing at Clemente. "Your conduct toward this gentleman is not only offensive and unbecoming of a gentleman, but your poor manners and boorish behavior here are beginning to spoil the taste of my brandy. So! Leave now, sir."

"Now, you soldier boys ain't running no plantation here. We ain't your niggers. You can't talk to us that way," riposted Fury as his hand slowly crawled up toward the opening of his frock coat.

"Yeah. You gots no call to talk to us likes that," corroborated Clemente. "You gots no right. 'Sides it ain't yo'r goddamn bizness."

Nate remained motionless in his seat, trying to remain in the background in what he viewed as a potentially explosive situation. Gaches, however, was enjoying being the aggrieved elderly cripple. The gambler contorted his face in such a fashion as to reflect a sense of wounded pride, and the anguish in Gaches's face fueled Major Prescott's indignation and impatience with the henchmen.

"Sir. Do not move your hand any farther," cautioned the major sternly. He saw that Fury's right hand was slowly creeping toward the opening of his coat and assumed that the rogue was reaching for a weapon.

Vincent Clemente took a step forward and removed the toothpick from his mouth and threw it on the floor in a confrontational manner, indicating that he was prepared to support his associate.

"I caution you two, leave now." Prescott took a step backward and wrapped his right hand around the pommel of his sword while his left held the scabbard.

"You ain't tellin' us nuthin', soldier boy." Simon Fury's hand had penetrated the inside of his coat and the major was convinced he was reaching for a derringer or a knife.

The abrupt sharp sound of polished steel sliding out from its metal sheath made Nate turn his head just in time to witness the blade of Prescott's sword slash Fury's hand across the knuckles. The henchman yelped in pain while Clemente lunged at the major who turned to meet this new threat. Prescott skillfully raised the hilt guard of his sword and slugged it in the brute's face, sending him reeling backward onto a nearby table. The remaining attendants in the dining room who were clearing up and dusting furniture became spooked by the violent commotion in the room and hurriedly left the premises.

"You cut me!" accused Fury, pulling a used handkerchief and wrapping it around his injured hand as blood started to seep from the slash. Clemente was still lying on top of the table moaning and feeling disoriented.

"Lieutenant." Major Prescott turned to Lieutenant Seay.

"Yes, sir." The young officer was staring at Clemente's motionless body and found that the henchman's dangling long legs and boots looked comical as they hung down from the table.

The major elegantly sheathed his sword with an air of accomplishment and turned to Seay. "Lieutenant, have some of your men clean up this mess."

III.

Nate had been wide awake for about twenty minutes, lying on his cot in his adobe chamber, when he heard the wrought-iron latch snap and the big wooden door slowly creak open. He had spent a restless night thinking about Jacques Napoleon Gaches and was feeling pain in his lower back because he had remained too long lying on his backside. The throbbing discomfort in his head had completely subsided but he was again feeling hunger pains in his stomach.

"Did you have a good sleep, *Hotoa' e Gordon? Nepevomohta-*

*hehe?** Are you feeling good?" George Bent stood in the doorway and a sudden flood of daylight poured into the room. Nate had to shield his eyes from the strong rays of the November sun but managed to see that Bent was dressed entirely in beaded buckskin.

"I was restless," sighed Nate, rising slowly from the cot. He maneuvered his frame to the middle of the bed and sat at the edge, his eyes searching for his boots.

The half-breed gestured with his eyes. "You will find your boots under the bed."

Nate searched with his hands to find them and felt awkward and anxious feeling about in the void space, because a man without his boots on is in a state of vulnerability. He became quickly relieved, however, after his hands felt the smooth leather of one of his boots. He retrieved the footwear and slipped them on as fast as he could and stood up. The sudden movement made the top of his head throb and he was forced to place the palm of his hand on his temple in an effort to arrest the pain.

"You all right?" Bent made a move toward Nate to assist him, but Nate waved him off.

"I'll be all right. I'm jest little dizzy from lyin' down too long, that's all."

"You still weak. *Hotoa' e Gordon.* You need food, *Noheto meseestse!*† Let's eat."

George Bent led Nate through a series of small adobe rooms that reminded Nate of a layout of a military barracks, and out to the courtyard where he could view the exterior of Bent's fort. He immediately saw that half of the structure at the opposite side of the main gate had been reduced to rubble and only ruins remained. Nate concluded that the damage was the result of an explosion

---

*Are you feeling good?
†Eat.

caused by gunpowder and subsequent fire that had spread throughout much of the fort. During the war, he had seen similar damage to fortified structures, bridges, and storehouses. He reasoned that this was the explanation for the smoke stains on the walls of his room.

Bent motioned Nate to follow him toward the main gate where some horses and mules were saddled and tethered. As they made their way across the courtyard, they passed a parked overland stage. The six-horse team was eating some moldy hay while the driver and the man who rode shotgun shared a brown jug of rye.

"Mornin', Bent," cried out the man who rode shotgun and who held the jug. He rested the double barrel twelve-gauge weapon on his right shoulder and snapped back his head to take a swig of booze from the ceramic container. George Bent nodded his head in acknowledgment of his presence, but remained silent, his gaze transfixed on the snow and muddy ground before him. Nate looked at the stage and saw that the vehicle was completely splashed with dried and wet mud, indicating a hard journey for the passengers. He then looked at the horses and saw that they were also splattered with mud and that great clouds of steam rose from their perspiring winter coats.

"Looks like the breed found a nigger bluecoat amigo," snickered the driver, taking back the brown jug to get his turn to suck on the rye.

"Pay them no mind, *Hotoa' e Gordon*. They are ignorant white men," dismissed Bent.

"Oh, I know that," confirmed Nate with an air of resignation. "I figure that most teamsters are as bright as the beasts they whip," he added, loud enough for the driver and his companion to overhear.

"What you say, *boy*?" The driver only heard the last part of

Nate's reply, but he sensed that his remark was derogatory.

Nate and Bent continued to ignore them and walked toward where two mules and a fine horse with an Indian blanket draped over the saddle stood tethered to a hitching post.

"When my father left this place back in '49, the fort was being used to bivouac soldiers and now it's a stage station to change horses and rest up passengers along the Sante Fe Trail," explained Bent. "Take your pick from the mules and mount up," he instructed, mounting onto his horse's back. Nate looked over both animals and decided to take the bigger of the two mules. *"Neheto! Follow me,"* Bent commanded. Bent gently tapped his heels to his mount's flanks, and turned toward the main gate.

*"Tosa'e?"** Where are we going?" inquired Nate.

"To my father's ranch. It is not far from here."

"Naa eho?"† Nate wanted to know where they were going.

"A few miles south. At the mouth of the Purgatoire River."

The two men followed the trail along the Arkansas River for several miles. George Bent led the way and Nate rode his big mule behind his host. The day was relatively mild and the cloudless sky was a deep blue. Nate felt the hunger pains in his stomach groan, and he wondered how much longer they had to travel before they could eat. He therefore became relieved when a huge stockade filled with horses, mules, and Mexican jackasses came in view.

George Bent turned around in his saddle and faced Nate. "My father's ranch."

"Epeva'e," acknowledged Nate. All of a sudden the strong smell of bacon and coffee reached Nate's nostrils.

"Soon we will eat," confirmed Bent, urging his mount to pick up speed. He was also hungry and he knew that his father and his relatives were waiting for him.

---

*Where?
†Where is your father?

When they arrived at the modest ranch house, a Mexican hired hand appeared and took their mounts to a barn for a good feeding.

"Ninaasts. We will eat, now." George Bent opened the front door of his father's ranch house and entered with the confidence of an offspring. Nate removed his beaver cap that George Bent loaned him in anticipation of being introduced and followed his host closely, staring at the back of his buckskin jacket. They entered a room filled with boots, shoes, coats, buffalo robes, and hides from dozens of animals. There were also pieces of tack and various farming implements and tools. Nate followed Bent through another doorway that led to a very spacious room. As he stepped into the space, Nate could feel the warm blast of heat that came from a large cast-iron stove, and the inviting aromas of sizzling bacon, and stove-cooked biscuits, mixed with the smells of tobacco and horse.

Nate saw that there was at least half a dozen individuals sitting at a very long table, eating, sipping coffee, smoking, and talking in English, Spanish, and Cheyenne.

"Greetings, my son. We have been expecting you," hailed William Bent cheerfully. The legendary founder of Bent's fort, the castle of the plains, raised his arm from where he sat. His thick lips gave William Bent a relaxed smile as he sat cross-legged a few feet away from the table. He was formally dressed in baggy black wool pants that were pulled over his boots, with a matching black wool jacket with silk piping on the cuffs and lapel. The jacket was open, revealing a clean white shirt that was buttoned to the neck. The sun and wind had weathered his face and Nate thought that William Bent's facial features and coloring made him look more Indian than white. Unlike most white men who either wore beards, goatees, sideburns, or mustaches, the trader's face was clean-shaven. His hair and wide eyebrows were as dark as a raven's feathers, and he had high cheekbones with a huge forehead. His eyes were slightly slanted and his nose was large and pronounced. "I see you have brought a companion with you, my son." William Bent squinted his eyes to look at Nate. "Well, well, a *Mo' ohtae-ve' ho' e*! There seems to be more and more of you coming this way, lately."

Nate noticed a middle-aged Indian man, who was sitting next to William Bent. The Indian nodded and grunted in agreement when his friend mentioned the *Mo' ohtae-Ve' ho' e*. He held a little Indian girl on his left knee so Nate thought that she might be his daughter. He was also dressed in black wool pants and frock coat with a white shirt but wore the garments more casually than his host. His feet were clad in thick, beaded deerskin moccasins and his long unbraided black hair hung elegantly on his shoulders.

"This is *Hotoa' e Gordon*, Father. The *Mo' ohtae-Ve' ho' e ho'nehe* that Cougar Eyes saved at the Washita," introduced George Bent, speaking more loudly than usual because his father was hard of hearing. William Bent nodded and stretched his large hand to welcome Nate, his deep-set eyes looking over his unexpected guest.

"Welcome to my humble home," said William Bent softly. "I hope you are hungry for we have too much food." His voice was relaxed and hospitable but also sounded confident and strong.

Nate clasped William Bent's strong hand and bowed his head. "Thank you, sir. I could sure use a meal."

"Yes, of course. Please be seated." William Bent pointed to a wooden chair with a wicker seat, and offered Nate a place at the table. "Let me introduce my old friend, Little Raven." William Bent gestured toward the big Indian who was bouncing the child on his knee. "Little Raven is an Arapaho, and a chief of his tribe."

Nate nodded respectfully toward Little Raven and quickly removed his buffalo coat and placed the hide on the back of the chair. He then brought the seat near a place setting at the long table, and placed his kepi in his lap. In front of him lay a large

Indian ceramic bowl filled with boiled potatoes, near a porcelain Mexican plate that was loaded with pieces of ham, bacon, and venison. There was also an assortment of preserved vegetables, canned peaches and pears, and freshly baked bread and biscuits.

An elderly but well-preserved Mexican woman came up to Nate and asked, *"Huevos, señor?"*

Nate looked puzzled. He did not understand what she was asking.

"She's askin' you if you want eggs," said a man sitting across the table sipping on a cup of coffee. He was about the same age as Nate and his skin and features showed that he was also half white, half Indian. His skin was very bronzed with high cheek-bones and his chin looked sculptured. He had a Mexican mustache that slightly covered his handsome mouth and his dark, slightly wavy hair was neatly parted to the right.

"Sí, señora, muchas gracias." Nate nodded, turning around in his seat to face the *señora*.

"My name is Edmond Guerrier, but you can call me Ed." The half-breed stretched his hand across the table and Nate put down his fork to meet it. His voice was deep and he spoke with an accent. Nate felt his strong grip as the breed looked straight into the eyes as his own right eye slightly drooped. He then gestured with his head toward a young and pretty half-breed woman who was sitting next to him. "And this is my wife, Julia." He had several silver bracelets on his wrist that rattled every time he moved his arm. He wore a heavy black velvet vest and had a blue silk scarf wrapped several times around his neck tucked under the collar of his red, store-bought stroud-cloth shirt.

Nate had heard about the half-breed and sometimes Custer scout, Ed Guerrier. His departed friend, Medicine Bill Comstock, had mentioned his name several times during conversations, and told him that he rarely told the truth to Custer about Indians, and that his father was a French trapper and his mother was a Cheyenne squaw.

"I see you met my brother-in-law," cracked George Bent. He was moving around the table talking to guests and family members as he nibbled on a large biscuit coated with red-eye gravy.

Nate's mouth was full of ham but he quickly chewed the meat and swallowed the piece so he could speak. "Your brother-in-law?"

"Julia is my sister," stated George Bent as he reached for the bread basket to grab another biscuit. "Our mother was Owl Woman, and when she died, my father, following the Indian custom, married Yellow Woman, Owl Woman's sister."

Off to the side of the table, near the cast-iron stove, was a middle-aged man with a gray mustache and shoulder-length hair lying on his back, tickling a three-year-old Mexican boy. The child was laughing so loudly that Nate had to turn his head to see what was occurring. He thought that the little man looked rather frail to be roughhousing, and thought that the child might even hurt the man. The three-year-old kept trying to place his little hands into the pockets of the man's blue coat and reach for something. The old man would laugh and tickle the youngster every time he got close, but would not allow him to reach far enough to seize the item in his pocket. Nate was intrigued that the man was speaking fluent Spanish to the child. He was not a Mexican or a breed, and his skin was very fair. His long hair and mustache, although gray, showed that his head was once very blond. Only when the old man decided that the youngster suffered enough frustration, did he reach into his pocket and give him a piece of hard candy. The three-year-old would then yell in triumph and stuff the candy in his mouth.

"The general sure loves kids," commented Ed Guerrier.

"He is always playing with them," added Julia, casting a smile in their direction. "Kit has seven children of his own." Julia paused for a moment and bowed her head in sorrow. "I feel so sad for him. Loosing Josefa last month. She was everything to him."

"Was Josefa this man's wife?" asked Nate, indifferently, breaking a piece of bread into two.

"Yes, and Kit worshiped her," responded Julia. "This is the first time I have seen him laugh since she passed."

"Yes, it's good to see the general have a good time," added Ed Guerrier.

"Why do you call him 'General'? Was he in the army during the war?" asked Nate.

"Well, Kit only became a brevetted brigadier general two years ago, but men called him general a long time before." Ed Guerrier beckoned the Mexican servant for more coffee. "It's just that the men who followed him always called him that because he was such a good leader."

"Was he a scout for the army?"

"For the army, the railroad, the government, hell! If it wasn't for *Kit Carson*, John Frémont's body would have been eaten by the wolves in the middle of the goddamn Rockies!" proclaimed Guerrier.

Nate was about to take a sip of coffee but almost spilt the liquid on the table when he heard that the frail little man playing with the child was that legendary scout, hunter, and Indian fighter, Kit Carson.

"That's Kit Carson?" he exclaimed in astonishment.

"Well, yes, didn't you know?" replied Guerrier, bemused at Nate's ignorance.

Kit Carson saw that Nate was staring at him as he lay on the floor. He felt self-conscious so he quickly rose and straightened his blue frock coat, and dusted his sleeves with his delicate hands.

"O qué, está aconteciendo compadres?" said Carson in perfect Spanish, slowly walking over to the table toward Nate. Although

he looked sickly, and his walk unsteady, his voice was strong and his deep-set blue eyes reminded Nate of a rattlesnake that was poised to strike if provoked.

"*Quien es tu amigo negro?*" inquired Carson, pointing to Nate.

William Bent noticed his brother-in-law addressing Nate and saw that his guest was a little stunned by this face-to-face meeting with the great scout. "Kit, this is *Hotoa' e Gordon*, he's a friend of George's."

"Heard about you," stated Carson, in a matter-of-fact manner, but with an air of great politeness and modesty. The Indian fighter came closer, and Nate could see that his face was smooth and fair, much like that of a white woman's and his head, although large, was well proportioned. He held out his feeble hand and Nate quickly rose from his chair and took it eagerly. Although he was shocked that the hero of so many dime novels was so short and gentle-looking, he was gratified that Carson's grip was still strong. The scout smiled and Nate thought that his mouth was firm but possessed a melancholy expression.

"You smoke *Hotoa' e Gordon*?" queried Carson as he cocked back his head to look at Nate's face.

"Yes, I smoke."

"Good, good. I got some Mexican tobacco that is of excellent quality." Carson slightly closed his left eye. "Want to try some?" he asked, as if he were throwing Nate a dare.

"Sorry, I lost my pipe."

"Oh, I gots lots of pipes. You can borrow one of mine," insisted Carson.

Nate was surprised at such an offer. Men usually did not lend out pipes. Like a man's woman, the practice was simply not done. Nate recognized, though, that to offer a complete stranger and a man of a different race a personal item such as a pipe was not only a selfless act but also an offering of friendship.

"I be obliged."

"You finish eatin', I'll be back in a moment." Carson turned his back and left the room.

Nate raced to finish the food that he had heaped on his plate before Carson returned. He was still hungry but he also wanted a good smoke after the meal and he certainly did not wish to insult Kit Carson by telling him that he was not ready to share his tobacco.

"He sure loves his tobacco," observed George Bent, taking a seat near his sister. The elderly Mexican servant woman brought him a plate with a large omelet stuffed with peppers and George Bent thanked her in Spanish.

Carson returned with two corn pipes and a large tobacco pouch made from buffalo scrotum. The sack looked well used but the colorful beadwork still retained its artistic attractiveness. Carson pulled up a chair and sat near Nate, but away from the table, and crossed his legs. Nate had just cleaned his plate of food and felt stuffed.

"Would you mind fillin' the pipes? My fingers feel real stiff right now," asked Carson as he handed Nate the pipes and tobacco pouch. "And, take your pick of the pipes. Makes no difference to me."

"Be glad to," responded Nate, taking the items. He examined the beaded detail of the pouch and admired its work. "That is a beautiful tobacco pouch."

"That ol' cuss Jim Bridger gave me this back at the rendezvous of 1840," recalled the scout, looking at the pouch.

Nate quickly filled a bowl and handed one of the corn pipes back to Carson. The scout eagerly took it and placed the article at the corner of his mouth. He then removed a small tin circular container from his jacket pocket and separated the lid from the container with some difficulty. Nate felt sorry for him as he watched Carson's delicate fingers struggle to eject a wooden match from the small container and wanted to assist him, but decided that the gesture might be construed as insulting. The great scout finally managed to take hold of a match with his right hand and pointed the fire stick at the table. He then leaned forward in his chair and struck the head of the match underneath the wooden surface. Nate heard the flash of flame igniting the twig and watched Carson quickly take the flaming piece of wood, place it near the long corn cob bowl, and puff on the stem to get it lit.

"I heard about the rendezvous," remarked Nate, taking the burning match from Carson and rapidly lighting his own pipe before it burned his fingers. "I heard they were like the fairs of medieval Europe."

"Medieval Europe, you say?" Carson's mild blue eyes suddenly lit up at Nate's analogy. The elderly frontiersman puffed vigorously on his pipe and reflected on the statement. At first, Carson wanted to laugh at Nate's comparison of the raucous rendezvous meetings in the Rockies with the urban festivals of ancient Europe. After some reflection, however, he recalled the stories that Frémont and other army officers had read to him about medieval life. How the Europeans would partake in jousting, trading, wenching, drinking, and other amusements for days on end. "I believe you might have a point there," Carson mused, puffing on his pipe with obvious relish. He blew a large cloud of white smoke near his face and then gently used his hands to slowly lift the fumes from burning tobacco over his head and closed his eyes in meditation.

"Which rendezvous did you like best?" asked Nate, intrigued by Carson's quiet, melancholy demeanor.

"Oh, the one of 1840, up on the Green River, I suppose. I like that one 'cause my daughter, Adaline, was baptized by Father de Smet, and it was the last and largest rendezvous to take place.

After that, the days for trappin' and tradin' were 'bout over."

"Tell him about Adobe Walls, General," clamored Ed Guerrier, as if he were some schoolboy who never got tired of hearing the same tale over and over again.

"Leave the man alone, Ed. Can't you see that he's tired of telling stories," chastised William Bent, waving his gnarled and pawlike hand in the air in front of him. He was sitting at the head of the table listening to his old friend.

"Oh, that's all right, Bill, I don't mind. And sometimes I do feel like talkin' when I smoke." Carson recrossed his legs and folded his hands in his lap. He then hunched his small frame forward in the chair to look at Nate. "At Adobe Walls, three things saved my command from annihilation from howling clouds of Comanches and Kiowas." Carson raised his index finger for emphasis. "The first one was the cover that the ruined adobe fort provided my men, number two, my two twelve-pound mountain howitzers, and number three, the disciplined fire of my men."

Nate had heard of the big fight at Adobe Walls near the Canadian River. He remembered that it took place during the late fall of 1864, and that Carson and his small force of volunteers had defeated thousands of hostiles.

"Fact is, I failed to carry out my orders and"—Carson stretched his right arm forward, the palm of his hand facing downward, then suddenly jerked the limb across his chest— "nearly got my command *wiped out.*"

Nate was surprised to hear the great Indian fighter's negative assessment of the battle.

"Come now, uncle, you are far too modest. You did destroy the Kiowa village and left them impoverished in the middle of winter," gibed George Bent, thinking about his own experience when Colonel Chivington and his drunken Colorado Volunteers ruthlessly attacked Black Kettle's peaceful village at Sand Creek and massacred women and children. He still felt the wound in his hip where he was wounded and nearly killed by Chivington's Colorado Volunteers.

"You know very well that those fiends deserved it!" snapped back Carson. "And my men didn't kill no women and children, neither." Nate saw the Indian fighter's eyes ignite with passion. "Them Comanche and Kiowa raidin' parties kilt women and children and looted like locusts along the Sante Fe Trail. And we found plenty of evidence when we burnt the village too. White children's clothing, military uniforms, photographs, bloody red hair scalps, books, and even a fancy buggy with a harness." Carson suddenly bowed his head and sighed. "I only have one regret: *the white captives,*" he mumbled. "You see, later after the fight, we found out that there were seven white women and seven children that were held captive by the Kiowa but at the time we didn't know 'bout them so we couldn't locate them. God knows what became of them after we fired the village."

Nate thought about the chaos and needless carnage that he had witnessed at the Washita. He especially thought about the poor, emaciated, white captive child, who had a knife plunged into his breast when the hysterical Cheyenne squaw chose to kill him and, in turn, be killed by the troopers rather than surrender.

"Tell him about the Mexican boy and the scalp," said Little Raven slowly, with a deep voice. He was sitting next to his friend William Bent, and still chewing on a piece of venison. He was a tall and portly man with large gold earrings that dangled almost to his shoulders.

Carson took a few deep drags from his pipe and coughed so loudly that most people in the room lowered their eyes out of embarrassment or concern for the great scout. Carson's loud hacking confirmed for Nate that the Indian fighter was in failing health, and might not have long to live.

"There was this young Mexican lad who rode with us into the fight." Carson slightly moved his big head from side to side as if he regretted something. "I'm afraid that I forgot his name. He stood next to me, along with my Jicarilla Apache and Ute scouts. Anyways, he was very young, maybe thirteen, fourteen years old. At the height of the battle, the smoke was so thick, hundreds of Comanche and Kiowa braves would suddenly swoop out from under the huge clouds of gunfire and appear at our skirmish line at point-blank range. They were a-howlin' war whoops and a-blowin' on bone whistles, and shooting wildly into our ranks. One tall buck"—Carson's blue eyes suddenly became very focused—"a Comanche, dressed in full battle regalia, and riding a beautiful white stallion, appeared in front of our line and threw his long lance at one of our men, who managed to duck and avoid being run through. But before the warrior could turn his war pony, the Mexican lad had shot him off his magnificent mount. The boy lowered his rifle and slowly made his way toward the body, keeping his head down, through a hail of gunfire. I shouted at him to get back on the skirmish line, but he never heard me or ignored my command." Carson took several more deep puffs off of his pipe but did not hack on the smoke and refolded his delicate hands. "Anyways, I saw that the Comanche was only wounded though, and as he lay helpless on the ground on his back, he suddenly raised his arm meekly, as if he was beckoning to one of his fellow braves to come and take him away. Well, when the boy saw that, he quickened his pace toward the wounded man as he removed his skinning knife from its sheath. When he reached the Comanche, he looked down at his victim for a moment but then placed his right knee on the brave's face and slit his throat like a prairie chicken. He cocked back his sombrero with the skinning knife and seized the warrior's ponytail and pulled it taut. He then sliced the top off from the Comanche's head and lifted his scalp and held it in the air in triumph, yelling war whoops. When my Jicarilla and Ute scouts saw what he had done, they went wild with excitement and some of them started to chant and dance scalp jigs."

"Tell *Hotoa' e Gordon* what the Jicarilla and Ute scouts did after the fight," reminded Little Raven, as he lifted his daughter from his knee and placed the child on the floor. The toddler immediately ran toward Kit Carson and gently placed her tiny hands on the scout's left knee. Nate could detect a sense of anticipation in the Arapaho chief's voice as if he had heard the tale before, but enjoyed hearing about it again.

"That scalp lifted from the Comanche was the only scalp taken at Adobe Walls. The Jicarilla and Ute scouts had failed to take any during the fight and they felt ashamed that such a young boy, and a Mexican to boot, had bested them in that respect. So they coveted the Comanche's hair that rightly"—Carson again removed his pipe and pointed in the air for emphasis—"belonged to the Mexican youth. So, after the fight, the Jicarilla and the Utes bidded for the hair because they wanted to do the scalp dance. At first, the boy refused to sell it, but the scouts were insistent. He was offered fine buffalo robes, skins, brass tacks, beads, and blankets, but the boy refused to sell. When my chief of scouts, a Ute, offered the boy two war ponies that he had taken from the Comanches, the Jicarilla matched the bid." Carson removed his corn pipe from the corner of his mouth, and pointed the stem at Nate. "Now, that Mexican was no fool. He saw an opportunity, and took it. He had the Jicarilla and Utes bidding for that lonely scalp as if it was the last drop of water in a canteen while crossin' the Mojave Desert." Nate saw that Carson's firm lips cracked a slight smile in admiration.

"Tell him about the scalp dance." Little Raven wanted Carson to recount what he considered the best part of the story.

"Well, the Jicarilla and the Utes saw that he was getting the best of them, so they decided to band together and make the Mexican a flat and final offer. For the scalp, they offered four ponies, all were taken from the Comanches and Kiowa during the fight, and two fine buffalo robes. The boy, seeing that this was the best offer he was going to get, accepted."

"How long did the scouts dance around the scalp?" asked Nate.

Nate's question impressed Carson. Obviously, this man knew something about Indians and was not a stranger to life east of the Missouri.

"Those scouts danced around that piece of Comanche hair for *twenty-one days.*"

"Twenty-one days? Well, that's a lot of celebrating for a bunch of Indians for one lonely, miserable scalp," commented William Bent dryly. The room, without warning, burst into laughter at William Bent's remark. Even Nate laughed heartily. It was not so much that his guests were amused by his observation, but rather it was the way the old seasoned trader had expressed it.

Nate heard the front door open in the boot room and heard it being quickly shut. Nobody at the table broke their conversation or interrupted their meal to acknowledge that someone had just entered the ranch house. This surprised Nate, for he was always watchful and suspicious when it came to unfamiliar sounds, or the prospect of facing imminent danger. He kept looking toward the entranceway that led to the boot room and expected the door that led to where everyone was seated to open at any second.

Nate was about to take another puff on his pipe when he heard the iron latch of the door snap open. A very tall man, his head bowed, walked into the big room. He was wearing a fine muskrat coat that almost touched the floor. The stranger had the collar of his coat unfolded upward, covering his ears, and he wore a sombrero so Nate could not see the newcomer's face.

"Mawnin', y'all. It's a fine mawnin'," said the stranger cheerfully. He gazed at Julia and touched the right side brim of his hat with his fingers. Ed Guerrier's wife smiled and Nate could see that her face became flushed with embarrassment.

There was something in the way the stranger said "Mawnin' " that drew Nate's attention. The accent sounded very familiar, and reminded him of his own. The newcomer removed his coat and gave it to the Mexican housekeeper who waited nearby. He then pinched the rim of his sombrero and elegantly lifted the hat from his head and gave it to the Mexican woman.

"Well, well, what we got for breakfast? That coffee sur' smells fine." He turned his body to face the long table and Nate saw that he was a black man. He was about twenty years older, and his short-cropped hair was peppered with specs of gray, but the stranger was about the same height and talked with the same language rhythm.

"Now we have two *Mo' ohtae-Ve' ho' e* in the room. A rare occasion, indeed," averred William Bent as he crossed his arms against his chest. "*Hotoa' e Gordon*, meet *Wasicun Sapa*. He is of your tribe, the Black-White Man." Nate recognized that the Negro's name was in Lakota and wondered if he was a scout or a hunter.

Wasicun Sapa walked over to Nate and gave him his right hand. "Name's Dorman. Isaiah Dorman," he said with a confident smile. He looked over Nate's uniform and saw his chevrons. "You with the Tenth?"

"Sergeant Major Nate Gordon. Yes, I'm with the Tenth." Nate clasped Isaiah Dorman's hand, and felt its strong grip. The two men smiled at each other as if they were already old friends.

"I've not seen 'nother black man for *long* time"—laughed Dorman—"and neva in a uniform."

"Well, I've neva seen a muskrat coat before on a black man," replied Nate, taking a puff from his pipe.

"Oh, this old rag? I've had that when I first came to the land of the Utes back in '51."

Nate was astonished by Dorman's response. "You've been free that long?"

"Longer than that, my man. Mind if I pull up this chair? I'm half starved." Without waiting for a reply, Isaiah Dorman took the seat in between Nate and George Bent.

"Wasicun Sapa is always hungry. Does your Lakota squaw not feed her man?" asked George Bent teasingly, watching Dorman help himself to the meat plate.

"Oh, she ain't with me. I left her back at Rice." He seized a biscuit from the bread basket and broke it in two. He turned to Nate with a smile. "Somebody gots to look after the stock while I'm gone."

Nate took note that Dorman had mentioned the place Rice. He presumed that he meant Fort Rice, which he knew was near Bismarck, Dakota Territory. "You work for the army?"

"Sometimes," replied Dorman as he chewed on a piece of venison.

"Wasicun Sapa cuts wood for the bluecoats," quipped George Bent. "Like squaw." George Bent did not care for *Wasicun Sapa*. He considered him a shameless self-promoter who had married a Santee Sioux woman because of the rich dowry of horses and mules her father had given him. What really bothered Bent, however, was that now the bluecoats, at one hundred dollars a month, employed him as a courier.

"I haven't cut wood for the army in a long time, and *you know it,*" shot back Dorman defensively. "And when I did, I was the bestest and fastest cutter in the territory. Why, the stacker could never keep up with me."

"Do you still work for the army?" Nate took a sip of coffee and peered at Dorman over the rim of his tin cup.

"I'm a courier," replied Dorman as he crudely maneuvered his fork and table knife on a piece of buffalo steak. "An' I gets a hundred dollars a month for deliverin' dispatches." Isaiah Dorman glanced into Nate's eyes with an expression of smug satisfaction. "An' that's mo' than most white men git out here."

Nate downed the last bit of the coffee in his cup and reflected for a moment. He had never met a black frontiersman before. He was fascinated at the notion that this fellow black man had been free most of his life and that he had successfully carved out an existence for himself by getting well paid for the army, while seemingly getting along with the Indians.

"Did you run from slavery?" asked Nate. He wanted to know more about whom the Indians called *Wasicun Sapa*.

"Ran all the way from *Louisiana,* and didn't stop till I came to the Black Hills. There, I trapped beaver and muskrat, and hunted game, for Lawd knows how many years." Dorman shifted his sitting position in his chair and gazed at the low ceiling. "I spent years hidin' from the white man." Nate noticed a change in Dorman's tone of voice, as if he was hiding some discomforting memory from the past. "Only after the war," he continued, "did I *dare* go to a white settlement an' show my black face."

"I ran too," stated Nate, recalling his own travails as a runaway. " 'Cept I joined the Yankees to fight fo' freedom, an' earn respect 'cause I wear these stripes." Nate pointed toward his wide chevrons. "I didn't' hide in no hills till the war was won."

"Well, you made your choice to fight. I wanted to be my own man."

"Well, you makin' a good livin' now, off the *Ve' ho' e,* aren't you?" jested Nate. He enjoyed calling the white man by the Cheyenne term, *Ve' ho' e*. He wanted to let Dorman know that he was not some novice that had recently arrived on the plains.

"I'll take 'em fo' every dolla I can git!" retorted Dorman, chewing on a piece of venison.

"Wasicun Sapa takes money from the bluecoats with contempt, but one day he will betray his Lakota brothers for money," accused George Bent, raising his voice.

"Now, son, hold your tongue," chastised the father, William Bent. "As long as Mr. Dorman is in my house, he will be treated as a guest, and not insulted or baited." William Bent's normally sedate demeanor had suddenly turned excitable. *"You know,"* yelled the old man, "that I have seen enough death and misery take place on this land to fill several lifetimes. I will not tolerate bad blood under my roof."

William Bent's rebuke had the effect of quieting the room. Nate saw that George Bent had shifted his eyes from Dorman to his half-empty plate as he nervously turned a fork in his hand.

After a few moments, the room became animated with conversation and the sounds of people eating again. William Bent's small tirade had passed, and family and guests were once again enjoying each other's company. The big room resumed its cacophony of frontier languages and Nate's ears discreetly wandered about the room to listen. Kit Carson was playing with several children on the floor as he spoke in rapid Spanish to them, while Little Raven conversed sharply with William Bent in Arapaho, using sign language for emphasis. Ed Guerrier was whispering in broken French to William Bent, and Nate could tell by the tone of the scout's voice, that he was offering moral support to his friend regarding what the younger Bent had said about *Wasicun Sapa*.

Isaiah Dorman knew enough French from the years he spent in the Rockies with seasoned *coureurs du bois* to gauge what Ed

Guerrier was saying about him. He turned to Nate who had resumed smoking the pipe that Kit Carson had loaned him, and
spoke softly but with a defensive edge.

"They don't know what it was like bein' a *slave*." Dorman
slightly moved his head contemptuously where Ed Guerrier and
George Bent were seated. Nate could see that Dorman's blood was
up and that he felt maligned. "Why shouldn't I get top dollar for
my services from the white man if they be willin' to *pay*?" Dorman's eyes peered into Nate's, seeking commiseration. "I was a
slave, same as you." He then nodded his head in bitter memory.
"And worked Master D'Orman's fields pickin' cotton as soon as I
could walk, 'cause my little hands an' fingers was small 'nough to
pluck off the cotton bulbs faster than the fully grown hands."

"I hear you," confirmed Nate softly as he nodded approvingly.
Dorman's harangue about slavery and injustice conjured up memories of his own miserable experience as a slave. He briefly thought
about his mother and lost sister, but the memory of them was too
painful for any deep thought. He slammed his eyes shut and shook
his head, as if awakening from a bad dream. He didn't want to
think about the past. "But out here," Nate said slowly, as if he
had given the matter some thought, "it's a new beginning." He
removed the pipe from his mouth and pointed the stem at Dorman. "Don't matter if a man's white, black, Mexican, breed, or
Indian, we *all* here just tryin' to survive an' live another day."

"You right 'bout that. And be that as may be, I plan to make
as much money from the army as I can get," sneered Dorman as
he plunged his fork into the meat plate and stabbed a large piece
of buffalo steak and transported it onto his own plate.

IV.

George Bent and Nate were en route, returning to Adobe Walls
to spend the night. They had spent most of the day at William

Bent's ranch, eating, talking, smoking, and drinking strong coffee, and it was only the imminent arrival of the early December dusk that forced them to leave because George had promised Magpie that he would return before nightfall.

Nate had thoroughly enjoyed the day. The conversation with the legendary Kit Carson, though, had somewhat affected him. He had been initially shocked by the scout's frail physical condition and modest height, but then became impressed by the man's quick mind, penetrating eyes, and a confident and commanding voice that still could lead men into battle. He also liked William Bent. The stalwart but embittered patriarch of a large, diverse family that seemed so representative of the kinds of people that made their lives on the frontier.

Nate liked everyone he had met at Bent's ranch but could not make up his mind about Isaiah Dorman. The older black man whom the Lakota had named *Wasicun Sapa* seemed amiable enough, and Nate did envy his independence. He shook his head in disbelief, however, when he thought about how he was only making twenty-one dollars a month in the army, while Dorman was pocketing over one hundred as a simple courier carrying dispatches from fort to fort.

"You know Dorman long?" asked Nate as he maneuvered his mule alongside George Bent. The moon was out and the sky was clustered with millions of stars, which enabled them to easily follow the trail.

"Many years," replied George Bent curtly. His wide scarf covered the lower part of his face so his voice was muffled by the proximity of the wool to his mouth. The younger Bent spoke in a taciturn manner, leaving Nate longing for more information.

"Where did you meet him?"

"I used to trap in the lands of the Santee, where *Wasicun Sapa*'s wife is from."

"You think that *Wasicun Sapa* is not to be trusted?" inquired Nate cautiously.

At first, George Bent remained silent, and the only sounds that could be heard were the plodding of their mounts' hooves against the frozen, partially snow-covered ground.

"Wasicun Sapa cannot be trusted. He will betray the Indian if the price is right. One day, his scalp will garnish a lodge pole."

Nate was stunned by this prediction and for an instant he envisioned Dorman's curly salt-and-pepper scalp attached to a tipi pole blowing in the breeze in the middle of some Indian camp.

"What you said earlier to *Wasicun Sapa*"—Bent adjusted the Navajo blanket that covered his lap and legs—"about how all men from different tribes are the same here because we are all trying to survive is true." Bent bowed his head to shield his face from a sudden cold blast of wind and Nate followed his lead. When the wind had passed them, Bent turned to Nate. "But there are two differences between the Indian and all the rest." Nate thought that Bent looked spooky when he spoke because the wool scarf was so close to his lips that the rag moved as if it were a sock puppet.

"And what are the differences?" asked Nate after Bent became silent again.

"Money and *land."* Bent's tone of voice suddenly became sharp and Nate detected bitterness in his heart. "Indians have no use for money and the land does not belong to the individual. But the white man and the black man and the brown man and even the breed hunger for money and land at the expense of the Indian."

"You're a breed yourself. Where do you stand in all of this?"

"I am with the *Tsitsitas,"* responded Bent resolutely.

"And do you ride with the Dog Soldiers, the *Hotame Ho' nehe?"* retorted Nate, remembering the horrific devastation that those warrior societies had inflicted upon wagon trains, stage stations, unsuspecting travelers, and defenseless homesteads.

"I have ridden with them, that is true, but never against help-less settlers. Only against the pony soldiers." Bent shifted his weight to the rear of his Indian saddle as his mount descended a small knoll. When the ground had become relatively flat again, he turned to Nate. "After the disaster at Sand Creek, we, the *Tsitsitas,* sent the war pipe to the other tribes and asked them to join us in going to war. All the tribes of the plains smoked the war pipe. First the Lakota smoked, then the Northern Arapahoes, and then of course the Hotame Ho' nehe. We were all eager for revenge. There was one night I remember well, when the whole valley along the South Platte was lit up with the fires of burning stage stations and homesteads. It looked like the sky when full of stars."

"Did the Hotame Ho' nehe ever catch any of the militia who attacked Black Kettle's village at Sand Creek?" inquired Nate, conscious of his own involvement in the recent attack on Black Kettle's camp at the Washita.

George Bent nodded, and again turned to his riding compan-ion. Although Nate could not see Bent's mouth because of the wool scarf, he saw that his eyes squinted in satisfaction.

"A few weeks after the disaster at Sand Creek, some warriors came upon nine white men who were traveling east, back to the states, who had ridden with Chivington. The warriors attacked and killed all of them as they attempted to flee. When they went through their valises, they found several scalps belonging to their friends that had been killed at Sand Creek. This so enraged them"—Bent clenched his fist and held it slightly aloft—"that they hacked the dead bodies to pieces and chopped off their heads."

V.

Nate had left Bent's fort at first light. He had spent the night at the ruins and George Bent had been kind enough to loan him the mule to make the trip to Fort Lyon. Nate promised that upon arrival at the post, he would hand over the mule to the fort's horse depot where George Bent could pick up the animal at his leisure. His head wound was sufficiently healed and he was eager to return to duty and longed to see Cara. Fort Lyon was half a day's ride from Bent's fort so Nate was hoping to reach the post by early afternoon, barring any trouble with the weather or with hostiles.

The morning was damp and cold, and a low canopy of heavy gray clouds made the flat and sparsely treed landscape more dreary than usual. As he kept his eyes on the trail, he thought about George Bent. He had thanked the half-breed for his hospitality and kindness and gave him a message for Cougar Eyes if he should see him before he did. Nate realized that he was in debt to Cougar Eyes for twice saving his life. First from freezing to death from the blizzard after Wild Bill Hickok had left him behind, and the second time by rescuing him from the fate that befell Major Elliott's men at the Washita. *"How can I eva repay him?"* he murmured softly to himself.

A bald eagle appeared in the sky circling for food. Nate followed the beautiful bird's wing span with his eyes and admired his flying prowess with an air of contentment. *"I wish I could be like you,"* he whispered enviously as he watched the eagle use the gusts of wind to remain aloft in the sky.

Nate became startled by the report of a gunshot that came from his immediate right. He reined in his mule and the animal obeyed immediately, although the beast's long ears moved erratically. Nate heard another shot ring out from the same direction, and then another. For a moment, he thought that it might be some hunters shooting at the eagle or blasting away at some fleeing coyote, but then the sounds of galloping horses on the frozen ground became audible. He drew his Walker-Colt and held it at the ready, but refrained from pulling back the hammer on the big horse pistol. Just when the mule snorted, Nate saw about a dozen Indians galloping past him about a quarter mile from his position. They were moving fast, and it was obvious that the band was being attacked because Nate noticed several warriors turning around on the backs of their ponies to either fire their revolvers or to let loose arrows from their bowstrings. Nate was too far away to fully distinguish the riders, but managed to identify them as Dog Men because he could distinguish their characteristic large bow-lances. They were also attired in bright winter trade-cloth clothing such as red breeches and turbans.

About two hundred yards behind, a pursuing troop of cavalry emerged from a grove of cottonwood trees, their blue greatcoat capes flapped smartly in the wind. They were giving chase, firing their Colts and hollering as if they were a pack of hounds that had become excited by the hunt. Way out in front of the troop was a rider whose horse Nate recognized almost immediately.

"Good Lawd. It's Cailloux and Jesse!" Just when he identified horse and rider, Jesse fired his revolver at a fleeing Dog Man who was about to release an arrow from his bow-lance. The bullet hit the warrior in the chest, propelling his body to roll off his pony. Nate felt his blood rise in excitement and dug his heels into the mule's flanks. The beast responded instantly, and Nate headed for the line of pursuing troopers. As he advanced, a Dog Man spotted him and lowered his revolver in his direction. He fired the weapon, and Nate felt the round whiz by his head. Nate then fully cocked the hammer of his weapon and pointed it at the brave who was now placing an arrow in front of his bowstring as he yelled, *"Hi, hi, hi!"* Nate took a deep breath and held the air in his chest as he took careful aim at the warrior's head. At the end of exhaling, he squeezed the trigger and sent the lead ball into the Dog Man's face. The force of the shot caused the brave's head to violently snap back and eject his body from the back of his pony.

When Jesse saw the man with the mule shoot the Dog Soldier, he abandoned the pursuit and ordered his men to slow down and move in Nate's direction. Jesse decided that the hostiles were traveling too lightly for the troop to catch them in comparison with his men's heavily laden mounts. In addition, the cavalrymen's horses were showing signs of fatigue over the last few miles and Jesse did not want to wear them down in hostile country. At first, Jesse thought that the man who had killed the Dog Soldier was a hunter. He was too far to properly identify him, but noticed that he wore a heavy buffalo coat.

Jesse approached the body of the dead Indian and viewed the giant hole in the middle of the man's face that made him look like a collapsed, rotten pumpkin. He found this peculiar because the damage to the dead man's face was so severe that Jesse believed that only a .50-caliber bullet or higher could have inflicted such destruction. This would mean that the stranger would have shot the Dog Man with a rifle or carbine, but from what Jesse could see, the man in the buffalo coat did not carry one.

"*Sweet Jezus,*" whispered Jesse to himself as if he just experienced a revelation. "I knows that there's only one kinda side arm that can do this kinda damage to a man at a great distance." He cocked back his forage hat and nodded his head. "And that be a .52-caliber Walker-Colt." He looked at Nate and placed his hand at the rim of his visor and squinted. "*Boy?* That you?"

"*Boy.* You smile when you call me that," responded Nate with a big grin as he returned the Walker-Colt to its holster. He then gently took the reins of the bridle and led the mule toward Jesse.

"Glory. I thoughts you was *dead,*" exclaimed Jesse. He also led his horse by the reins and marched toward his companion to meet him halfway.

"Who in the hell tol' you that? Some damn coyote?" jested

Nate. Jesse could see Nate's face now, and noticed that he was smiling with smug satisfaction.

Jesse dropped the reins and walked up to his friend and opened his arms to hug him. Nate obliged him and both men wrapped their huge arms around each other in a bear hug.

"Boy! You ought to know to neva drop yo'r reins, 'less you got a man holdin' the animal," chastised Nate.

"To hell with that," scoffed Jesse. "Where you been all these weeks?" asked Jesse loudly. "I searched all 'round the Washita, hopin' just to find yo'r body, an' now you here as if you took time to go fishin'."

"I ain't been fishin', that's for gawddamn sure," replied Nate defensively. His mind quickly returned to the fate of Major Elliott and his slaughtered command. He still had trouble accepting that he would have been killed along with the other troopers if not for Cougar Eyes' intervention. "How come you always find me after I've been gone?"

"Reckon dat it takes a black man to find another black man." Jesse smiled.

"Oh? An' you be that man?" challenged Nate, who was devoted to his comrade, but questioned his tracking abilities.

"Well, I seems to be the one who finds you when you gits lost," he boasted as he playfully slapped Nate's shoulder.

"Jess"—Nate took a deep breath—"I never been lost, jest left for *dead.*"

VI.

Nate and Jesse were at the head of the troop on the road returning to Fort Lyon when Jesse heard an abrupt noise coming from a grove of cottonwood trees.

"What was that?" he asked, alarmed. Jesse was listening to Nate tell him about his experience with George Bent and how Cougar Eyes had saved his skin at the Washita when he heard the noise. He raised his hand in the air to command the troop to halt and stared at the trees. "Someone is in that grove!"

"Why we halted?" complained one trooper who was in the rear.

"Quiet in the ranks, damn ya," snapped Jesse, trying to concentrate his vision toward the trees.

Nate saw the scant outline of a horse and rider standing still in the grove, but could not make out if he was an Indian or not. The rider's horse's coat was completely white and blended so well with the partially snow-covered landscape that Nate would not have seen them if it was not for the rider's dark buckskin coat. He tapped Jesse on the arm and pointed.

"Over there. Toward the right."

"Oh, yeah. I see him." Jesse pulled his Army Colt from the holster and pulled the hammer halfway back. "Come out of there, *now*, mister, you spookin' my horse."

The rider remained motionless, however, and Jesse became impatient. "Damn you, mister, if you don't come out from them trees, I'll start shootin'."

"Wait, Jess. Let me try." Nate did not want Jesse to start shooting blindly at the man without provocation. *"Ninaasts!** *Nidonshivih?*† *Nitsisdah?"*‡ he barked.

"What you tellin' him?" asked Jesse who was convinced that the rider was a hostile, possibly a scout for a war party.

"Just inquirin' if he is Cheyenne, and to come out and tell us his name."

---

*Come here.
†What is your name?
‡Are you Cheyenne?

"Nasaatsistah!" responded the man as he emerged from the cottonwood grove.

The man's voice and the way he sat in the saddle with his left hand on his hip, as if he were posing for a painting, were familiar to Nate and Jesse. His horse was fresh and walked with energy and confidence toward them while the rider seemed to float in the air.

"It appears that your Cheyenne has much improved, Sergeant Major," said the rider as he stroked his mustache with his index finger.

"Well, well, Mr. Cody. I didn't figure runnin' into you so soon," responded Nate, eyeing the plainsman's custom-made buffalo coat with matching gloves.

"Heard some shots fired yonder, you boys get into a fight?" inquired Cody as he shifted his weight in the saddle.

"We chased some Dog Men for 'bout twenty miles and killed two of them," reported Jesse proudly.

"Just two of them?" mocked Buffalo Bill.

"Well, they were well armed and movin' like a bunch of banshees."

"Banshees?" exclaimed Buffalo Bill. "Why, my ol' grandmother used to call me that when I was a young-in and misbehaving."

"Oh, so you sayin' that you was a hell-raiser when you were a young-in?" gibed Nate.

"A *hell* of a hell-raiser," boasted Buffalo Bill. "And still am, when called upon." The plainsman laughed and Nate and Jesse chuckled at Cody's remark.

"You boys returning to Fort Lyon?" Cody removed a thick stick of tobacco from his coat's pocket and offered the men a chaw. Nate politely declined, but Jesse seized on the opportunity, even though Nate had never seen him chew tobacco.

"We returning to Lyon, then probably return to Wallace," replied Jesse, breaking off a piece of tobacco from the stick.

"Hear about the fuss over at Wallace?" queried Buffalo Bill casually.

"What fuss?" asked Nate, thinking about Cara.

"That Creole whore peddler, Vasco, kidnapped a breed woman who was a laundress at the fort in the dead of night."

"Was the breed half Comanche, half Mexican?" asked Nate anxiously, feeling his temperature rise and his flesh flush at the mention of Vasco's name.

"Don't know what kind of breed she was, but I was told that she was a pretty little gal with long ebony hair."

Jesse stopped chewing on the tobacco and looked at Nate. "Sounds like Cara to me."

"It sure gawddamn does!" exploded Nate. He became instantly struck with intense anxiety, and his heart started to beat faster.

"Do you know where Vasco has taken her?" Nate was trying to think, trying to organize his thoughts to deal with this brutal news.

"She your woman?" asked Buffalo Bill somewhat naively.

"Yes, she's my woman. Do you know where that bastard took her?" yelled Nate, causing Cody to be taken aback by Nate's impatience and anger.

"All I know is that Sharp Grover saw her and Vasco in Dodge City sometime back . . ."

"Where's Sharp Grover?" snapped Nate.

"He's at Fort Lyon, prospecting for a job scoutin' for the army."

Nate turned to Jesse. "I gots to finds him fo' he leaves the fort."

"Well, go on ahead. Find Grover. I'll see you back at Lyon," Jesse said with a nod.

Nate turned the mule's head and dug his spurs into the beast's flanks and got the animal into a fast trot. Dissatisfied by his mount's slow speed, he started to whack the mule's rump and yell for him to move faster.

"I didn't know that the girl was his woman," muttered Cody to Jesse.

"I am afraid that she's more than just his woman," replied Jesse.

VII.

Sharp Grover was walking out of the sutler's store where he had purchased ammunition for his Spencer, tobacco for his pipe, and coffee beans for his grinder, when Nate rode up on the mule. It was late afternoon and the light was quickly fading as the bugler sounded Stable Call. The scout noticed that Nate's mule was well lathered, and its rider's face wracked with consternation.

"How have you been, Sergeant Major?" asked Grover. He had not seen Nate since the engagement with Dog Soldiers last summer and was surprised to see him looking so disheveled, unlike his usual spit-and-polish appearance.

"You saw that pimp, Vasco, in Dodge?"

The scout was taken by surprise by this question and for a moment couldn't find his tongue. "Yeah," responded Grover hesitantly and slowly. He was not sure why Nate would ask him such a question. "I saw Vasco in Dodge, and paid him two dollars to poke one of his whores."

Nate's face stiffened at the scout's cavalier response about poking a whore. *My Gawd, did he poke Cara?* he thought to himself. He felt disgusted by the prospect of Cara forced into becoming a prostitute for the fat flesh peddler. He then dismissed the possibility, realizing that she was strong-willed and loved him and would resist. But for how long?

"Did you see a tiny woman with very dark hair and eyes? She's a breed, half Comanche, half Mexican."

Grover thought for a moment and nodded. "Well, the morning after my poke, I did see a short but slender girl wearing a Mexican blanket over herself. She was carrying two pails of water for the whores' washbowls. I remember real good 'cause at the time, I wondered why she looked so sad for such a pretty woman who was carrying a child."

Nate's eyes flashed with agitation. "Did she look all right?"

"She kept her head bowed and didn't say a word. She did walk with a limp though."

"A limp, you say?" Nate was afraid that Vasco was beating Cara again.

"Yup, she walked like a wounded animal."

"Gawddamn his hide! I'll kill him, so help me," muttered Nate. He was off to see Colonel Grierson whom he hoped was present at the fort.

VIII.

On the way to Officers' Row, where he hoped to find Grierson, Nate changed his mind. He decided that it would be best to get rid of the mule and see the regimental quartermaster sergeant and get a new uniform and other necessary accoutrements and supplies to replace what was lost during the Battle of the Washita. Nate then took a long hot bath where he organized his thoughts and devised a plan to search for Cara. He would need to get permission to take a leave of absence, and for that, he wanted General Grierson to grant him this request. After bathing, cleaning his Walker-Colt, dressing, and polishing his boots and brass spurs, he went to see Grierson at his house on Officers' Row but was told that the general was at the post commander's residence where he was having dinner with high-ranking officers. Undeterred, he proceeded to make his way to General Hazen's house where a white sergeant told him that no one could interrupt the dinner party unless there was an Indian attack. The noncommissioned officer also told him that not only was Grierson and Hazen present, but that Generals Sheridan and Custer were also present. Nate decided to wait on the porch and sit on a bench near the window of the dining room where the officers had gathered, and wait.

General Phil Sheridan and his staff, as well as General George Custer, were seated at the dining-room table with General Benjamin Grierson and the post's commander, General William Hazen. Hazen had invited his distinguished visitors to dinner and the officers were attired in their double-breasted dress uniforms complete with yellow waist sashes and shoulder plates. With the exception of Ben Grierson, all the officers had gold-colored ripcord cordage with medallions and tassels that decorated their chests and shoulders. "Little Phil's" wartime physical fighting trimness, however, had softened and fat had established itself around the cavalry general's face and waist. His recently acquired potbelly touched the edge of the table, and when Nate quickly looked through the window, he noticed that the hero of the Battle of Cedar Creek's shiny brass buttons were bulging. The boy general, George Custer, sat erect in his chair, his long curly dirty blond hair was combed back over the scalp and his mustache was elegantly waxed. Colonel Grierson had a more relaxed, less military posture as he stroked his beard while listening to Custer's bravado in recounting his "triumph" against Black Kettle's village.

"At the Washita, my command killed more hostiles than any other regiment since before the war against the South," proclaimed the boy general as if he were a peacock that just fanned his tall.

Nate could hear almost every word because most of the officers were speaking loudly and the voices carried through the thin windowpanes.

"It was good work, Autie," confirmed Phil Sheridan, calling Custer by his boyhood name. "Any dead hostile is a good thing for the country," he added as the fiery Irish cavalryman took another helping of wild turkey meat from a plate that an orderly was carrying to each dinner guest.

"It was a great victory, sir! A great victory," boasted Custer, sipping on a glass of warm eggnog. "The men performed excellently, and Cook's sharpshooters performed perfectly."

"Correct me if I am mistaken, General, but after you discount the women and children that were killed at the Washita, there were more troopers killed than warriors. Especially when you take into consideration what happened to Major Elliott's command," commented Grierson dryly as he took a sip of eggnog but then quickly placed the glass on the white tablecloth because he did not care for the drink. Grierson disliked Custer. He considered him a shameless self-promoter who enjoyed exaggerating the facts and toadied to Sheridan's every whim.

An awkward silence descended upon the small room and the only sounds that were audible to Nate were the clanging of silverware against porcelain plates and the shuffling of boots as some of the guests shifted nervously in their seats.

"Men, women, papooses—makes no difference," dismissed "Little Phil," taking his glass of wine and gulping the liquid to wash down a piece of wild turkey meat. "They are *hostile* and should be treated accordingly. Those Southerners that betrayed the Union during the war also suffered for their treacherous ways." Sheridan nodded his head in conviction as if he had absolute power to judge and execute. "I see no reason why the redskins should experience any *leniency* from us when they break treaties, burn stage stations, kill our civilians, and run off with thousands of head of stock."

"Hear, hear," bellowed General Hazen who agreed with Sheridan that hanging hostiles was the best solution in curing the Indian problem.

"With all due respect, General, we would not have an 'Indian problem' if we would fulfill our obligations toward them," responded Ben Grierson whose relationship with Sheridan was decidedly cool and whom he referred to as "Sherry Dan" in his letters to his wife. On several occasions, Sheridan had given choice commands to his West Point pets, such as Custer and Wesley Merritt, rather than to him even though he had seniority. Grierson also disapproved of Sheridan's Indian policies and considered them the equivalent of "The Irishman at the fair," which meant hitting every head in sight.

"They get their annuities," scoffed Sheridan as he looked around for the waiter because he wanted to try one of the venison steaks.

"Never on time, General, and *never* enough," shot back Grierson.

"They are always hungry and they feel that we treat them without honor."

"That might be true but the fact remains that Indians by nature are born to raid and pillage," commented Custer. "And furthermore, if the army would be responsible for issuing annuities rather than corrupt and greedy civilians, we would do a better job. It is not our fault that Washington ties our hands in this matter."

"So you think that by killing a few braves here and there at a huge financial cost while slaughtering scores of women and children is the answer?" challenged Grierson. His eyes were bright and wide with passion and he gave Custer an accusing look.

"What huge financial cost?" asked Custer, acting surprised at

Grierson's financial assessment regarding the warrior kill count. "Goldilocks" was intimidated by Grierson, who reminded him of his father and was of superior rank.

"According to my calculations, General Custer, for each male Indian killed over the past year, about two hundred thousand dollars was spent for *each* dispatched warrior." Grierson paused and took his time to look at his dinner guests. "Gentlemen! I hardly believe that this is a good return on the country's investment for pacifying the frontier from hostiles."

Sheridan winced, then loudly placed his knife at the edge of his plate, much to Hazen's consternation because it was his wife's fine china from back East.

"The simple truth is that there are too few of us to cover the thousands of miles of territory to corral all of the hostile tribes," replied Sheridan defensively, but firmly.

Nate could hear that the Irishman's blood was heating up. He whispered to himself and nodded, *"Good ol' Grierson, always pissin' off his superiors."* Nate recalled the incident on the parade ground at Fort Leavenworth when Grierson confronted Hoffman, the post's racist commandant, in defense of the regiment's right to march in dress parade.

"You know perfectly well, General"—Custer stabbed at a chunk of venison meat on his plate and started to cut off a piece— "that we live like paupers out here, and our army pay is barely sufficient to feed our families. If each brave killed costs Washington two hundred thousand dollars apiece, it is not because we are getting any of the money. I suggest that you look toward the current administration and their business cronies, and not at the army for finding fault."

"Are you insinuating that President Grant is involved in misappropriating government funds, General Custer?" Grierson became angry at Custer's insinuation that his beloved General Ulysses

Grant was involved in any way with the administration's current problems regarding accusations of corruption and graft.

"Gentlemen, I usually do not order my officers to cease discussing topics that I find distasteful, but I will order that any mention of our president and his current difficulties be omitted in my presence," insisted Sheridan.

Little Phil's stern order had the desired effect. Nate noticed that the dining room became void of any conversation and that the officers shifted their attention to their plates. After a few moments, however, General Sheridan started peppering Grierson with questions about building a new fort to replace Fort Cobb and the logistics involved in containing the Southern Cheyennes and Arapahoes.

Nate waited for over an hour for the senior officers to finish their dinner party. When the repast ended, Phil Sheridan and General Custer left General Hazen's home together. Sheridan briefly looked at Nate who towered over the tiny Irishman while Custer chatted into little Phil's ear about how he and the Seventh were ready to pursue more hostiles and ignoring Nate's presence. When Grierson emerged from Hazen's house, Nate accosted his commanding officer and came to attention.

"General Grierson, sir. Request permission to speak with you about an important matter."

Grierson was surprised to see Nate. The commander of the Tenth Cavalry was under the impression that he had gone missing during the action at the Washita and he feared that his favorite noncommissioned officer was dead. "Sergeant Major! I thought you were dead, but here you are in the flesh."

"Reports on my demise have been much abused, sir."

"Apparently so, Sergeant Major." Grierson eyed Nate's buffalo coat and new uniform. "Nice coat," he commented, a little envious that he did not possess such a warm garment.

"Sir, I need to take an immediate leave of absence."

"Family?" queried Grierson who sensed that Nate was not his usual composed self.

"Yes, sir, you could call it that." Nate knew that he was telling Grierson only the half-truth, but as far as he was concerned, he was prepared to make Cara his wife and that made her family.

"Well, there's not going to be much campaigning for the rest of the winter, and since I have known you, you have never requested a leave of absence. How much time do you need?"

Nate thought for a moment and was at a loss to give his commanding officer a precise time span. "I am not sure, sir, maybe a month or two."

Grierson nodded his head. "Take two months, Sergeant Major, you've earned it."

"Yes, sir, thank you, sir."

IX.

Nate was saddling his horse, a big sorrel that he had selected from the post's corral, when Sharp Grover came over to him leading his own horse, a young pinto that was green broke.

"Heard you goin' after your woman," said the scout.

"Who told you that?" Nate finished tightening the cinch and turned to face Grover.

"Half the fort knows 'bout it," replied Grover as he smacked the side of his horse's face because the animal kept brushing up against him. "Stop it, *damn you*. I ain't no scratchin' post."

"So? What is it to you?"

"I want to come with you," responded the scout smartly. He was cradling a Spencer in his arms and was dressed in a baggy and thick brown wool coat while his large floppy felt sombrero made his face look small. "You're goin' need help, Sergeant Major."

"Aren't you scoutin' for the army?"

"Nope, they got all the scouts they need right now an' I don't want to stay here doin' nuthin'."

"This is my bizness, not yours."

"I don't question that, Sergeant Major, but the fact is, I'm a better tracker than you, an' I can help you find her." Grover waited for Nate to reply, but all he received was a blank stare. "Besides, I know Dodge," he added as if he were trying to seal a deal by offering something extra.

Nate thought for a moment and agreed that the veteran scout had a point. Another pair of eyes on the trail would be an added advantage, and another man who knew how to shoot a gun could make the difference in a fight between living or getting killed.

"All right, Grover, you can come with me, but I won't be slowed down. If your horse goes lame or if you can't ride 'cause you wounded or get sick, I'll leave you on the trail, you understand me?"

"I can fend for myself, Sergeant Major, always have."

"Well then, let's mount up an' get goin'."

X.

Nate and Sharp Grover followed the Sante Fe Trail to Dodge traveling east, skirting the Arkansas River. The pair pushed their animals hard, alternating between trotting and cantering for most of the morning and early afternoon. They had not stopped at midday to feed, water, and rest their mounts and Grover became anxious.

"We're pushin' the horses too hard," protested the scout. Nate ignored him and continued to canter his sorrel. "If we don't slow down a bit, they goin' go lame."

"How many miles to Dodge?" asked Nate who continued to stare at the horizon.

"'Bout a hundred fifty miles," he hollered back.

Nate pulled on his reins to slow down his mount to a walk. "A hundred and fifty miles?"

"Yup, that's right," confirmed the young scout, relieved that Nate had slowed his horse down.

"Let's dismount by those drooping cottonwoods and give the horses a break," suggested Grover.

"Yeah, you right." Nate felt some embarrassment that he had to be told not to wear down the horses, and he was surprised by Grover's information that Dodge was a hundred fifty miles away. He had assumed that the town was not more than a hundred miles at most, and expected to be there in a day and a half.

When Nate dismounted he noticed that both horses were heavily lathered. He also saw that their nostrils were crimson, indicating great exertion. He went over to his saddlebag and removed a hoof pick while Grover loosened the cinch on his Mexican saddle as his pinto bowed his head to nibble on some brown short buffalo grass.

Nate looked at the gray overcast sky as he hoof-picked his mount. "We'll stay here long enough to rest the horses an' give 'em a feed. Then we push on, we can cover another ten miles 'fore night come."

"I reckon the horses can do that. I know a place along the trail where we can hold up for the night," said Grover as he led his horse toward the Arkansas where he was going to water him.

"Oh? Where would that be," asked Nate, half interested in what Grover had to say. His mind was preoccupied with thoughts about Cara and what he was going to do to Vasco once he had caught up with the thieving flesh peddler.

"It's an abandoned stage station. It ain't much, but we can stay dry and the horses will be sheltered," explained Grover.

Nate had removed his horse picket and rope from the Mc-Clellan and had tethered the animal to the iron stake. He experienced difficulty in driving the spike sufficiently into the hard ground, however, and had to use a rock to pound it so it would keep the horse from fleeing. He only managed to drive the picket in about a quarter of the way when he gave up because he had to make water. The combination of several cups of hot coffee and the quick morning ride had now made him uncomfortable. He had wanted to empty his bowels for quite some time, but decided that he would rather wait than take the time to dismount. He was now glad that Grover had insisted on stopping and went over to a big cottonwood and urinated up against the trunk. As he watched the steam cloud rise, Nate sighed with relief and then felt anxious as he thought about Cara and how she must be waiting for him to save her from Vasco. He was about halfway through relieving himself when he heard a loud thump next to his head. He became startled and thought it might be an animal in the trees, but then he looked up and saw that an arrow had penetrated the bark of the cottonwood. Another arrow came flying in his direction and landed in the ground near his feet. Nate fell on his knees and unflapped his holster and drew the Walker-Colt. Using the underbrush for cover, he turned to look at his horse and saw that the animal was tugging with all its strength at the picket to flee from the commotion.

"*Indians*. Get behind the trees!" hollered Sharp Grover as he scurried up the riverbank leading his spooked pinto that was bucking and violently moving his head and neck in an attempt to break free. Several other arrows landed near Nate as he heard shots fired, the bullets slamming against the cottonwood trees and hitting the sandy bank of the river. Nate cursed himself for making a cardinal mistake. He should have kept the sling and rifle across his shoulder but had carelessly removed it along with the Spencer and placed the items on the ground near his horse. Although the attackers were secluded, he decided that they were surrounded. The arrows were coming from multiple directions and were dangerously close, indicating that the hostiles had taken up good positions. Nate watched in increasing consternation as his horse continued to pull on the picket and slowly pull it free. He dreaded that he might not reach his mount in time before the sorrel would yank it out and bolt, leaving him on foot.

As Grover came running toward him, Nate started to worm his body on the ground as fast as he could to get to his repeater and horse as several more arrows came from the sky and struck the earth dangerously near him. When he was a few feet away he got on his feet and bolted for the rifle and sling and with his right hand he seized the weapon and with his left pulled the knot free that tethered his horse and made for the grove of cottonwood trees.

Sharp Grover had already taken up a crouching position in the underbrush. He had securely tethered his pinto to a low branch and held his Spencer at the ready, but was unable to see any of the attackers. He did look at one of the arrows that protruded from the bark of one of the cottonwood trees and determined that the length and arrangement of the gray feathers on the rear of the shaft was neither Cheyenne, Kiowa, nor Comanche.

"Dog Men?" asked Nate, taking up a position next to his companion. He had lashed his horse with Grover's as a means of keeping both animals under control. It was an old trick that he had learned during the war. When two or more horses started to act up, one way to keep them from bolting under fire was to tie them closely together and tether them with a line to a secure object.

"Think they are Prairie Apaches."

"Apaches?" Nate was surprised at this news. "This far north?"

"They live south of the Arkansas and come up to join the Kiowas and Comanches to spend the winter or hunt," explained the scout in his typical plainspoken manner.

"How can you tell?" Nate searched the area in front of him and then turned his back to survey the rear but saw nothing.

"The feathers on the arrows are from birds usually found south of the Arkansas. The Comanches and the Kiowas use different feathers for their arrows, so I'm assumin' that they're Prairie Apaches." The area became very quiet. And Nate and Grover waited for their attackers to make their next move.

"These Apaches behave like their southern cousins in that they never rush ya like Cheyenne, Lakota, or Comanche. They like to sneak up to you and git as near as they can 'fore they start shootin'."

"They got to show themselves sometime." Nate could still not see anything. He was hoping that they would fire their guns so he might be able to see their smoke, but for the moment they were clever enough to shoot only arrows that came flying in as if they were angry hornets.

"Maybe, but most likely they goin' to wait till the sun goes down an' rush us in the dark."

"I thought . . ."

"That Indians don't attack at night?" interrupted Grover.

"In their religion . . ."

"Oh, you can thank the French and Spanish missionaries for that! The priests tol' the Apaches that there are no bad spirits after the sun goes down." Grover turned his head and looked at Nate. "And many of the bucks believed them, especially the young ones."

Two more arrows came flying in, hitting the cottonwood trees only a few inches above their heads. The thudlike noise that the projectiles made when the arrowheads hit the bark spooked Grover's young pinto, causing him to kick.

"They after our horses 'cause they would have hit them by now," speculated Grover in a low voice that sounded soothing to Nate. "Them boys are careful. All the arrows have come in real close to us, but not at the horses. At Beecher Island, the Cheyennes didn't care much 'bout the horses, so they killed them all so we couldn't ride out."

"That means they goin' have to kill us from afar, or they goin' have to come and get us, if they want our horses," replied Nate, still searching for any signs from the besiegers. He was angry that these secluded hostiles were holding him back from his mission and wasting valuable time. He thought about mounting up and riding out and take his chances in a running fight, but without knowledge of their positions, he would be too vulnerable a target, or the Apaches might shoot his horse rather than see him get away.

Without warning, an Apache emerged from a small boulder on their right, about eighty yards away, and started running across their field of fire. He was short in stature and his torso was bent forward as if he were running on his feet and hands. Nate saw that the fast-moving brave carried a rifle, bow, and quiver, but the main distinguishing feature that Nate found haunting was his long, black, and thick mane that fell on his back, making him resemble a wolf on the run. Both Nate and Sharp Grover took aim and fired their Spencers at the fast-moving Apache, and although they got off multiple rounds from their repeaters, the warrior managed to safely take cover behind another, even smaller boulder directly in front of them.

"Man's got strong medicine," noted Grover. "I swear I hit him."

"He was moving as if he was chased by hounds," replied Nate, recalling his experience running away from Bloodhound Jack's slave-catching dogs.

"Yeah, I reckon you would know about that," quipped Grover, pulling back the lever on his Spencer to place another round in the chamber.

The big sorrel snickered loudly and Nate turned his head around to see another fast-running Apache in a crouched position advancing toward them as if he wanted to seize the horses. Nate fired his Spencer, but the brave slammed his body on the ground just as he fired, avoiding the round.

"Did you get him?" asked Grover hopefully, staring at the boulder where the other Apache remained hidden.

"Nope."

"Get ready. One of them is goin' make a move," cautioned the scout. Grover slowly raised his head slightly above the brush to get a better view of the terrain, but then an arrow penetrated the top of his sombrero, lifting the hat off his head.

"Sweet Jesus!" he yelled as he ducked back into the brush.

"Bastards are all around us." Nate also lowered his body into the brush while he kept an eye on the Apache who was slinking in front of him in the buffalo grass. He did not have to wait long. Hoping to take advantage of Nate and Grover's caution, the Apache suddenly raised his body from the ground and bolted toward Nate, releasing an arrow from his bow. Nate ignored the projectile that went over his head, and stood up, aimed, and fired, hitting the Apache in the chest. He heard the man grunt loudly as he dropped his bow and fell backward, then watch him violently kick his feet and twist his limbs in the buffalo grass for a few moments until his body became motionless.

"Did you kill him?" Grover heard the loud grunt and knew that Nate had hit the Apache.

"Oh, he's dead all right." Nate resumed his crouching position behind the brush.

With the exception of the noises that came from the fidgeting horses, the site became quiet, void of any human movement, and Nate made up his mind that there would be no more assaults on their position while it was still daylight.

"I think they goin' wait till night 'fore they make another move." Nate quietly crept through the low brush to get to his horse and unhooked the tin canteen. He first took a little water to rinse out his mouth and spit, then took another sip to quench his thirst. "You want some water?" asked Nate as he passed the canteen to Grover.

"Don't mind if I do," replied the scout softly as he reached for the container through the brush. He uncorked the canteen and took a sip. "You probably right," concurred Grover. "I figure that there were four of them, and now that you killed one, there are only three. The way I see it, they can't afford to lose another man."

"Then we wait." Nate checked to make sure that the flap on his holster was free so he could quickly grab the pommel of his Walker-Colt. If the Apaches came into the brush and cottonwood his Spencer would be useless in close-order fighting, so he wanted to make sure he could draw his horse pistol.

"If they come in after us, we'll be ready."

XI.

Nate watched the winter sun descend on the horizon, while keeping a clear eye for any movement from the Apaches. It would be about a half hour before the light would disappear and while the two men waited for the hostiles to make a move, Nate used the time to contemplate what Kit Carson had said about the twelve-pound howitzer at the fight at Adobe Walls. He also contemplated what the famous Indian fighter would do in his place.

"Hey, Grover," whispered Nate.

"Yeah?"

"What do you think Kit Carson would do in our place?"

"Oh, heavens, I don't know." Grover paused to think. "Probably sneak out from where we are hidden and then attack the Apaches from the rear."

"Sounds 'bout right," agreed Nate, recalling the story that Carson had told him about the time when accompanied by only a handful of men, he attacked a band of thirty Cheyennes who had stolen horses from Old Bent's fort.

Nate's thoughts returned to the twelve-pound howitzer at Adobe Walls and Carson's insistence that the small piece of mobile artillery was the most important determinant in saving his command from annihilation at the hands of the Comanches and Kiowas.

"What we need is a howitzer, like Carson had at Adobe Walls."

"Is that what he had?" replied Grover, half-interested. He was more concerned with the Apache that was still hiding behind the boulder, and as he peered into the darkening landscape, he remembered what he learned at Beecher Island. Stay behind good cover, remain vigilant, and make every shot count.

"During the war, at the fight at Baxter Springs, we had a howitzer that saved us from being butchered by Quantrill's bushwhackers," whispered Nate.

Sharp Grover did not reply to Nate's comment. He was too preoccupied with lurking Apaches and the approach of night.

Nate's thoughts, however, returned to the Battle of Baxter Springs and how he once again nearly lost his life at the hands of ruthless Missouri guerrillas.

XII.

Nate and Private Randall Garland were on picket duty at the horseshoe-shaped crude fort that was located at Baxter Springs.

The post was built to protect the Fort Scott–Fort Smith road that skirted the Kansas–Missouri border. Each man stood at attention on either side of the open-end part of the four-foot-high earth and timber embankment. It was midday and the men of the Third Wisconsin and First Kansas Colored Infantry were lining up at the chow line that was a hundred feet away from the fort.

"I can smell that salt pork and beans," remarked Private Randall Garland, sniffing the air and savoring the fragrance of the fumes that came from the cook fires. His right forearm rested where the socket bayonet was attached to the barrel of his Springfield infantry rifle and he had positioned his body to use the long rifle as a resting pole.

"We'll get our turn soon enough," replied Nate, standing in the correct position, rifle resting on his shoulder, feet at forty-five degrees apart.

"Not soon enough," scoffed Garland. "I'm hongry."

Lieutenant James B. Pond of the Third Wisconsin Cavalry, commander of the Union fort, was walking toward the entrance of the fortification where Nate and Garland were on guard duty. He was in the process of adjusting the knot on his yellow sash because he was irritated that the garment did not fit properly around his waist and that the tassels did not fall precisely along the thin gold trim at the seam of his trousers. He wore an officer's frock coat with both flaps folded back and buttoned to the sides, cavalry style, revealing his sky-blue wool vest.

"How you boys doing?" asked the lieutenant cheerfully.

Both men presented arms, but Garland had to move faster than Nate because he was not standing in regulation position.

"At ease, boys. You may speak freely if you wish."

"When can we be relieved, Lootenant?" asked Garland, who was famished and apprehensive that there would not be enough food for him after the rest of the hundred fifty men from the

Third Wisconsin and First Kansas Colored Infantry had had their midday meal.

"I'll have you men relieved shortly," replied Pond. "You boys seen anything unusual?"

"Just jackrabbits," answered Nate as he watched two of the big creatures feed on winter grass and leap around the prairie as if they did not have a care in the world.

"Well then, all is calm, eh?" replied Pond as he removed the folded gauntlets from his saber belt and slapped the gloves against his high-top boots to chase the dust away.

"Yes, sir, all is calm," reaffirmed Nate.

"Good, good," replied the lieutenant, trying to make small talk. As was the case with most officers who led black troops on the frontier against Rebels and Missouri guerrillas, James Pond was an abolitionist. Nate had made up his mind, however, that Pond was of the milder sort of abolitionist. He did not demonstrate the fire and brimstone anti-slaver zealotry such as James Lane, or like Colonel James Williams, who preferred to hang Secesh Missourians rather than waste a bullet.

"We goin' see any Secesh, Lootenant?" queried Garland.

"Oh, they might come. Depends if the bushwhackers can surprise us," replied Pond, eager to talk and listen to what a black enlisted man had to say. Although he felt that he had little in common with his black troops except their emancipation, he felt it was his duty to at least try to converse with them if it would improve morale. The young lieutenant moved himself to the very front of the entrance of the fort, and turned to face Nate and Private Randall Garland. "Those cowards never attack you honestly." Pond kicked his right toe in the dust in a gesture of contempt, then gazed at the open prairie that surrounded the crude encampment. "If I learned anything about these devils is that you can never let them get the jump on you."

Nate could not have agreed more with the lieutenant's assessment regarding the ruthlessness of the men who served with Quantrill and the other guerrilla leaders. He was grateful that the lieutenant had spent the time and effort drilling and training the men of the Third Wisconsin and First Kansas, especially after his earlier horrific and disastrous experience with Quantrill.

Nate had learned that Pond had spent most of the six months prior to his posting at Baxter Springs chasing and fighting bushwhackers along the Missouri–Kansas frontier. He consequently showed a healthy respect for these formidable and ruthless foes and learned to appreciate some of their fighting techniques. Before his arrival, the soldiers at Baxter Springs were facing lapses in discipline and were quarreling over petty thievery. In addition, small but potentially explosive disputes were developing between black and white troops. Within a few weeks, however, Pond had shaped the men from both regiments into a respectable fighting force. He ordered that they march side by side in close order drill and strongly encouraged the men to mingle with each other. Both black and white infantrymen, however, mostly ignored this encouragement, although some commerce did take place among the troops such as trading for tobacco and tins of food.

A mild but long breeze from the northeast descended upon the area and Nate smelled horseflesh. It was that particular aroma blend of perspiration, dirt, equine hide and mane that was so familiar to him, going back to the time when he worked Mas'a Hammond's horses.

"Sir, I smell horses," cautioned Nate. He looked toward the Fort Scott–Fort Smith road but saw no activity. He then shifted his gaze toward a ridge to the northeast where a large stand of timber stood.

"Boy, you an Indian or whut?" mocked Garland. "I don't smell nuthin' but corn bread comin' frum the cook fires."

"Well, you would," riposted Nate. He then looked at Pond. "Sir, I swear riders are comin', they probably in the timber near that ridge over yonder." Nate pointed toward the northeast but the lieutenant could not smell or see anything unusual.

"At ease, Private," commanded Pond in a reassuring manner. "General Blunt and the supply train are due to pass here on their way to Fort Smith. I am sure what you smell are the mounts of the advance flankers."

Nate was not soothed by the lieutenant's reasoning so he cocked back the hammer on his Springfield while the three men waited in silence, staring at the smoothly sloping ravines. Another gust of wind blew by and this time the distinct odor of horse became very apparent to Lieutenant Pond, and the crude aroma rudely diverted even Private Garland's attention away from the smells of the mess fires nearby.

"Fall back," ordered Pond, drawing his .44-caliber Army Remington revolver and walking backward. Pond sensed something was wrong. The horse smells did not come from the direction of the road where General Blunt and his wagon train were supposed to be traveling, but farther north among the ravines, indicating sleuth guerrilla tactics. "Private." He turned to Nate. "Find a bugler and sound assembly." Nate saw that his dark eyes were calm but that the lieutenant's chest was breathing more rapidly.

"Yes, sir." Nate bolted into the earth and log embrasure to find a bugler but discovered that most of the soldiers and noncommissioned officers were still eating their chow a few hundred feet from the fort. He turned on his heels and ran out of the fort to find a bugler.

"Get ready, boys, let's make this another Lawrence!" shouted Coleman Younger as he kept digging his spurs into his swift horse's flanks in order to keep up with the advancing guerrilla horde. The bushwhackers were racing among the trees in the woods making for the clearing.

"Amen to that," roared Frank James, pulling out another Colt revolver with his left hand. The bushwhacker now carried two revolvers, obliging him to place the reins between his teeth as most of his confederates had done, relying on the lead riders to steer the swarm of attackers toward their target.

The bulk of the Missouri riders suddenly emerged from a cutting that was a quarter of a mile away. Their horses were galloping at full speed, and once in view of the fort commenced hollering at the tops of their lungs while withholding their fire until they were in close range.

Pond could hear the strained notes from the trumpet calling for the men to take up their posts but he realized that the bushwhackers would be on top of them within seconds. Nate had rushed back to the lieutenant's side as the noncommissioned officers barked orders for the men to return to the encampment and seize their Springfields that were neatly stacked in rows at the center of the fort.

"*You two men, follow me,*" ordered Pond as he raced back into the fort and got behind the twelve-pound howitzer that was close to the entrance. "Help me move this piece to the opening." He started pushing the artillery piece, but the wheels had sunk into the soft ground and he could not dislodge the gun.

"Stand back, Lootenant, we'll get it." Nate grabbed one wheel and Garland took the other, all three men pushed the piece free and wheeled the howitzer in the middle of the horseshoe entrance.

The guerrillas were galloping toward the mess area and some of the bushwhackers started firing their revolvers at the Federals who were returning to the fort.

"Private, get to the caisson and get a round from the ammunition crate," barked Pond to Nate as he seized the sponge-and-rammer and ran the rod through the barrel. "You there!" He gestured to Garland who was staring at the attacking bushwhackers. "Take that round and drop it in the muzzle." Garland went over to Nate and took the round of canister from him and hurriedly lowered it down the muzzle as Lieutenant Pond gave the sponge-and-rammer rod to Nate. "Ram the round with the rammer!" shouted Pond as he went to the breech to cut a piece of fuse and aim the howitzer.

"Cut 'em off 'fore they reach the fort," order Coleman Younger, urging his mount forward, trying to take the lead. He wanted to kill as many of the bluecoats as he could before they were behind their protective fortifications. Frank James and a dozen men broke off from the main guerrilla body and galloped toward the entrance of the fort.

The men of the Third Wisconsin and First Kansas were running pell-mell for the fortification, but some of the slower ones were being cut down, mostly shot in the back, by Colt revolver fire.

"Don't shoot! We surrender," begged two soldiers, one black, another white. They had stopped running and had raised their arms high in the air. They had become afraid that they might be run down by the bushwhackers' horses. The white soldier got down on his knees and started to cry as he pleaded with Coleman Younger not to be shot.

"Go fornicate yourself!" sneered Coleman Younger; his lips became twisted in a spine-chilling expression as he lowered one of his Colts and shot the hapless infantryman in the forehead. "You too, nigger! Go fornicate yourself," and again the guerrilla aimed his revolver and shot the black soldier in the chest.

The wounded man staggered but remained standing, his face showing defiance. "Oh, you a tough buck, ain't you?"

Younger shot the man again in the chest, but he still remained on his feet. "Damn your black hide!" he bellowed. He moved his excited and lathered mount within a few feet away from the blue-coat and shot him in the right temple. The last shot caused the man's eyes to roll in their sockets as his mouth gaped. He stood erect for a moment, then keeled over on his back, his body making a large thump as it hit the ground.

Lieutenant Pond, Nate, and Jesse hustled to get the howitzer ready to fire. Pond knew that his men were caught in a terrible state of unreadiness. Most of the soldiers were still running toward the fort, creating more confusion as dozens of men packed the entranceway making the task of readying the artillery piece for action more difficult.

Pond had quickly cut a piece of fuse rope and had shoved the pick through the barrel vent of the howitzer and into the powder bag.

"Hand me that lanyard and friction primer," he ordered Nate as he pointed to the rope that was attached to a metal pin. Nate handed the friction primer to Pond. "Stick the pin into the vent." Nate hesitated. "Stick it, man! Stick it into the powder bag." Pond saw that the guerrillas were almost at the entrance of the fort. If he did not get off a round immediately, they would pour into the fortification and overwhelm its defenders. He saw that his infantrymen were either still frantically trying to avoid being gunned down as they fled, or scrambling for their stacked Springfields.

"Hurry, man, hurry," shouted Pond, urging Nate to stick the metal friction primer into the vent as he took up the slack on the lanyard. "Stand back, clear the area, damn it." Pond dropped back and grabbed the trail handspike to move the artillery piece slightly toward the northeast where the majority of the bushwhackers were approaching. "Fire," he commanded to himself. He jerked the lanyard and the howitzer jumped into the air, nearly knocking Garland and Nate over because they were standing too close. The sudden blast from the howitzer had the desired affect. The twelve-pound case shot sent a cloud of little cast-iron balls in the direction of the guerrillas.

The Missourians became stupefied by the unexpected artillery shot and both horses and riders were hit. Three of the guerrillas that were charging out in front were particularly badly torn to pieces by the shot as multiple rounds tore into their flesh, severing limbs and creating horrific wounds.

"Fall back," ordered Frank James as he stood up in his stirrups waving a pistol.

"Fall back, fall back, boys," repeated Coleman Younger upon hearing his comrade's command.

"Reload," ordered Lieutenant Pond as he rammed the sponge-and-rammer rod down the smoking muzzle of the twelve-pounder. Nate took another round of case shot from Garland and dropped the round down the muzzle. The three men loaded the howitzer much faster this time and the lieutenant fired off another round at the Rebels, sending them into full flight.

"Reload," he ordered again. Although the bushwhackers were retreating in disarray, the lieutenant wanted to get off another round for good measure and give more time for his men to get into position. Once again Nate and Garland assisted Pond in loading the howitzer and the lieutenant pulled the lanyard, sending the artillery piece into the air as the mouth of the gun belched flames and smoke. The last two rounds did not cause any casualties among the guerrillas, but did produce the desired effect of scattering the Missourians back into the timber.

"We best wait for Quantrill," said Frank James to Coleman Younger who was reloading his Colts. The bushwhackers had returned to the safety and seclusion of the timber to regroup.

"Yeah, the boys didn't like that howitzer, all right," Younger said with a laugh.

"Well, I ain't attacking that fort again without more men," decided Frank James.

"I ain't arguing with you, Frank, we'll rest the horses, reload our Colts, and wait for Quantrill. Besides, I still need to cut me an ear or two, 'fore I call it a day." Coleman Younger smiled as he stuffed one of his freshly reloaded revolvers back into its saddle holster.

Union Major General James G. Blunt was mounted on a superb Thoroughbred stallion. He was riding at the head of his hundred-man personal escort and headquarters wagon train on his way to take command of Fort Smith, on the Arkansas–Indian Territory border.

"How far till we stop, General?" inquired James O'Neal. The artist-correspondent for *Leslie Weekly* had ridden up to the front of the wagon train to ask how much longer the trip would take because he had developed a saddle sore and was in much discomfort.

"We still have a ways to go, Mr. O'Neal," responded the fiery abolitionist general in a gruff manner. He had no patience for whiny civilians and was more concerned in controlling his young, fast horse than with the correspondent's comfort.

"Aren't we going to stop and rest at some point?" pleaded O'Neal. The artist longed to dismount and take care of the open blister on his rear end.

"I know that you are not cut out for this sort of travel, young man," mocked Blunt. "After all, you are delicate in body and you have the face and hands of an artist. So, I don't expect you to put up with the rigors of army travel."

"Sir, we will be in view of Fort Baxter Springs within twenty minutes," suggested Major Curtis, who was General Blunt's aide-de-camp. "The command has traveled some forty miles and the horses need a noon rest, and quite frankly, General, most of our men are green and are in just as much pain as Mr. O'Neal here."

"Oh, that's right, *Major,*" shouted Blunt in a theatrical manner. "That wretched encampment you call a fort was your brainchild. I suppose you wish to take a looksee at your creation," teased the general. "Maybe you want to inspect the troops, ha, ha, ha."

As was his place, Major Curtis remained silent, but did not enjoy being teased by his overbearing commanding officer.

"Oh, very well, we will stop at your little fort and rest and water the horses," agreed Blunt, trying to soothe his aide-de-camp's feathers.

"Riders coming, General," shouted an advance flanker. "Looks like two of our boys."

Nate and Randall Garland were galloping fast. Lieutenant Pond knew that Blunt's wagon train of forage and supplies was due to pass through, and he wanted to warn the command that there were Missouri bushwhackers in the area. The lieutenant did not want to spare any of his cavalry to warn Blunt because he thought that he might need them if the guerrillas returned, so he dispatched Nate and Garland after they had volunteered and insisted that they could both ride.

"Go see, Major," ordered Blunt. Major Curtis lashed his horse with his long reins and cantered his animal toward the two riders.

Nate and Garland reined in their mounts as soon as Curtis was close enough. "Sir! Beg to report," said Nate as his chest heaved with excitement.

"Guerrillas, sir! Hundreds of guerrillas attacked us not one hour ago," reported Nate, trying to catch his breath.

"Collect yourself, Private!" Curtis waved the palm of his right hand downward, in a calming manner. "Now, how many guerrillas did you say?"

"I reckon at least two hundred, Major, and they probably still around." Nate pointed to the timber that was only a few hundred yards away from the Fort Scott–Fort Smith road. "And they probably hidin' in the woods."

Quantrill was furious with Coleman Younger and Frank James for disobeying his orders. "I ordered you not to attack the fort until we combined our forces!" The bushwhacker chieftain always had trouble maintaining discipline among his very young recruits and resented spending countless hours debating with some of his men who always seemed to question his leadership and military decisions. "Bloody Bill" Anderson was not the only one who ignored his orders in favor of extracting revenge on Union sympathizers or for loot.

"We didn't know they had a howitzer," protested Coleman Younger.

"Did you reconnoiter?"

"No, but now with our combined forces we outnumber the Yankees two-to-one! We can sweep 'em, Colonel, sure as wheat on harvest day," insisted Frank James eagerly.

"They are behind their works and they have the howitzer!" shouted Quantrill angrily. He was mad that his plan of attack had been spoilt by Frank James's and Cole Younger's zealotry. He was even more tipped, however, that he now had to attack the Federals behind fortified works, for to retreat would be to lose face in front of his men.

"Colonel Quantrill, Colonel Quantrill, sir," shouted a rider who was trying to make his way through the big trees in the timber to get to the guerrilla leader.

"What is it?" demanded Quantrill.

"*Oooh, oui,*" cried out the rider, excited about his information. "I just saw the biggest wagon train in my life, Colonel. Must be a hundred or more wagons, filled with supplies, forage, furniture, ammunition, enough for a whole goddamn army!"

"How many men in the escort?" inquired Quantrill anxiously. This was good news indeed. The guerrilla leader now had a choice of either assaulting the entrenched soldiers at Baxter Springs or attacking the fat wagon train that promised much booty and easy killing.

"Don't think they more than a hundred men at the most, Colonel. And whut's more, they look as green as apples in June."

"*Excellent.*" Quantrill was very pleased. With his superior and better armed force, he could now overwhelm the wagon train, kill the Yankees at minimum loss to his command, procure supplies, and save face in front of his men by avoiding a direct attack on the fort. As an added bonus, the Missourians would be pleased with this decision because the wagon train promised rich plunder. "Where are they?" he demanded to know.

" 'Bout a quarter mile up the road, north, toward Fort Scott."

"Show me."

The rider nodded and turned his mount around and led Quantrill through the woods where he could view the slow-moving Yankee command. The guerrilla leader gave orders to his men to wait for him in seclusion until he and a few chosen men reconnoitered.

Quantrill was impressed with the size of Blunt's command. "*My God.* Look at all them plumb wagons, just bursting with goods. Hell! If they wanted to make a run for it, the wagons

393

would either turn over or lose half the stuff." He removed his spyglass from its case and gazed at the column of men and wagons. Through the glass, he spotted Blunt's personal colors. *"By Jesus,"* he said gleefully. "We got us a Yankee general! Probably the commander of the District of the Frontier."

He turned to Frank James and Coleman Younger. "Have the men fan out from the woods and approach the Federals at a slow pace. Wait for my order to charge. Do not proceed hastily. Try and control the men. Do you understand my orders?"

"Why yes, Colonel, we'll wait for your orders." Coleman Younger gave Quantrill a sardonic smile and the guerrilla leader felt that Younger was mocking him.

"Federal cavalry up ahead," announced a lieutenant on General Blunt's staff.

"General," proclaimed Major Curtis, "these men say that Baxter Springs has been attacked by hundreds of bushwhackers and that they may still be in the area. I suggest that we place the wagon train in a defensive position . . ."

"I do not need your suggestions, Major!" chastised Blunt as he looked at Nate and Randall Garland. "Here comes our cavalry now. Probably Pond's men out exercising their horses, or to provide us with an escort, if what these two men claim is true."

Nate took one look at the riders and knew that they were not Pond's cavalry, but guerrillas disguised as Yankee troopers. "Major, those are not our men."

"Are you sure, Private?" asked the major, trying to focus on the riders. He realized that their formation was not regulation, and that sharpened his suspicions.

"General, I request that I go and see."

"Very well, Major, take the lieutenant here, and find out who those people are. In the meanwhile, order my personal bodyguards to form a skirmish line."

"Yes, sir." Curtis executed the general's orders and then proceeded to ride with the lieutenant toward the unidentified riders.

Quantrill, Frank James, and Cole Younger were out in front along with another bushwhacker, George Todd, one of Quantrill's chief lieutenants. Quantrill had ordered the bulk of the command to stay well behind them so as not to alarm the Yankees.

"Let's shoot those bastards down, now," suggested George Todd.

"*Wait*. I want to see the expressions on their faces," snapped Quantrill.

When Major Curtis and the lieutenant had advanced their horses far enough for them to clearly see that the approaching riders were not Pond's mounted cavalrymen, but Missouri bushwhackers, Curtis quickly turned his horse around.

"Return to the command!" The major did not have to tell the lieutenant twice. Both men dug their spurs into their horses' flanks and rode back to the command as if they had just seen Satan.

"They bushwhackers, General, sure enough. Probably advance flankers for Quantrill and his boys," reported Curtis hurriedly.

"Oh, nonsense, Major. It's probably some of Jackman's guerrillas from South Missouri. Give them a few rounds and those cowards will run for cover," ordered Blunt, placing his hand in front of his mouth to cover his yawn.

"Have the men fan out, now," ordered Quantrill. He could see the Yankee officers conferring and knew that the element of surprise was quickly running out.

George Todd motioned for the men to spread out and form a battle line and the guerrillas quickly advanced their horses into position. The Missourians were still at a walk but eagerly waited for their chieftain to give the order to charge.

"*Yiii, ha,*" screamed George Todd. "*Charge.*" The sudden yell startled Quantrill. Todd yanked both Colts that were stuffed in his wide belt and dug his spurs into his horse's flanks. The big beast responded instantly, and George Todd galloped toward the rich-laden Yankee wagon train.

"*Yiii, ha!*" The green troopers that escorted the wagon train could hear a chorus of shouts, yells, and acclamations pouring forth from the guerrillas.

"Goddamn his hide!" cursed Quantrill, watching dozens of his men ride past him in an effort to be one of the first to reach the wagon train. Coleman Younger and Frank James also joined in the fray and Quantrill had to lash and spur his mount to catch up.

"*Bushwhackers, bushwhackers*" went out the wail among the green troopers in Blunt's command. The dreaded cry, combined with rapid revolver fire and Rebel yells, produced an air of panic. Some of the officers shouted for their men to form skirmish lines, but their orders went unheeded as dozens of them took flight. Most of Blunt's command consisted of infantrymen who walked along both sides of the wagons. Therefore, it was almost impossible to get them into battle formations to repel an onslaught of hundreds of swiftly mounted attackers pouring a hot and accurate fire.

The attack by the Missourians quickly developed into a rout and within a few minutes the guerrillas were among the fleeing Yankees, shooting them down as they ran. Nate and Randall Garland were still with General Blunt and his staff behind the general's bodyguard detachment. Blunt's thin skirmish line only managed to get off two rounds when it became clear that they were going to be overrun. They too broke ranks and fled, abandoning their rifles and packs to avoid being encumbered.

"Damn your souls. Stand and fight, you cowards. Stand and fight," bellowed Blunt, watching his men break ranks and flee, causing his horse to rear up, nearly throwing him off his custom-made saddle. "Come back here, or I will have you all shot for treason and cowardice!" he shouted to no avail at the top of his lungs.

The guerrillas were almost among them, and Frank James and Cole Younger saw that Blunt was a Yankee general and motioned to each other to cut him off.

Seeing that his person was in immediate peril, Major General James Blunt decided to join the rout.

"Sauve qui peut, gentlemen," he commanded with flair, as if he were exiting a scene on a stage. He dug his brass eagle spurs into his fast horse's flanks and charged in the direction of Baxter Springs. Since Nate, Garland, James O'Neal, and all of Blunt's staff were mounted, they followed suit, galloping pell-mell to escape the Missourians.

Almost immediately, Major Curtis's horse was shot from beneath him, catapulting him into the air. He fell on his back and as he tried to get up was immediately surrounded and shot to death by grinning, mocking guerrillas who emptied their Colts into his body at point-blank range.

"Let's get out of here," shouted Nate to Garland. "Make for the timber."

"I hear that," agreed Garland, turning his mount to follow Nate into the timber. Before Nate entered the woods he looked back and saw that the young civilian that he had noticed earlier among Blunt's staff had halted his mount and had thrown his hands into the air, surrendering to a half-dozen guerrillas that had cut him off.

"Get that Yankee general, Frank," egged on Cole Younger. His companion's horse was faster than his. Blunt's Thoroughbred, however, sensed Frank James's horse catching up, and he did not like being passed. Blunt's big mount bucked sideways at James's horse, striking the beast in the face. This gave the general the few precious moments that he needed to jump a wide gorge that was in front of him. Not trusting his mount to jump over the gorge, Frank James reined in his animal and watched the Yankee officer kick up a cloud of dust as he galloped full speed at the other end.

In frustration, Frank James fired his pistol several times at the fleeing Union commander, but his rounds failed to find their target. Seeing that his companions were now happily engaged in killing and looting the Federals, Frank James turned his mount and galloped toward the wagon train, hoping that he would not be too late to partake in the traditional festivities.

Nate and Garland had found a spot in the woods where they dismounted and hid behind a huge boulder that shielded their horses and provided cover. They peered through the trees and past the thinning and yellowing autumn leaves, and could discern some of the action that was taking place. They could hear much gunfire and men pathetically pleading for their lives as they attempted to surrender. Nate and Garland cringed as they heard the bushwhackers yell and curse at their victims or laugh with glee before shooting them to death.

"Bastards are killin' them afta they surrender," whispered Nate in abhorrence.

"Neva seen white men kill their own wounded as if they rabid dogs," commented Garland, shaking his head in disbelief as he watched and listened in horror to the cries of a wounded man who was on his knees. He saw that the left side of the soldier's head was bleeding and that his ear had been cut off and that one of the guerrillas was showing off the item to his companions. The hapless soldier had his hands clutched in prayer and held them in the air as if he were appealing to the Almighty.

"Please, mister, I got a wife and baby. Don't kill me," Garland heard him beg.

"Shut up, bluebelly! My brother's wife and child were burnt by you sons of bitches," retorted one of the Missouri riders as his horse pranced around the infantryman. The guerrilla contemptuously spat a wad of spent tobacco juice on him, aimed his Colt, and shot the top of his head off, forcing the torso to collapse backward as if it were a kicked sack of potatoes.

Nate's and Garland's attention was suddenly diverted to one of the wagons that had managed to break free from the train and was making a run for it. Nate saw that it was stuffed with soldiers and on the canvas cover, Nate recognized the military band's insignia. It was General Blunt's musicians' wagon and the teamster was whipping and shouting at his mules as the wagon twisted and bounced on the road toward Baxter Springs. Sitting next to the teamster was a young drummer boy that Nate thought could not have been more than twelve years old. As the wagon rattled on the rough road and dangerously listed from side to side, the drummer boy clutched his side drum in his lap with one hand while he held the edge of his wooden seat with the other.

"Stop that wagon. Rein in those mules and surrender," shouted a guerrilla who had caught up with the rear of the vehicle and was holding his fire.

Nate saw a rifle barrel suddenly protrude from the back of the wagon and saw a shot ring out. He saw the bushwhacker fall from his horse and crash to the ground, but his left boot became caught in the stirrup and the horse continued to gallop after the vehicle, dragging its rider.

Some of his companions saw what had happened to their comrade and became enraged. They turned their horses around and caught up with the fleeing wagon. They shot the teamster and then shot the lead mule in the head, causing the beast to tumble forward and forcing the craft to come to a violent halt.

"Get out of that goddamn wagon, you bastards!" shouted George Todd as he pointed his Colt at the rear opening of the wagon. Todd was a very tall man and older than his companions. He wore his brown hair short and his chisel-cut face was clean-shaven. He wore high cutoff boots and his hat had a star embroidered on the left side brim that was pinned to the crown. The terrified musicians slowly emerged from the wagon one by one.

"Get your hands in the air," commanded Todd. *"Raise 'em high, bluebellies."*

One musician did not have his hands raised high enough and that irritated Todd. "Damn you for not listenin' to me!" The bushwhacker lieutenant pointed his Colt at the hapless bandsman and shot him in the head.

"Line up against that wagon," shouted Todd who had now dismounted. He saw the drummer boy and gestured with one of his Colts. "You too, boy!" His head bowed, the lad walked timidly over to the side of the wagon, clutching his drum. As he walked past Todd who was shouting orders, the Missourian whacked the drum from his arms, sending the instrument on a roll. "You won't be needin' this!" he sneered. Mortified, the drummer boy tried to retrieve the drum but the bushwhacker seized him by the collar and while his musician buddies silently looked on, threw him backward on the ground.

"Please, God. Don't let that man kill that boy," whispered Nate to himself in prayer.

As soon as the members of General Blunt's band were lined up against the side of the wagon, George Todd stood in front of them.

"You shouldn't have killed my friend," lectured the tall Missourian.

"He did it, mister! I tol' him not to shoot, but he wouldn't listen," cried one of the bandsmen, pointing to his neighbor.

"*Shut up,*" ordered the guerrilla. "All right, boys, let's do it for ol' Bill Blesdoe." The guerrillas started firing at the musicians at point-blank range and Nate cried out when he saw the little drummer boy collapse to the ground in a hail of bullets.

"Those bastards! They jist kilt a chil'!" whispered Garland in horror.

"They aren't done yet," cautioned Nate, expecting to see more atrocities.

"*Burn the goddamn wagon,*" ordered Todd as he pressed his shoulder against the vehicle and started to push and rock the wagon. Other bushwhackers gave him a hand and within a moment the craft was tipped over on its side. "Throw the bodies on top of the wagon."

Another guerrilla found a kerosene lantern that had fallen off the vehicle. He emptied its contents on top of the corpses, making sure that he sprayed each body with the kerosene. Nate sighed with apprehension as he watched the tiny body of the drummer boy be the last of the executed bandsmen to be thrown onto the human pile.

"Gawd, I hope they all dead," whispered Nate.

Todd removed a matchstick from his vest pocket and struck the head against the tailgate of the wagon and watched the twig light up. He stared at the burning match for a moment, mesmerized by the slow-moving flame as the fire moved toward his fingers. Just when the blue and yellow flame was about to burn him, he tossed the match on top of the drummer boy. The kerosene had the desired effect and Nate's heart jumped as he watched the bodies and the wagon abruptly go ablaze into a giant ball of flame and smoke.

"Ouu wee! Look at them corpses burn," remarked a bushwhacker, starting to dance a jig with a companion who had a bottle.

George Todd walked over to where the side drum lay and picked up the instrument that had belonged to the drummer boy. He gazed at it contemptuously, his mouth still twisted in anger.

"That wet-nose brat can take his little piece of shit straight to hell," he commented casually, throwing the article on the burning pile.

"I sure wish I had some liquor," lamented another Missourian as he wiped his mouth on the sleeve of his light beige frock coat.

"All right, boys, let's see if we can find some more Yankees to kill," suggested Todd who began to feel uncomfortable as the stench of burning human flesh started to permeate the air.

Nate and Garland felt somewhat relieved by this statement because it meant that the bushwhackers would leave the immediate area in search of the fleeing Federals who were running in the direction of Fort Scott. Nate was going to suggest that they start moving but a man with a dark and devillike beard appeared and called out to some of his fellow Missourians.

"Look what I found hidin' behind a stump!" shouted "Bloody Bill" Anderson triumphantly. He was leading the artist-correspondent, James O'Neal, at gunpoint from on top of his horse. Quantrill's rival chieftain had arrived with his band on the scene a few minutes earlier and Anderson had found the cowering illustrator hiding.

"Take a look at these," he demanded, throwing O'Neal's large sketchbook on the ground.

Some of the guerrillas started going through the pages and looking at the sketches. O'Neal had sketched a couple of skirmishes that he had witnessed and had presented the Federals as clean, noble men in blue, fighting gruff and filthy Southern riff raff. After the Missourians had looked at several of the sketches, "Bloody Bill" commented dryly, "Makes you want to vomit, don't it?"

The guerrillas stared haughtily at O'Neal, but the journalist remained silent. "Is that the way you see us?" asked one guerrilla menacingly.

"Well, I draw what I see and I. . . ."

"Boy, your illustratin' days are over!" snapped Bloody Bill, lowering his Colt. O'Neal placed his hands over his face and Anderson started to laugh hysterically as he emptied his revolver into the journalist's body and head.

"That will learn 'em," commented a youthful-looking bushwhacker who had removed his big Bowie knife from its fringed deerskin sheath. He walked over to O'Neal's bullet-riddled body and squatted on his haunches next to the dead man's right hand. "Well, I need me a little souvenir from this here son of a bitch." He started to slice off O'Neal's right hand as if it were a piece of meat on a spit. He wanted that particular hand because it had a wide wedding band, but Anderson became irate.

"Stop that. He's mine," warned Anderson, wild-eyed. He was starting to froth at the mouth and drips of white spit started to fall on his black bib shirt. The guerrilla with the Bowie knife suddenly became cautious because he had learned over the past few months that any man who rode with Bloody Bill would be best advised to give him a wide berth if he knew what was good for him.

"Oh, hell, Bill. We all a band of brothers, native to the soil, live and let live." The bushwhacker with the Bowie smiled.

"To hell with that! I found him, I kilt him, so he's mine, damnit. Now, get away from him," ordered Bloody Bill as he dismounted.

The guerrilla with the Bowie saw that Anderson was about to explode and decided to back off. "No harm done. Meant no disrespect."

Grinning and wild-eyed, Anderson removed his own Bowie knife that was much larger than the one owned by the guerrilla whom he had browbeaten into leaving O'Neal's body alone.

He started to make grunting sounds as if he were a hog that was rooting, causing some of his fellow bushwhackers to stare at him strangely. Bloody Bill stooped to pick up O'Neal's right arm and with one clean slash eviscerated the dead journalist's limb. Bloody Bill then held the pale crumpled hand high in the air and proclaimed: "Another token taken on the long road to justice!"

"God bless Bill Anderson and Robert E. Lee," shouted the older guerrilla, raising his plumed hat into the air. Following his lead, most of the bushwhackers also raised their hats and cheered while others cried out that Bloody Bill was the most fearless of them and that he should be their leader and that they wanted to kill more Yankees. They spurred and lashed their already excited horses in the direction of the wagon train where the bulk of their comrades were busy pilfering, shooting fleeing and wounded Federals, and mutilating and stripping the dead.

"Don't move a muscle," warned a guerrilla, pointing both fully cocked Colts at Nate's and Garland's backs. The two men nearly jumped in the air from fright but did not turn around to see who had gotten the jump on them. "Drop those rifles," he ordered. Nate and Garland complied, resting their Springfields on the ground.

"You niggers should have hidden your horses better. I had no trouble seeing 'em through these dying leaves. Now, get up real slow like and turn round."

Nate and Garland obeyed and gently turned around only to

be shocked at the bushwhacker's age. The boy could not have been more than fourteen years old and he was dirty-looking and half of his front teeth were either gone or chipped. Although he carried four Colts, two in his hands and another brace squeezed in between his gut and a Union saber belt, he wore work clothes. Unlike his more flamboyant companions, he was not attired in fine linen ruffled shirts, silk cravats, brocaded silk vests, and light-colored frock coats and trousers with satin piping. Nate thought that the boy probably came from a dirt-poor farm and had run off seeking adventure and loot.

"I saw you boys duck into the woods, an' I been trackin' you," he commented smugly. "Now, let's go join my friends."

Nate knew that if he did not do something he was going to be executed in the same brutal manner as O'Neal, the drummer boy, the bandsmen, Major Curtis, and all the others. The guerrilla youth, however, had his Colts trained on them and was close enough that it would be almost impossible for him to miss.

The youth led them to where most of the Rebels had gathered and Nate saw that Colonel Quantrill was riding about in a crazed manner in General Blunt's personal buggy. He was shouting in a drunken stupor while holding a five-gallon demijohn of gin aloft.

"By God, Shelby couldn't whip Blunt, neither could Marmaduke, but I sure whipped the hell out of his ass." The guerrilla chieftain would then take a long gulp from the demijohn, repeat the boast, and lash the buggy horse.

Nate saw that Quantrill was not the only bushwhacker who was inebriated. Many of the Missourians were also reeling from drinking the canteens that had belonged to Federal infantrymen that were filled with whiskey.

"Bring me those two niggers," ordered "Bloody Bill" Anderson, towering over a captured black man who was a civilian. The

Negro was on his knees, as if he were about to be beheaded. There were several other guerrillas standing with him and Nate assumed that they were part of his outfit.

Nate and Garland were brought within Bloody Bill's presence as the guerrilla leader continued to snort like a hog and drool over his black bib shirt. When they were within a few feet of Anderson and his henchmen, Bloody Bill kicked the black man over with the heel of his high-top boots.

"You're a goddamn thief!"

"No, sir! Not me, I didn't do nuthin'," he pleaded.

"Don't lie to me, boy. I know you committed criminal acts in Jackson County 'fore you ran off to Kansas to help that bastard Jim Lane and his Jayhawkers."

"I don't know no Jayhawkers!" cried out the kneeling man.

"Shut up, you black rascal." Bloody Bill lowered his Colt and fired the revolver at the back of his prisoner's skull, spattering pieces of brain, bone, and blood onto his trousers. Anderson started to laugh hysterically and only stopped when Nate and Garland came within eyeball range.

"Well, well. What do we have here? More niggers?" mocked the guerrilla leader as his devillike gaze and cruel mouth examined the two new preys that had been delivered to him. "Jody! Give that big buck that shovel over there." The bushwhacker picked up a shovel that had fallen off from one of Blunt's supply wagons and threw the digging implement at Randall Garland's feet. "Dig, nigger," ordered Bloody Bill. "Dig three holes big 'nough to fill a corpse, *he, he, he.*"

Garland stared at the shovel and hesitated to pick it up.

"Don't try an' sass me, boy." Anderson cocked back the hammer all the way and pointed the Colt at Garland's head.

"Don't be a fool, pick it up," whispered Nate.

Garland looked at Nate with a sense of great doom as he

slowly stooped to pick up the shovel. He gave Bloody Bill a look of disgust and contempt as he placed the pointed tip against the topsoil and pushed his right foot on top of the head of the shovel and broke ground.

"Dig faster, nigger. I don't got the whole goddamn day." Bloody Bill looked about him and saw that most of his men were busy loading their saddles with pilfered sacks of flower, coffee, meats, and clothes. "I got a lot of lootin' to do 'fore the day's over, ha, ha, ha!"

Nate looked about in horror as he witnessed the guerrillas stripping the dead as they engaged in a drunken babble, while others slashed at the corpses with their Bowie knives. Sliced-off fingers, hands, arms, feet, and privates were thrown about as if confetti, but ears were enthusiastically pocketed or placed in the Missourians' haversacks or saddlebags.

Randall Garland had dug one hole and was about to start on the second when Colonel Quantrill had halted his appropriated buggy to talk with Anderson. All of Bloody Bill's men had left him to partake in the killing and looting of the wagon train and Anderson was becoming impatient.

"I told you that I shoot any body that arrives late," lectured Quantrill. He took another sip on the five-gallon demijohn and placed the long-necked jug on the horsehair seat. Nate saw that he was completely sloshed and that his head reeled about as if it were going to roll off his torso.

Anderson was taken aback, because like him, when Quantrill said he was going to shoot someone, he usually meant it.

"If you think you can shoot faster than me, then shoot. Damn you!" challenged Bloody Bill, turning to face the drunken Quantrill.

Garland glanced at his companion and Nate gently nodded his head as his eyes pointed to the shovel. Garland understood completely. Pretending to be oblivious to Anderson and Quantrill's argument, he rammed the shovel into the ground and filled the head with a small pile of black soil. He then slowly maneuvered the digging implement toward the dirt pile and dumped his load. Without losing his composure or raising his head to attract attention, Garland quickly lowered his left hand to the base of the shaft converting the shovel into a club. He then abruptly turned toward Bloody Bill and violently swung the shovelhead at his tormentor's face, knocking over the guerrilla leader and sending his prized hat flying. Seizing the moment, Nate leaped into the buggy and grabbed Quantrill by his double-breasted Confederate jacket and picked up the bushwhacker as if he were a sack of potatoes. He lifted Quantrill's slender body into the air and threw him out of the vehicle, sending the guerrilla chieftain aloft. Still carrying the shovel, Garland also vaulted into the buggy and Nate lashed the reins against the horse's rump, while yelling "*Ya, ya!*" The already excited beast dug his hind hooves into the ground as if he were going to jump over a fence and bolted, throwing huge clumps of dirt into the air.

The buggy sped down the road toward the fortification at Baxter Springs. The fast-turning high wheels spun the vehicle from side to side, sending huge clouds of dust into the air. Although he was too drunk to feel the pain of being thrown into the air and landing on the ground, Quantrill was also too inebriated to get up. His fellow bushwhacker "Bloody Bill" Anderson sat on his backside holding his head as he reeled from the sharp blow, muttering about the whereabouts of his hat.

XIII.

"Here they come," shouted Sharp Grover as the remaining three Apaches emerged from their places of seclusion and charged

Grover and Nate. The moon was shaped as if it were a nail sliver that came from a thumb, casting just enough light to enable the defenders to see the attacking Apaches' clothing.

The Apache who resembled a black wolf had pulled out a tomahawk from his belt and bolted from behind the rock and charged where Grover was positioned. The Apache remained noiseless, preferring to attack his enemies in silence. Fortunately for Grover, he had remained vigilant even though he was becoming fatigued and had to ward off sleep by repeatedly slapping his face. He was about to strike his right cheek again when he saw the white hand band of the attacker in the moonlight. The Apache was zigzagging as he ran toward his prey in a low crouching position. Grover recognized the erratic pattern and adjusted his aim and started firing his Spencer. The Apache, however, was too fast on his feet, running as if he were a wild animal. He was about to leap into the brush where Grover was stationed when the scout cried out: "I can't see the bastard."

Nate reacted quickly. He yanked his Bowie knife from its leather sheath and turned around to where he was next to his companion. Nate briefly saw the white headband of the attacker in the lunar light and threw the knife at the Apache. Nate and Grover heard a loud thud and then a long groan followed by the Indian crashing into the brush, a foot away from Grover. The dying Apache was lying on his back. Nate and the scout stared at the body while watching out for the remaining two that lurked on their flanks. Nate was amazed at the expiring Apache's height. He was very small and Nate thought that he had the body of a child. He remained silent as the Indian ogled him and Nate decided that he was going to cut his throat if he did not perish soon. That did not become necessary, however, because the Apache gasped his last breath and Nate could hear the air escape from where the knife projected from his chest.

Grover squatted on his haunches and grabbed the pommel of the Bowie and yanked the knife out. He then carefully wiped clean both sides of the blade on the Apache's smock and held the knife by the tip and handed it back to Nate.

"Thank you. I owe you one," whispered the scout.

"Anytime," replied Nate, taking back his knife.

XIV.

Hiram Mackenzie was cleaning his .54-caliber Hawken rifle and thinking about Cara. As the seasoned mountain man rammed some oiled swabs of cloth in and out of the long octagonal barrel, he fretted about his current circumstances. He thought that it was unjust that Silas Quinn should have such a fine woman as the Comanche-Mexican half-breed while he slept alone. Ever since the death of his wife several years ago, a Ute princess who he had spent nearly thirty years with, Mackenzie's heart had been heavy with loneliness. He looked around his cave where he had been living for several years and sighed. When his wife was alive, no matter where they chose to dwell as they were always on the move, she would make the place warm and fill the air with laughter and song as she cooked and went about her daily tasks of serving her husband.

The mountain man had disassembled his Hawken. The fifty-inch-long iron barrel rested on a table in a corner of his large cave along with the deadly weapon's elegant brass trigger guard and butt plate, steel nipple, and hammer and maple stock. He lovingly picked up the barrel and pointed the muzzle toward the brightly lit oil lamp that hung on the cave wall and peered into the breech to make sure that the bore was clean. His right eye blinked and quivered from the bright light that flooded the interior of the barrel when he placed the rim of the breech to his eye to inspect the bore. He was satisfied that the gun was perfectly stainless and gently placed the barrel back on the table as if it were an infant.

"Yup, I remember you when you were brand-new," he reminded himself with pride. Mackenzie frequently spoke to himself. It was a habit he had developed when he was young and traveled alone on the plains spending long solitary winters holed up in crude cabins or damp dugouts.

"Yes sir-ree, I can recall when I bought you in St. Louie." Mackenzie stroked his long wild gray beard in contemplation.

"Them Hawken boys sure knew how to make a gun," he added admiringly, thinking of Jake and Samuel Hawken, the two brothers who had invented the big bore plains rifle in St. Louis. "Must have been in the spring of '32. Before I set out for the Platte that I got you."

He took a moment to gaze lovingly at the other finely crafted parts of the Hawken that were neatly arranged on the surface of the table.

"Well, time to put you back together." He sat down at the table and methodically and expertly reassembled and loaded the Hawken.

"Maybe she will be down by the creek," he told himself, thinking about Cara and how he would frequently see her carrying water to Silas Quinn's cabin. He had accompanied her several times and spoken his best Spanish in an attempt to curry favor, but their brief meetings had been tense because she feared her keeper's wrath.

He put on his beaver coat and matching hat and placed his doeskin haversack around his left shoulder and took his Hawken into his arms. When he opened the door of his cave that he had constructed out of heavy timber, he had to shield his eyes from the bright early morning sun. The day was very warm for the season, and Mackenzie thought that a January thaw might be taking place.

The creek was about an eighth of a mile from the mountain man's cave and Mackenzie followed the deer trail that led down the side of the mountain into the valley. As he surveyed the ground before him, he noticed an inordinate amount of animal tracks, indicating that he was not the only one who believed a January thaw was at hand. Tracks were everywhere. Mule deer, coyote, rabbit, bighorn sheep, and coyote crisscrossed each other in the fast-melting snow and mud.

One set of tracks gave Hiram Mackenzie pause however, and the mountain man squatted on his haunches to inspect the big imprint on a patch of snow.

"Sweet Jesus. Ol' Prowler is out, damn him." Mackenzie looked up and smelled the air seeking Ol' Prowler's scent. "Don't that bear know it ain't spring yet?"

Ol' Prowler was a notorious middle-aged grizzly known by the inhabitants of South Pass as more than just a nuisance. Miners and stock alike spent the warm months of the year in fear of his excursions into their camps searching for food to feed his insatiable appetite. What really riled the occupants of the area, though, were the grizzly's bad manners in killing donkeys, mules, cows, dogs, and the occasional miner. The grizzly had become very fond of these types of meats and found it easier to kill than fast-moving game. Many a man had shot at the beast but somehow they would either miss the bear or inflict only minor wounds on his thick hide and skull leaving him to quickly escape into the woods.

"Damn bastard probably lookin' for a meal."

He knew that Ol' Prowler liked lurking in the timber and low brush at the edge of the trail where miners, sutlers, and travelers used to descend to the river. He cocked back the hammer on the Hawken and placed his finger gently against the safety trigger. He cautiously proceeded down the mountain trail. After following the bear's tracks for a few yards, Mackenzie saw that the grizzly's tracks led into the woods. Although somewhat relieved that the beast was not meandering along the narrow trail, he walked slowly and kept a sharp eye as he sniffed the air for any signs of the animal.

Silas Quinn and Cara were filling their buckets from the fast-moving water of the creek. The temperature of the water was ice-cold and although the weather was warm, she felt chilly because her fingers had become numb from dipping into the creek. She finished filling her containers and since Silas Quinn still had one bucket to fill, she lifted her head toward the warm winter sun and closed her eyes. She smiled slightly as she felt the warmth of its rays bake her cheeks.

"Le-let's go," ordered Quinn. He was carrying four containers, two in each hand, and he was eager to return to the cabin. He hadn't had breakfast yet and his stomach was growling.

Cara remained silent and avoided eye contact as she always did when Quinn spoke to her. She picked up her two buckets and followed the miner along the river back to the cabin.

Ol' Prowler had made his way toward the river and had downed several gallons of creek water to quench a burning thirst. The creek was filled with river trout and the grizzly successfully snagged several of the big fish with his giant paw. He was about to snag another when he picked up Silas Quinn's and Cara's scent. The wind had shifted and the grizzly's curiosity had been aroused. The bear drew up on his hind legs and stood up and faced down-river. He sniffed the wind as his snout quivered and identified the scent as human. He was weak and famished from his hibernation and decided that it would be easier to investigate the humans rather than chasing antelope and mule deer.

"St-st-stop fa-fallin' b-behind, damn you," barked Quinn over his shoulder. Cara had been slowing down and began to straggle.

She ignored the miner's order because she was too tired to respond and too busy catching her breath. Every step her little feet and legs took, the weight of the buckets became increasingly burdensome and she started to drip water from the rims. Cara was about to call out to Quinn and ask him to take a break when she heard some rustling of branches to her left. At first, she thought it was a rabbit or a whooping crane, but when she heard the crisp sounds of bushes being trampled and the cracking of snapping twigs, her heart leaped from fear.

"Oso!" she exclaimed as she froze in her tracks. Her heart was beating very fast and her eyes searched the timber for any sign of the animal, but the woods were too dense to see anything.

"Wh-wh-what's th-the ma-matter?" Quinn did not hear the noises in the timber and had become irritated that Cara had stopped walking.

"Oso!" explained Cara in a strong whisper and pointed toward the timber.

"What you blabbin' 'bout, girl?" snapped Quinn impatiently. He turned around to face her. "You know I can't understand that spic lingo."

Although a hard man Quinn was not unsympathetic regarding Cara's condition. He knew that she was pregnant and the burden of lifting the water containers uphill was hard for her. He was about to put down his four buckets and help carry hers when Ol' Prowler burst from the timber, howling and charging Cara on all fours.

Cara screamed and abandoned her buckets of water and started to run back down toward the river, hoping to gain some speed from the charging grizzly. Quinn could have retreated back to the safety of his cabin but he became so enraged that the bear was attacking Cara that he threw one of the buckets at the grizzly and managed to hit the beast on the head, diverting the bear's attention away from her. The miner was only armed with a Navy Colt that was wedged in between his belt and trousers. He frantically drew the revolver, cocked back the hammer, and prepared himself to confront the bear. The beast had now also become incensed and had lifted himself on his hind legs and was stepping slowly toward Quinn as he growled and made hideous noises.

Quinn was determined to hold his ground as he raised his pistol at the towering carnivore. The grizzly continued to growl appallingly at him and the miner winced when he saw the bear's sharp teeth protruding from his quivering, drooling mouth. As the animal approached closer, Quinn could feel the hot stench of the beast's breath on his face as if it were a dry, putrid wind.

Quinn could not see whether Cara had put sufficient distance between herself and the grizzly because the bear was so large and blocked his view of the path. He knew he would have to go for a head shot and pray that the .36-caliber ball would either kill the bear or at least seriously injure the animal enough to disable him.

The grizzly was about twenty feet away from Quinn and the miner decided that was as far as he was going to let him approach. He aimed at the bear's forehead and fired the Colt. The round missed its mark but did take a piece of the bear's ear off, outraging the beast even more as he wailed from the fresh wound.

"God damn it! I can't believe that I missed the bastard. God-damn it!" Quinn was so agitated that he had not realized that for the first time in days he did not stutter. He took several steps backward as he recocked his revolver, but Ol' Prowler's front paws came crashing down on the ground. He shook his great neck forward and opened his snout to its full extent and roared defiance.

"Ka-ka-come on! U-u-you devil, I—I—I'm ready for you!" hollered back Quinn defiantly in a futile attempt to outroar his antagonist.

Ol' Prowler swiped the ground back and forth with his huge right paw, lowered his trunklike neck, and charged Quinn. The miner fired his Navy Colt again at the head of the grizzly, but all he heard was the hammer hitting the nipple on a spent cap.

"Shit!" cursed Quinn. There was no time to run. Ol' Prowler was a few feet away, so Quinn placed his arms and hands into the air in an effort to protect his head and await the shock of the grizzly's impact.

Ol' Prowler threw himself on top of Quinn and forced him to the ground as the miner screamed and kicked with his feet while the carnivore mauled him. The grizzly worked his jaws around the miner's skull as if he were bobbing for an apple and dug his enormous claws into his back, shredding Quinn's clothing and ripping flesh.

Hiram Mackenzie heard Quinn's revolver shot and Ol' Prowler's familiar unnerving reverberating roar. His first thought was Cara and her safety. He bolted down the mountain path that led to the creek as if he were a bighorn sheep while holding his Hawken close to his chest. By the time he arrived at the scene, the grizzly was still mauling Quinn on the ground while the miner wailed in pain and horror. Mackenzie faced Ol' Prowler's back side and hind legs. The bear's ass was wobbling wildly from his efforts in mangling his prey and the mountain man could see Quinn's legs kicking savagely under the grizzly's underbelly. Mackenzie paused and looked anxiously about as he squeezed the safety trigger to its off position. He knew perfectly well that damage from a .54-caliber ball fired from his Hawken could inflict great and lethal harm, but he also realized it would be useless to shoot the bear in the rear. The shot might prove lethal in the long run if the beast bled to death in the woods, but the immediate result would be drawing his attention away from Quinn to himself, and there would not be enough time to reload the Hawken for another shot.

He decided to fire his big bore rifle at point-blank range at the bear's head, thereby ensuring the round's maximum effect. He ran over to the front of the bear and nearly stumbled on a stump, but recovered his balance and moved into position where he was as near as possible to Ol' Prowler's skull. The grizzly was so preoccupied with mauling Quinn that he had not noticed the mountain man's approach, and Mackenzie had the advantage of being upwind from the beast. Mackenzie was about five feet away when he leveled the barrel at the right temple of the bear's head. He tried pointing the muzzle as close as possible to the skull but that was proving difficult because the beast was thrashing madly at Quinn.

A thunderous crack rang out, followed instantly by an explosion from the bore of the Hawken that sent the .54-caliber ball slamming into Ol' Prowler's head. The grizzly suddenly slumped onto what was left of Quinn's body and became motionless. It was over. The mountain man had killed the scourge of South Pass.

Mackenzie kicked Ol' Prowler's rib cage with his boot to make sure that the animal was dead. Satisfied that he had been successful in accomplishing that task, Mackenzie wanted to see if Quinn was still alive but the mountain man failed to budge the dead bear because of the animal's great weight. He did manage to lift Ol' Prowler's huge head sufficiently to get a look at the miner.

Although Quinn had been badly bitten on his head, face, neck, and shoulders, and his flesh torn by the grizzly's claws, Mackenzie saw that he was still breathing. The miner was oozing blood from where the bear had bitten him and although he was a thoroughly seasoned plainsman, Mackenzie winced when he saw what Ol'

Prowler had done to Quinn's head. The bear had ripped off his victim's scalp and ears and he thought that the miner's head resembled a battered crimson melon.

Quinn's eyes suddenly popped open and the miner coughed up blood signifying to the mountain man that he was dying fast.

"You," whispered Quinn, knowing that he was at death's doorstep.

"Don't talk, save your strength."

"Can have her now," he blurted, trying to crack a smile. Mackenzie stared at him and watched his breathing grow slower and then cease altogether. For the second time in the day, Silas Quinn did not stutter while expressing himself.

XV.

Antonio Vasco was sitting at a table in his tent counting money. The greenbacks and coins were the week's proceeds from the labors of his whores and the Creole pimp took great pleasure in arranging the bills and silver coins into neat little piles based on their numerical value. Business had been good in Dodge City and Vasco had greatly improved his financial prospects by ruthlessly driving his horizontal workers hard and shortchanging and cheating as many drunk patrons as possible.

It was early Sunday morning and with the exception of the occasional barking dog, braying donkey, or neighing horse, Dodge was quiet. Vasco had just completed an early breakfast that consisted of a brandy, toasted bread, and a soft-boiled egg that Miguelito had brought him from a nearby saloon.

Vasco burped loudly after he had finished devouring the boiled egg and consumed the last of the brandy. He then searched his slit pockets on his vest for matches to light a tiny Mexican cigar. He found one stick and lit it on the back of the table. He was about to touch the flame to the stogie when a strong wind gust slammed into the side wall and roof of the tent. The flesh peddler became alarmed and stared at the moving canvas while his corpulent fingers held the burning match until the big flame singed the tips.

"*I-yaa,*" cried out Vasco in pain. He released the burning twig and sucked his burnt index finger and thumb. "*Miguelito, aquí. Rápido.*" Vasco wanted a glass of ice-cold water to soak his burns. The injured fingers were used to count money and it distressed him that he might have trouble engaging in that task if he was in too much pain.

"My, my. Look at all that money," commented Nate coldly as he slowly entered Vasco's tent cradling his Spencer. He left the tent flap loose and the canvas snapped in the wind. "The fruits of flesh peddling and thievery have been good to you, eh, *pimp?*"

Vasco's heart leaped in his chest, and his face became flush with guilt and dread.

"What you want? Why you here?" he demanded as his fingers slowly crept toward the inside pocket of his coat where he kept a .28-caliber mini Colt with folding bayonet.

"You know what I want, you lyin', thievin', fat bastard! Where's my woman?" Nate's voice was loud but he controlled his rage. He wanted Cara back safely before he would make Vasco pay for his abduction of her and their unborn child.

"She gone. She—she left over a month ago," stammered the pimp, trying to buy time. He was hoping that Miguelito would show so Nate might be distracted and he could reach for his pocket pistol.

"Gone where?" snapped Nate, slowly approaching Vasco's table, pointing the fully cocked Spencer toward the Creole.

"How should I know where? She just left—in the middle of the night." Vasco's hand stopped moving toward his inside coat pocket because he was afraid that it might provoke Nate.

"He's full of bullshit!" proclaimed Sharp Grover, pushing Miguelito into the center of the tent. Vasco's Mexican lackey was hatless and looked disheveled. "I found this one outside and he told me another story." Grover gestured with his head as he rested the butt of his Spencer on the ground. "The Mex told me that his boss sold her to a miner."

Vasco's face became so flushed that he thought he was going to pass out. He was afraid of Nate and knew that his life now hung on a thread. His only chance was to either bargain for his life or reach for his mini Colt and shoot the big black soldier in the head before he could get a shot off from his Spencer.

"You goddamn slaver, you sold my woman?" Nate's controlled rage now exploded into visible outrage. His voice became so loud that even Sharp Grover became stunned. Nate took two quick steps toward Vasco.

"I will tell you where she is if you spare my life," pleaded the pimp, rising from his seat and quickly getting behind his chair.

Nate stopped his advance toward Vasco and took a deep breath. "If you tell me this instant where she is I won't kill you."

"She is with a miner by the name of Quinn," blurted Vasco, clutching the back rim of his hickory and leather chair as if it were a blanket.

"Where?" demanded Nate.

"In the gold fields of South Pass," responded the pimp as beads of sweat poured from his scalp. Vasco wanted to reach for his linen handkerchief to wipe his face but was afraid that Nate might misconstrue the movement.

"That's 'bout five hundred miles as far as the crow flies," remarked Grover.

"Five hundred miles? Jezus. Take all winter just to get there!" lamented Nate. He felt his blood heat up and wanted Vasco to pay for this outrage. He raised his rifle butt into the air and was about to strike him in the head when the Creole pimp threw his arms in the air to protect his head.

"But we had a deal," he protested.

"I said I'd not kill you. Didn't say nuthin' 'bout not slammin' your fat head, flesh peddler." Nate whacked Vasco in the face with the metal butt plate of his Spencer as if he were a rattlesnake. The blow propelled the obese pimp into the tent wall where he collapsed to the ground.

Vasco moaned in pain as he held his nose. Blood was pouring forth from the nostrils and he felt that it was loose, indicating that it was broken.

"You *bastardo! You broke my nose.*"

"Be glad I didn't kill you for what you did!" leered Nate, watching Vasco hold his handkerchief to his broken nose and crawl on the wooden planked floor, dripping tiny pools of blood.

Nate and Sharp Grover turned their backs to leave when Miguelito cried out: *"Watch your backs."*

Vasco had suddenly lifted himself from his crawling position and charged Nate with his mini Colt. The pimp had removed the weapon from his inside coat pocket and Grover saw him press the button on the pistol that ejected the small but pointed bayonet from the bottom of the barrel. The pocket Colt now became a lethal knife in the hands of someone who had become so enraged at what Nate had done to his nose that all he could think of was slitting his throat. Nate did not turn around in time to meet his assailant and as a consequence felt a sharp pain in his lower back as the pimp grunted loudly and grinned repulsively while he twisted the blade, pressing hard on the pommel. Nate roared in pain as he felt the blade penetrate the tough hide of the buffalo coat, his uniform, and long johns. He instinctively rotated his body in an attempt to shake off Vasco as if he were some wild animal, but the pimp stubbornly clung to his coat with one hand while the other continued to push the short bayonet into his lower back.

Sharp Grover tried to intervene but Nate and Vasco were so violently thrashing about in the tent that he could not get close enough to pry Vasco off of his friend's back. The two men kicked over chairs and slammed into an armoire and stumbled into a spittoon before knocking over the table where all of the neatly piled money had been stacked, sending coins and currency aloft. Nate spotted the potbelly stove in the center of the tent and decided to maneuver himself and Vasco's clinging body toward it. He backed up onto the hot stove and shoved the fancy man's ass onto it, burning his fat rump. Vasco kicked and screamed in severe pain, and to escape being burned, finally released his hold on Nate. The bayonet of the .28-caliber Colt, however, remained in Nate's back as Vasco crawled away and retreated toward the tent flap.

"You're not goin' anywhere." Nate's anger had reached the boiling point. The heated struggle with Vasco and being stabbed in the back made him lose all self-control. He marched up to him, the heels of his cavalry boots and spurs caused the floor planking to vibrate as Vasco pathetically crawled and moaned as he made his way toward the entrance of the tent. Grover saw that Nate's face was contorted with hate and knew what he was about to do but remained motionless, unwilling to interfere in Nate's personal business. Nate placed the center of the barrel of his Spencer against the front of Vasco's neck and pulled it with both hands as he pushed his right knee down on Vasco's back. The pimp immediately collapsed onto the floorboards, his great weight making a loud thud, but Nate continued to strangle him until Sharp Grover heard the sound of his neck snap, making even the veteran plainsman wince.

Miquelitto stood in horror at the center of the tent and stared at his former employer's body. *"Madre mia,"* he bemoaned, bowing his head in reverence and making the sign of the cross.

Nate witnessed Miguelitto's religious expression and grimaced. The bayonet was still stuck in Nate's back but he had recomposed himself and his breathing had returned to normal, even though he had just killed a man.

"Don't waste your breath, *hombre!*" quipped Nate, turning his head and reaching for the pommel of the mini-Colt. He firmly bit his lip as Grover watched him slowly pull the bayonet out from his lower back without flinching. Holding the bloodied knife in the air to examine the weapon, he turned to gaze contemptuously at Vasco's corpse.

"Damn him to hell. He won't be needin' any prayers where he's gone to."

XVI.

Nate and Sharp Grover had arrived at William Bent's new fort along the Arkansas River by the middle of February. They had planned to stay at Bent's ranch for the night and acquire supplies and gather information regarding the trail north.

The pair had been so far fortunate that the weather had co-operated as they journeyed across the prairie toward the Southern Rocky Mountains. Before they had left Dodge City, the two travelers had pooled their money together and purchased supplies and a mule to carry the burden for the long trip to the South Pass gold fields.

Nate had given all of Antonio Vasco's money away to the whores, and Grover thought it was the right thing to do, considering that they worked hard for it. Nate also gave some money to Miguelitto because he realized that he was just a poor wretch who had also been exploited by Vasco. The Mexican had tears in his eyes when Nate handed the money over, embarrassing him as he repeatedly expressed his gratitude. *"Gracias, señor, gracias, señor."*

As Nate and Grover approached Bent's place, he noticed that the flag was at half-mast, and wondered who important had died. When they arrived at the ranch and dismounted, a military honor guard from nearby Fort Lyon had formed a line and were at ease. A half a dozen officers were also present, apparently waiting for something to come out of Bent's ranch house.

Nate and Grover were about to climb the few steps that led to the front porch when the door suddenly opened and a sergeant shouted in an authoritative voice: *"Make way. Make way for the colonel."* Nate and Grover stepped back and a crude wooden box carried by four troopers led by a colonel emerged from the doorway.

"Carson?" whispered Nate to himself. It had to be him, he thought. He remembered how frail and sickly the great scout looked on the last and only time he saw him. Several Mexican and Cheyenne women were wailing as they emerged from the house accompanied by equally upset children. Nate recognized one sobbing lad as the boy who had been playfully crawling all over Kit Carson's body on the floor just weeks earlier.

Following the coffin, George and William Bent and Isaiah Dorman emerged from the ranch house. Nate noticed that their faces were either grim with grief or strained from melancholy contemplation. They stood on the porch quietly as they stared at the flag-draped coffin. Nate removed his kepi and bowed in reverence and Sharp Grover, following his companion's lead, did the same.

"You jest ride in?" inquired Isaiah Dorman, separating himself from the Bents and going over to where Nate was standing.

Nate waited for the coffin to pass him by before he replied to Dorman's question.

"Yeah, we arrived right now. Say, that is Carson's body?"

"The man died early this morning. I was there along with a bunch of us. At the end, he hollered good-bye to us in Spanish and passed."

"He was a legend in his own time," remarked Nate in admiration.

"Probably the most decent white man I ever met," added Dorman. "He was always polite to me."

When Kit Carson's coffin passed where the honor guard had assembled, a lieutenant ordered: "Present arms!" Instinctively, Nate came to attention and as he stood ramrod straight noticed several troopers in the honor guard and one of the officers had tears in their eyes. One trooper gasped and cried out a pathetic sob, but none of the officers or the sergeant bothered to reprimand him. They were all too sad or struggling to keep a grip on their military comportment.

Nate watched Carson's coffin lifted into a military ambulance wagon and the detachment leave for the return trip to Fort Lyon where Nate assumed the scout's body was to be interred. As he watched the wagon leave and the troopers depart, he felt a sense of remorse but was thankful that he at least had the opportunity to have met and spoken with Kit Carson.

"The Indian lost a good friend today," said George Bent, bowing his head. His wife Magpie stood next to him, prostrate with grief.

"This is a sad day for our country!" warned William Bent from his porch as if he were a preacher on a podium cautioning about man's imminent demise. "I have lost an old and true friend," he added, lowering his head.

"Yes, sir, he was one of a kind," responded Nate, clutching his kepi and feeling awkward that he had nothing better to say.

XVII.

The next morning when Nate and Grover were at the corral, and had almost completed their tasks in preparation for getting back on the trail, Isaiah Dorman approached them, leading his pack mule.

"George Bent told me that your woman was stolen."

"Bent junior got a big mouth," retorted Nate, tightening the cinch on his horse. It irritated him that his business was rapidly becoming widespread knowledge.

"He didn't mean no harm. Fact is, I'm goin' as far as Denver and I like to accompany you all."

"I don't want you slowin' me down," bristled Nate.

Dorman became astonished by Nate's statement. His face tightened and he looked Nate straight into his eyes with a mixture of contempt and bemusement.

"Slow you down? Boy! Didn't your mama tell you to respect yo'r elders? I came to this country when you were still suckin' on the tit! I been travelin' these mountains, valleys, and prairies of this country for near twenty years. What's more, I speak half a dozen Indian languages. How many do you know?"

For the first time in a long while, Nate felt chastised. Dorman's reasoning rang true and he realized that he had made a mistake in judgment.

"I stand corrected," said Nate softly. "And sure, you can come with us."

"Well, that's fine, just fine. You know, normally I ride alone, but I thought you could use an extra pair of eyes and another gun on the trail."

Nate nodded in approval and mounted his horse.

"Let's get goin'."

XVIII.

"Where's the proprietor?" inquired Sharp Grover after the three men had entered the dimly lit hotel. The scout had addressed the question to an elderly man who was sitting in a wooden armchair leaning against the wall smoking a clay pipe with a very long stem.

Nate, Grover, and Dorman had arrived at Pueblo, Colorado, late in the evening and found lodging scarce in the river town that stood along the banks of the Arkansas. They had searched the town for accommodations but were turned away from all of them because the establishments were filled to capacity. They were told at their last stop that they should try a place called the Irish Queen. A "paper hotel" at the north end of town.

"Shut the goddamn door, mister. You lettin' in the cold air," barked a gruff half-asleep patron who was curled up on the floor next to the stove. Dorman hadn't properly shut the front door, and the flimsy portal had swung open again on its leather hinges. Nate looked at the patron and saw that he was wrapped in a filthy horse blanket and was using his money belt as a pillow.

"Where's the proprietor?" asked Grover again after Dorman had properly secured the front door.

The elderly man removed the pipe from his mouth and Nate noticed that most of his front teeth were missing.

"She's back in the kitchen, *drunk,*" replied the man, pointing the long curved stem toward the back. "Fact is, she's been drunk fo' *three days.*"

The response surprised Grover and Nate, but Dorman's face remained expressionless.

Nate and Grover went to go look in the kitchen and when they cracked open the door to peek in, they saw a middle-aged woman slouched over on a table snoring as a large hog slept by her feet.

"Hard to tell which one is snorin' louder, the drunk passed-out woman or the hog," mused Dorman, peering over Nate's shoulder.

"I swear! Are they both drunk?" questioned Sharp Grover.

Disgusted, Nate turned back and addressed the elderly man with the pipe. "Mister, we need a place to stay the night."

"Well, soldier boy"—the elderly man glared at Nate, trying to see his face in the dim light—"there's one bed upstairs that's empty 'cause no one wanted it on account that the last fella that slept there died of the *pox*." The geezer laughed heartily, daring any of the three travelers to sleep in a dead man's bed who had recently died from smallpox.

"Don't bother me. I been vaccinated," replied Nate, recalling getting the shot back at Fort Wallace.

"Same here," boasted Dorman, grinning smugly. "Courtesy of the United States Army."

"Well, well, ain't that nice fo' you black boys! How come the army vaccinatin' darkies while white civilians are dyin'?" cursed the man who was lying near the stove.

"Now, I don't want that kind of talk in here, mister," chastised the geezer. "Everybody has to get along here, and when Mrs. Riley is stone drunk, I'm the boss here!" The elderly man turned to Nate and Dorman. "Now, if you boys want to share the dead man's bed, it's all right by me."

"Much obliged, how much?" asked Dorman.

"That will be a dollar apiece," replied the old man without batting an eye.

"A dollar?" Nate was about to argue about the price. A dollar apiece to share a diseased bed sounded like robbery but then he knew this was probably the only bed left in town, and the geezer was prepared to take advantage of that fact.

Nate and Dorman paid him and Sharp Grover was told he had to hand over fifty cents for a spot on the floor.

Nate and Dorman climbed the rickety stairs to the large room upstairs where they were surprised to see over twenty cots two feet apart divided in two rows with two patrons per bed.

"Jeezus, I thought army barracks was bad," commented Nate, grimacing when he smelled the stench of body odor mixed with stale tobacco and urine, dirty feet, soiled socks, and long johns.

"I've seen wurse," replied Dorman, walking down the middle of the two rows of cots looking for the empty bed. There was one oil lamp that was turned down low that was the only source of light for the room, and even though both men proceeded cautiously, Nate almost tripped several times over empty boots that were carelessly discarded on the floor. Most of the patrons were snoring and Nate thought it was going to be difficult to get any sleep.

"Here it is," whispered Dorman, sounding relieved that he had found the empty bunk. He removed his beaded haversack, French trapper coat, and bobcat hat and sat at the edge of the double-wide cot to remove his boots. Nate followed suit and sat at the opposite side. Both men then maneuvered their bodies onto the cot and discovered that the bed was far too short, so half of their legs and all of their feet protruded from the foot of the cot. Nate threw the pillow on the floor because it was so covered with dust that when he tried to shake it out, he nearly choked. Both men also discarded the flea-bitten and filthy covers and chose to use their own saddle blankets to keep warm.

Nate and Dorman stared at the heavily cobwebbed and smoke-stained ceiling trying to close their eyes to go to sleep as they listened to the hideous sleeping sounds of their roommates. Nate was almost asleep when he was jolted by the blast of a steam whistle coming from the Arkansas River. The whistle rang out twice, each time causing the thin walls of the paper hotel to vibrate.

"Put a cork into it," shouted one patron who was awoken by the whistle.

"Shad up, damn ya," cried out another. "How can I get sober if I can't sleep?"

"Didn't you say that you once traveled on a steamer?" inquired Dorman, ignoring the noise.

"Yeah, on the Red River during the war."

"You were on the run, right?"

"Oh, yeah, I was on the run all right," confirmed Nate, thinking about his journey up the Red River on the paddle wheeler *Belle de Jour.*

"Didn't you say that you were hidin' with a Creole gambler?" probed Dorman.

"Jacques Napoleon Gaches," responded Nate reflectively, "and he was an octoroon not a Creole."

"What happened to him? He get away?"

"Well, yes and no," replied Nate ambiguously. "And right now, I don't feel like talkin' much. I jest want to get some sleep. We got a hard ride tomorrow and I don't want to lose any more time."

Nate shut his eyes but Dorman's mention of Jacques Napoleon Gaches reminded him of the last leg of the journey on *Belle de Jour* as the stern-wheeler steamed toward Shreveport.

The following morning after Major Prescott had corrected Vincent Clemente's and Simon Fury's bad manners in the dining room, Jacques Napoleon Gaches and Nate were readying themselves to go to breakfast. Hoping to get another *Dix* bill from the gambler, Red River Sam had suggested that he bring food to their cabin, but Gaches's vanity and overconfidence that his disguise would prevent detection got the best of him. He declined Red River Sam's offer and decided that he was safe from his pursuers.

"I don't much like goin' back to that dinin' room. Maybe Red River Sam is right. Maybe we should have our food brought here.

Suppose those two men are there?" Nate recalled asking Gaches.

"Nonsense. And tip my hand by our absence?" retorted Gaches, appalled that Nate would make such a suggestion. "Besides, my good man, we mustn't deny my creditor's solicitors one final act in our little masquerade ball before we reach Shreveport, *n'est-ce pas?*"

Resigned to Gaches's stubbornness in venturing forth from the snug confinement of their cabin, Nate grabbed the handles of the wheelchair and made for the door that led to the upper deck. As Nate wheeled the creaky contraption forward, Gaches gave his face a glance in his portable shaving mirror one last time to check his freshly made-up face.

"It's good," he remarked smugly to himself. "Let us go and perform."

"Watch out, boy. Watch for debris in the water, damn it!" bellowed the pilot at his young apprentice, chopping on his soggy cigar stub. The captain of *Belle de Jour* always became concerned with the last stretch of the Red River in approaching Shreveport. The river twisted and turned like a treacherous water moccasin and the night was very foggy.

"We goin' so slow now that I reckon that the gators can hitch a ride," commented the apprentice as his sweaty palms and fingers gripped the big wheel.

"Don't worry 'bout that, boy. Keep a sharp eye on the water, watch for currents."

"Aye, Captain."

Both Simon Fury and Vincent Clemente were in a foul mood. Their rough treatment at the hands of Major Prescott the previous evening had incensed them and Fury was still convinced that there was something not quite right with the elderly man in the wheelchair accompanied by a big Negro.

"I know that old octoroon is a goddamn fraud. It's Gaches, I tell you, his beard looked fake," he vented as he painfully tried to move the fingers on his right hand to make a fist. Prescott had whacked his hand so hard the night before that he feared that he would not be able to use his gun hand.

"So what are you going to do about it?" asked Clemente half-heartily. His face was still sore from the blow that he had received from Prescott's sword hilt guard and he had decided that he would rather stay in his cabin than risk more confrontation.

"Look, we know that Gaches is on board," explained Fury as he rubbed his bruised hand. "We both saw him jump onto this tub at Natchitoches, so he's got to be here somewhere and my sixth sense tells me that the cripple in the chair might be him."

"Well, if you think it's him, how you goin' get past that big buck of his and that meddling nigga-lovin' major?"

"Oh, I'm not worried about him. We just have to stay clear of him and his men. But you got a point about the buck, we might have to kill him to get to the octoroon."

Vincent Clemente sighed. "I don't think I'm up for this. My head hurts, and the way my back feels right now...."

"Do I have to remind you that our employers expect results and not excuses," retorted Fury. "Do you want to face them empty-handed?"

Upon reflection, Vincent Clemente did not relish the prospect of facing their ruthless employers without the money that Gaches owed them or his head.

"Well, let's get this over with."

"The morning fog is mysterious. Don't you agree, Nate?" exclaimed Gaches as Nate gently pushed the chair among the strolling passengers on the upper deck on the starboard side. Nate remained silent, he was too preoccupied with not hitting any of the passengers because the deck was narrow and he had to avoid hitting the brass cuspidors that were arranged on the floor of the deck near the railing. As the pair made their way to the stairwell in the forecastle to descend to the lower deck where the dining room was, Nate kept his head bowed but looked up every now and then, discreetly searching the faces of the white passengers for any unfriendly signs. Nate had wheeled the chair to the center of the boat. The pilothouse was located above them and he could hear the captain admonishing the apprentice.

"Boy, you've got to have the river in your veins if you going to be a pilot. You wait, boy, I'll learn you the river. In time, you will know every bluff and reef between Shreveport and Alexandria."

Nate slowly wheeled Gaches toward the double stairwell in the forecastle and was about to lift the wheelchair to descend the stairs when a sudden blast of steam rang out from a whistle.

"That was not us," remarked Gaches alarmingly.

"Must have come from another boat," suggested Nate who thought that the sound was so loud that it might have just as well come from *Belle de Jour*'s whistle.

Without warning, Nate felt the stern-wheeler suddenly turn hard to starboard, throwing his body off balance and causing him to fall on his backside and lose control of the wheelchair. He watched in dismay as the rickety contraption rolled the few remaining feet that separated the deck from the stairwell, and observed Gaches and the chair plunge down the stairs. Nate tried to grab the chair in vain but it rapidly became out of reach and all he could do was watch Gaches tumble off his seat and fly down the steps followed by the bouncing wheelchair.

When the captain heard the whistle from the oncoming steamer, he cursed God and shoved the panic-stricken apprentice away from the wheel and seized it in a frantic attempt to turn the vessel and evade a collision. As he lay on the deck, Nate looked up and saw the big boat suddenly appear from the thick fog as if it were a ghost ship emerging from hell.

Due to the captain's quick action however, *Belle de Jour* narrowly escaped being rammed in the stern on the port side. The captain's maneuver, however, had a price. Passengers who had been walking on the decks were also thrown off their feet and many of them sitting at the dining room eating breakfast were ejected from their seats while the shouts from male passengers and the screams from frantic women and frightened children added to the chaos.

Moments before *Belle de Jour* made the abrupt maneuver, Simon Fury and Vincent Clemente had been walking toward the dining room to have breakfast. When the two men had reached the staircase, they were also knocked down by the paddle wheeler's hard move to starboard. A few feet away from where Fury and Clemente had fallen lay Gaches. He was on hands and knees and had become disoriented and his head was spinning in a dizzy haze from the tumble down the stairs.

Belle de Jour had narrowly escaped being hit by the other steamer and had now straightened herself in the water. Passengers were slowly getting back on their feet and members of the crew hurriedly ran about.

Gaches's beard had become unglued from his face during the plunge down the steps. He moaned and held his head as he got up on his feet.

"It's Gaches," cried out Clemente, pointing his finger at the fugitive gambler.

"Seize him," ordered Fury, reaching for his gun.

"Run," yelled Nate from the top of the stairwell. *"Run."*

Gaches was wondering around aimlessly in tiny circles and was not conscious where he was or what had happened. Before he could get a grip on himself, Vincent Clemente had seized his collar and was dragging the hapless dandy gambler toward the outside to the lower deck.

Nate rushed down the stairs to assist Gaches but by the time he had descended to the lower deck, Clemente had dragged the gambler outside into the fog. Nate followed but was stopped by Simon Fury. The henchman pointed his pistol in Nate's face.

"Don't move. Don't move a muscle, you black rascal, or I'll blow your head off!"

Nate obeyed. He raised his hands in the air and watched helplessly as Clemente started to slap and punch Gaches.

"Where's the goddamn money?" he would demand every time he struck Gaches.

Gaches wanted to talk but Clemente kept hitting him so frequently that he could not find his breath to speak.

"Stop hittin' the bastard so much," ordered Fury.

Clemente complied and Gaches was able to regain his composure. "The money is safely put away," he said coolly and Nate was amazed at the gambler's casual attitude considering the circumstances.

"Where?" demanded Fury.

"In the boiler room."

Nate became stunned by this reply. Not only was it a lie, but he contemplated what was to be gained by such a reply. More time? he wondered.

"You lead the way," ordered Fury, pointing his pistol toward the stern of the steamer.

"What are we goin' do with the buck?" asked Clemente.

"He'll have to come with us, for now."

"You lead," ordered Fury, gesturing at Gaches. Clemente seized the gambler by the collar and made him walk while Fury hid his pistol within his frock coat but continued to keep his finger on the trigger. Although most of the passengers were too preoccupied with their own recovery after *Belle de Jour* had moved abruptly hard to starboard, Fury did not want to draw any attention but wanted to be prepared in case Nate might try something or if anybody attempted to intervene.

The four men proceeded toward the boiler room that was located near the stern of the steamer on the main deck and the fog was still so dense that Nate thought he was walking in a cloud. Taking extra precautions, the captain blew the steam whistle at regular intervals to prevent any further difficulties with other river crafts. The sharp bends on the Red River and nonexistent visibility also forced the captain to reduce speed and to rely on his experience and knowledge of the river to avoid going aground or hitting debris. He had given orders to the crew to watch for floating logs and stumps and to be prepared to use their long poles to ward off floating obstacles that came near *Belle de Jour*.

As they approached the boiler room, the roaring sounds of the engine grew louder. The heavy clamor that made the tremendous iron cranks rotate the huge stern wheel as steam escape pipes blew off the excess from the low-pressure boilers became increasingly deafening. Adding to this cacophony was the movement of hundreds of tons of river water as the stern wheel pushed its foreboding blades into the water.

The entranceway to the engine room had no door. It was a wide opening that allowed men and wood for the boilers to enter and leave the room easily. Gaches and Clemente had almost reached the opening that led to the hot engine room when two huge black men that were stripped to the waist and sweating rivers of perspiration came running out, laughing playfully. The first one was walking backward and collided into Gaches and Clemente, forcing the henchman to lose his grip on Gaches's collar. Although Fury was armed, Nate gambled that he had become distracted by this sudden obstruction. He quickly rotated his huge frame backward to face Fury and kicked his cane out from underneath him, forcing the man to lose his balance and collapse onto the deck.

"Throw him in the river, man, throw him into the river," shouted Gaches, struggling with Clemente who was trying to get a hold on him. Nate saw that Fury was about to pull out his pistol so he used his right foot to stomp on his hand and chest. The henchman grunted in pain and grabbed Nate's foot in an attempt to lift it off his chest. Nate, however, reacted by seizing Fury's frock coat and hoisted the man into the air as if he were a sack of grain.

"No, no, I can't swim," clamored Fury as his feet kicked the air as if he were an infant.

"Catch a ride with a gator," wisecracked Nate, throwing Fury's body over the railing into the Red River.

Clemente watched in consternation as his colleague fell into the water. The fog was so thick that Fury's body quickly disappeared from view and within a few seconds his pleas for help vanished as the strong currents pulled him quickly under.

Clemente had become sufficiently distraught by his companion's fate that Gaches was able to wiggle free and flee down the deck toward the stern, leaving Nate to face Clemente.

"You be needin' help?" asked one of the engine-room workers who had stumbled into Clemente and Gaches. The two tall and muscular boiler men had watched impassively as Nate threw Fury into the river, but now wanted to help their brethren.

"I can handle him," responded Nate as he started to move toward Clemente.

"Stand back, you black rascals," cautioned the henchman, but Nate kept coming at him and the two boiler men moved to corner him.

"I am warning you, niggers, I'll have you whipped and put in chains!"

"We free men, mister, and this our boat," responded one of the boiler men, pointing to himself and then to his companion.

Surrounded by three huge and defiant black men, Clemente started to panic. His back was up against the railing and there was no one else in view on deck. Desperate and cornered, he decided to kick Nate in the groin and make a run for it but Nate seized his foot when Clemente raised it, and rolled the brute over the railing. The fog was still thick so Nate and the three boiler men could not see him land in the water, but they did discern a loud splash that sounded as if a gator had just snapped its tail.

"Hope the man can swim." One of the boiler men laughed.

XIX.

"Press harder! *Mas fuerte*," ordered Cara as she breathed heavily and stood on all fours on top of Hiram Mackenzie's bed in the trapper's cave. The mountain man pressed with all his might with the palm of his hands against the small of Cara's back.

"Pant harder, girl. Pant like a dog," yelled back Mackenzie, encouraging her to breathe faster to relieve the pain and distract her mind from the labor.

After the bear attack, Mackenzie had found Cara down by the creek, trembling with fear and squatting on her haunches underneath some fallen timber. He lovingly took her back to his cave and for several weeks had nursed and taken care of her because of the sufferings she was undergoing due to the last stages of her difficult pregnancy.

Mackenzie was feeding his horse some hay in the cave when Cara felt the contractions in the early part of the evening and told the mountain man that her time had come.

Mackenzie quickly built a huge fire and had a pot of boiling water ready along with some clean linen. He had sterilized a skinning knife to cut the umbilical cord and made a pot of boiling black coffee in case Cara's labor was to endure into the dark hours of the night or longer. He had a bottle of laudanum and offered some to Cara but she declined to take any because she wanted to be fully alert.

Although the cave was not very warm, and the grizzly hide flap that served as a door occasionally blew open, allowing snow and wind to penetrate the grotto, Cara was sweating as if the cavern were an oven.

"Push, girl, push," repeated Mackenzie. The mountain man had much experience in delivering babies. He had assisted with all of his children when his squaw had given birth, often on the trail or in the mountains as well as witnessing countless squaws, pioneer women, whores, and mining camp women give birth.

"Madre mía! Madre mía!" she moaned over and over again as she panted and pushed. Her hair was so soaked from perspiration and matted together that it reminded Mackenzie of a wet mule's tail. He reflected upon this for a moment and smiled. He found it interesting how women always fussed with their hair but when giving birth, their hair always looked horrendous, but the difference was that they never gave a damn.

Isaiah Dorman had left Nate and Grover in Denver and now the pair were making their way up a narrow and winding mountain pass in the Antelope Hills, Wyoming Territory, not far from the gold fields of South Pass that were located at the northwest part of the Antelope Hills. The snow was deep along the path and huge drifts hindered their progress. The cold was tolerable but Nate feared that they would encounter a blizzard that would not only slow them down but also endanger the health of their horses, already weak from lack of sufficient feed.

The mountain path was a crust of thin ice on the top with soft snow underneath. The horses walked slowly and methodically but with increasing effort. The riders remained silent and the only noise that was audible was when one of the hooves from the horses crunched through the thin layer of crust.

While Nate kept his eye on the path and horizon, Sharp Grover kept glancing at the heavily laden snow-covered cliffs above. He was concerned that a sharp noise might trigger an avalanche. He had instructed Nate on some of the dangers in traveling the mountain passes during winter, but Nate's eyes just glossed over every time Grover suggested a longer but less dangerous route.

Nate's horse stumbled on a rock and struggled to keep his footing. The iron shoes, however, only made it more difficult for the beast to regain stability and Grover heard a sharp crack that came from above his head. He turned to look and saw a mountain of snow coming down on them.

"Avalanche," he hollered, but it was too late. No sooner had Nate's mount regained his footing than he felt a tremendous weight on his head and shoulders. The horses neighed in terror as both man and beast became buried under tons of snow.

Hiram Mackenzie was becoming greatly concerned that Cara's birthing was going to be either lethal to her or both mother and child. It was over five hours ago that she had started labor and her breathing had become heavy and her moans had grown louder and more agonizing as the night wore on. Besides verbal assurances and encouragement the mountain man would wipe her brow and face with a cool rag and tried to make her comfortable by making her change positions in order to facilitate the delivery, but nothing seemed to work.

In desperation Mackenzie went over to an old parfleche that had belonged to his wife and reached into the bag. His fingers briefly searched the interior and he quickly found what he was looking for. His wife's rosary beads. The threaded set of dark beads that came from northern France had been given to her by a French Jesuit missionary when she was a very young girl. His dead wife had converted to Catholicism and she carried them all of her life. His wife always clutched her rosary and mumbled her prayers every time she had given birth to their children or when she said her daily prayers.

Mackenzie handed the set to Cara, and she warmly received them hoping that it would relieve her pain and save her child.

"Over here, boys, over here," cried the miner to his comrades. A small party of miners, traveling up the mountain path to a dig and mounted on mules, had heard the crash of snow falling from the cliffs and the neighing of panic-stricken horses.

"I can see their horses. They seem to be all right," shouted another miner. The rescuers moved quickly. They dismounted from their mules and grabbed their shovels and started digging furiously. Because of the full moon, visibility was sufficient for the men to work accurately. Although Nate and Sharp Grover were completely buried, the layer of avalanche snow was not deep and the miners had soon uncovered their faces and were slapping them to come to.

Nate groaned as he regained consciousness. A miner had to loosen Sharp Grover's belt and pump his chest for him to start breathing. Nate felt his head, shoulders, and back ache from the weight of the crushing snow and for a moment could not stop his head from spinning.

"You all right, soldier boy?" queried one of the miners.

Nate's head stopped spinning and he looked into the miner's eyes. He was an old man with a white flowing beard.

"I think so. The horses, mules?" mumbled Nate, trying to get up.

"Oh, they seem no wurse fer wear. . . . Now, you boys jest take it easy. You all had quite a load fall down on your asses."

Although Grover felt weak he managed to get back on his two feet and, with the help of some of the miners, started to gather the two horses and pack mules.

"Much obliged for you all helpin' us out the way you did," acknowledged Grover, shaking the snow from his sombrero and clothes.

"You miners know a half-breed woman that might be livin' with a Silas Quinn?" asked Nate as he also got back on his feet and brushed the last of the snow from his person.

The miners starred at Nate and Grover as if they just saw a ghost.

"Quinn's dead. Kilt by a grizz," answered one miner finally.

"What 'bout the woman?"

"We haven't seen her much. She bein' heavy with child an' all, but after Quinn gots himself tore up by the grizz, ol' Hiram Mackenzie, the mountain man, took her in an' she livin' with him."

"Can you show me where?" asked Nate eagerly.

"Well, soldier boy, I'm headin' to a new dig where some nuggets were found the other day . . ."

"Please, mister," admonished Grover. "We traveled for weeks to find her." Grover hesitated for a moment before continuing, "It's his woman and baby that's in her belly."

"Well, considerin' that, I su'pose I can show you boys where Mackenzie lives, though he don't cotton too much to visitors."

"Push, woman. You've got to push if you wants this baby to see the light of day!" encouraged Mackenzie in desperation.

Cara had her back against the wall of the cave and was pressing hard on a horse blanket that Mackenzie had placed in between her sweating and clammy body and the cold surface of the rock wall. Her legs were stretched apart and she used her hands, the right clutching the rosary beads, to push on her stomach to force the infant from her womb. The mountain man was also sweating, not from exertion but from fear that something bad was going to happen.

Cara was moaning so loudly that Mackenzie feared that her sounds might draw attention from the nearby mining huts and camps. She was pressing down hard with her hands and the mountain man felt the child move forward.

"Push. You're almost there. Push, woman. Breathe harder, keep the momentum goin'!"

Cara cried out so loudly that it spooked Mackenzie's horse. The mountain man was about to yell at the beast to simmer down when he felt something drop into his huge hands. It felt as if a large wet trout had just jumped into his hands from a riverbed.

The infant, however, had her umbilical cord wrapped around her neck and she was not breathing. Mackenzie seized his knife and sliced the cord and unwrapped the cord from around the baby's neck. He spanked the child on the buttocks, and the infant, eyes wild with life, gave a roaring cry that spooked the horse again.

"By Jesus, it's a girl, woman. It's a *girl*."

Nate had heard Cara's scream as he neared the cave. He was following the miner who had volunteered to show him Mackenzie's grotto, and as they advanced on foot leading their horses and mules, he heard the scream and immediately recognized her voice. He hastened his pace and passed the miner, nearly knocking him over.

He reached the entranceway of the grotto and threw back the grizzly hides that curtained the opening and stood there, in silence. The bright but soft light of the two burning oil lamps that were in the cave gave Nate's buffalo coat and kepi a statuesque pose. Both coat and hat were speckled with melting snow, and his chest was heaving with dread and anticipation.

Mackenzie had wrapped Cara in a trader's blanket and she lay on her back holding her daughter. Although weak from exhaustion she managed to turn her head in Nate's direction. She noticed that he had a full beard and also looked tired and worn.

"Come here, *mi hombre*. Come see your daughter."

Nate smiled at the sound of Cara's strong voice and knew that everything was going to be all right. He slowly walked over to the bed and hoped that he had the strength to hold back the moisture that was forming in his eyes.